THE SEARCH FOR THE MISSING DWARVES

MANURO
GOROBEI

QUIRK BOOKS
PHILADELPHIA

Originally published in France as *Hocus & Pocus:
Duo de choc* in 2016 by Makaka Éditions.

Copyright © 2017 MAKAKA. All rights reserved.

Story by Manuro
Drawings by Gorobei

First published in the United States in 2019
by Quirk Productions, Inc.

Translation copyright © 2019 by
Quirk Productions, Inc.

Library of Congress Cataloging
in Publication Number: 2018943031

ISBN: 978-1-68369067-2

Printed in China
Translated by Mélanie Strang-Hardy
Typeset in Sketchnote
Cover design by Andie Reid
Production management by John J. McGurk

Quirk Books
215 Church Street
Philadelphia, PA 19106
quirkbooks.com

10 9 8 7 6 5 4 3 2

STOP!

THIS IS NOT A REGULAR COMIC BOOK!

In this book, you don't read the story straight through from the first page to the last. Instead, you begin at the beginning but then soon you are off on a quest where you choose which comics panel to read next. On your adventure, you will solve puzzles, collect clues, rely on your magical creature for help, and fulfill your quest— because the main character in this story is YOU!

It's easy to get the hang of playing the game once you see it in action. Turn the page for an example of how it works!

POCUS

HOCUS

HOW TO PLAY COMIC QUESTS

1 Pick where you want to go—doors, paths, signs, and objects can all have numbers, so keep your eyes peeled!

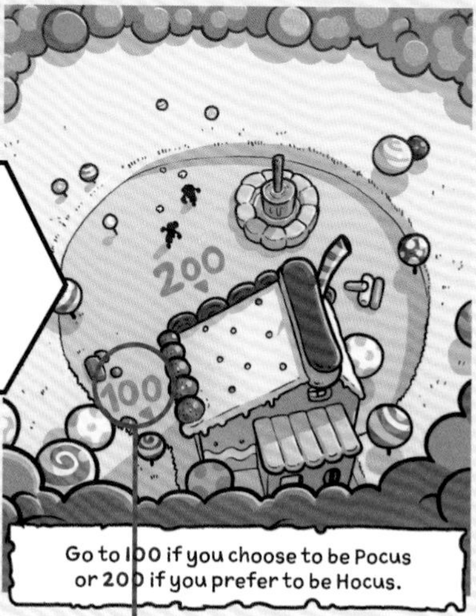
200
100
Go to 100 if you choose to be Pocus or 200 if you prefer to be Hocus.

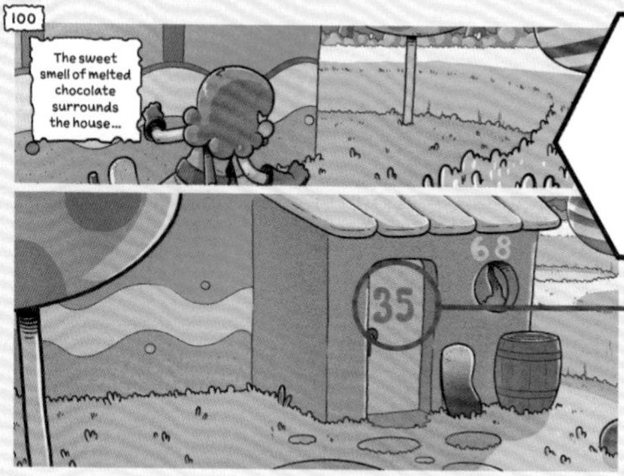
100
The sweet smell of melted chocolate surrounds the house...
68
35

2 Flip to the panel with the matching number.

3 Continue reading from there, making more choices as you go, and complete the quest!

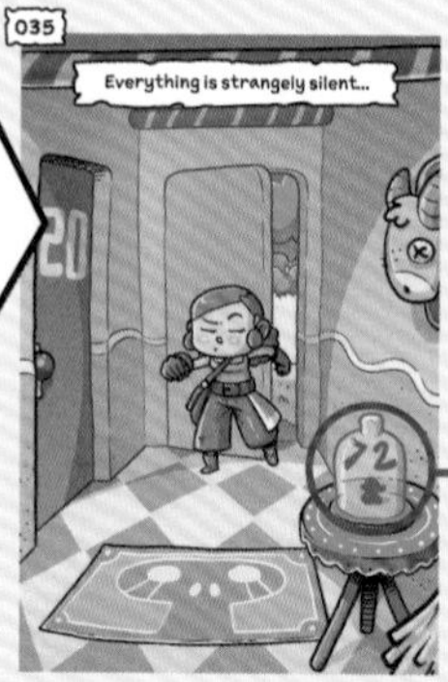
035
Everything is strangely silent...
20
72

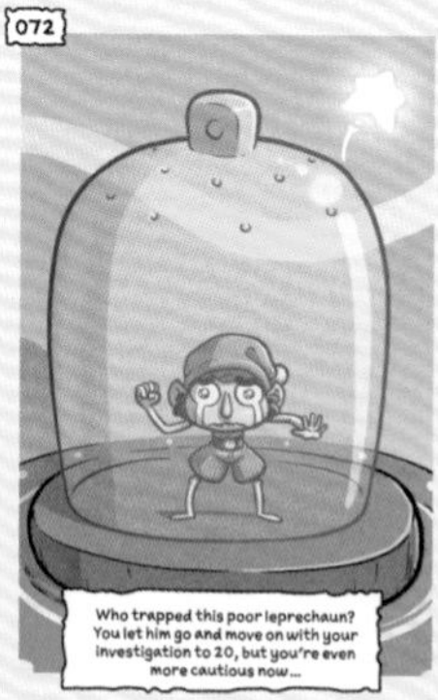
072
Who trapped this poor leprechaun? You let him go and move on with your investigation to 20, but you're even more cautious now...

HOW TO PLAY COMIC QUESTS

Use the Quest Tracker sheets (reproduced on the next few pages) to log your progress. Write with a pencil so you can erase your marks. (You can also use a notebook and pencil, or download extra sheets at ComicQuests.com). As you progress through the book, you'll also collect clues to solve puzzles, so keep some scratch paper handy.

Here are some of the things to watch for as you go.

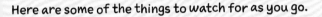

THE MAGICAL CREATURES

Choose which magical creature you want to help you. Your magical creature will allow you to access unique pathways.

AWAKE OR ASLEEP?

♣ At the beginning of the adventure, your magical creature is awake.

♣ Each time you call on your creature for its powers, it will help you, but then it will fall asleep from exhaustion. To keep track of when your creature is sleeping, check the ZZZ box on your Quest Tracker.

♣ If your creature is asleep and you need its help, you will have to feed it. (See "Food for Your Creatures," below.) Once your creature has eaten, it will wake up. Erase the checkmark on the ZZZ box on your Quest Tracker.

FOOD FOR YOUR CREATURES

♣ At the beginning of your quest, you will need to build up your reserves of food. Each creature eats something different. For example, Trampoturtle eats dandelions, and Whirlybird eats worms. Your Quest Tracker will tell you which food each creature eats.

♣ Look closely in each panel for your creature's food. If you find it, check a box beside that food item on your Quest Tracker.

♣ Every time your creature needs energy to wake up, you must feed it two units of its food. Uncheck two boxes on your Quest Tracker. You just used up those units.

THE STARS

Throughout your adventure, you may see shining stars. They appear when you have done a good deed or have shown yourself to be particularly clever. Gather as many stars as possible to impress your headmistress at the end of the quest. Keep track of them by checking the corresponding boxes on your Quest Tracker.

PUZZLE-SOLVING SYMBOLS

When you're confronted with a puzzle to solve, you'll see a little symbol near the number of the panel. If you solve the puzzle correctly, you will turn to a panel where the same symbol is shown. (Nice work!) If the symbol is different, or there is no symbol at all, that means you did not solve the puzzle correctly. Go back to the puzzle and try again.

HOW TO BEGIN

Start your adventure at page I and follow the narrator's instructions, turning to the panels you choose based on the choices you make.

♣ Either the narrator will tell you where to go...

♣ Or you'll pick a number based on where you want to go.

GOOD LUCK! LET THE ADVENTURE BEGIN ...

QUEST TRACKER

TRAMPOTURTLE

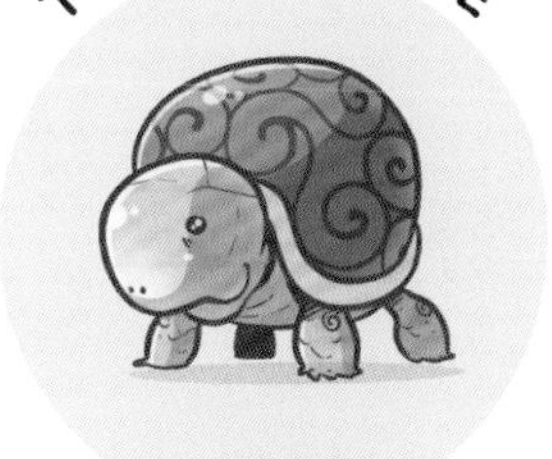

○ ZZZZ

BOXOBULLFROG

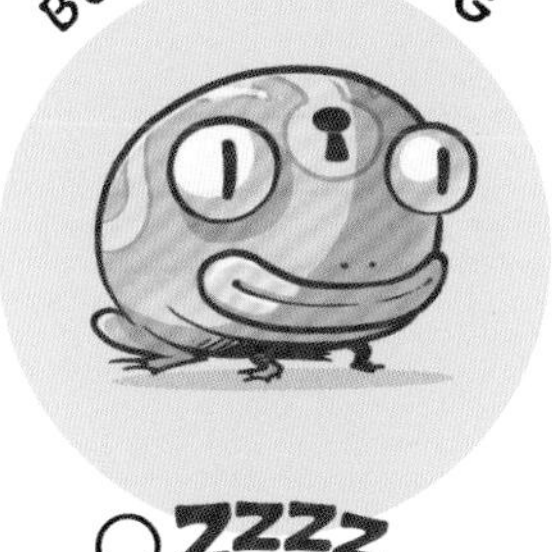

○ ZZZZ

WHIRLYBIRD

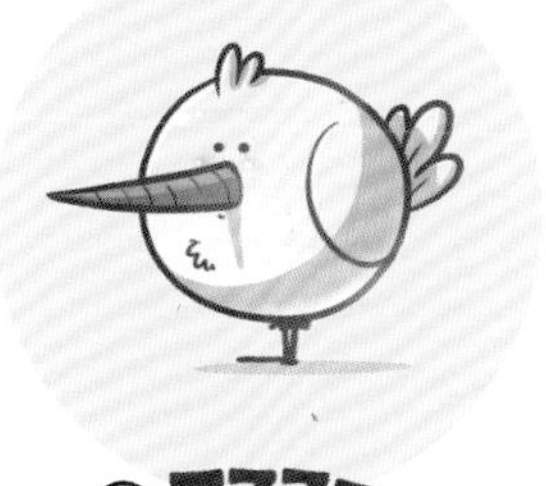

○ ZZZZ

OTHER MAGICAL CREATURES

.... ○ ZZZZ

.... ○ ZZZZ

NOTES

....

....

....

FOOD FOR YOUR CREATURES

DANDELION (Trampoturtle) ○ ○ ○ ○ ○ ○ ○ ○ ○ ○ ○ ○

FLIES (Boxobullfrog) ○ ○ ○ ○ ○ ○ ○ ○ ○ ○ ○ ○

WORMS (Whirlybird) ○ ○ ○ ○ ○ ○ ○ ○ ○ ○ ○ ○

STARS

☆ ☆ ☆ ☆ ☆ ☆ ☆ ☆ ☆ ☆ ☆ ☆ ☆ ☆ ☆

☆ ☆ ☆ ☆ ☆ ☆ ☆ ☆ ☆ ☆ ☆ ☆ ☆ ☆ ☆

☆ ☆ ☆ ☆ ☆ ☆ ☆ ☆ ☆ ☆ ☆ ☆ ☆ ☆ ☆

QUEST TRACKER

TRAMPOTURTLE

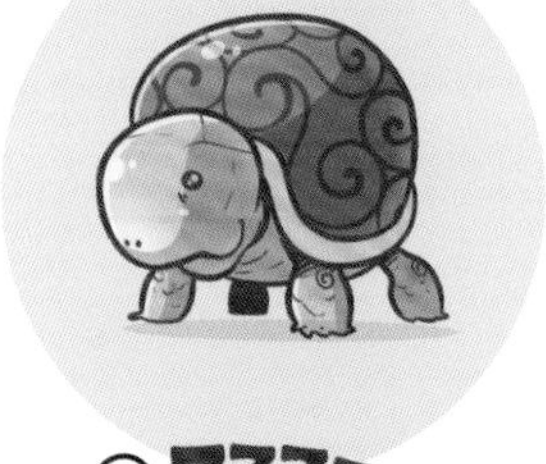

○ ZZZZ

BOXOBULLFROG

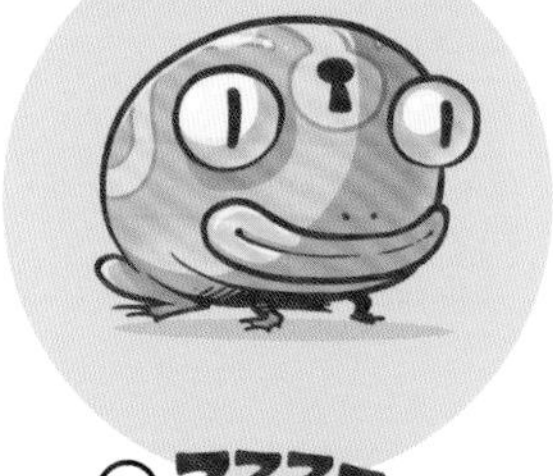

○ ZZZZ

WHIRLYBIRD

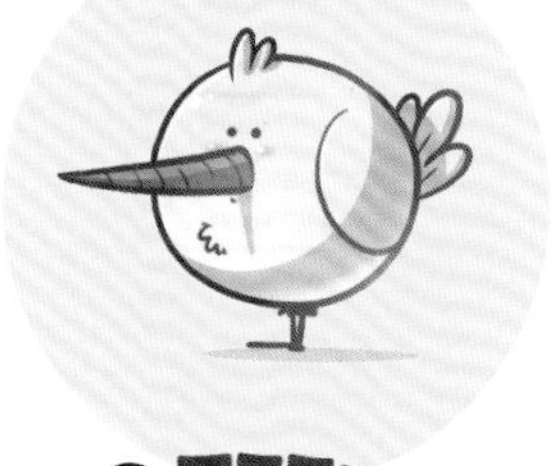

○ ZZZZ

OTHER MAGICAL CREATURES

.... ○ ZZZZ

.... ○ ZZZZ

NOTES

....

....

....

FOOD FOR YOUR CREATURES

DANDELION (Trampoturtle) ○ ○ ○ ○ ○ ○ ○ ○ ○ ○ ○ ○

FLIES (Boxobullfrog) ○ ○ ○ ○ ○ ○ ○ ○ ○ ○ ○ ○

WORMS (Whirlybird) ○ ○ ○ ○ ○ ○ ○ ○ ○ ○ ○ ○

STARS

☆ ☆ ☆ ☆ ☆ ☆ ☆ ☆ ☆ ☆ ☆ ☆ ☆ ☆ ☆

☆ ☆ ☆ ☆ ☆ ☆ ☆ ☆ ☆ ☆ ☆ ☆ ☆ ☆ ☆

☆ ☆ ☆ ☆ ☆ ☆ ☆ ☆ ☆ ☆ ☆ ☆ ☆ ☆ ☆

QUEST TRACKER

TRAMPOTURTLE
○ Zzzz

BOXOBULLFROG
○ Zzzz

WHIRLYBIRD
○ Zzzz

OTHER MAGICAL CREATURES

.... ○ Zzzz

.... ○ Zzzz

NOTES

....

....

....

FOOD FOR YOUR CREATURES

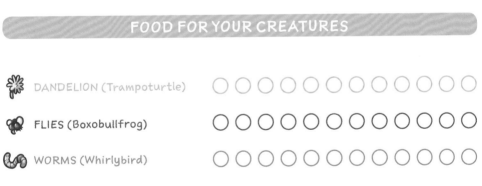

DANDELION (Trampoturtle) ○○○○○○○○○○○○

FLIES (Boxobullfrog) ○○○○○○○○○○○○

WORMS (Whirlybird) ○○○○○○○○○○○○

STARS

☆☆☆☆☆☆☆☆☆☆☆☆
☆☆☆☆☆☆☆☆☆☆☆☆
☆☆☆☆☆☆☆☆☆☆☆☆

QUEST TRACKER

TRAMPOTURTLE

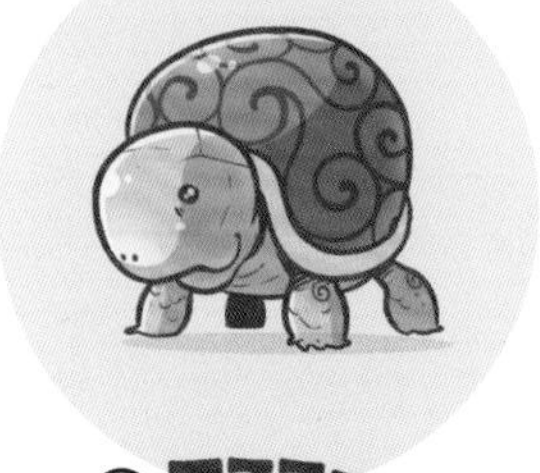

○ ZZZZ

BOXOBULLFROG

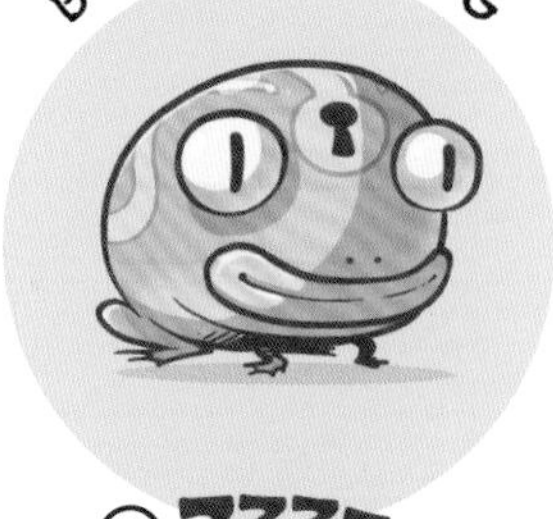

○ ZZZZ

WHIRLYBIRD

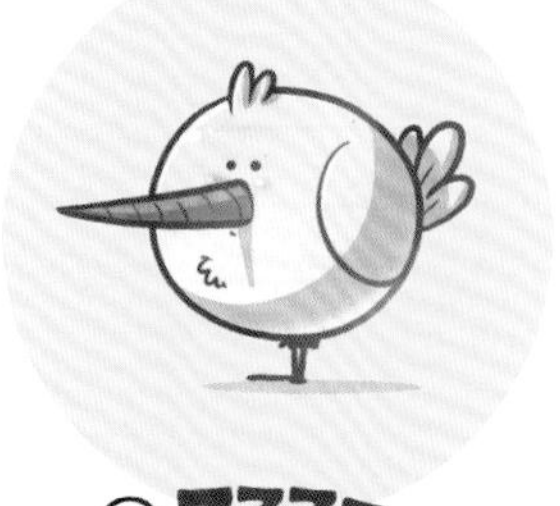

○ ZZZZ

OTHER MAGICAL CREATURES

.... ○ ZZZZ

.... ○ ZZZZ

NOTES

....

....

....

FOOD FOR YOUR CREATURES

DANDELION (Trampoturtle) ○ ○ ○ ○ ○ ○ ○ ○ ○ ○ ○ ○

FLIES (Boxobullfrog) ○ ○ ○ ○ ○ ○ ○ ○ ○ ○ ○ ○

WORMS (Whirlybird) ○ ○ ○ ○ ○ ○ ○ ○ ○ ○ ○ ○

STARS

☆ ☆ ☆ ☆ ☆ ☆ ☆ ☆ ☆ ☆ ☆ ☆ ☆ ☆ ☆

☆ ☆ ☆ ☆ ☆ ☆ ☆ ☆ ☆ ☆ ☆ ☆ ☆ ☆ ☆

☆ ☆ ☆ ☆ ☆ ☆ ☆ ☆ ☆ ☆ ☆ ☆ ☆ ☆ ☆

QUEST TRACKER

TRAMPOTURTLE

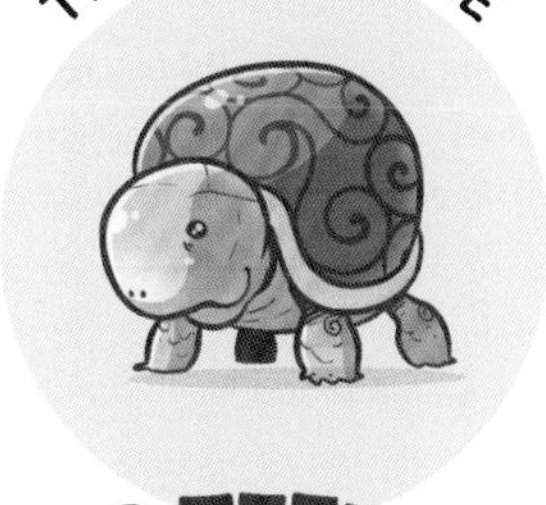

○ Zzzz

BOXOBULLFROG

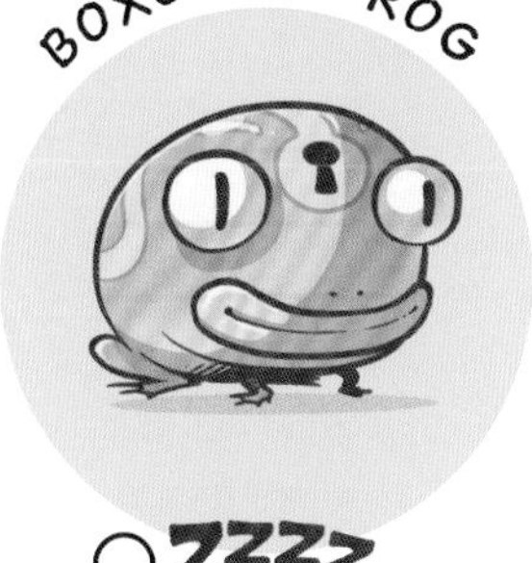

○ Zzzz

WHIRLYBIRD

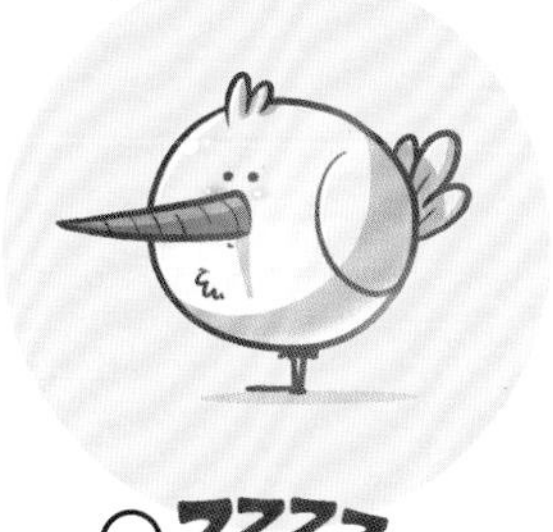

○ Zzzz

OTHER MAGICAL CREATURES

.... ○ Zzzz

.... ○ Zzzz

NOTES

....

....

....

FOOD FOR YOUR CREATURES

DANDELION (Trampoturtle) ○ ○ ○ ○ ○ ○ ○ ○ ○ ○ ○ ○

FLIES (Boxobullfrog) ○ ○ ○ ○ ○ ○ ○ ○ ○ ○ ○ ○

WORMS (Whirlybird) ○ ○ ○ ○ ○ ○ ○ ○ ○ ○ ○ ○

STARS

☆ ☆ ☆ ☆ ☆ ☆ ☆ ☆ ☆ ☆ ☆ ☆ ☆ ☆ ☆

☆ ☆ ☆ ☆ ☆ ☆ ☆ ☆ ☆ ☆ ☆ ☆ ☆ ☆ ☆

☆ ☆ ☆ ☆ ☆ ☆ ☆ ☆ ☆ ☆ ☆ ☆ ☆ ☆ ☆

BEGIN YOUR QUEST!

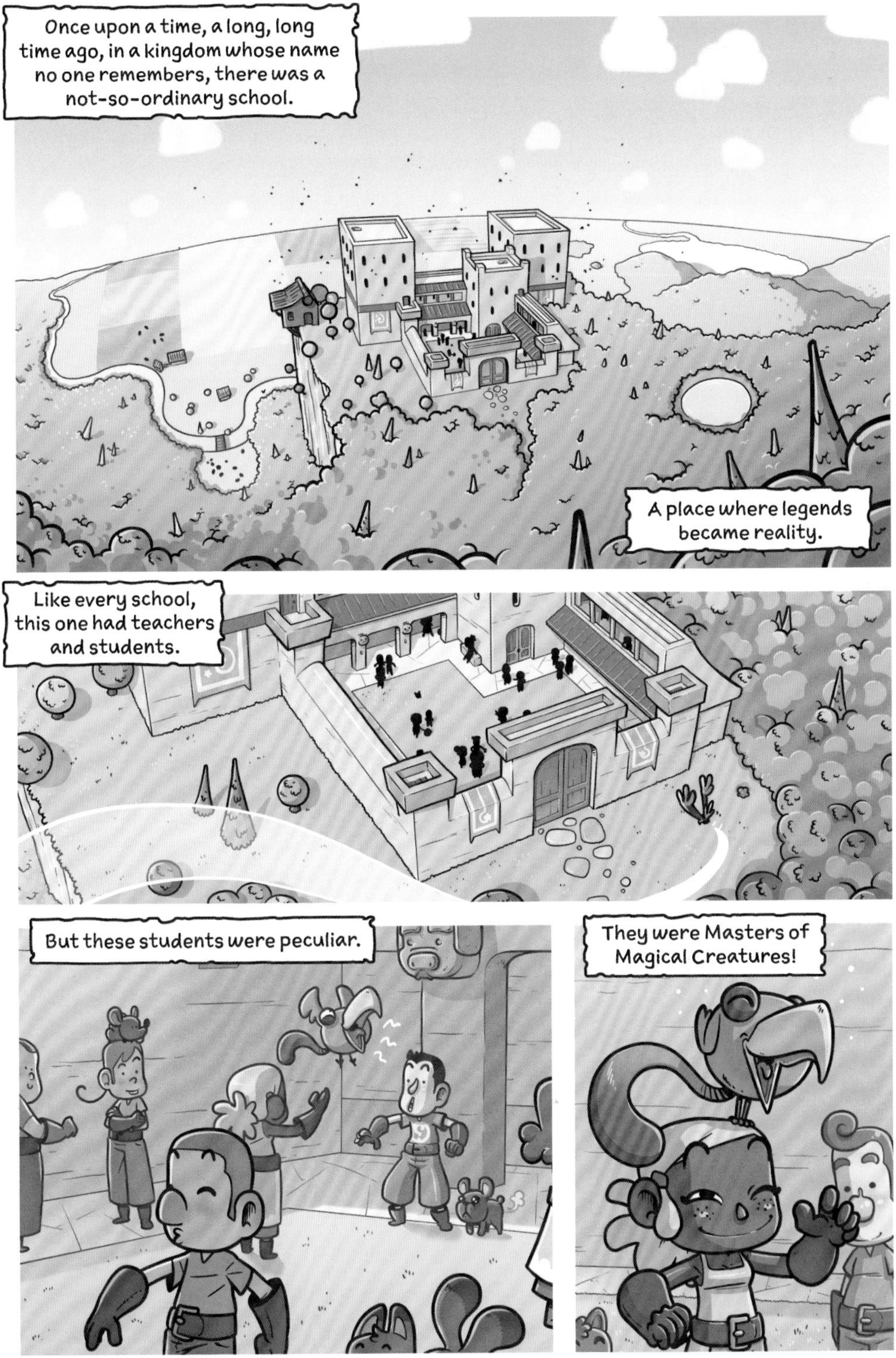
Once upon a time, a long, long time ago, in a kingdom whose name no one remembers, there was a not-so-ordinary school.
A place where legends became reality.
Like every school, this one had teachers and students.
But these students were peculiar.
They were Masters of Magical Creatures!

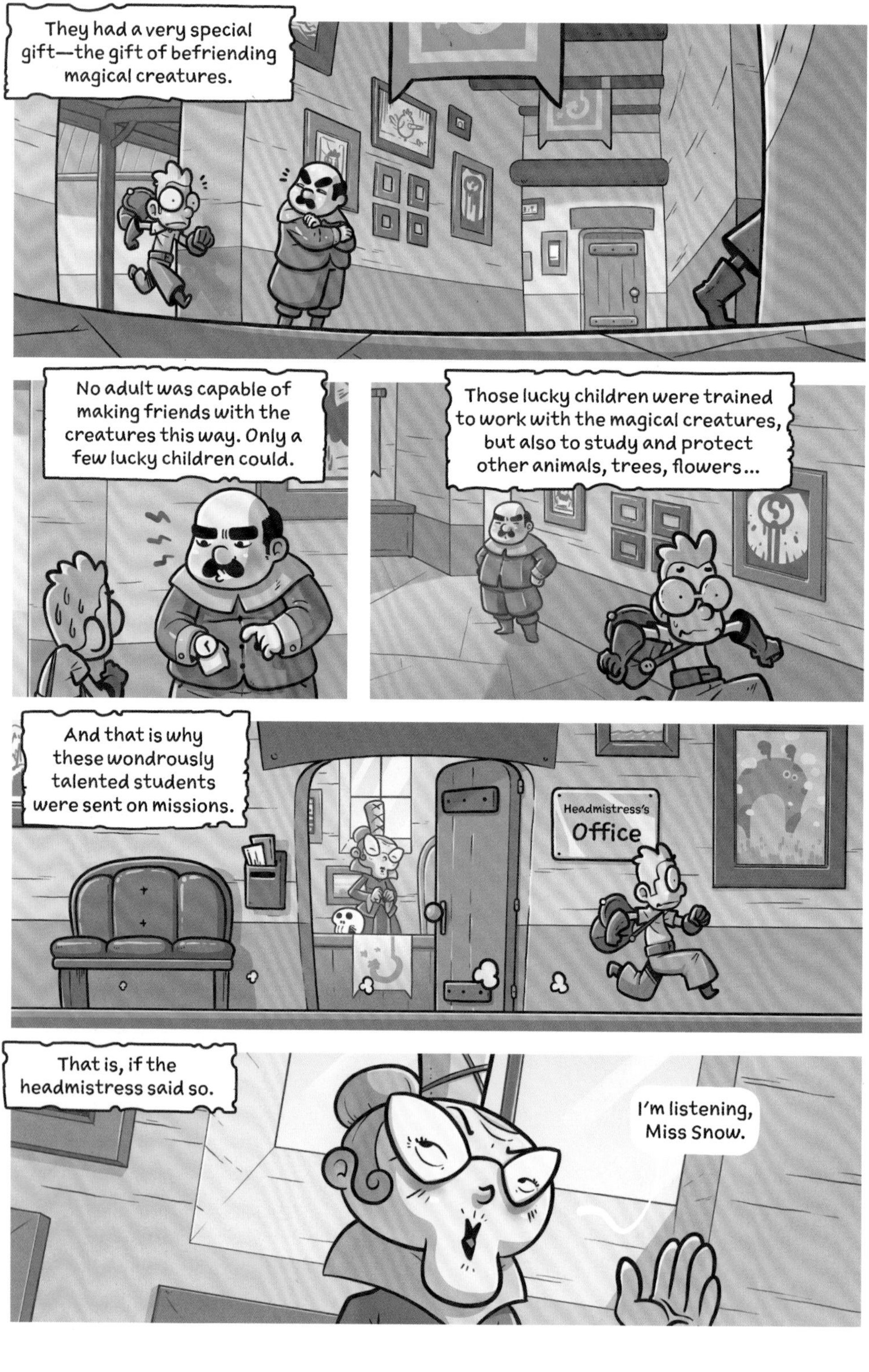

They had a very special gift—the gift of befriending magical creatures.
No adult was capable of making friends with the creatures this way. Only a few lucky children could.
Those lucky children were trained to work with the magical creatures, but also to study and protect other animals, trees, flowers...
And that is why these wondrously talented students were sent on missions.
Headmistress's Office
That is, if the headmistress said so.
I'm listening, Miss Snow.

It's my cousins! There're seven of them. They left for work two days ago and never came back!

Curious. But why fret over it?

Because, well, they work in the mines.

The mines in the Bramble Forest.

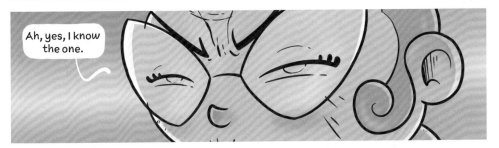

Ah, yes, I know the one.

I've heard such good things about your students and your school, so I was wondering if maybe...

You did well to come here, Miss. Hocus, Pocus! Go find your magical creatures and start looking for these seven unfortunate souls!

Right away, Ma'am!

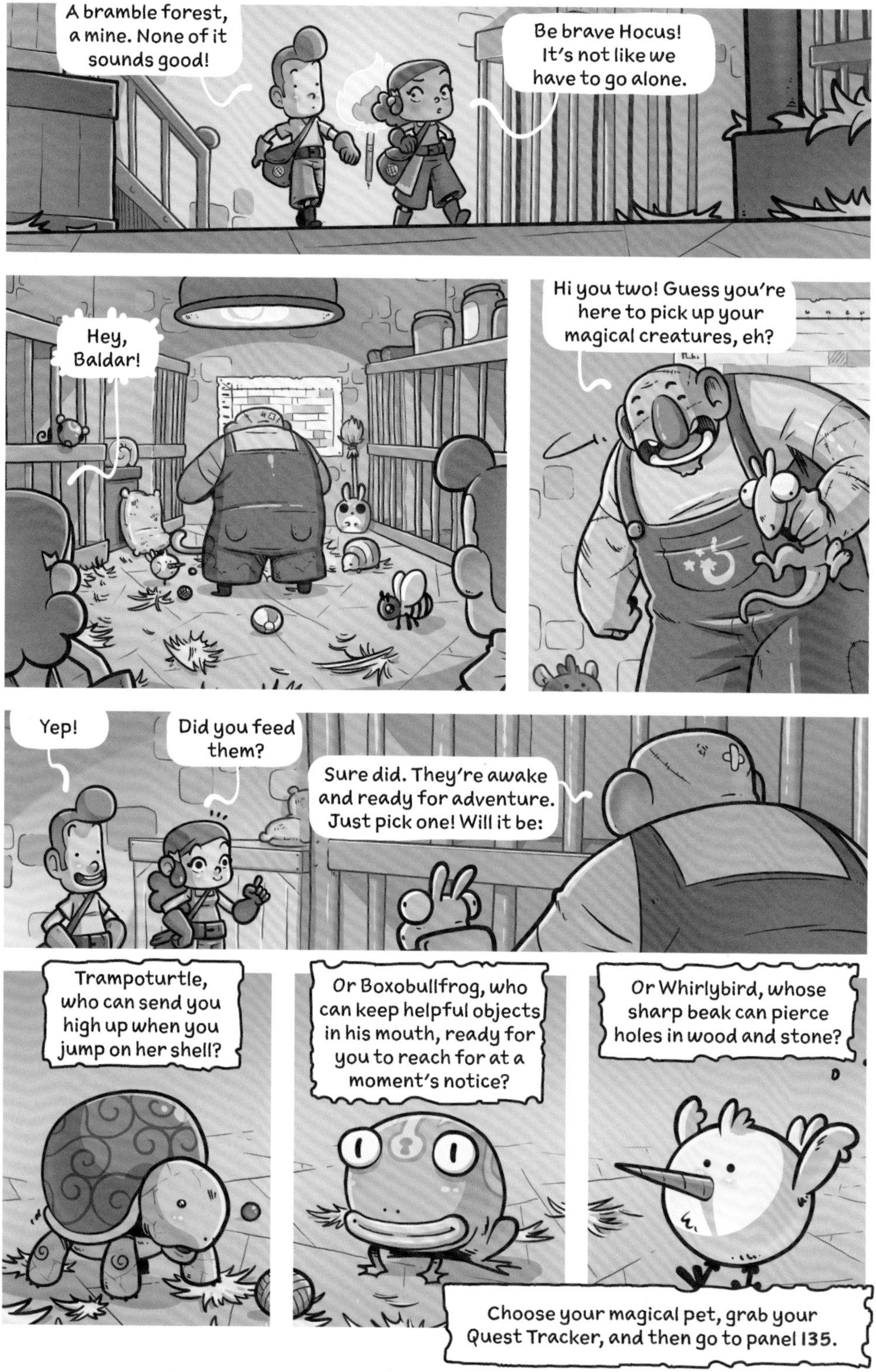
A bramble forest, a mine. None of it sounds good!
Be brave Hocus! It's not like we have to go alone.
Hey, Baldar!
Hi you two! Guess you're here to pick up your magical creatures, eh?
Yep!
Did you feed them?
Sure did. They're awake and ready for adventure. Just pick one! Will it be:
Trampoturtle, who can send you high up when you jump on her shell?
Or Boxobullfrog, who can keep helpful objects in his mouth, ready for you to reach for at a moment's notice?
Or Whirlybird, whose sharp beak can pierce holes in wood and stone?
Choose your magical pet, grab your Quest Tracker, and then go to panel 135.

001

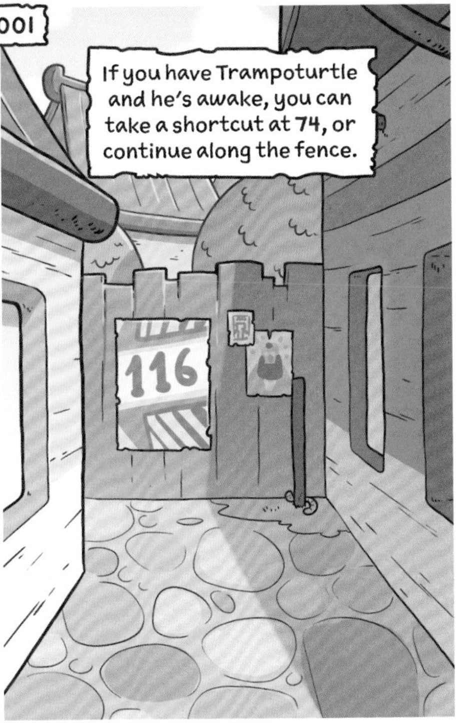
If you have Trampoturtle and he's awake, you can take a shortcut at 74, or continue along the fence.
116

002

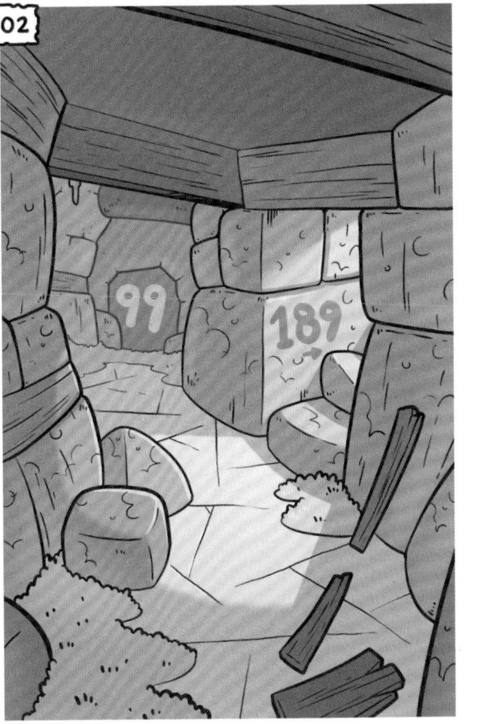
99
189

003

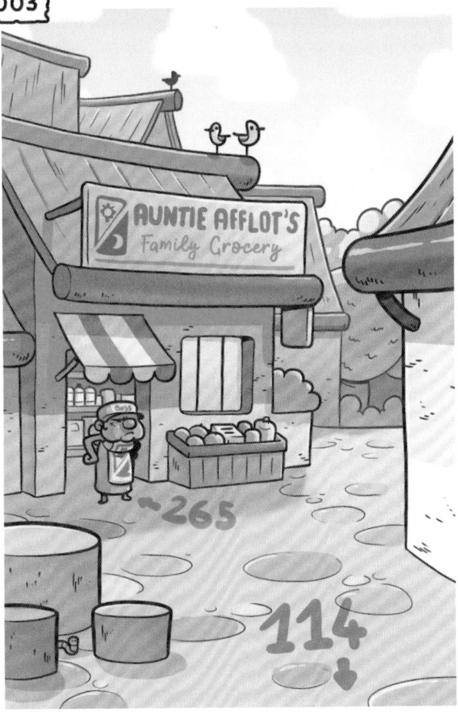
AUNTIE AFFLOT'S
Family Grocery
265
114

004

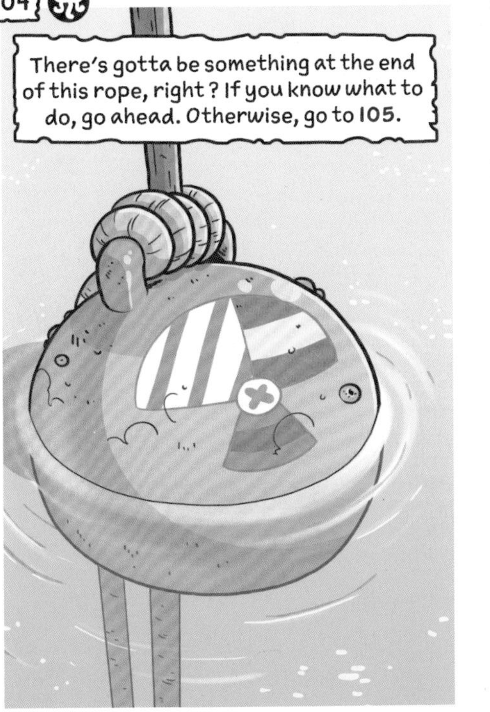
There's gotta be something at the end of this rope, right? If you know what to do, go ahead. Otherwise, go to 105.

005

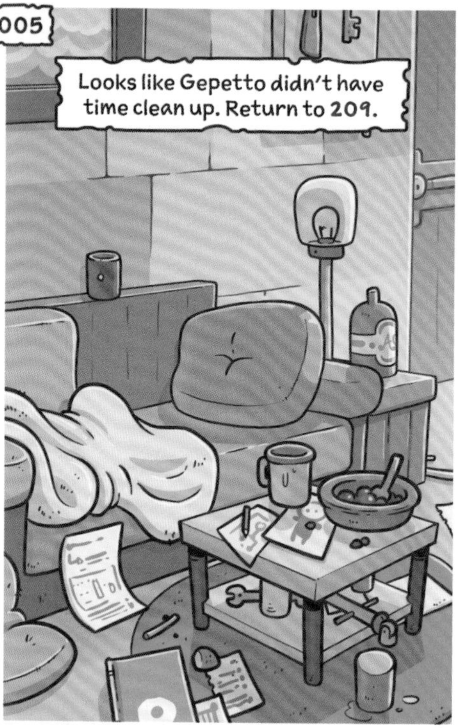
Looks like Gepetto didn't have time clean up. Return to 209.

006

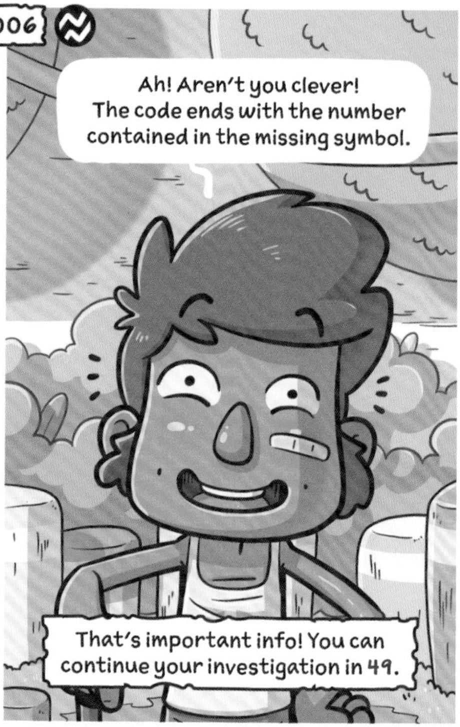
Ah! Aren't you clever! The code ends with the number contained in the missing symbol.
That's important info! You can continue your investigation in 49.

007

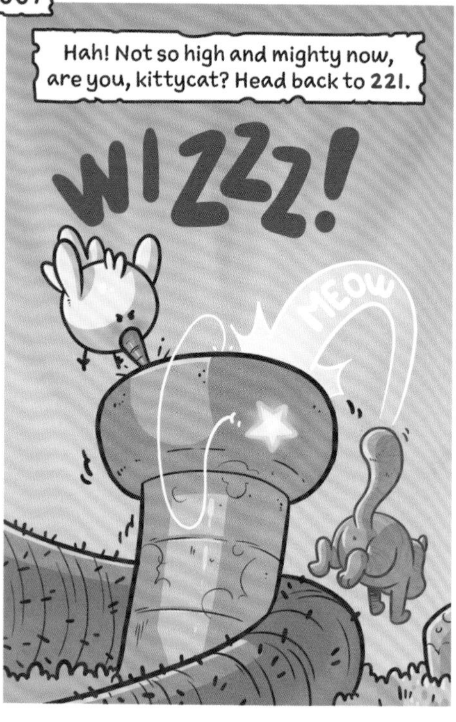
Hah! Not so high and mighty now, are you, kittycat? Head back to 221.
WIZZZ!
MEOW

008

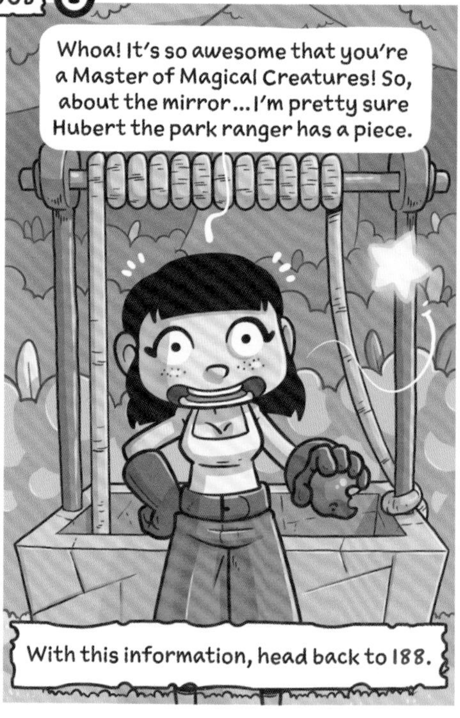
Whoa! It's so awesome that you're a Master of Magical Creatures! So, about the mirror... I'm pretty sure Hubert the park ranger has a piece.
With this information, head back to 188.

009

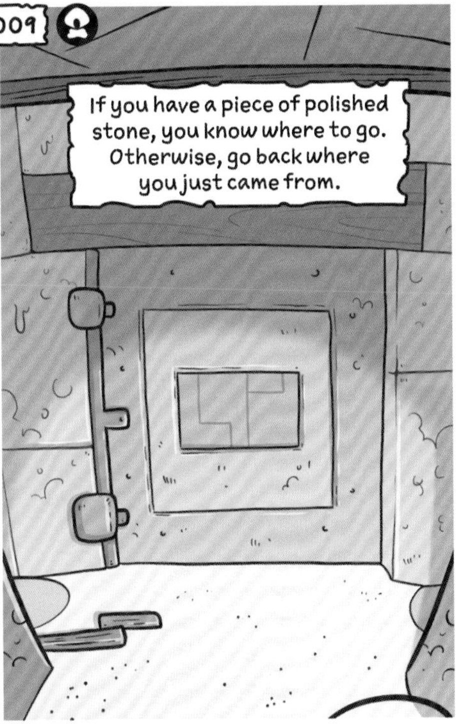
If you have a piece of polished stone, you know where to go. Otherwise, go back where you just came from.

010

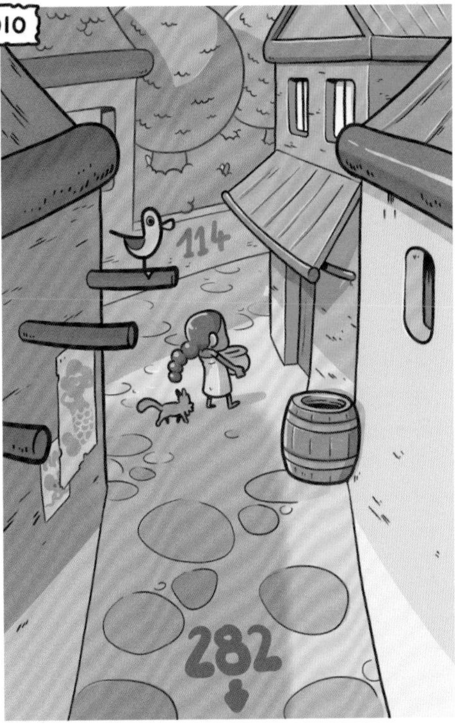
114
282

011

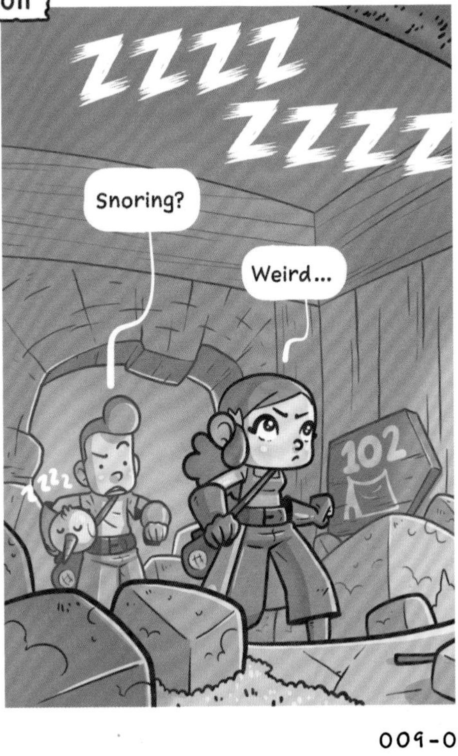
ZZZZ
ZZZZ
Snoring?
Weird...
102

012

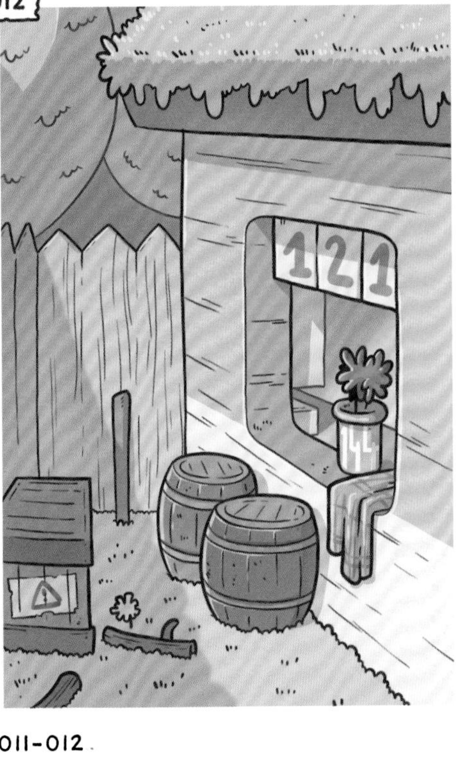
121

013

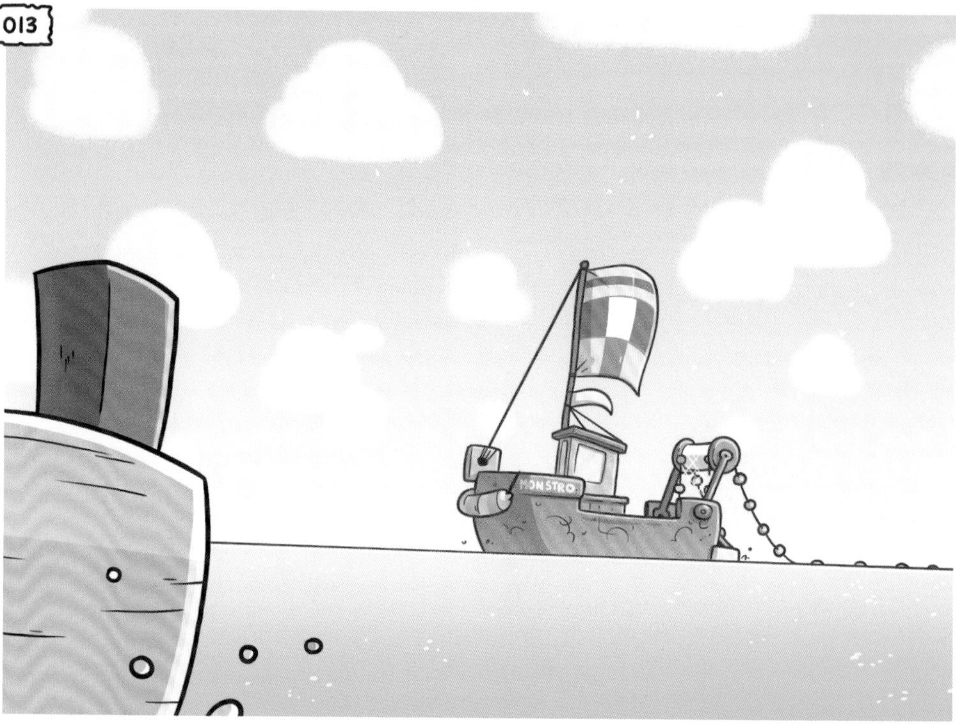
MONSTRO

014

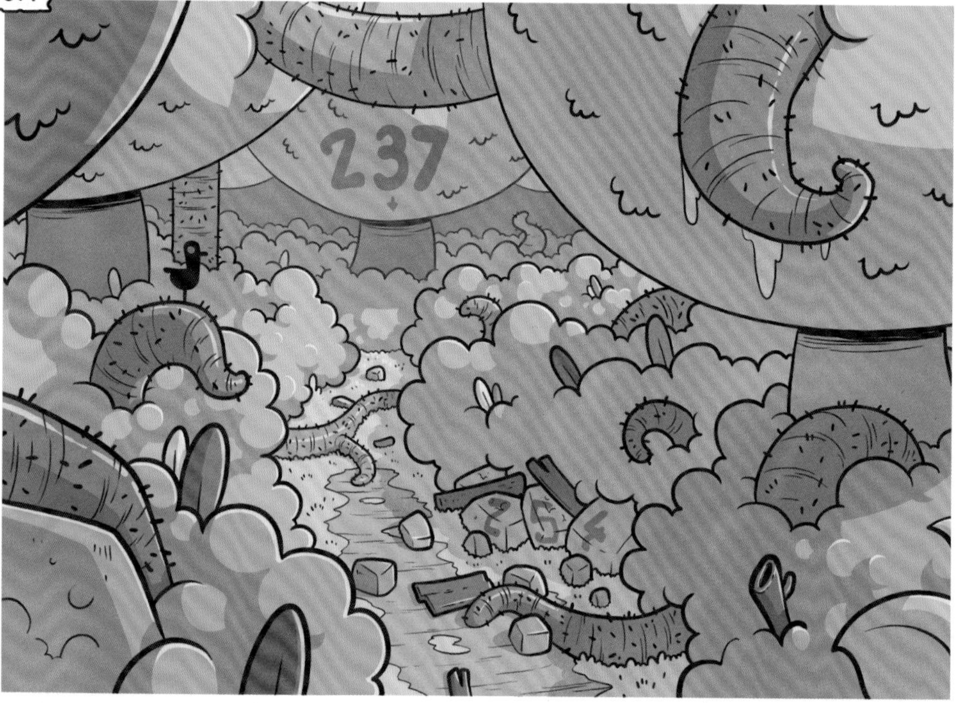
237

015

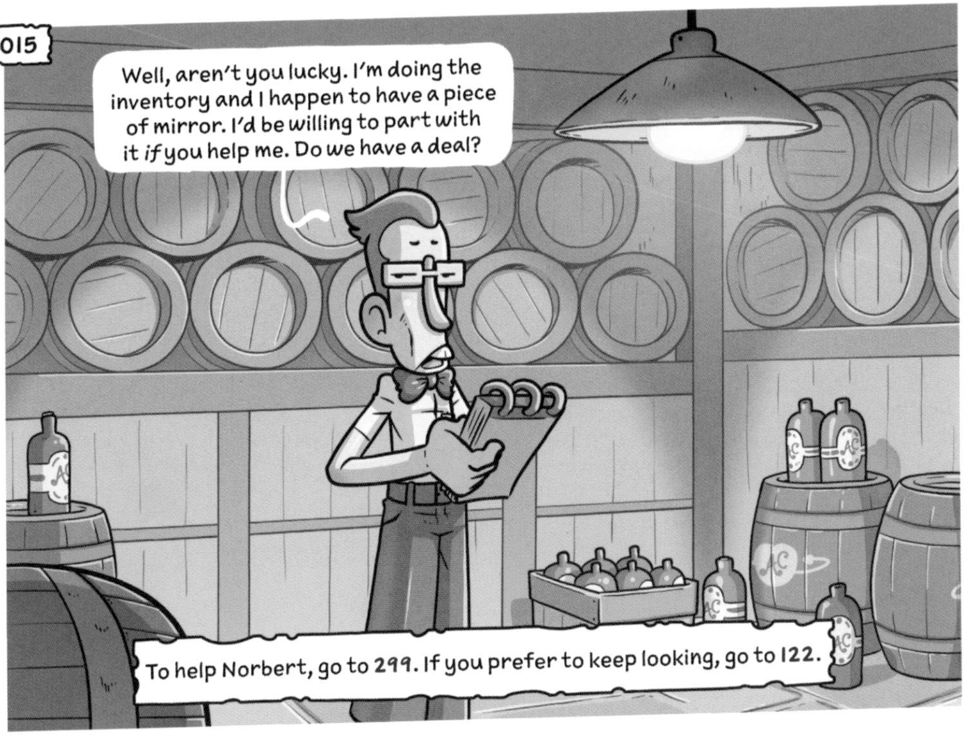
Well, aren't you lucky. I'm doing the inventory and I happen to have a piece of mirror. I'd be willing to part with it *if* you help me. Do we have a deal?
AC
To help Norbert, go to **299**. If you prefer to keep looking, go to **122**.

016

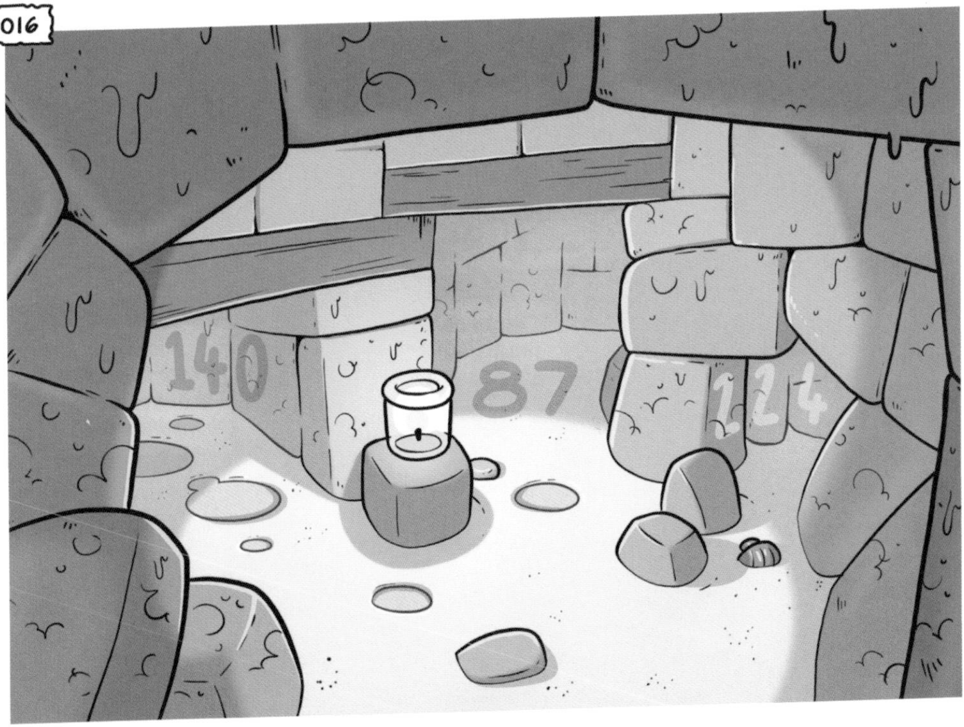
140
87
124

017

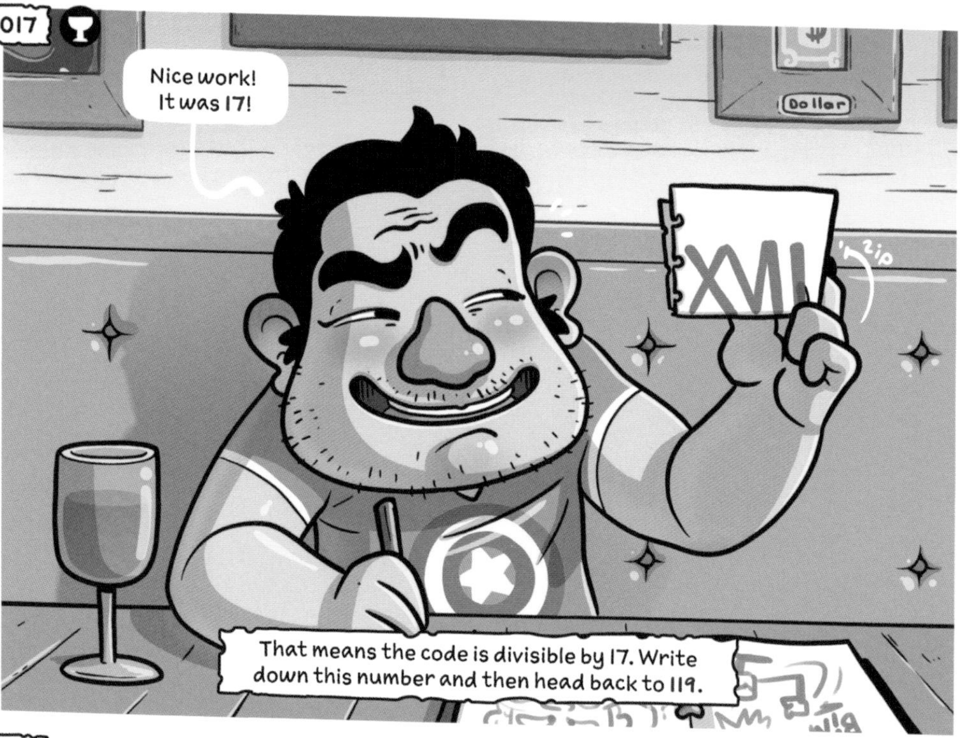
Dollar
Nice work!
It was 17!
XVII
zip
That means the code is divisible by 17. Write down this number and then head back to 119.

018

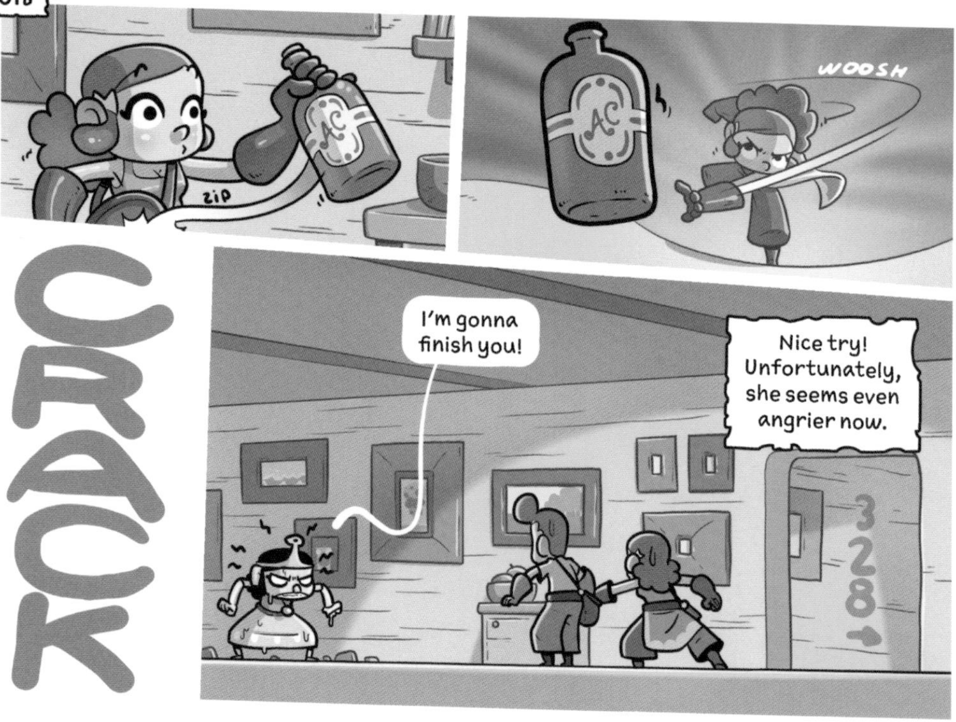
AC
zip
AC
WOOSH
CRACK
I'm gonna finish you!
Nice try! Unfortunately, she seems even angrier now.
328

019

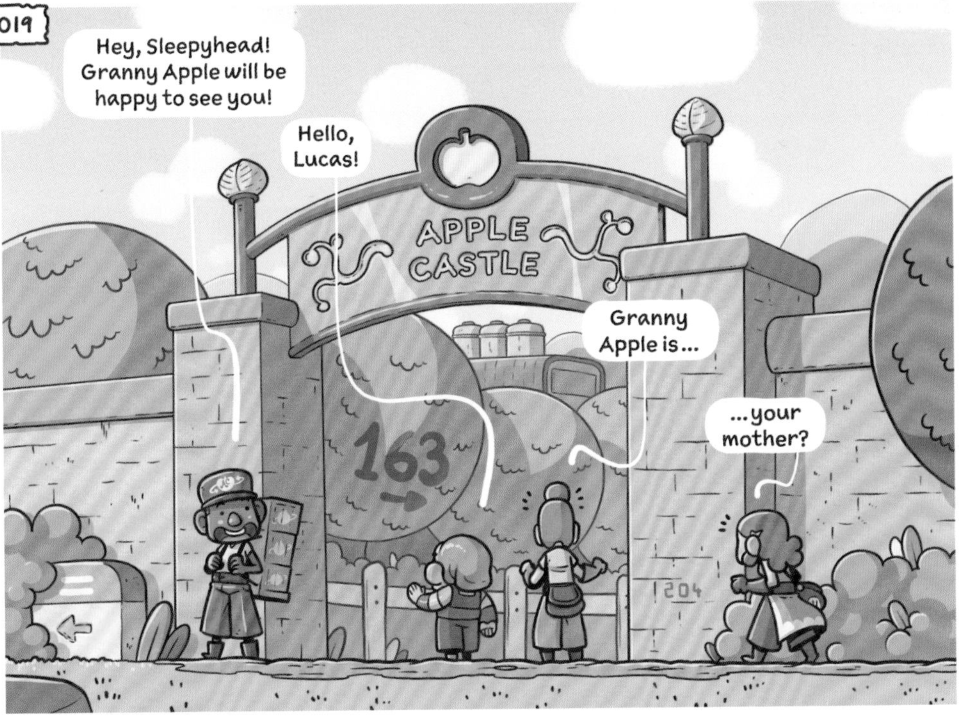
Hey, Sleepyhead!
Granny Apple will be
happy to see you!
Hello,
Lucas!
APPLE
CASTLE
Granny
Apple is...
...your
mother?
163
204

020

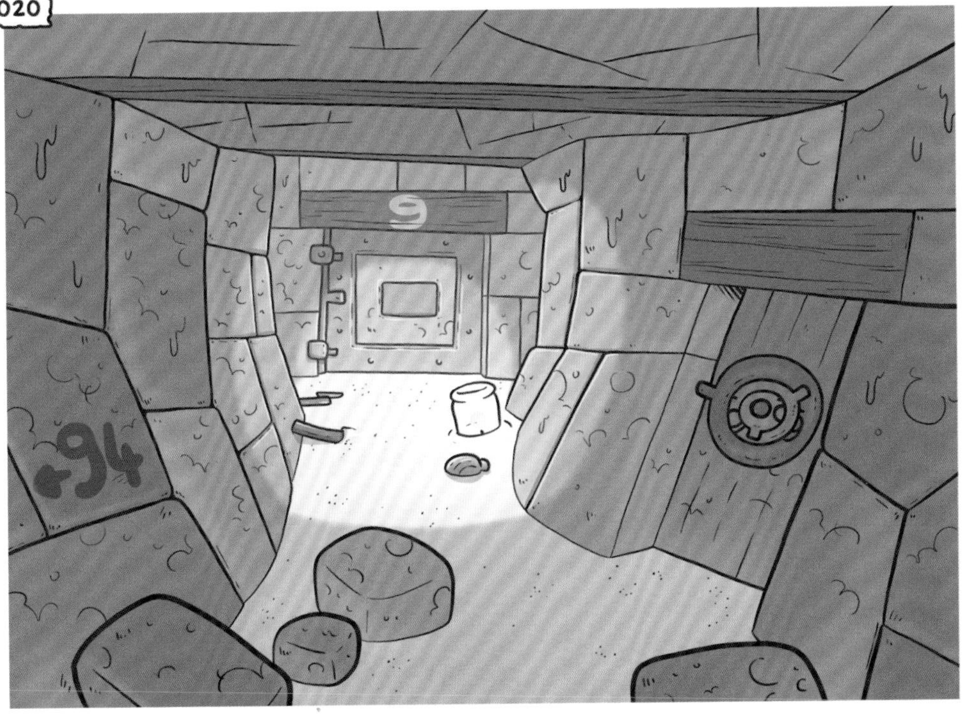
9
94

021

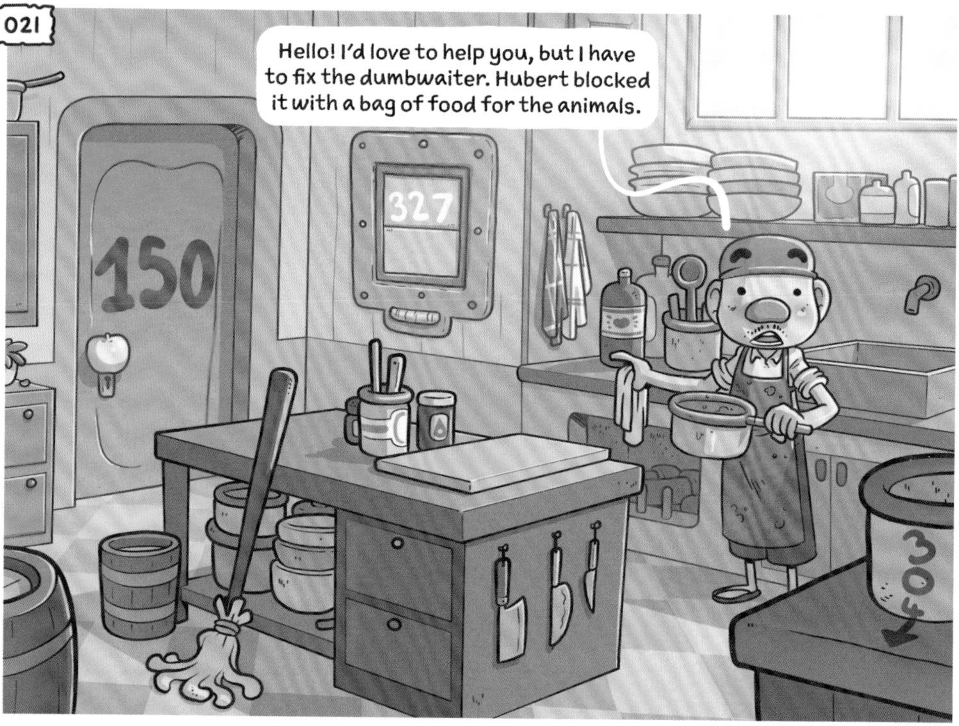
Hello! I'd love to help you, but I have to fix the dumbwaiter. Hubert blocked it with a bag of food for the animals.
150
327
303

022

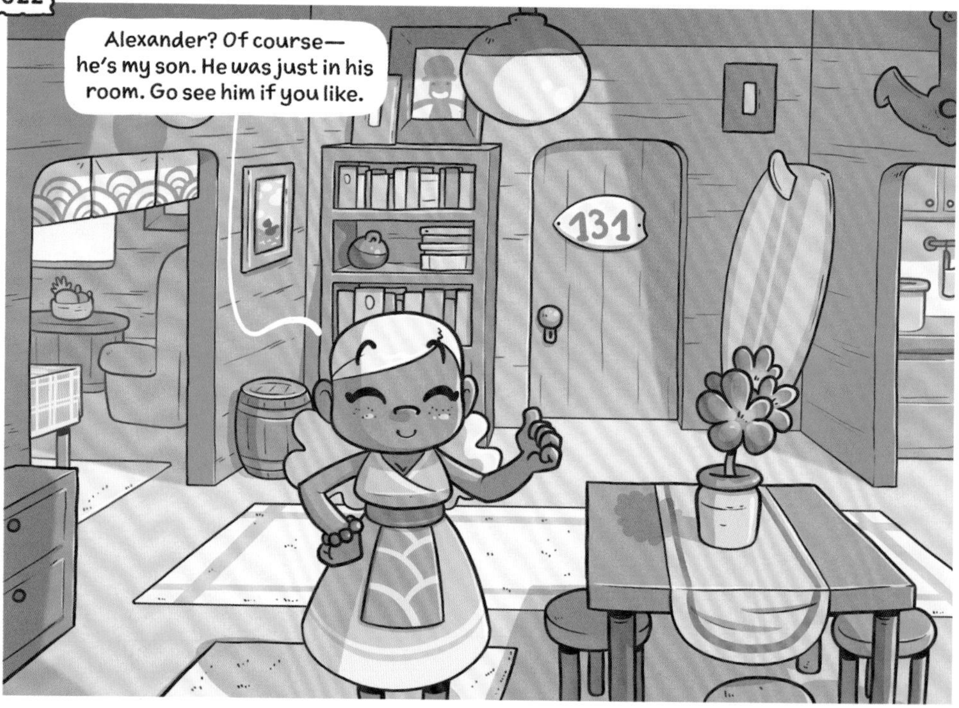
Alexander? Of course—he's my son. He was just in his room. Go see him if you like.
131

023

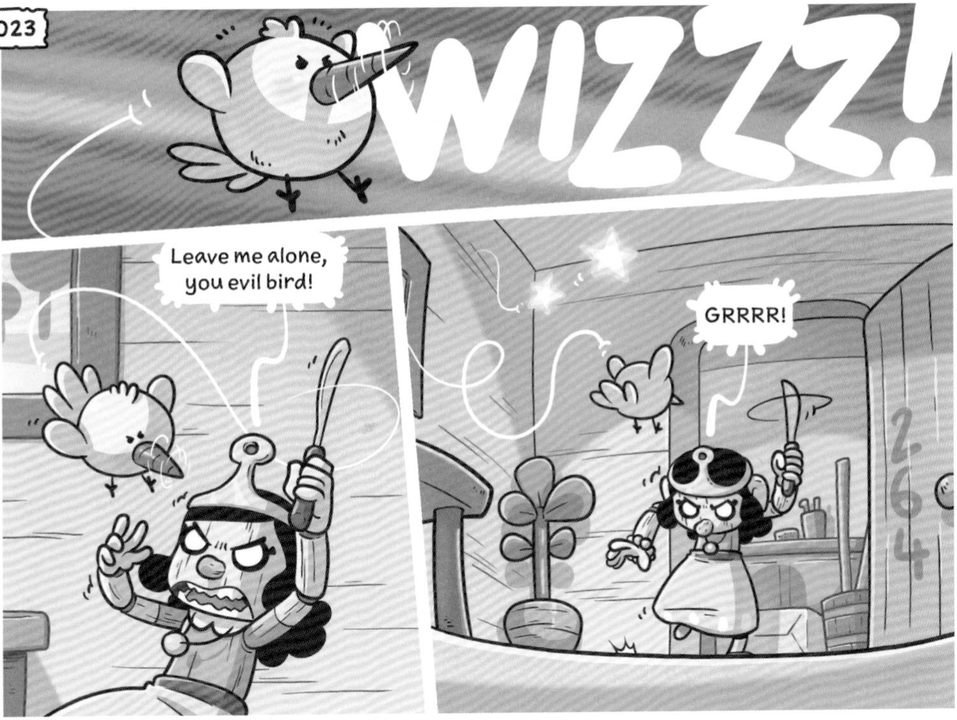
WIZZZ!
Leave me alone, you evil bird!
GRRRR!
264

024

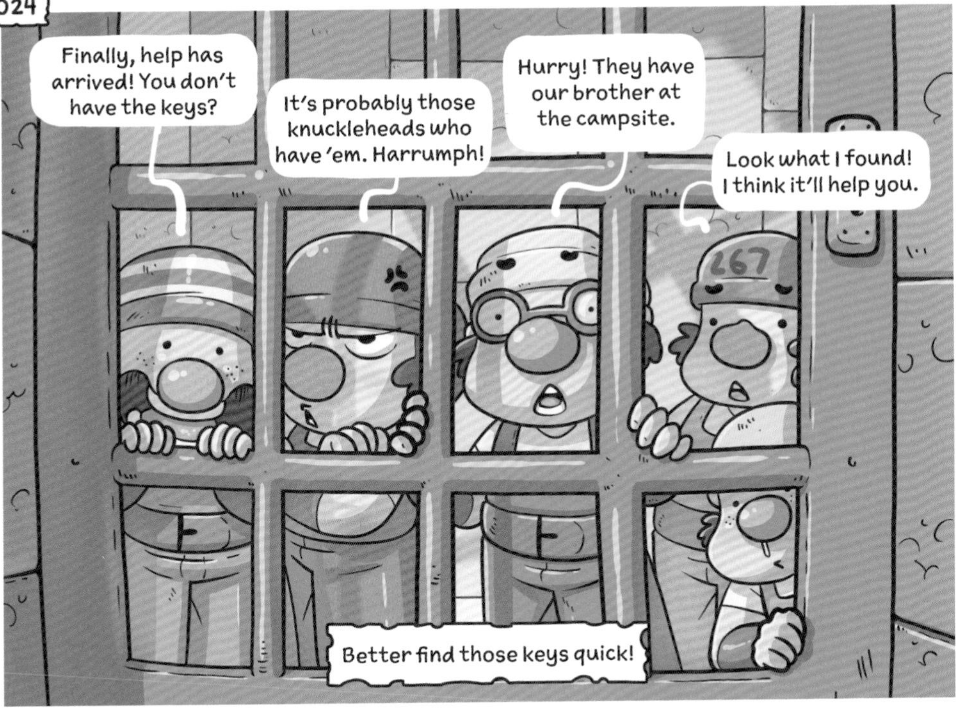
Finally, help has arrived! You don't have the keys?
It's probably those knuckleheads who have 'em. Harrumph!
Hurry! They have our brother at the campsite.
Look what I found! I think it'll help you.
267
Better find those keys quick!

025

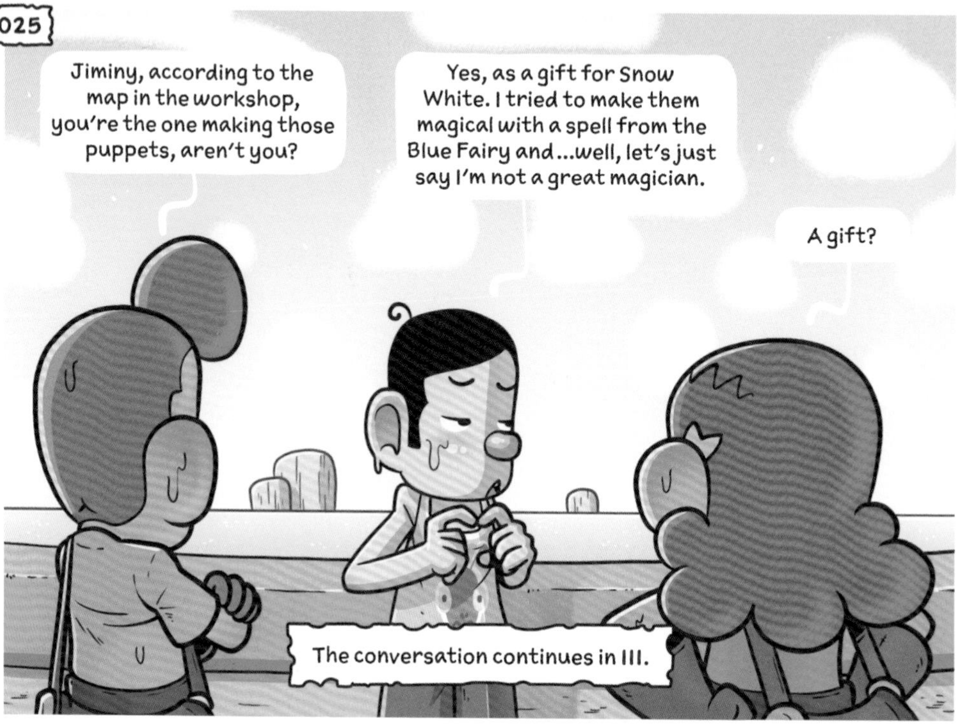
Jiminy, according to the map in the workshop, you're the one making those puppets, aren't you?
Yes, as a gift for Snow White. I tried to make them magical with a spell from the Blue Fairy and...well, let's just say I'm not a great magician.
A gift?
The conversation continues in 111.

026

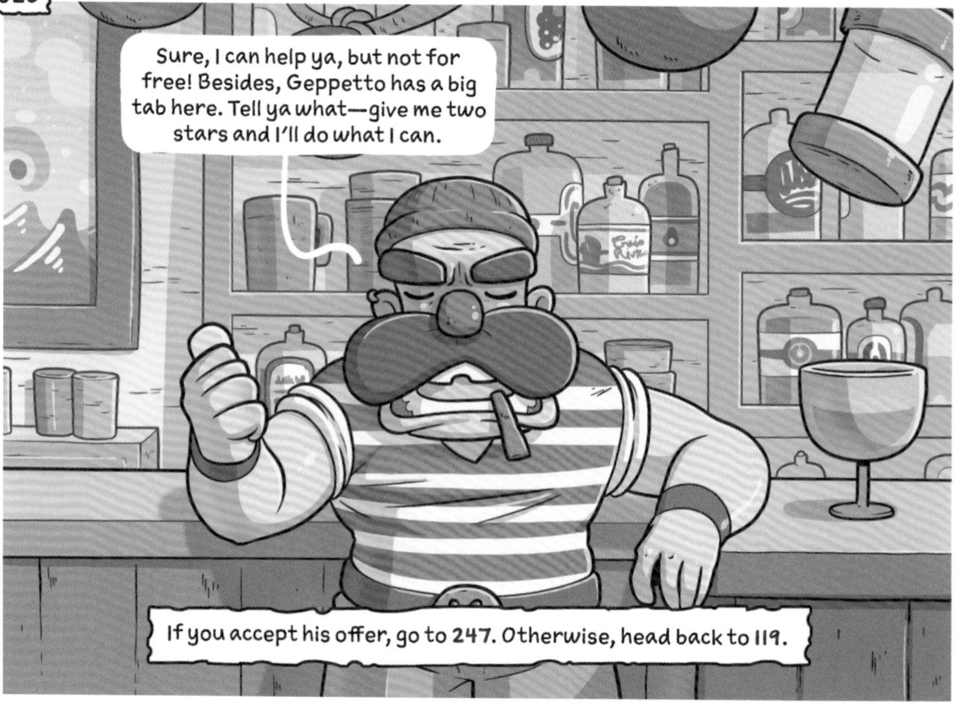
Sure, I can help ya, but not for free! Besides, Geppetto has a big tab here. Tell ya what—give me two stars and I'll do what I can.
If you accept his offer, go to 247. Otherwise, head back to 119.

027

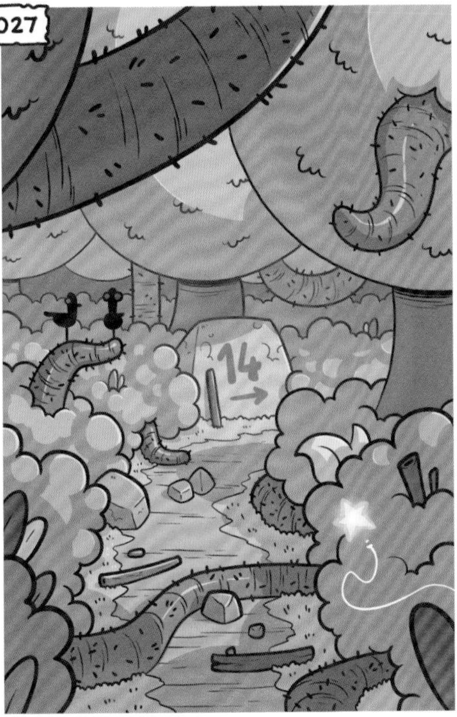
14

028

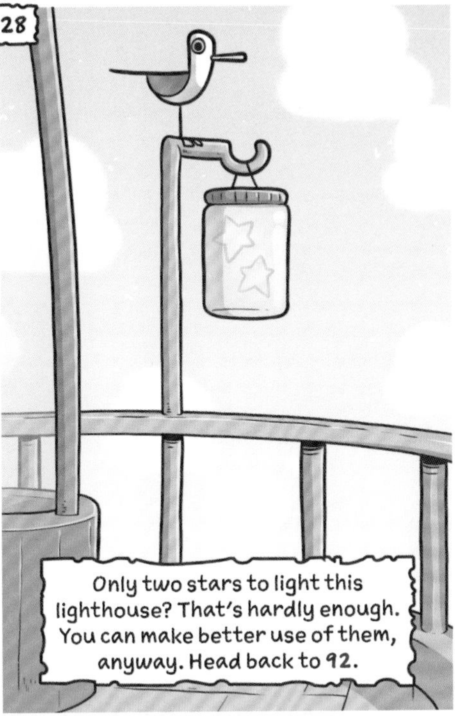
Only two stars to light this lighthouse? That's hardly enough. You can make better use of them, anyway. Head back to 92.

029

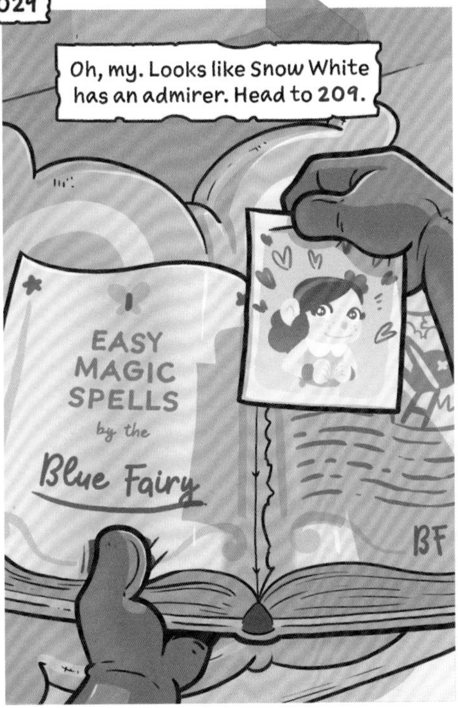
Oh, my. Looks like Snow White has an admirer. Head to 209.
EASY MAGIC SPELLS
by the
Blue Fairy
BF

030

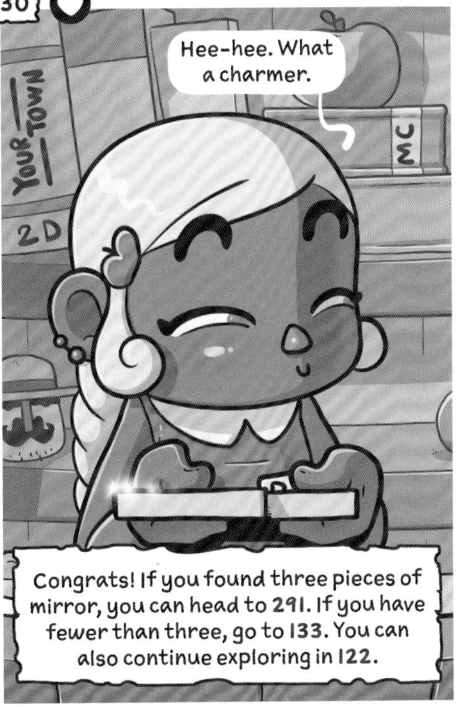
Hee-hee. What a charmer.
YOUR TOWN
2D
MC
Congrats! If you found three pieces of mirror, you can head to 291. If you have fewer than three, go to 133. You can also continue exploring in 122.

031

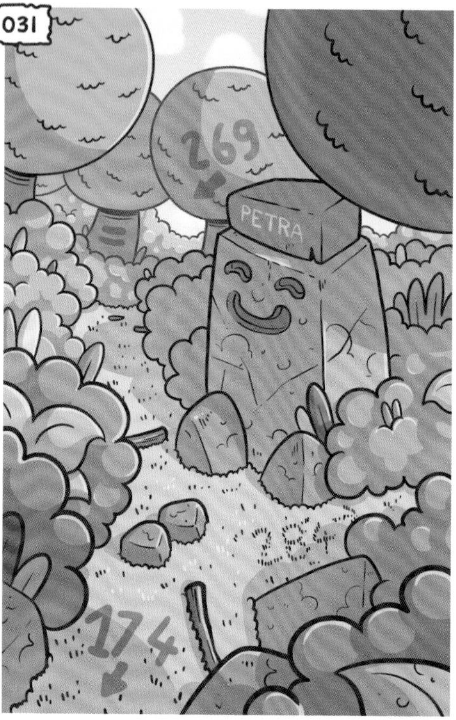
269
PETRA
284
174

032

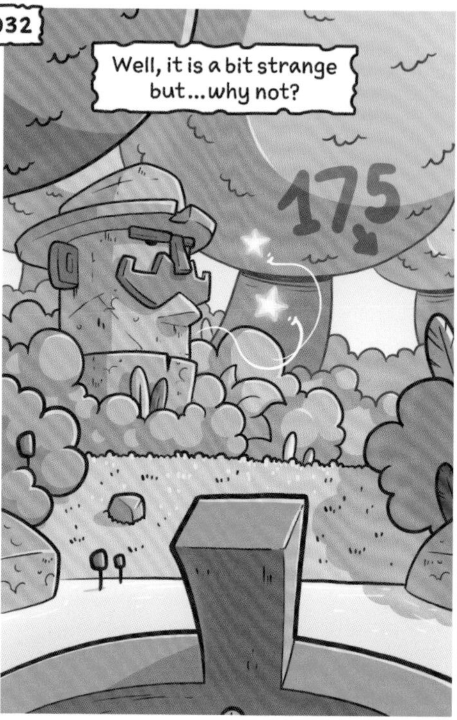
Well, it is a bit strange but...why not?
175

033

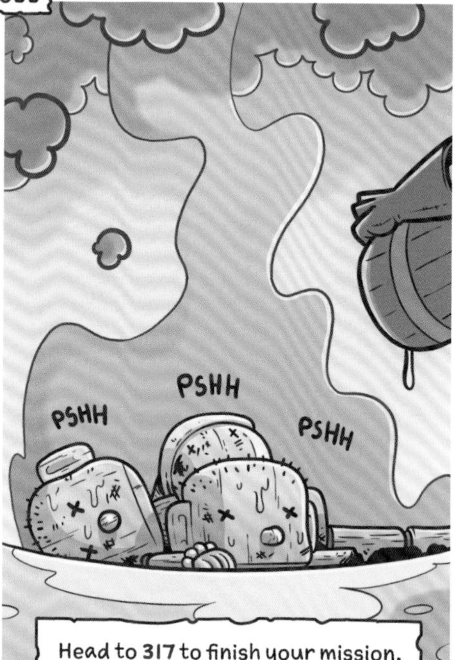
PSHH
PSHH
PSHH
Head to 317 to finish your mission.

034

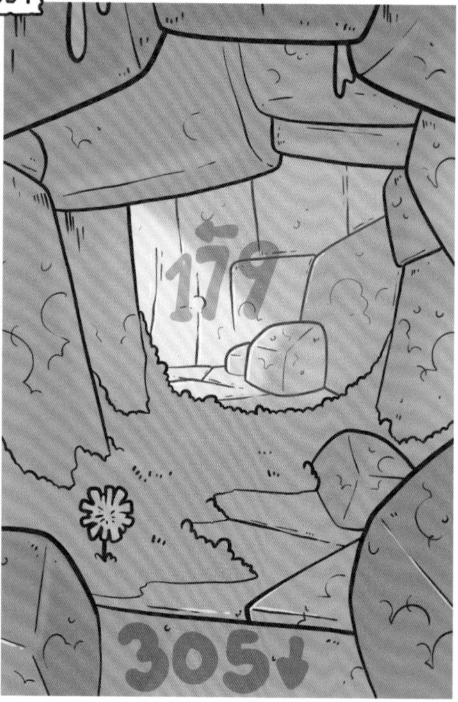
179
305

035

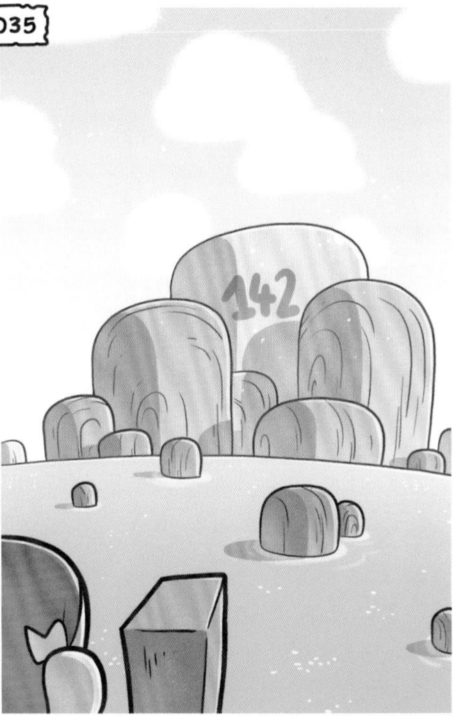
142

036

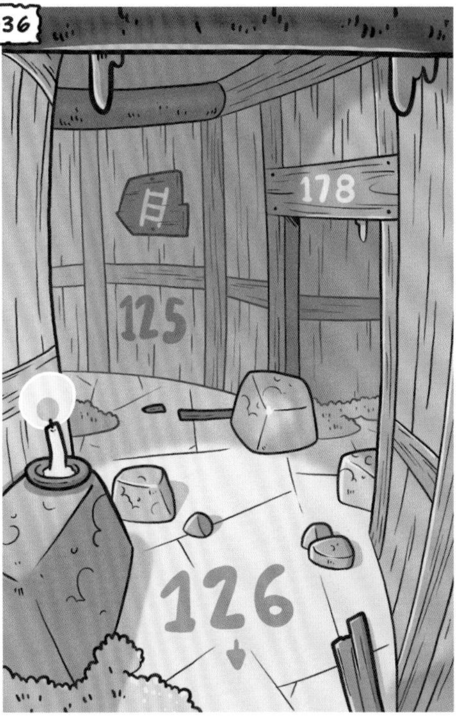
178
125
126

037

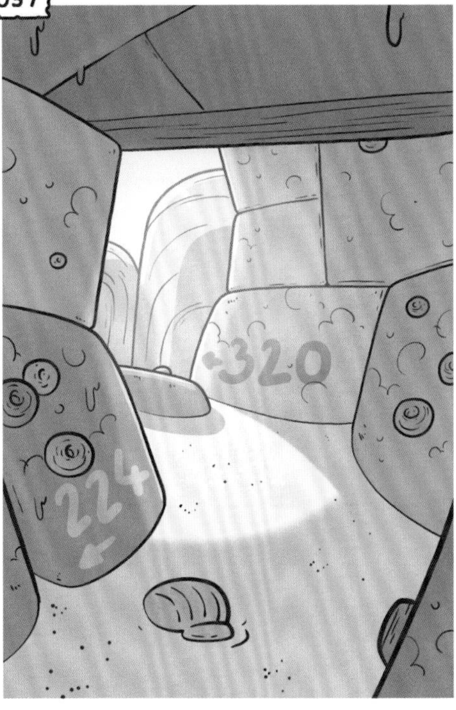
320
224

038

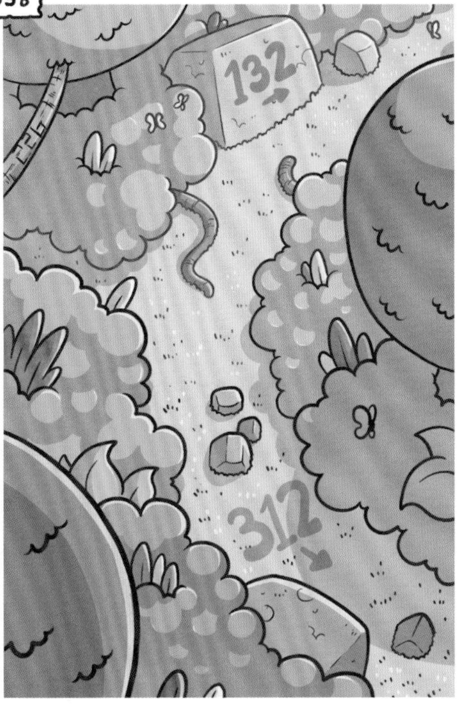
132
312

039

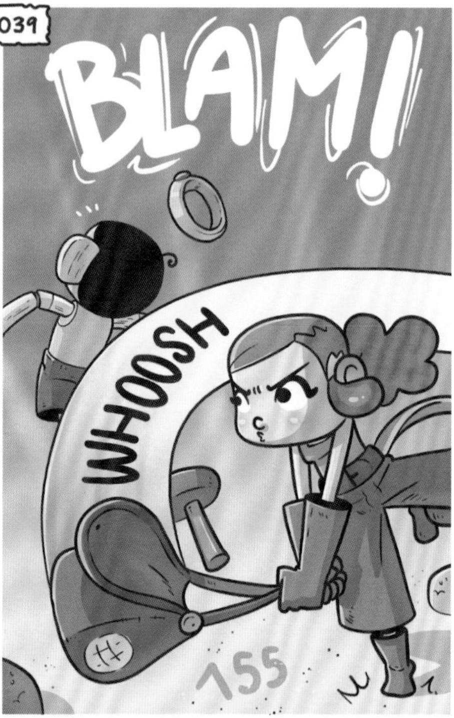
BLAM!
WHOOSH
155

040

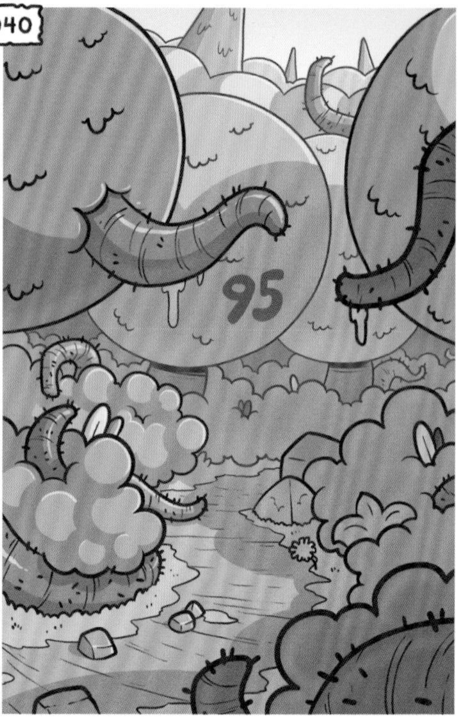
95

041

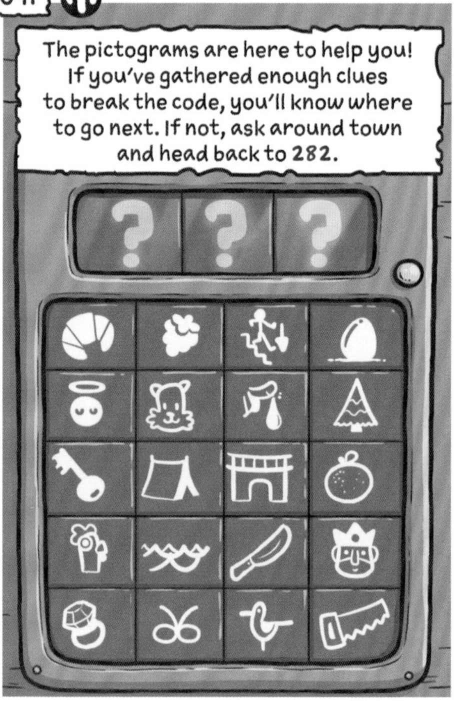
The pictograms are here to help you! If you've gathered enough clues to break the code, you'll know where to go next. If not, ask around town and head back to 282.
? ? ?

042

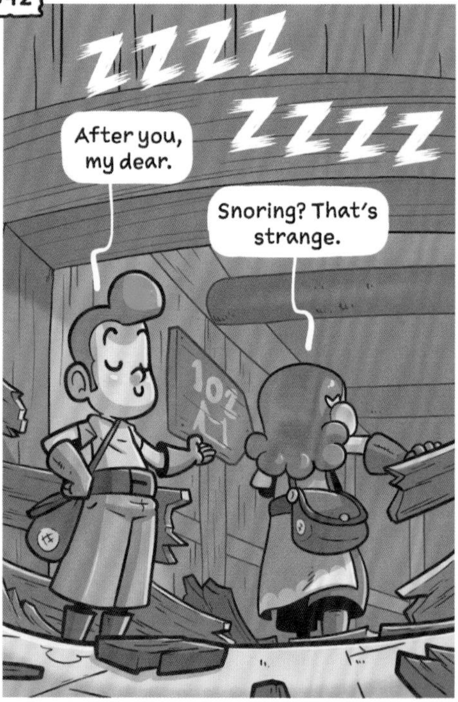
ZZZZ
ZZZZ
After you, my dear.
Snoring? That's strange.
102

043

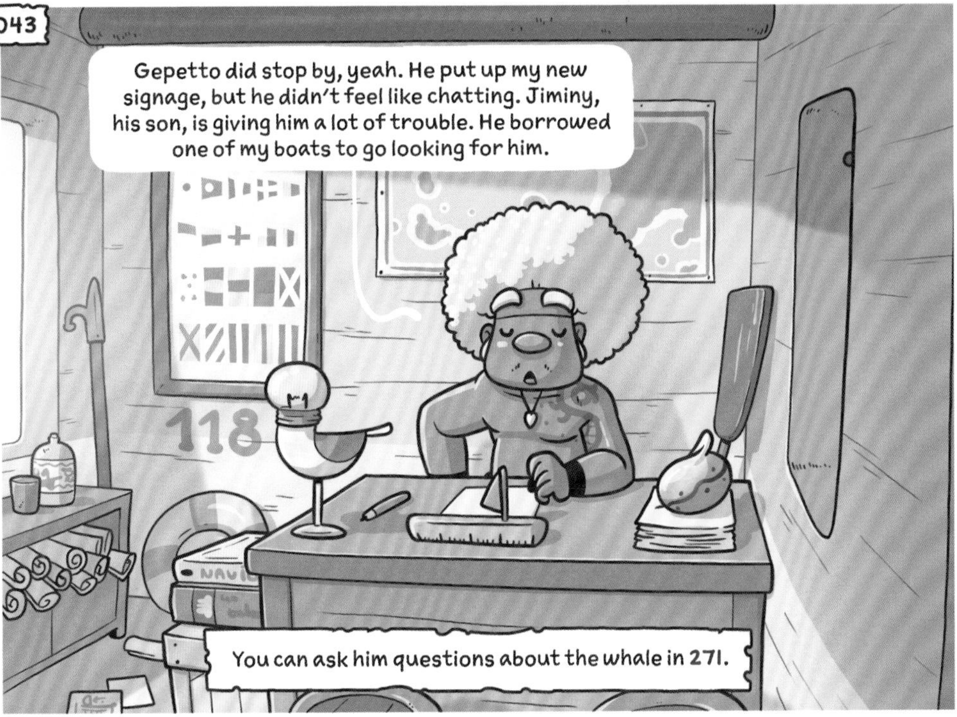
Gepetto did stop by, yeah. He put up my new signage, but he didn't feel like chatting. Jiminy, his son, is giving him a lot of trouble. He borrowed one of my boats to go looking for him.
118
You can ask him questions about the whale in 271.

044

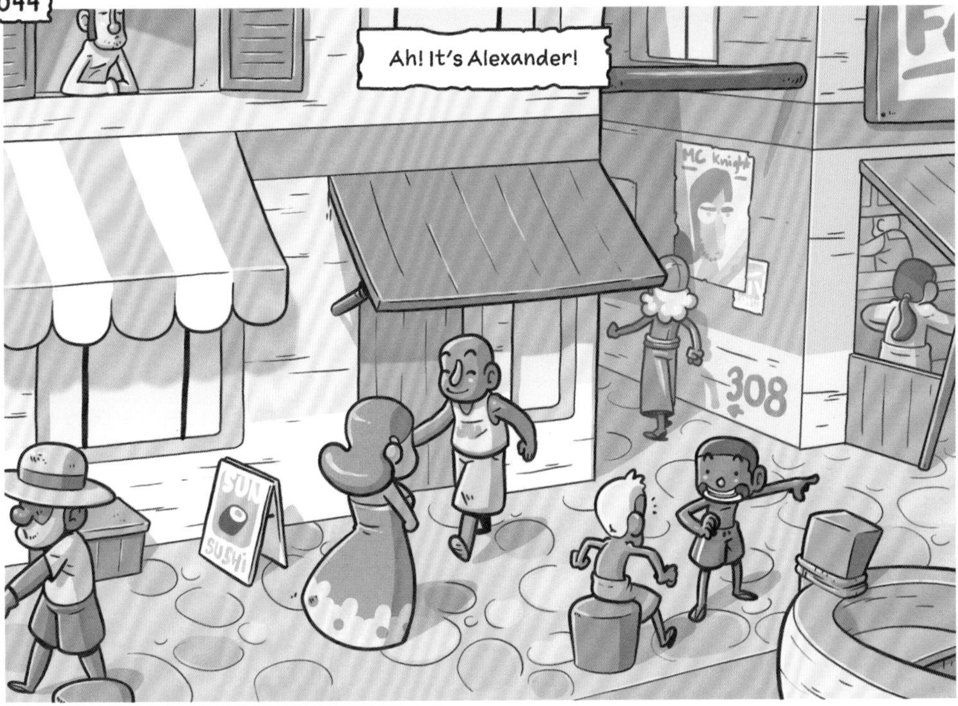
Ah! It's Alexander!
MC Knight
308
SUN
SUSHI

045

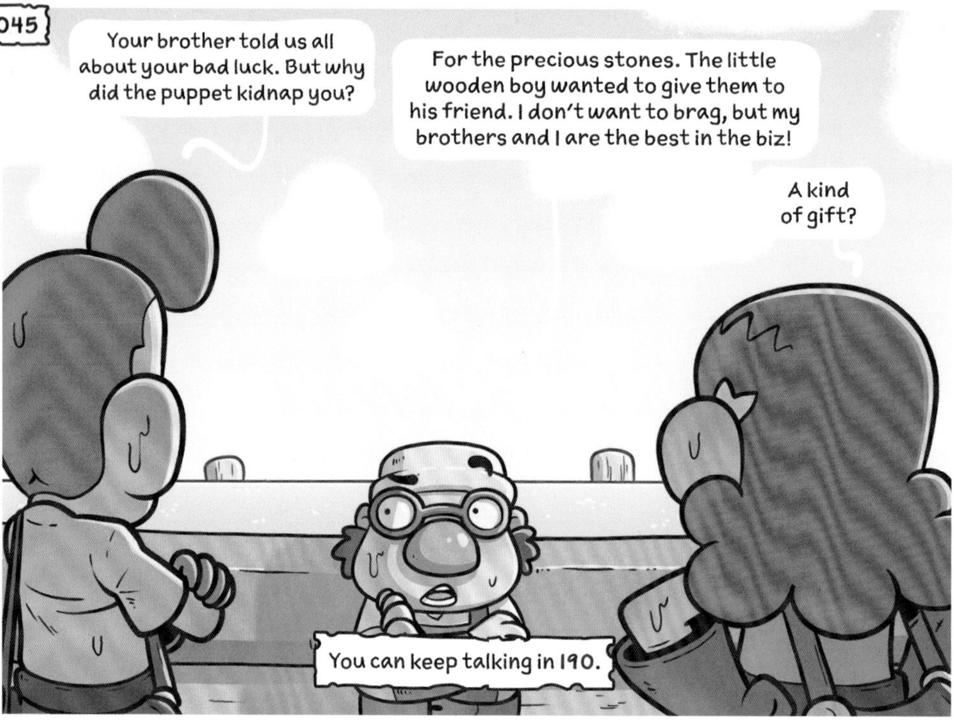
Your brother told us all about your bad luck. But why did the puppet kidnap you?
For the precious stones. The little wooden boy wanted to give them to his friend. I don't want to brag, but my brothers and I are the best in the biz!
A kind of gift?
You can keep talking in 190.

046

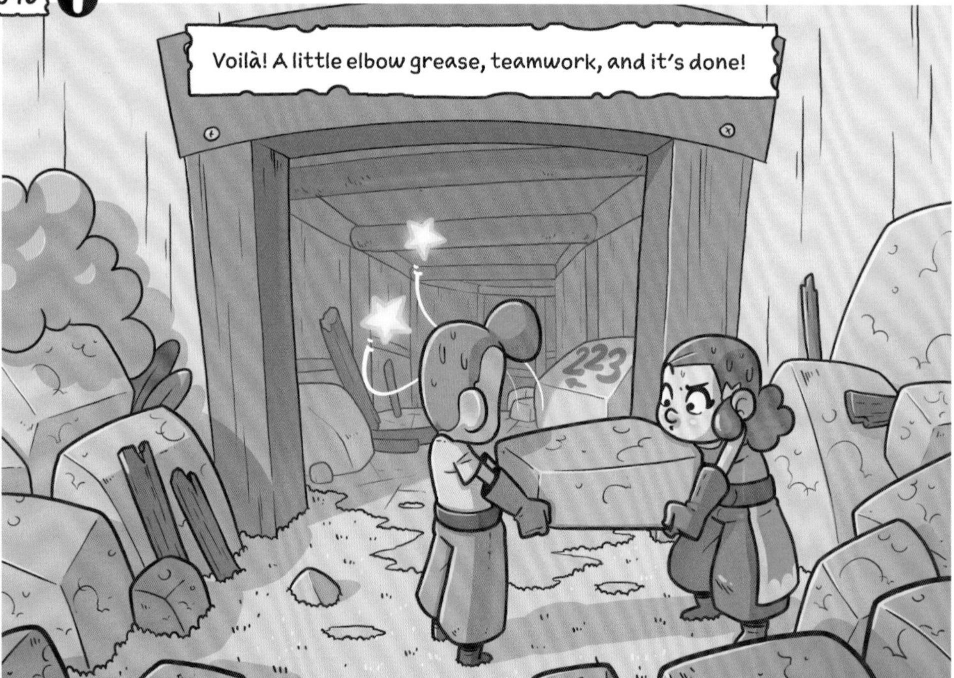
Voilà! A little elbow grease, teamwork, and it's done!
223

047

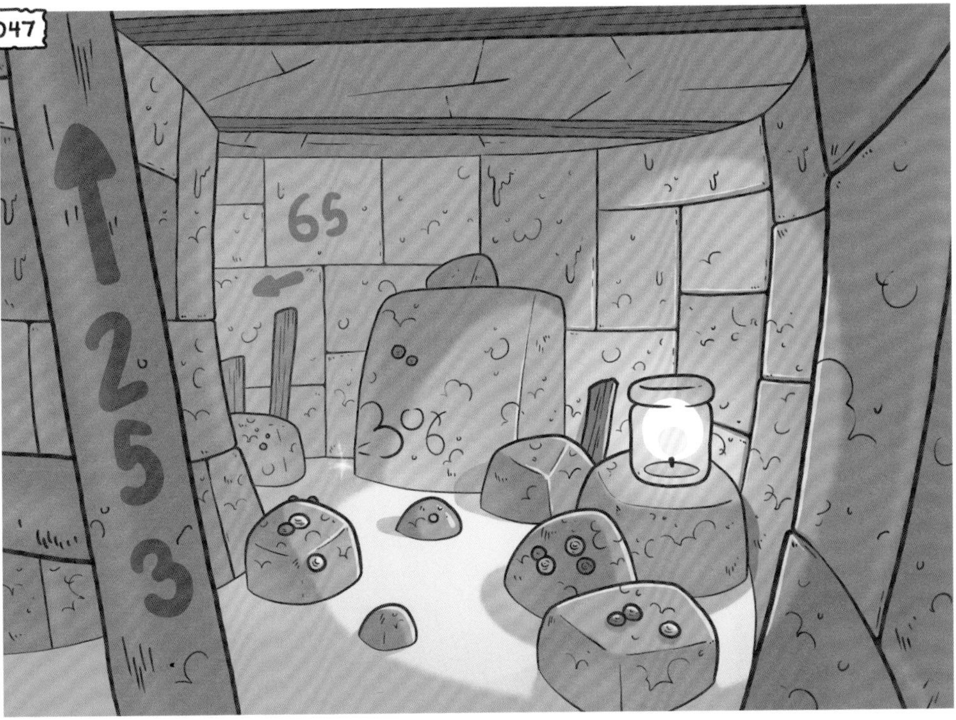
65
253
306

048

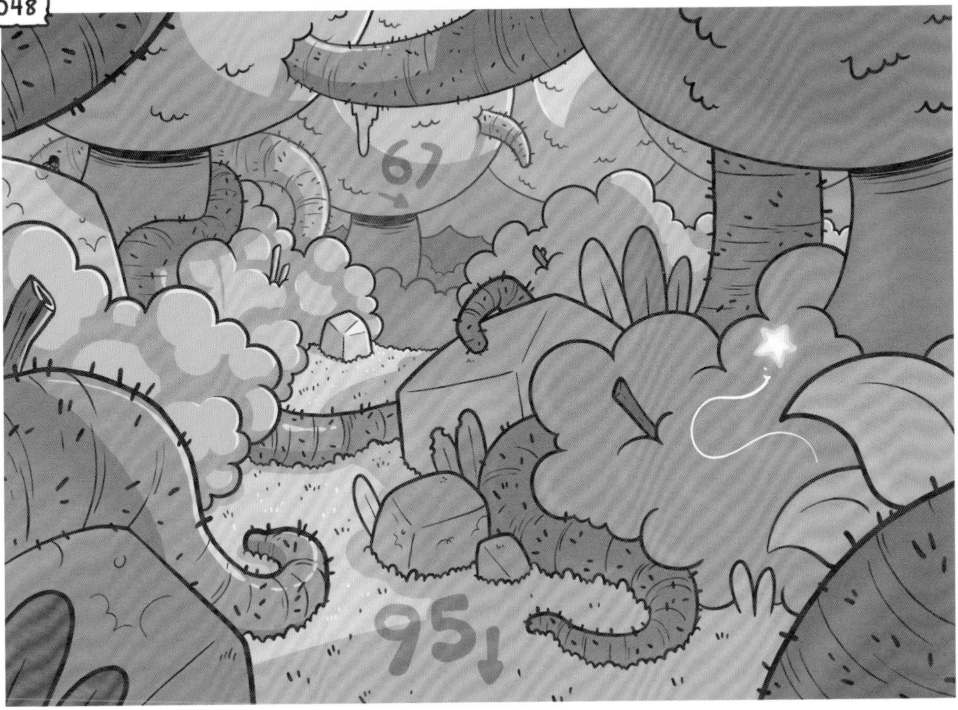
67
95

049

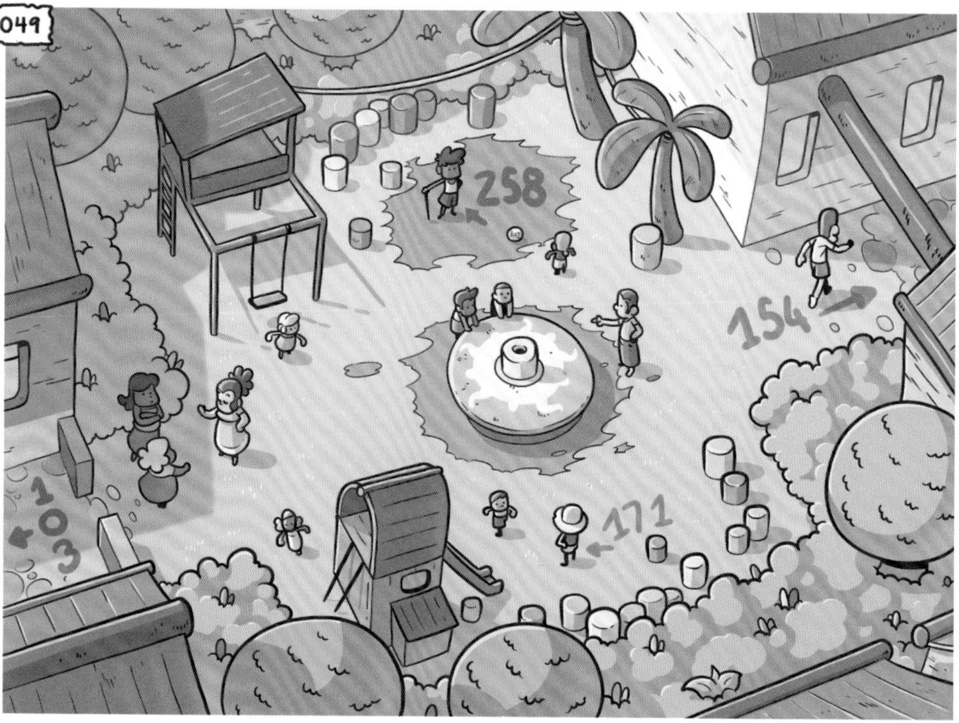
258
154
171
103

050

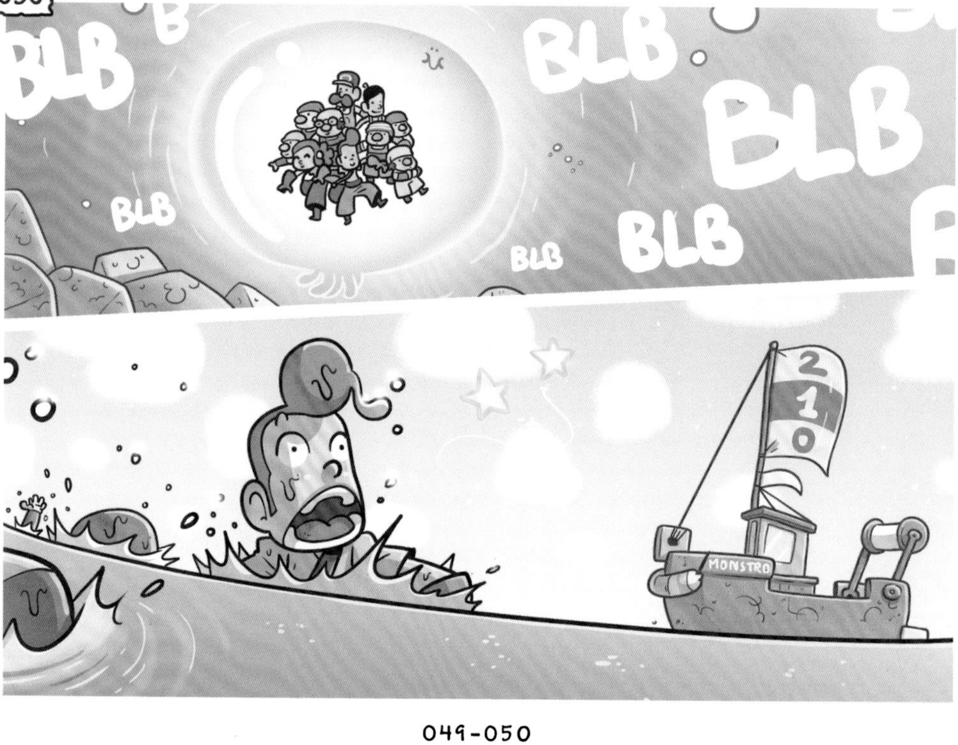
BLB
BLB
BLB
BLB
BLB
BLB
210
MONSTRO

051

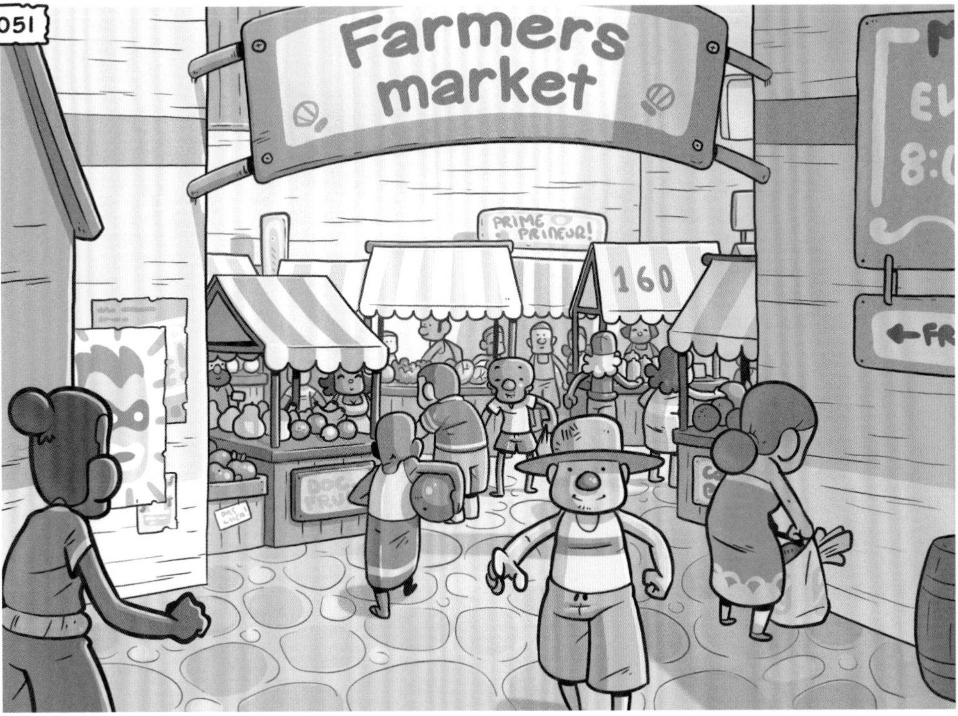
Farmers market
PRIME PRIMEUR!
160

052

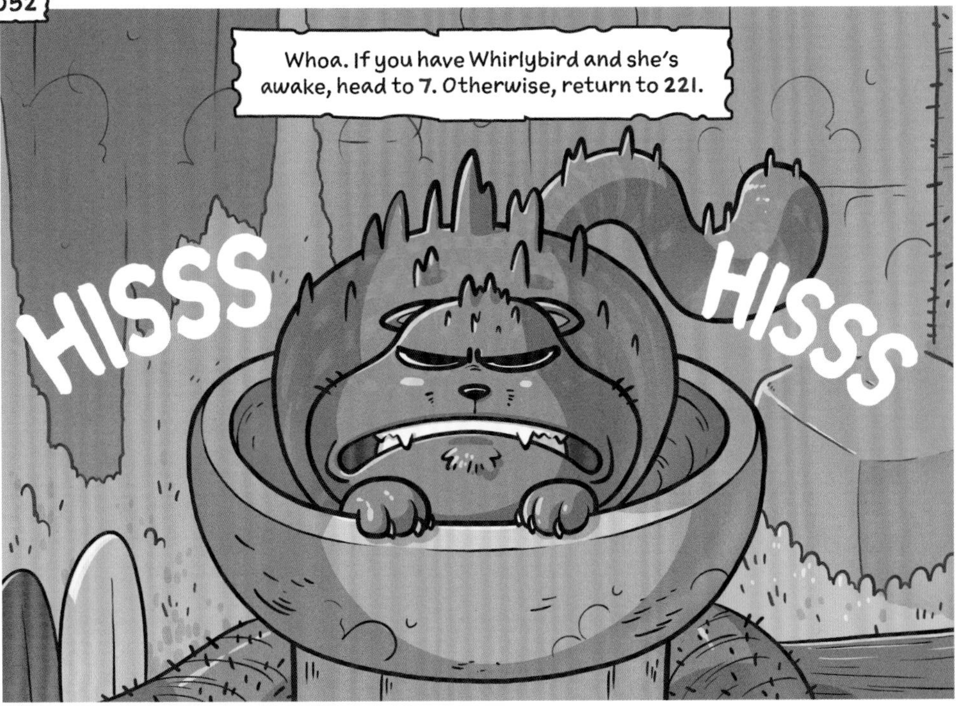
Whoa. If you have Whirlybird and she's awake, head to 7. Otherwise, return to 221.
HISSS
HISSS

053

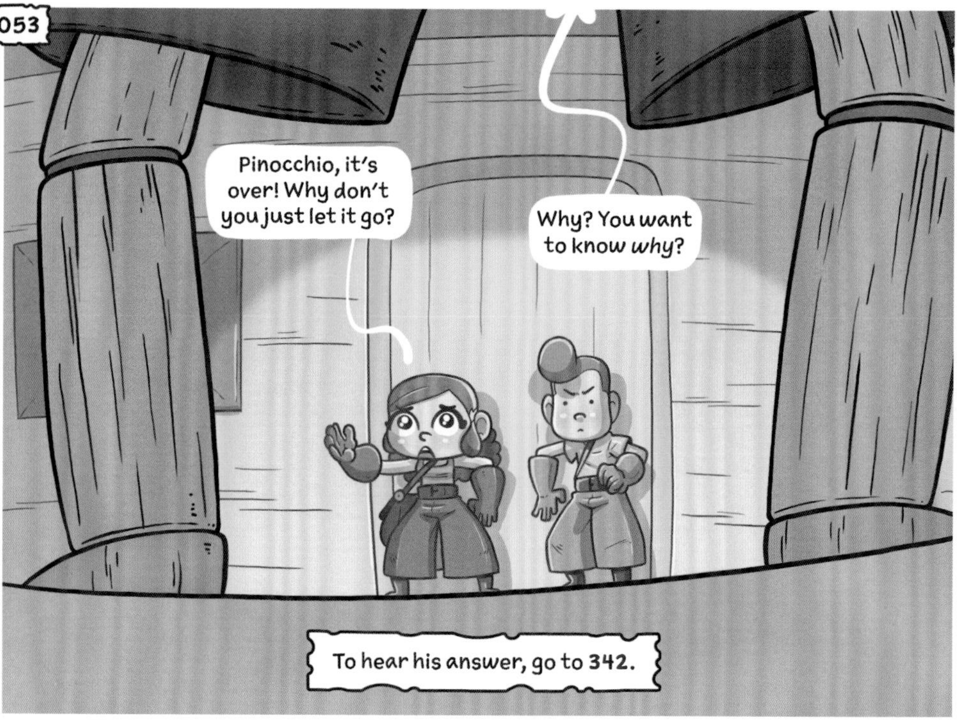
Pinocchio, it's over! Why don't you just let it go?
Why? You want to know *why*?
To hear his answer, go to **342**.

054

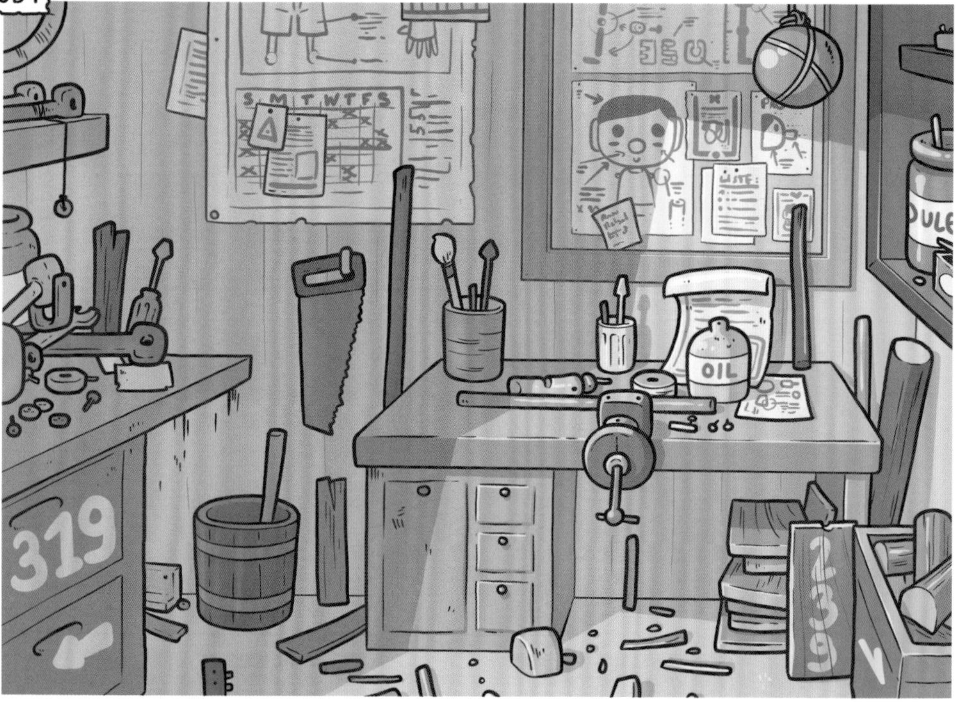
S M T W T F S
OIL
319

055

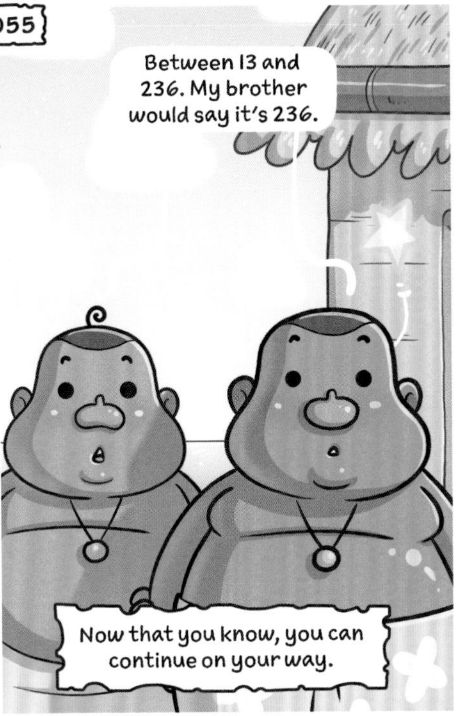
Between 13 and 236. My brother would say it's 236.
Now that you know, you can continue on your way.

056

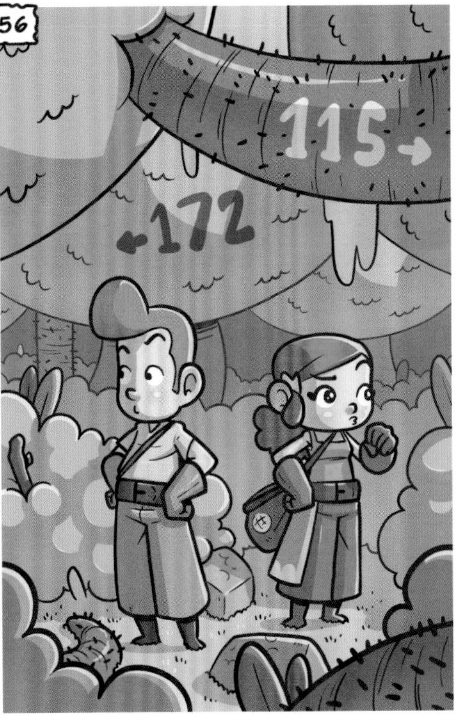
115
172

057

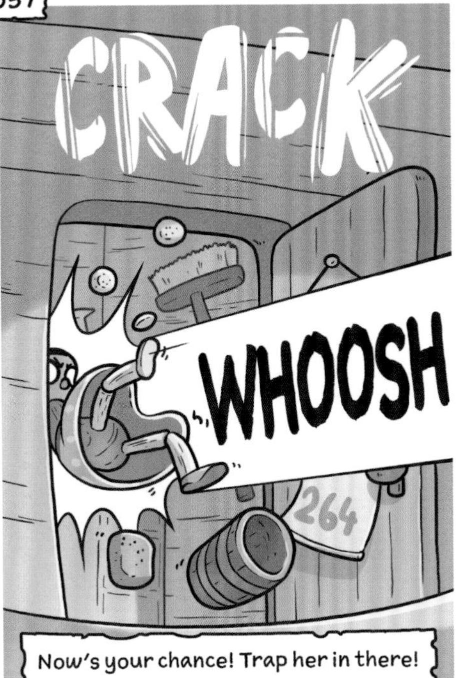
CRACK
WHOOSH
264
Now's your chance! Trap her in there!

058

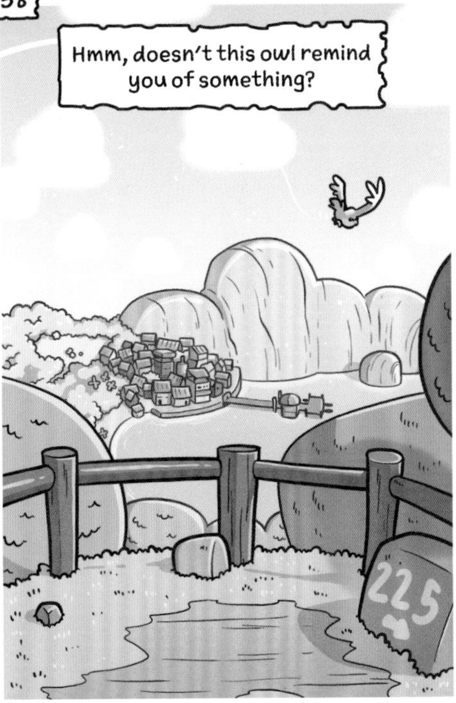
Hmm, doesn't this owl remind you of something?
225

059

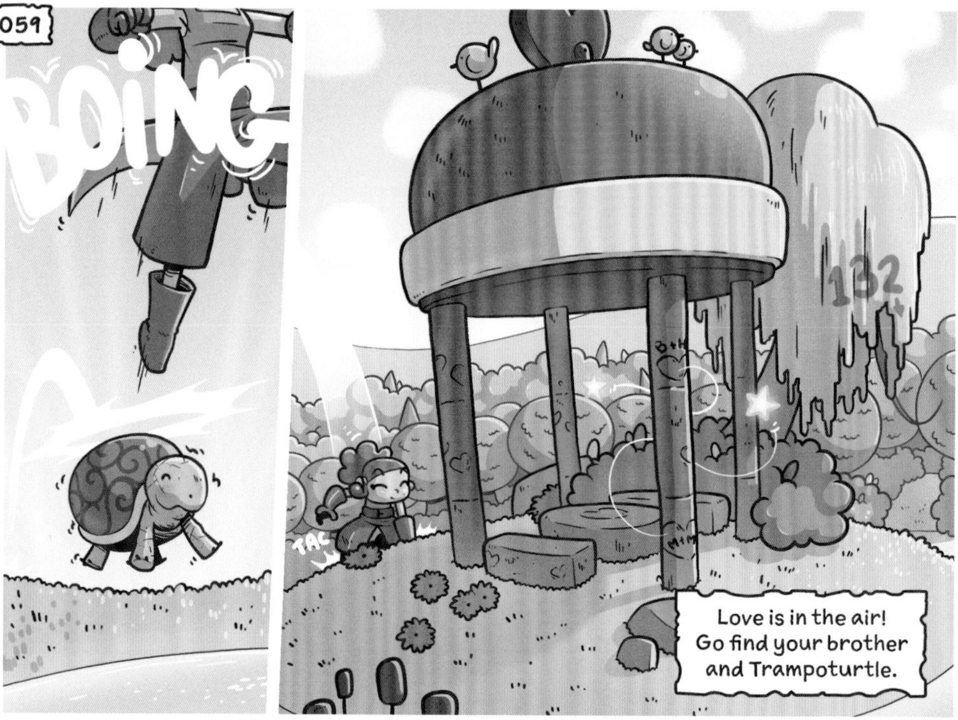
BOING
132
Love is in the air!
Go find your brother
and Trampoturtle.

060

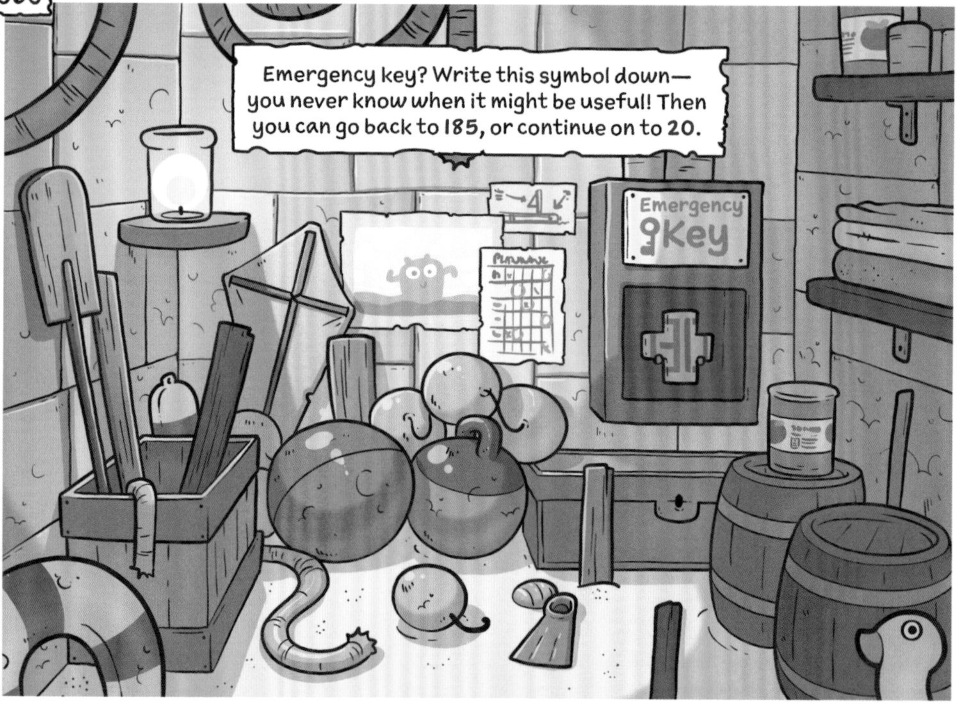
Emergency key? Write this symbol down—
you never know when it might be useful! Then
you can go back to 185, or continue on to 20.
Emergency
Key

061

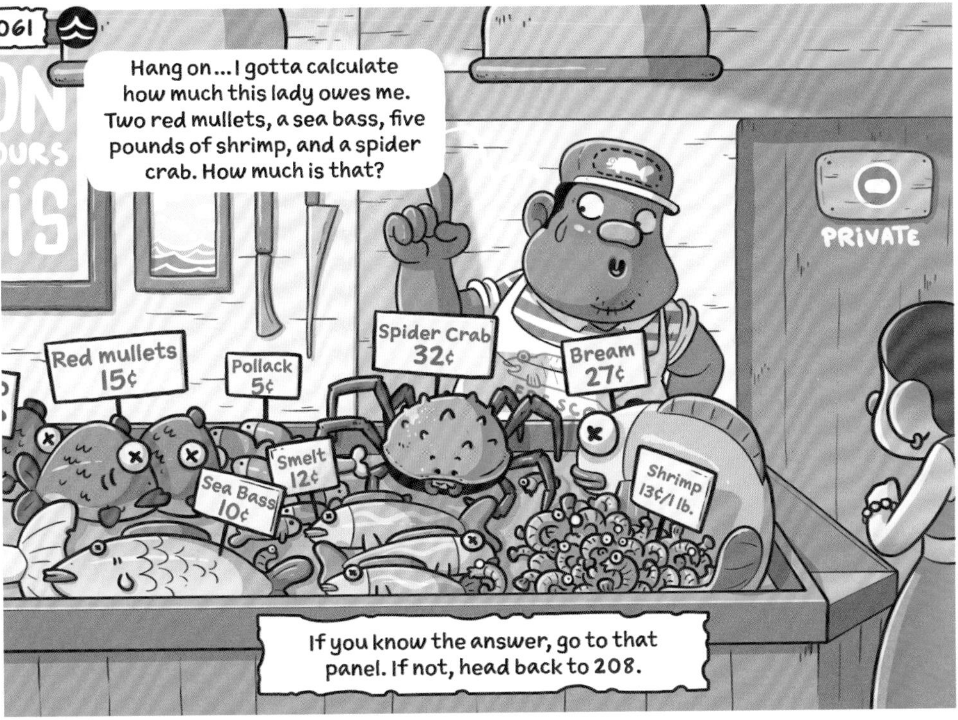
Hang on... I gotta calculate how much this lady owes me. Two red mullets, a sea bass, five pounds of shrimp, and a spider crab. How much is that?
PRIVATE
Red mullets 15¢
Pollack 5¢
Spider Crab 32¢
Bream 27¢
Smelt 12¢
Sea Bass 10¢
Shrimp 13¢/1 lb.
If you know the answer, go to that panel. If not, head back to 208.

062

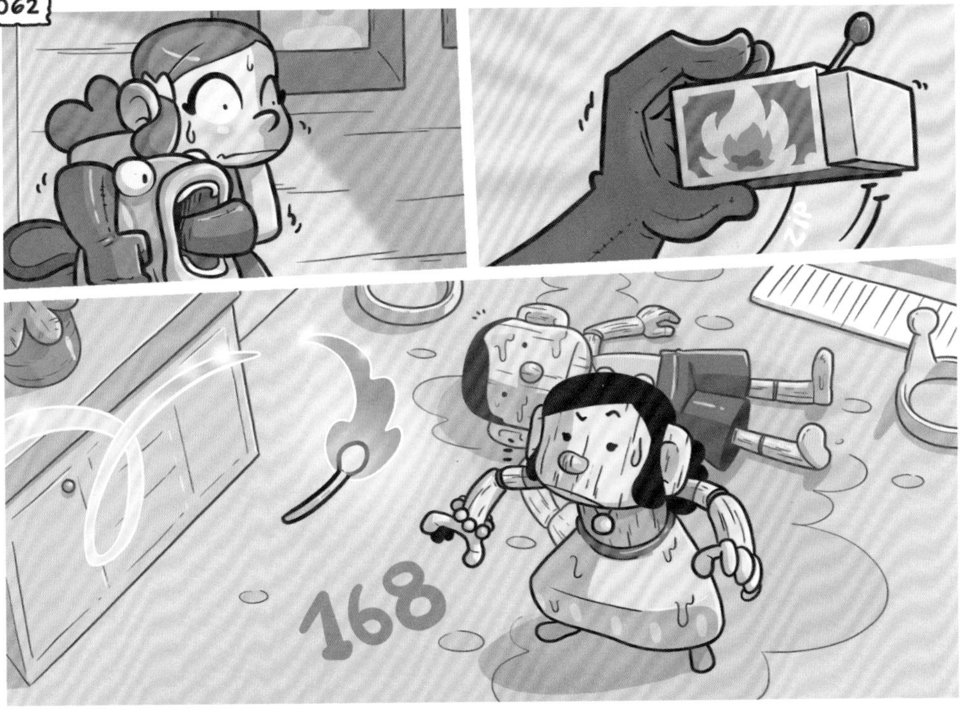
168

063

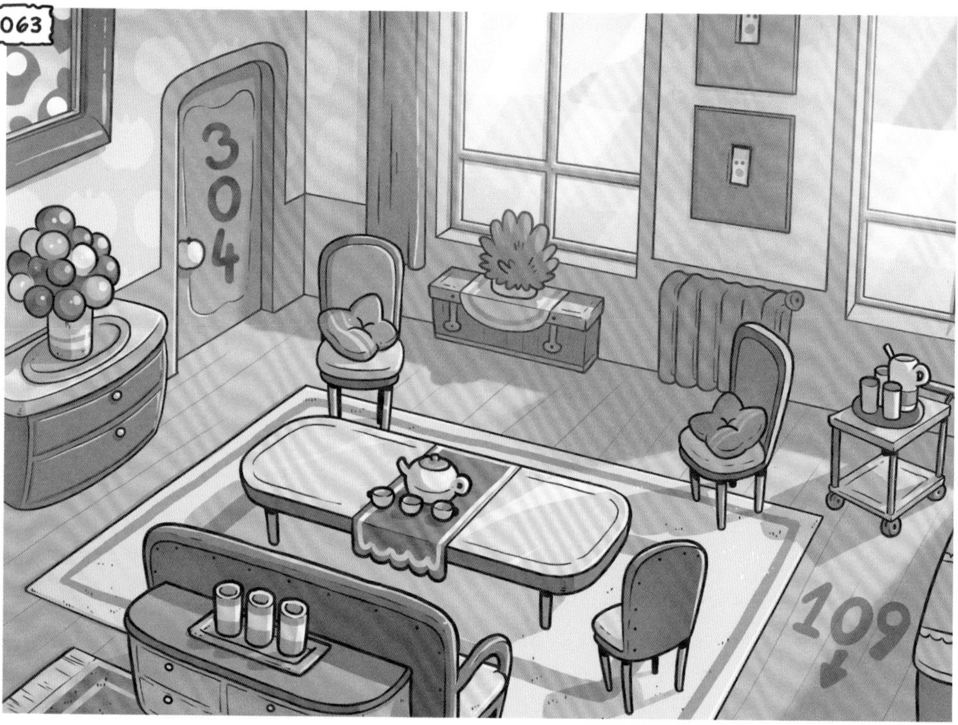
304
109

064

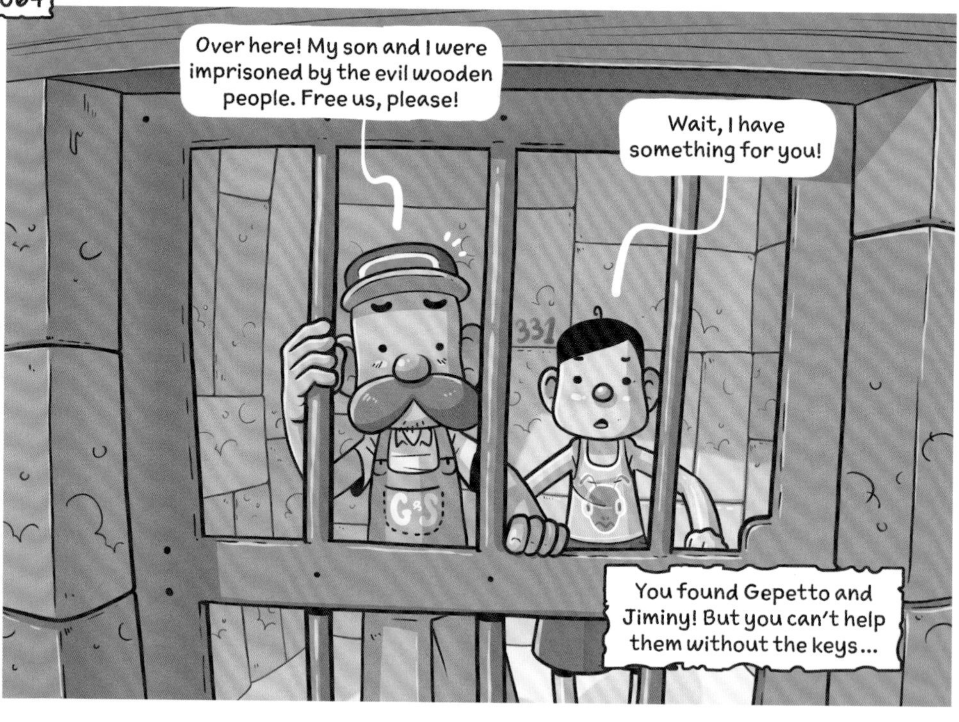
Over here! My son and I were imprisoned by the evil wooden people. Free us, please!
Wait, I have something for you!
331
You found Gepetto and Jiminy! But you can't help them without the keys...

065

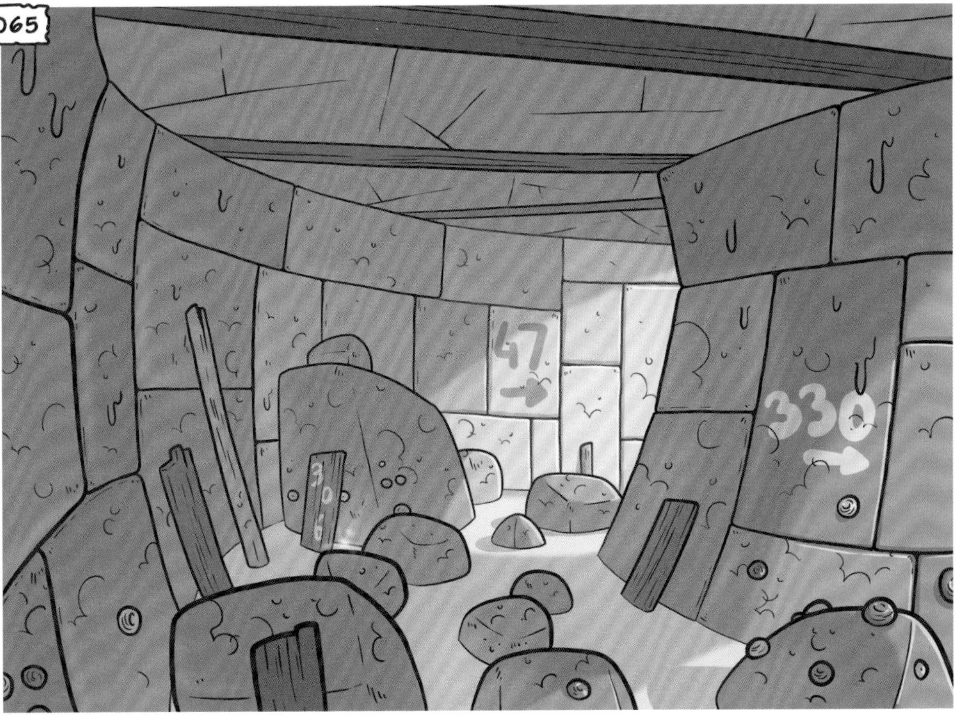
47 →
330 →
306

066

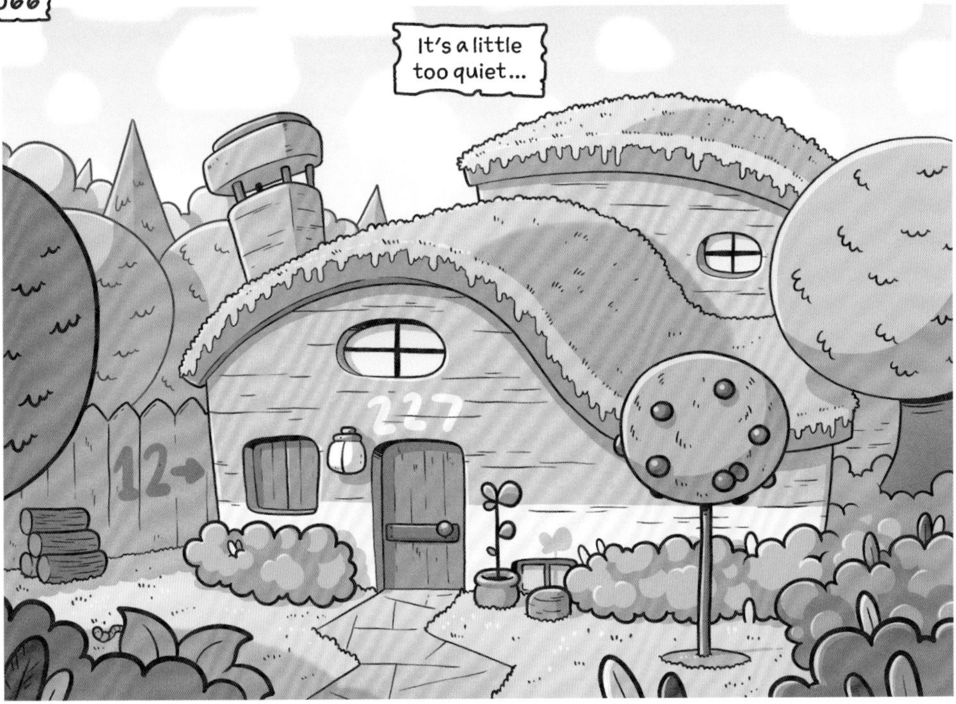
It's a little too quiet...
227
12 →

067

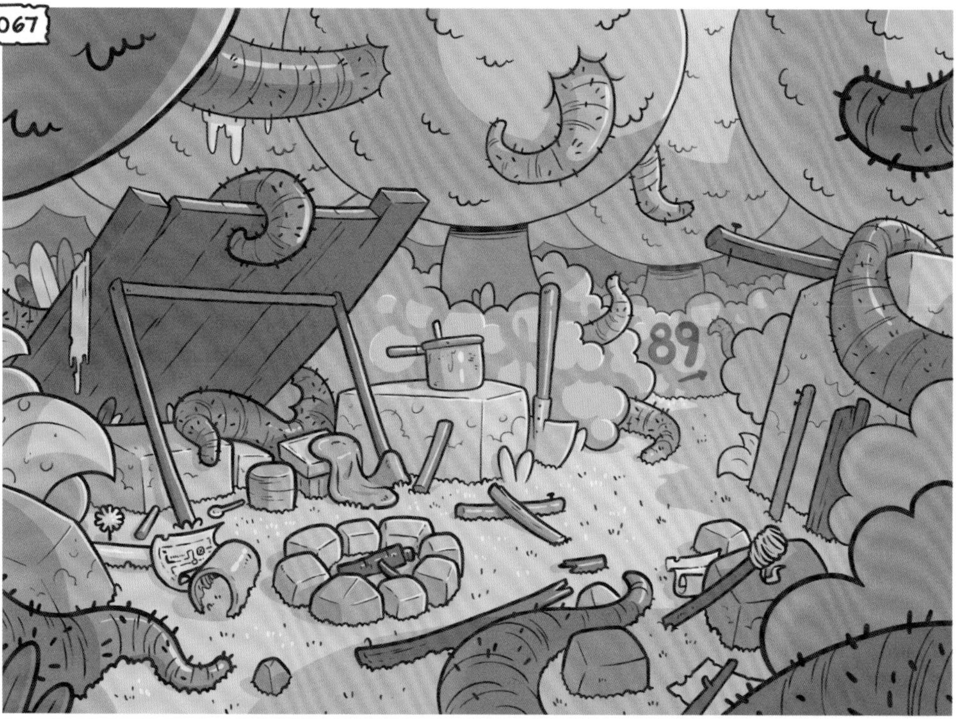
89

068

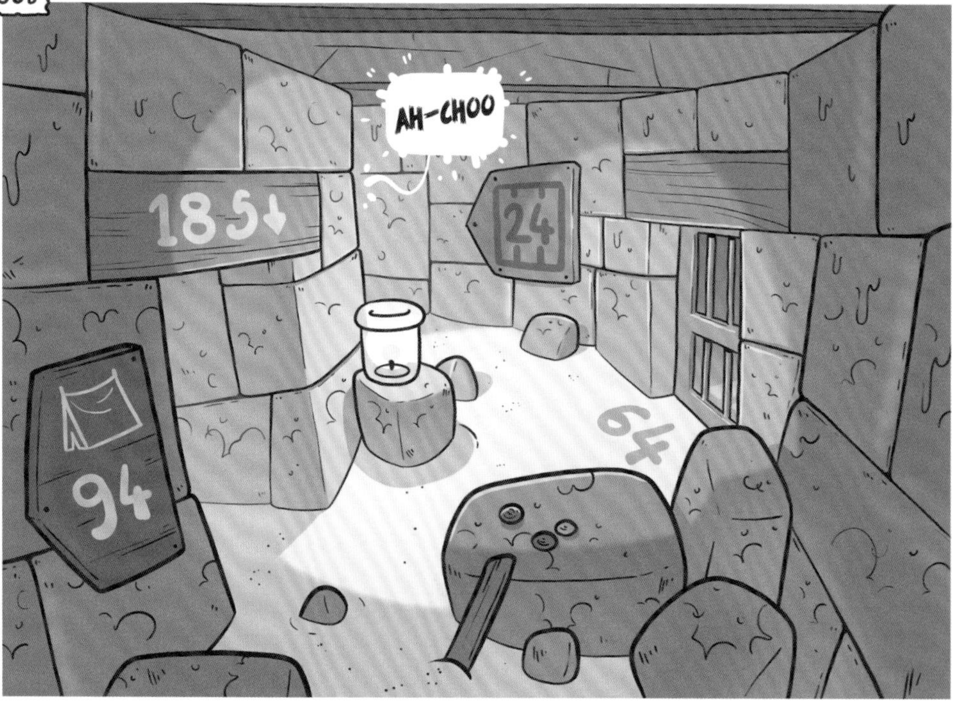
AH-CHOO
185↓
24
94
64

069

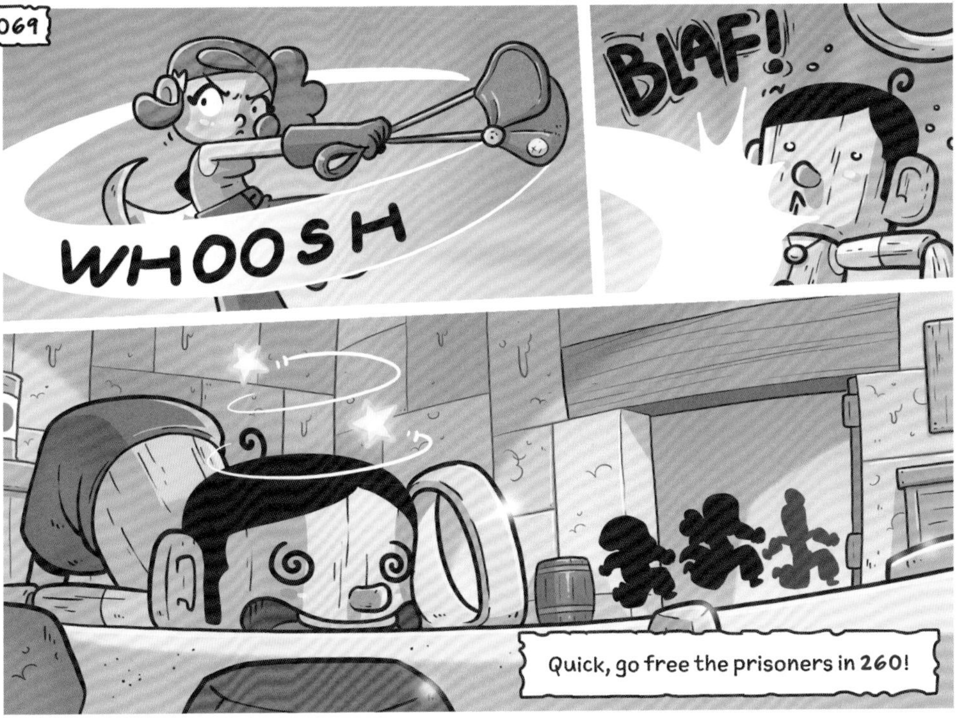
WHOOSH
BLAF!
Quick, go free the prisoners in 260!

070

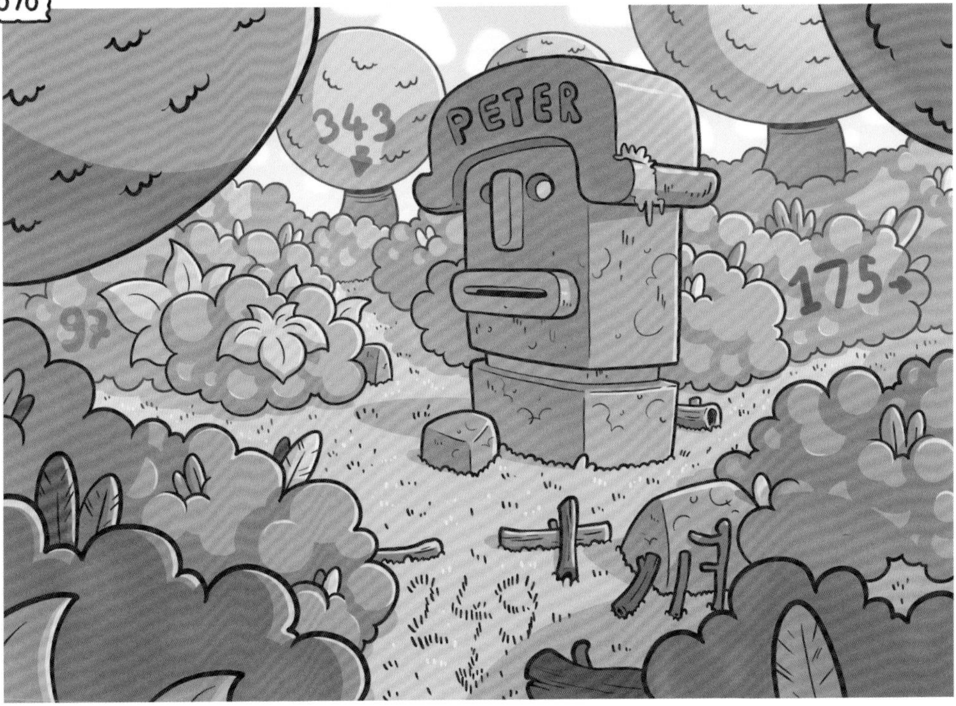
PETER
343
97
175

071

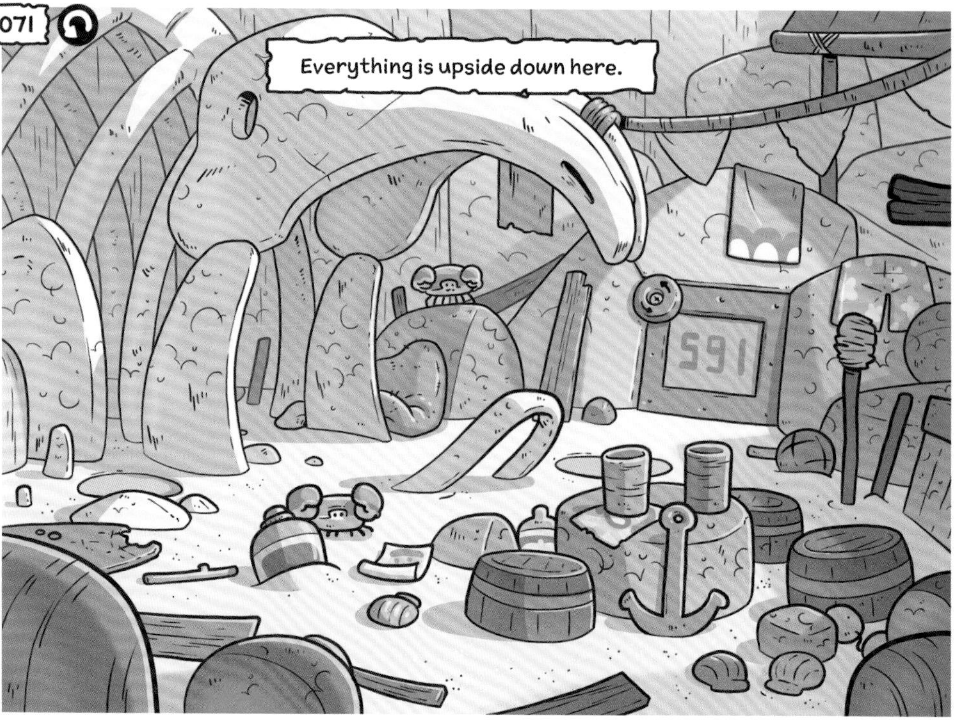
Everything is upside down here.

072

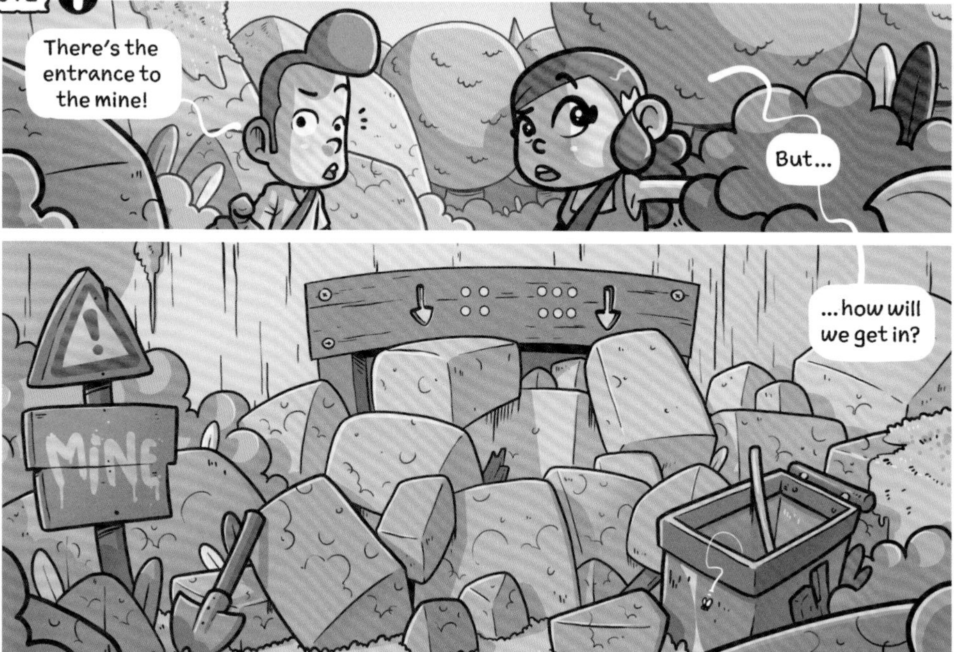
There's the entrance to the mine!
But...
...how will we get in?
MINE

073

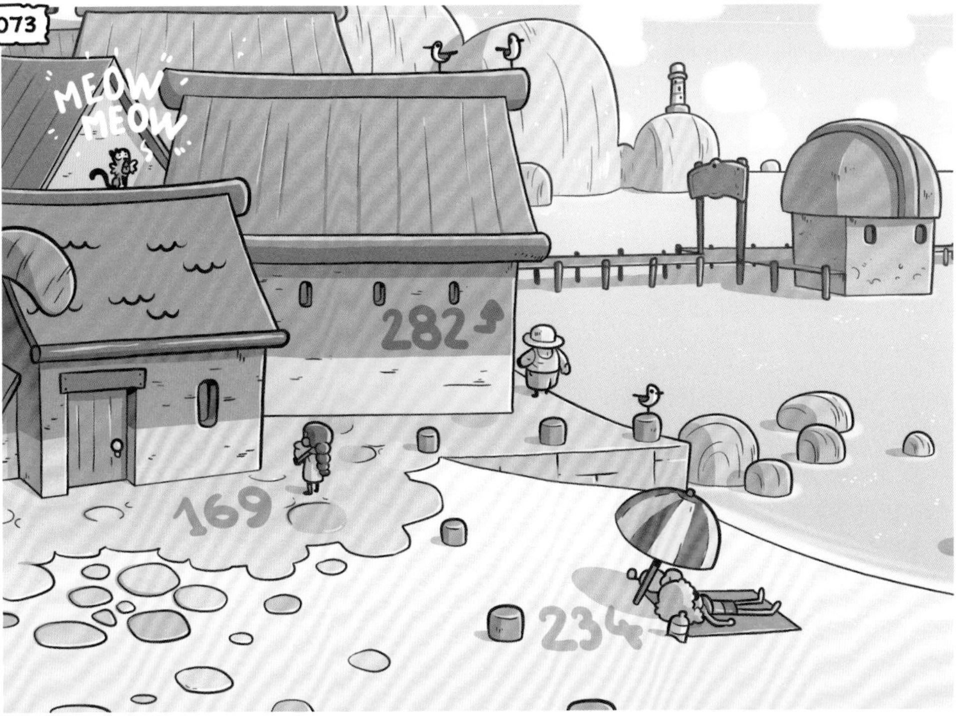
MEOW
MEOW
282
169
234

074

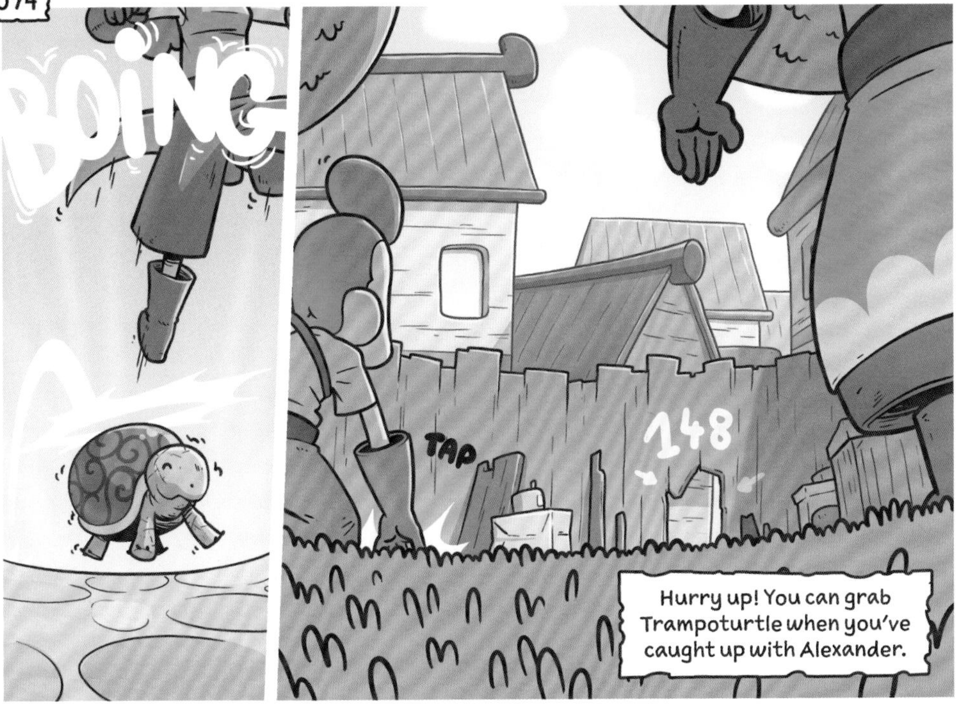
BOING
TAP
148
Hurry up! You can grab Trampoturtle when you've caught up with Alexander.

075

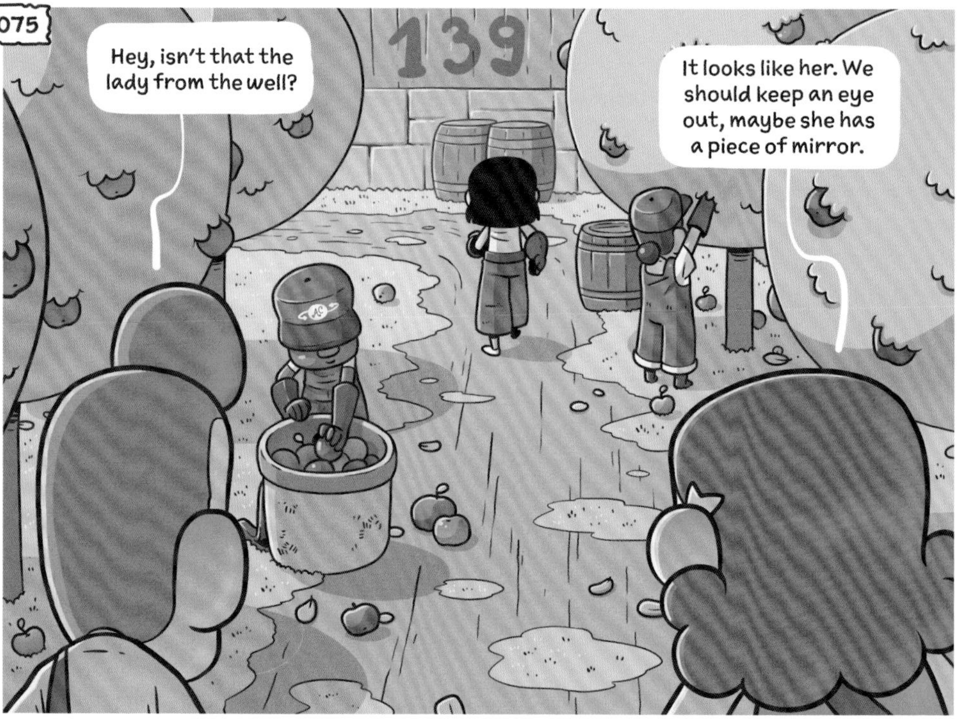
139
Hey, isn't that the lady from the well?
It looks like her. We should keep an eye out, maybe she has a piece of mirror.

076

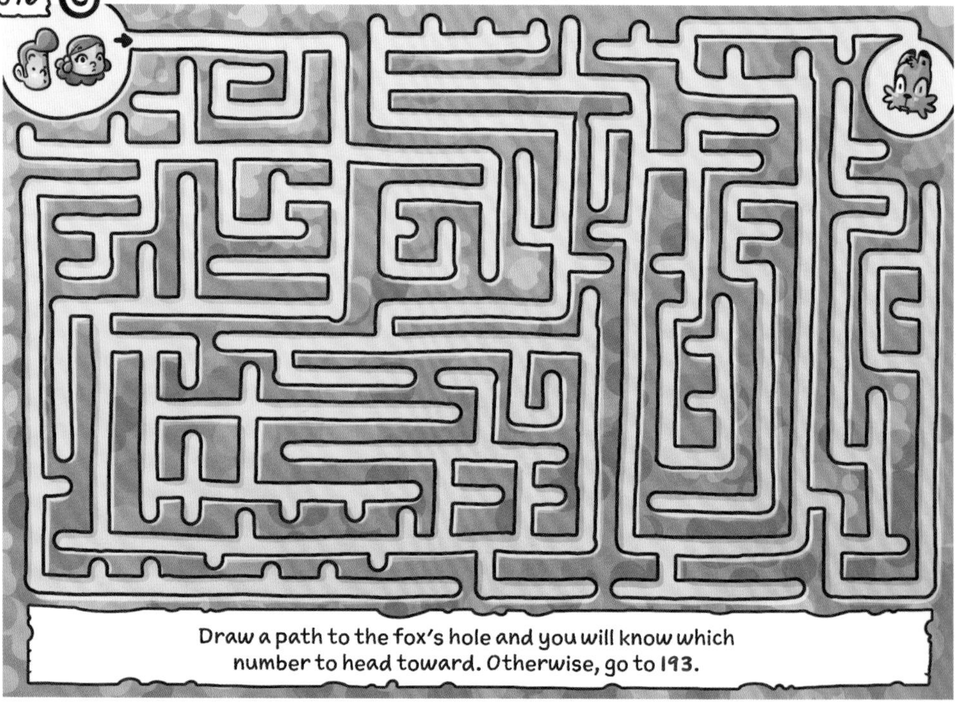

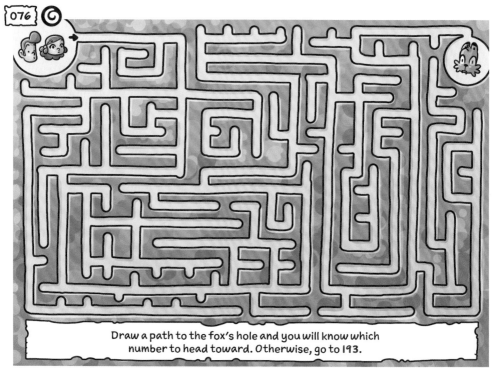

Draw a path to the fox's hole and you will know which number to head toward. Otherwise, go to 193.

077

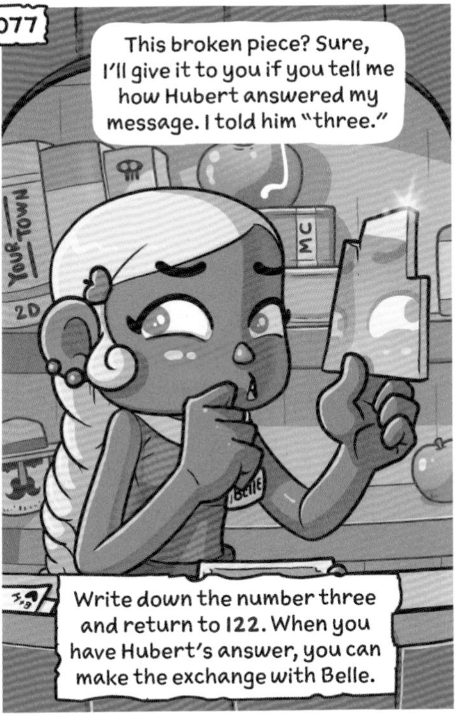
This broken piece? Sure, I'll give it to you if you tell me how Hubert answered my message. I told him "three."
YOUR TOWN
MC
2D
BELLE
Write down the number three and return to 122. When you have Hubert's answer, you can make the exchange with Belle.

078

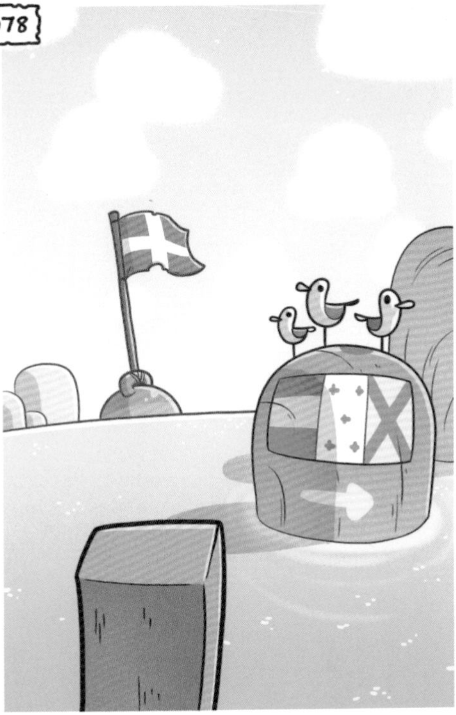

079

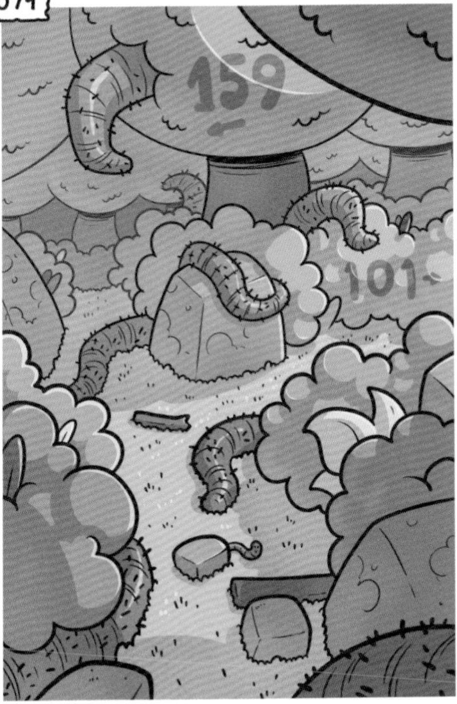
159
101

080

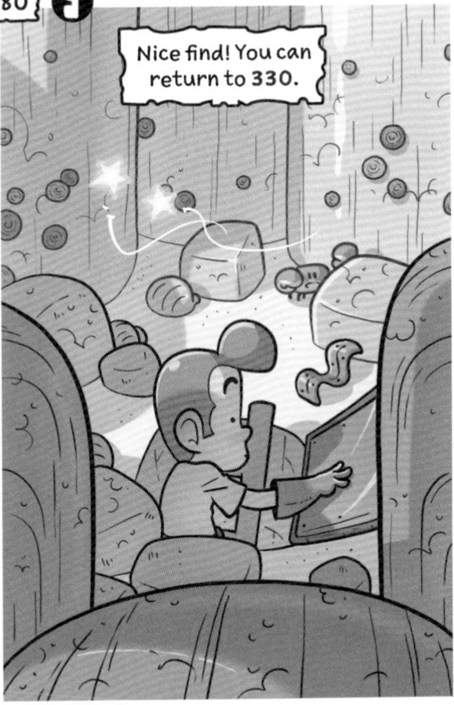
Nice find! You can return to 330.

081

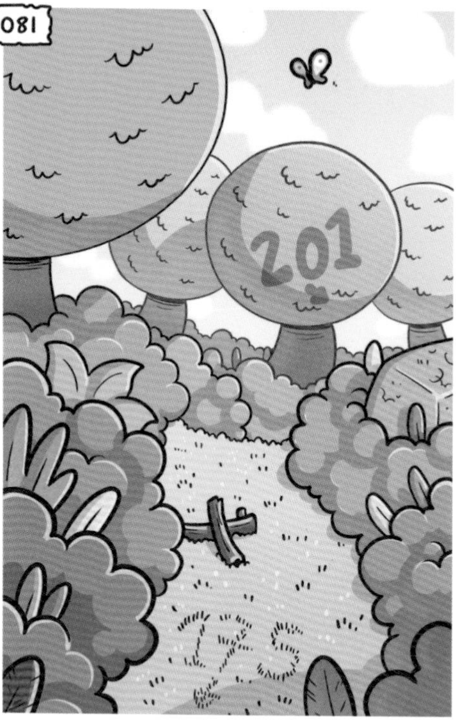
201

082

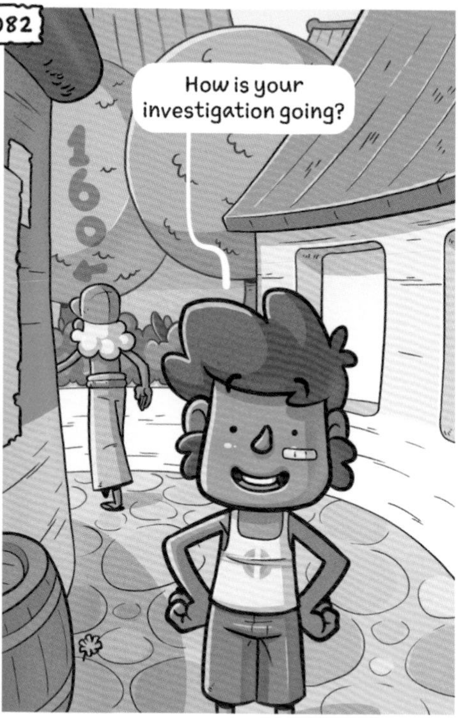
160
How is your investigation going?

083

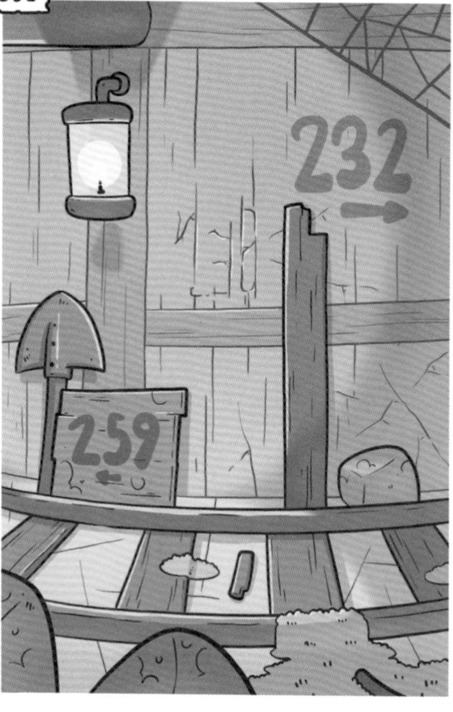
232
259

084

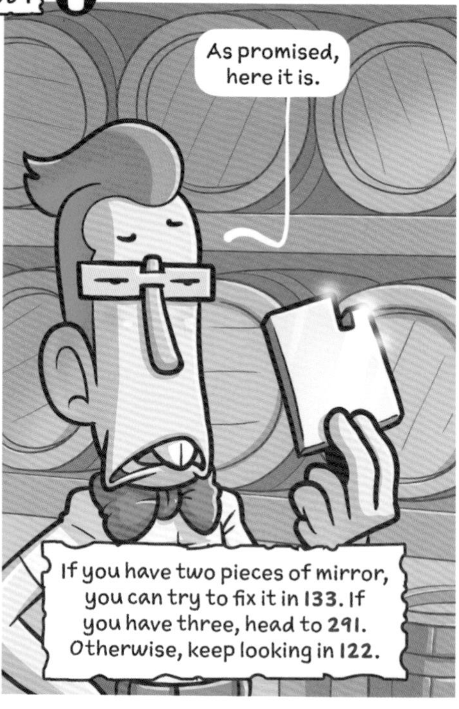
As promised, here it is.
If you have two pieces of mirror, you can try to fix it in 133. If you have three, head to 291. Otherwise, keep looking in 122.

085

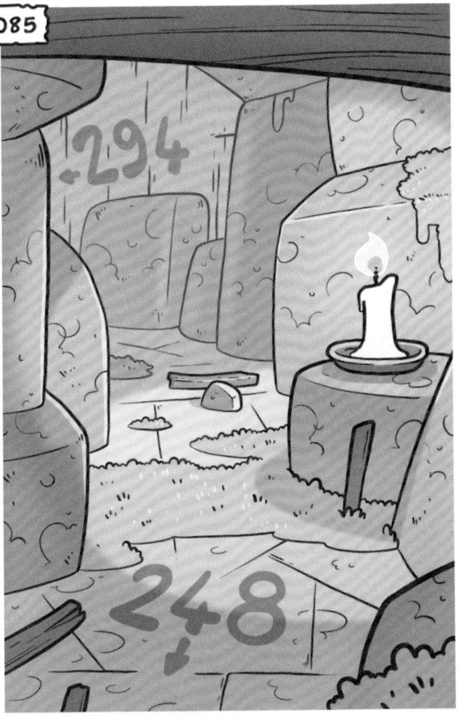

294
248

086

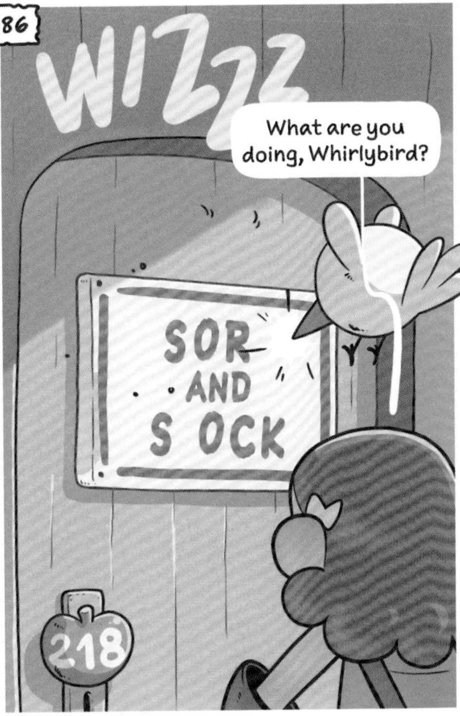

WIZZZ
What are you doing, Whirlybird?
SOR AND S OCK
218

087

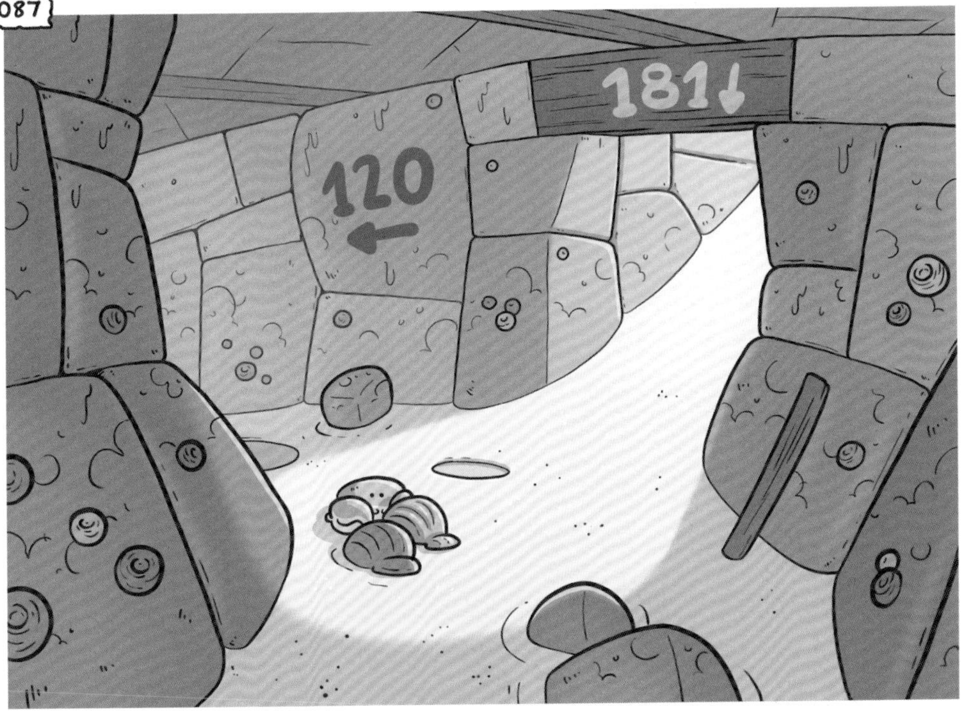

181
120

So you're looking for Gepetto?

Yeah.

We hope he can help us find Snow's cousins.

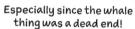

If I've seen him, it was a long time ago. And he didn't even say hi.

Shoot, what are we gonna do?

Especially since the whale thing was a dead end!

A whale?

Yes.

Ha ha! There are no whales around here. Or there haven't been in a long time, anyway...

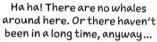

This just keeps getting better and better.

Wait! My son often talks about a place called the Whale. You should pay him a visit. He's probably hanging out in the village. His name is Alexander; we look like twins.

To head back to land, go to 244.

089

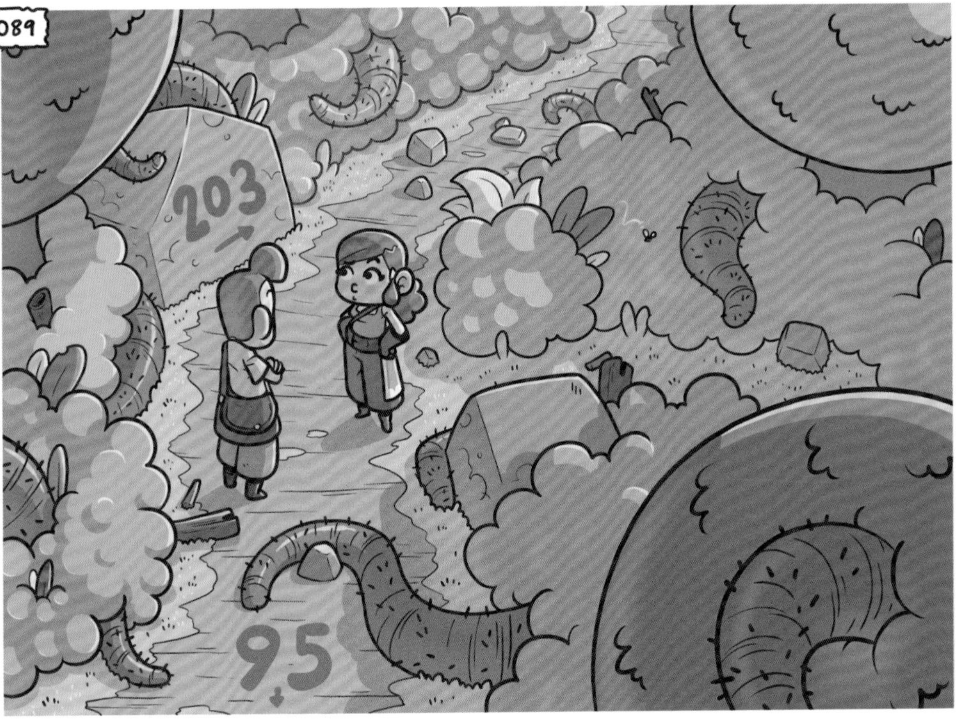
203
95

090

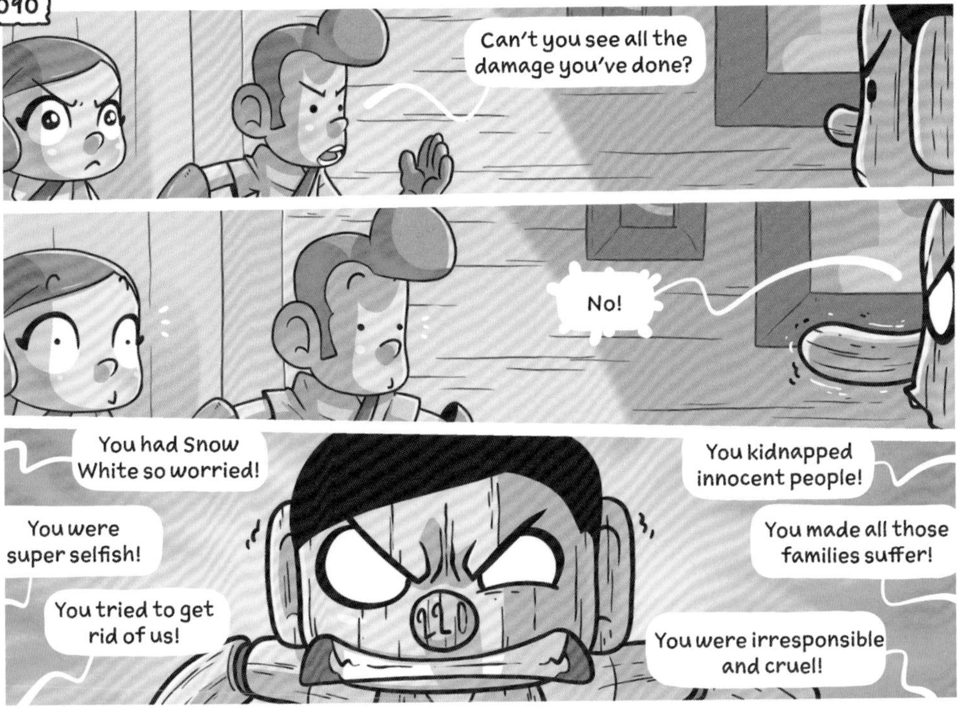
Can't you see all the damage you've done?
No!
You had Snow White so worried!
You were super selfish!
You tried to get rid of us!
You kidnapped innocent people!
You made all those families suffer!
You were irresponsible and cruel!
220

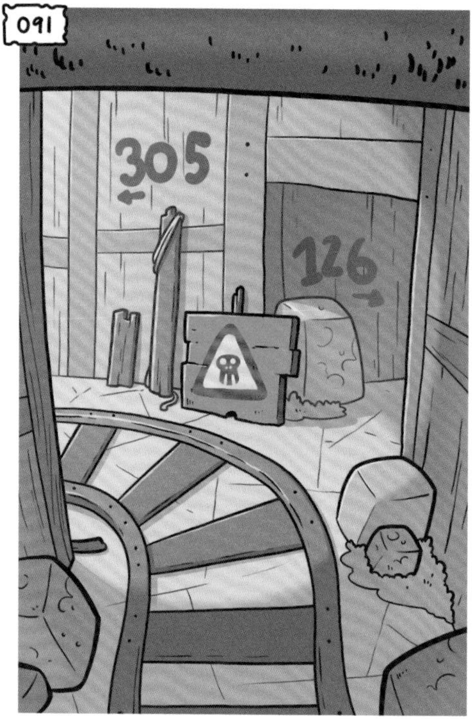
091
305
126

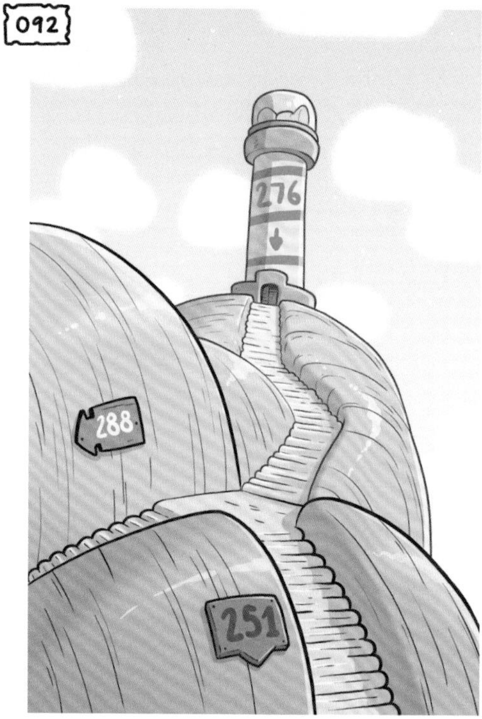
092
276
288
251

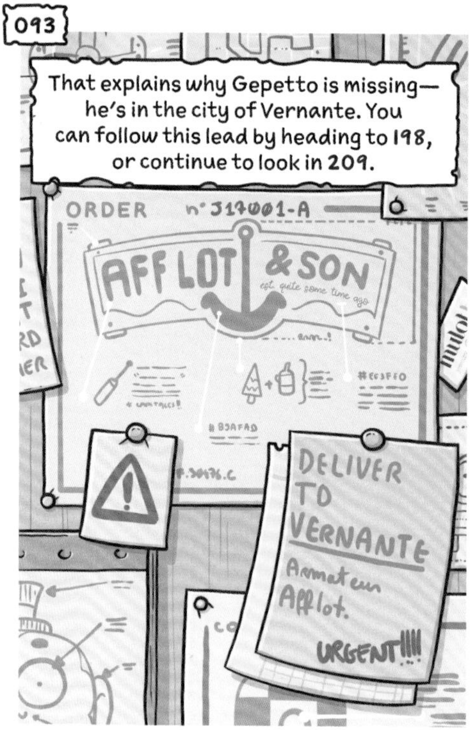
093
That explains why Gepetto is missing—he's in the city of Vernante. You can follow this lead by heading to 198, or continue to look in 209.
ORDER n° J17001-A
AFF LOT & SON
est. quite some time ago
DELIVER TO VERNANTE
Armateur Afflot.
URGENT!!!!

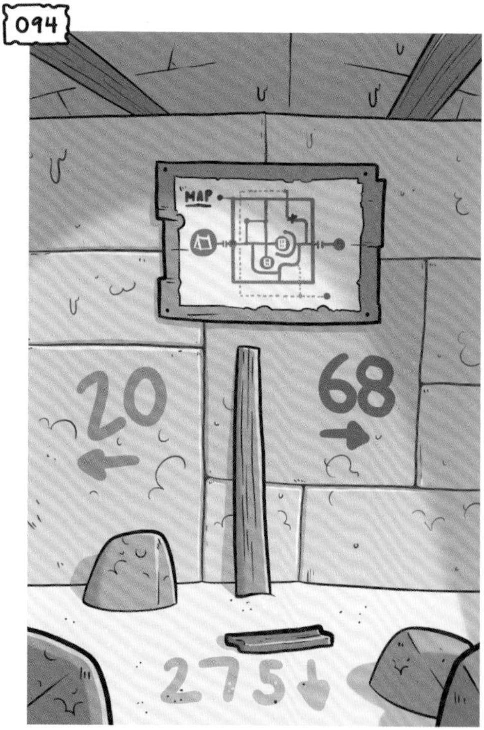
094
MAP
20
68
275

095

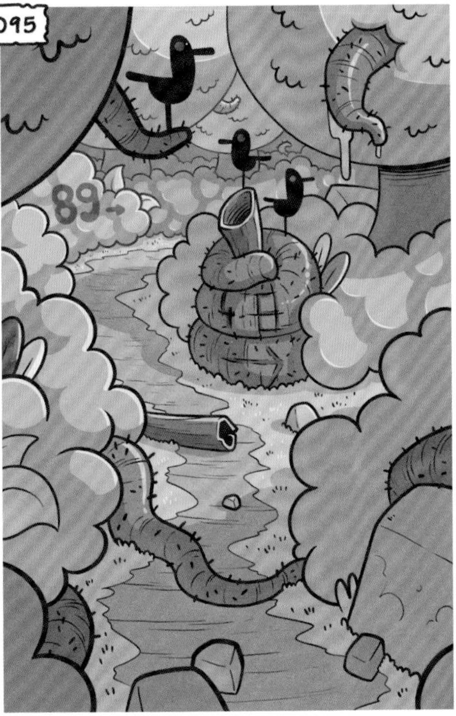
89→

096

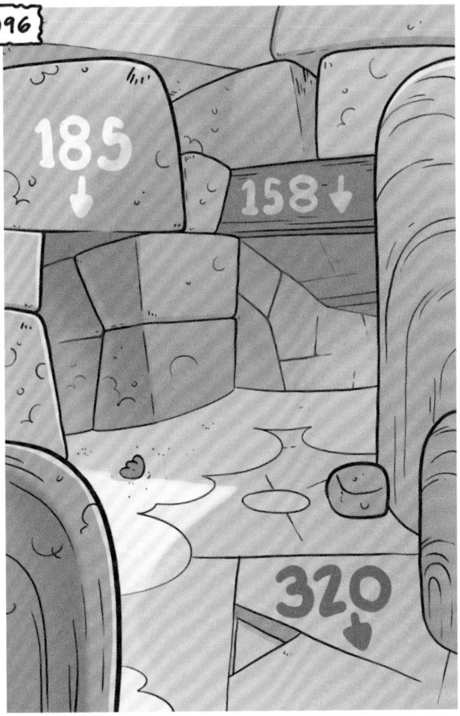
185 ↓
158 ↓
320

097

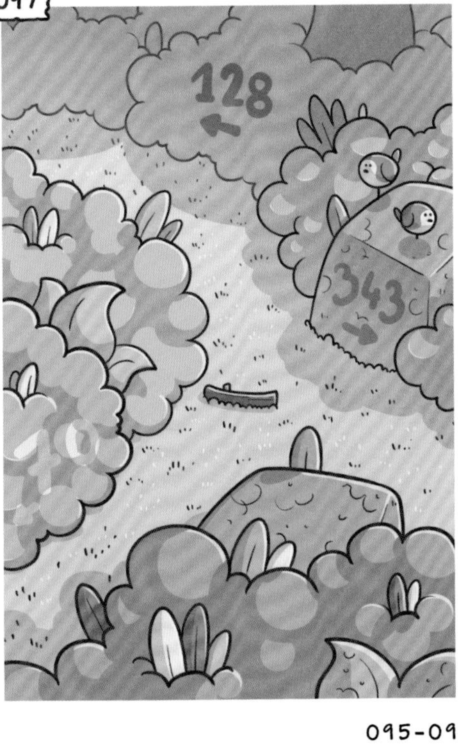
128 ←
343 →

098

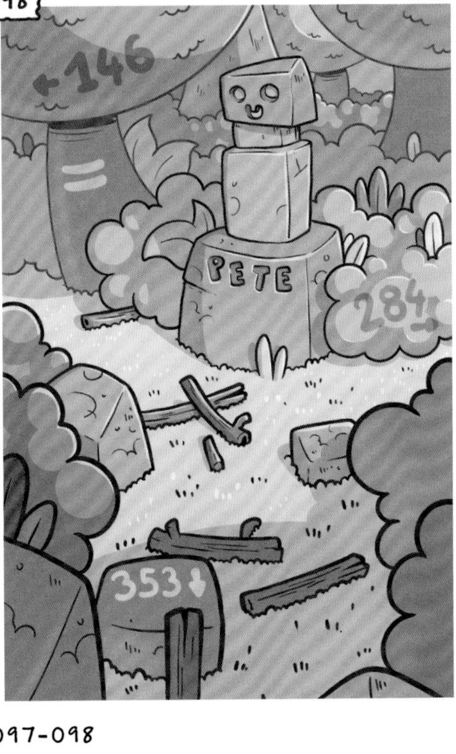
← 146
PETE
284 →
353 ↓

099

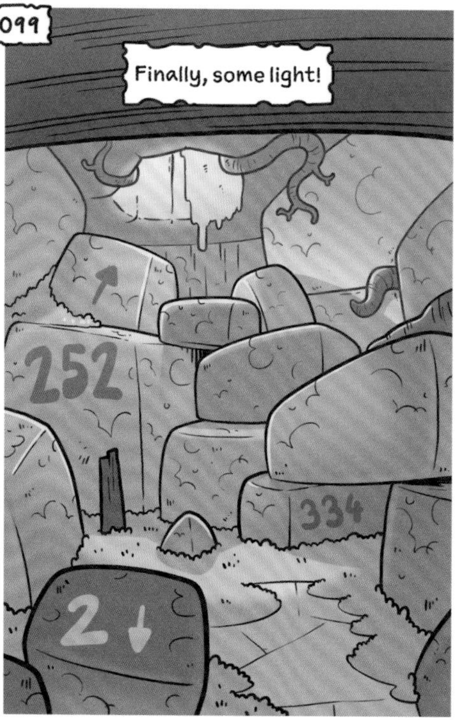
Finally, some light!
252
334
2

100

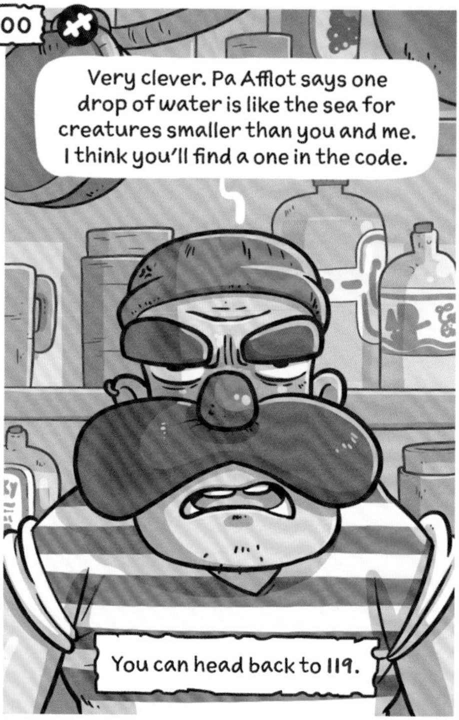
Very clever. Pa Afflot says one drop of water is like the sea for creatures smaller than you and me. I think you'll find a one in the code.
You can head back to 119.

101

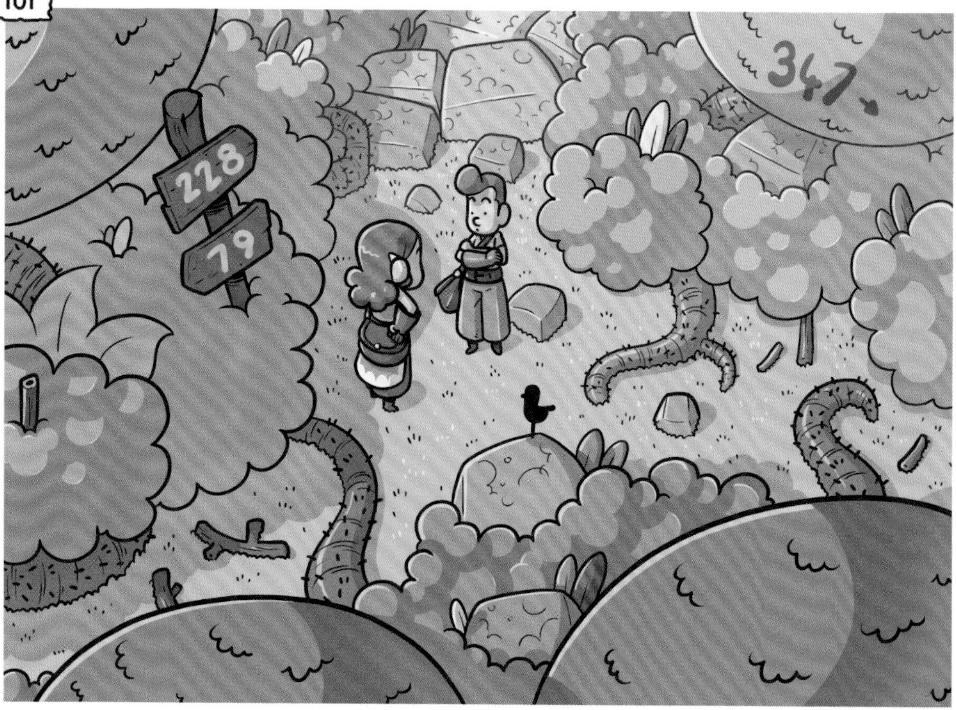
228
79
347

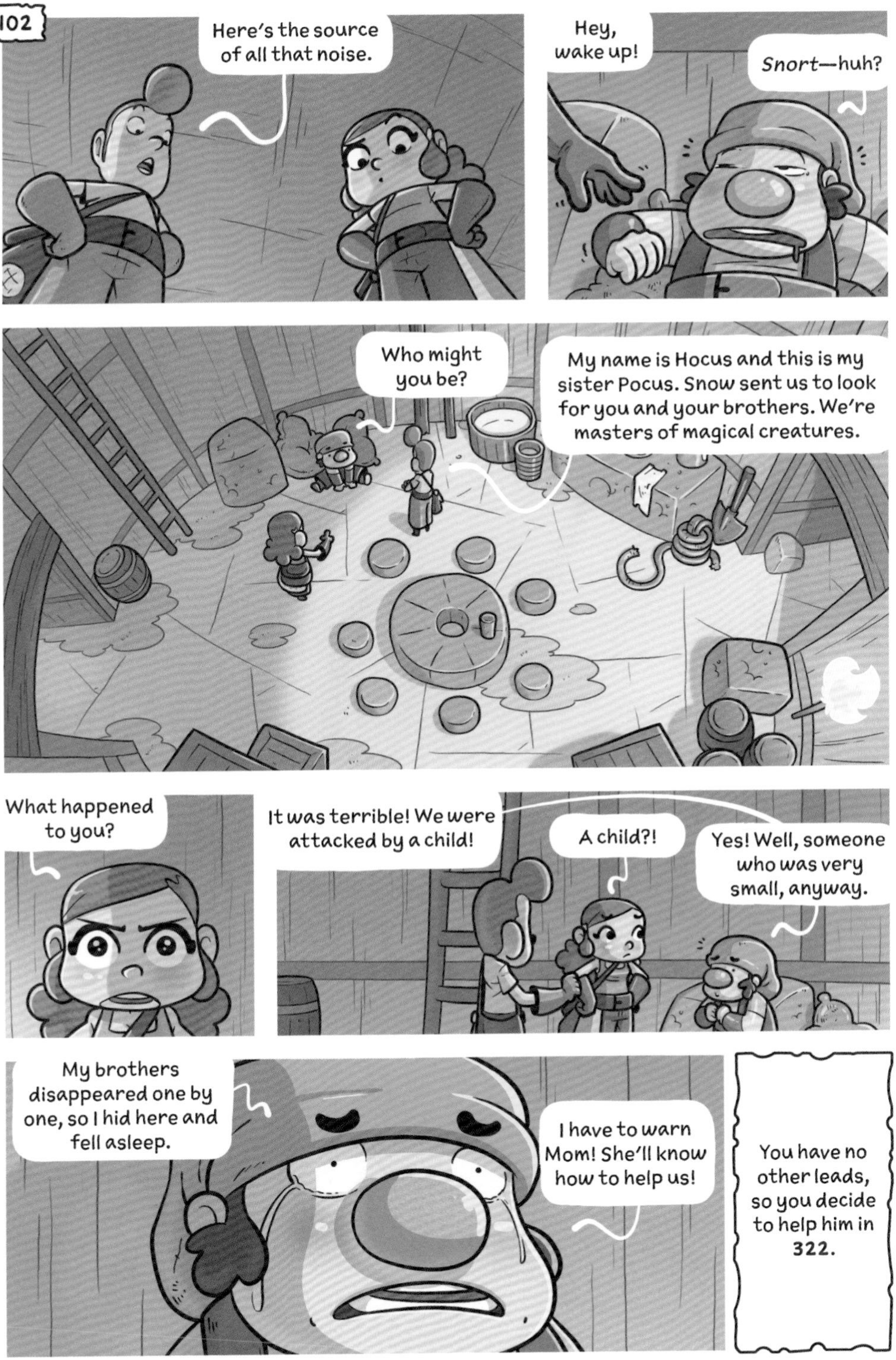
Here's the source of all that noise.
Hey, wake up!
Snort—huh?
Who might you be?
My name is Hocus and this is my sister Pocus. Snow sent us to look for you and your brothers. We're masters of magical creatures.
What happened to you?
It was terrible! We were attacked by a child!
A child?!
Yes! Well, someone who was very small, anyway.
My brothers disappeared one by one, so I hid here and fell asleep.
I have to warn Mom! She'll know how to help us!

You have no other leads, so you decide to help him in **322**.

103

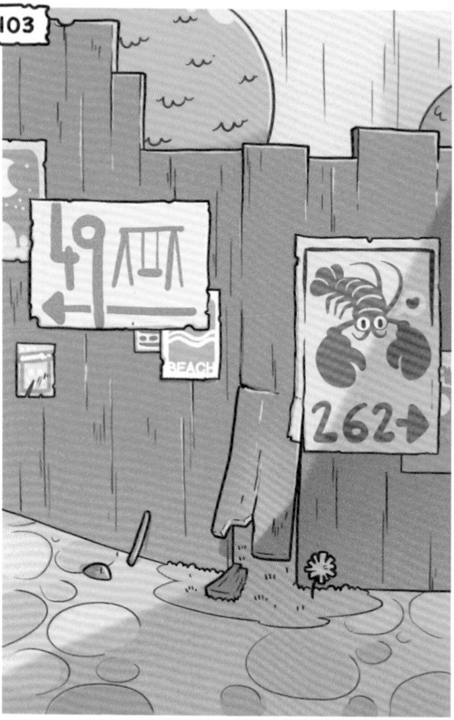
49
BEACH
262→

104

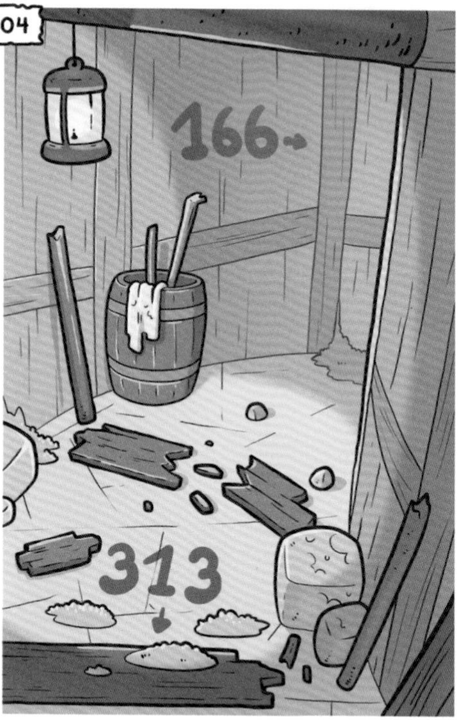
166→
313

105

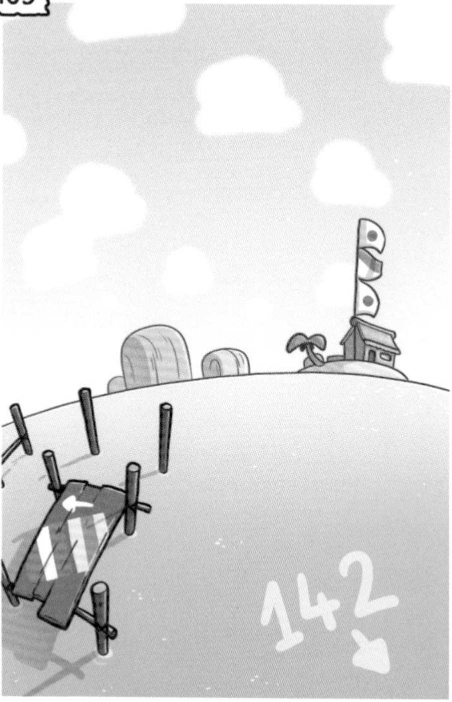
142

106

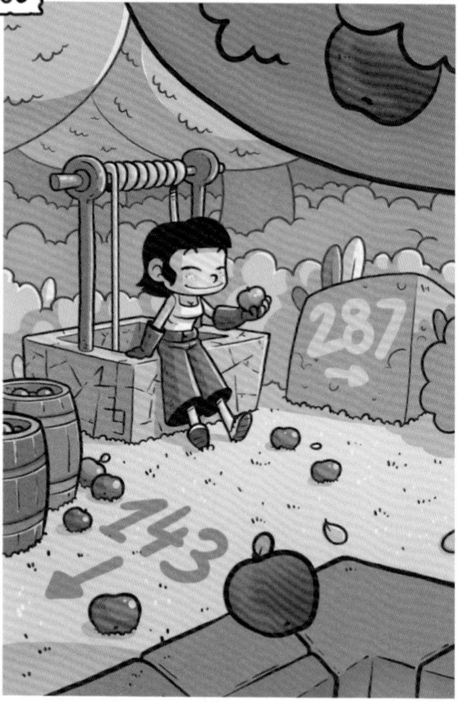
287
143

107

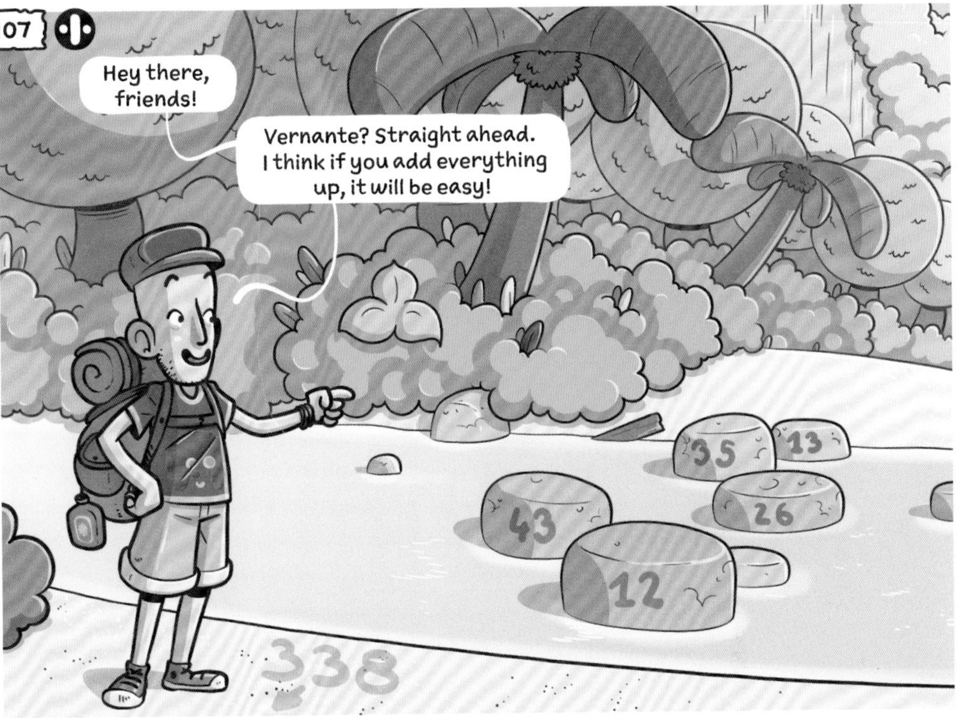
Hey there, friends!
Vernante? Straight ahead. I think if you add everything up, it will be easy!
35
13
43
26
12
338

108

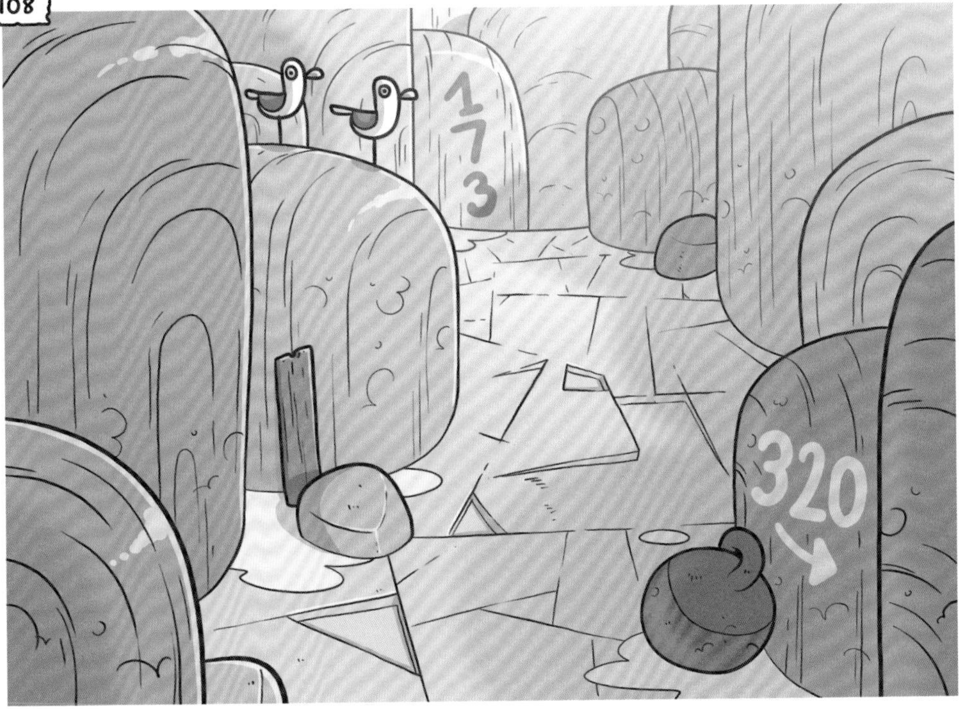
173
320

109

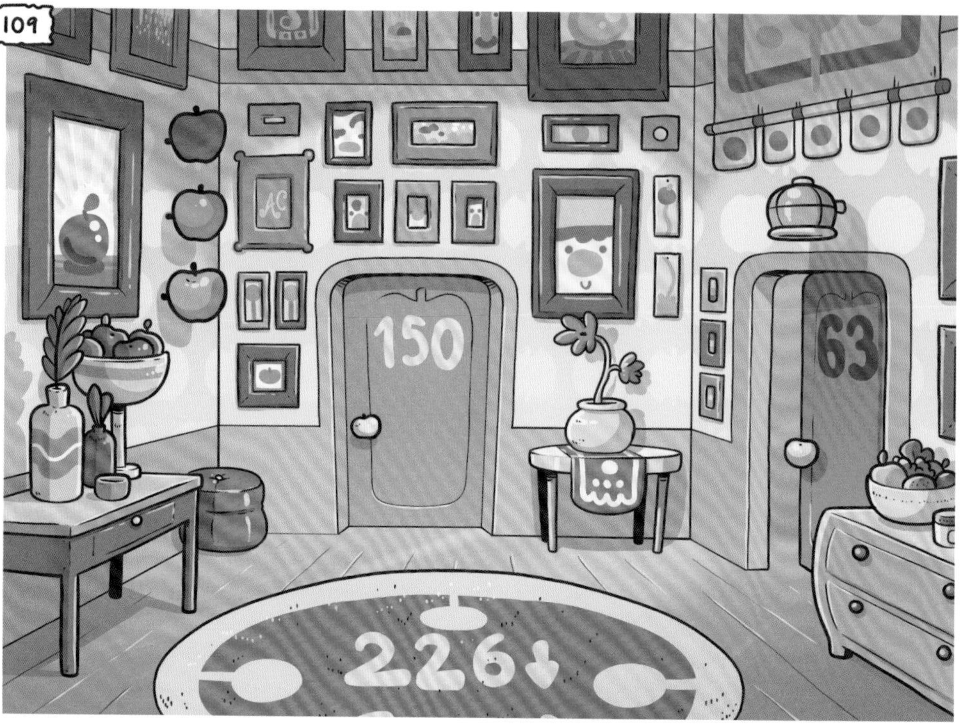
150
63
226↓

110

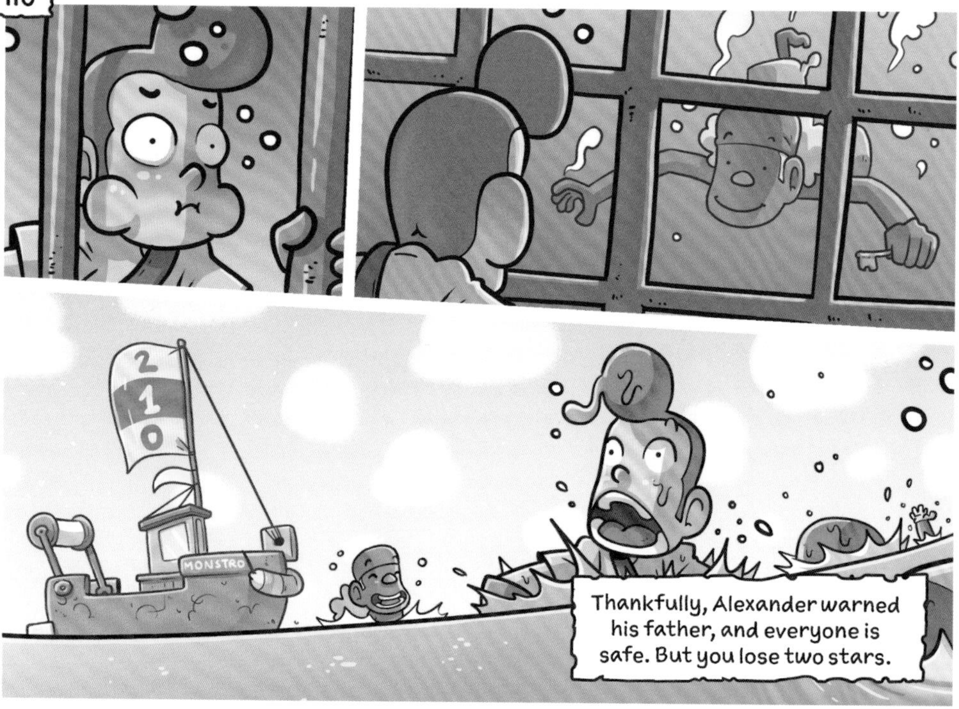
210
MONSTRO
Thankfully, Alexander warned his father, and everyone is safe. But you lose two stars.

111

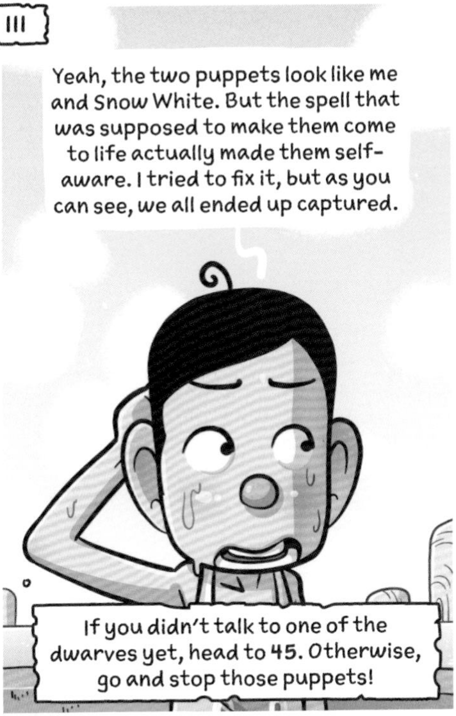
Yeah, the two puppets look like me and Snow White. But the spell that was supposed to make them come to life actually made them self-aware. I tried to fix it, but as you can see, we all ended up captured.
If you didn't talk to one of the dwarves yet, head to 45. Otherwise, go and stop those puppets!

112

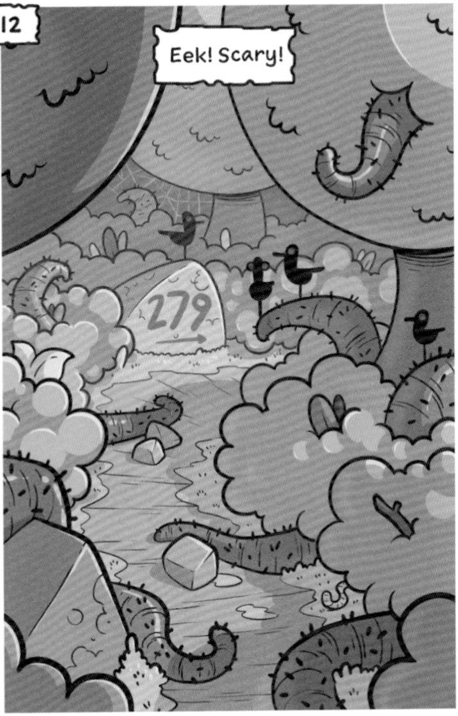
Eek! Scary!
279

113

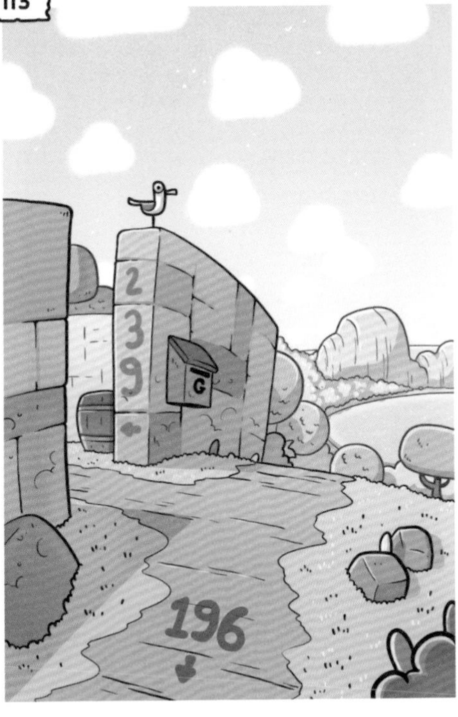
239
G
196

114

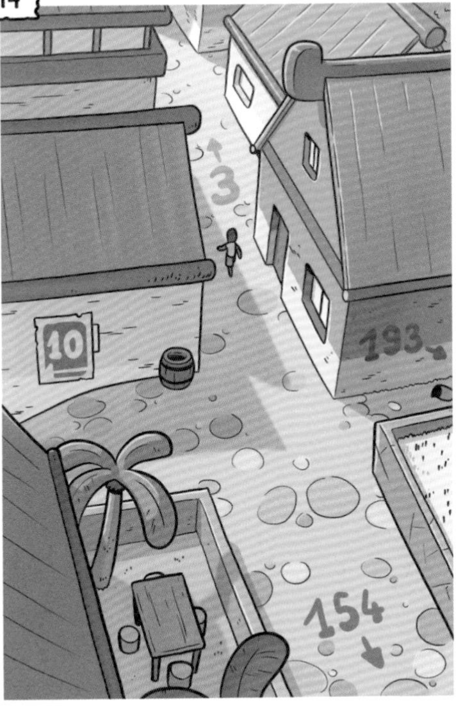
3
10
193
154

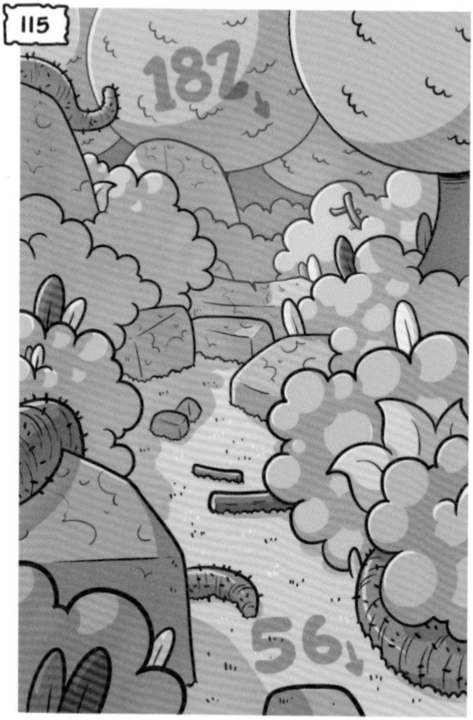
115
182
56

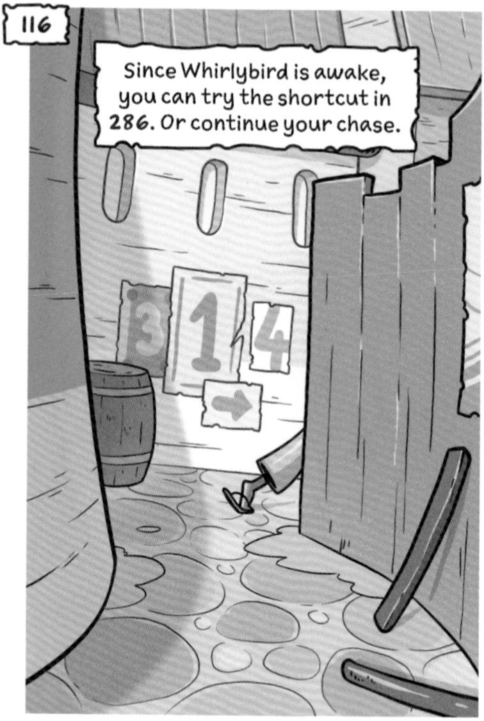
116
Since Whirlybird is awake, you can try the shortcut in 286. Or continue your chase.
3
1
4

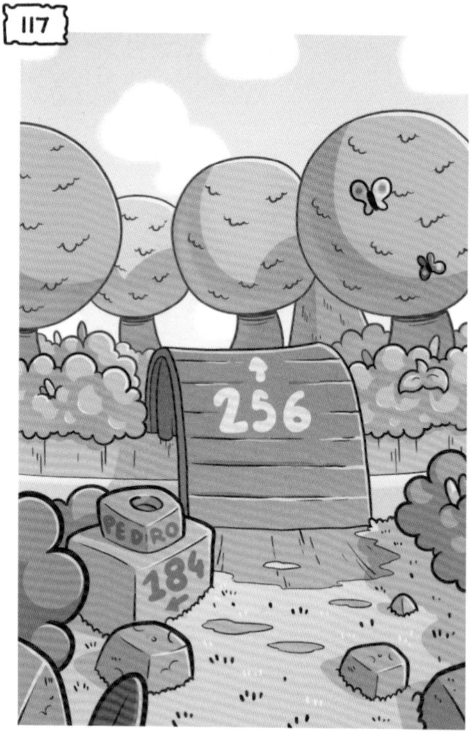
117
256
PEDRO
184

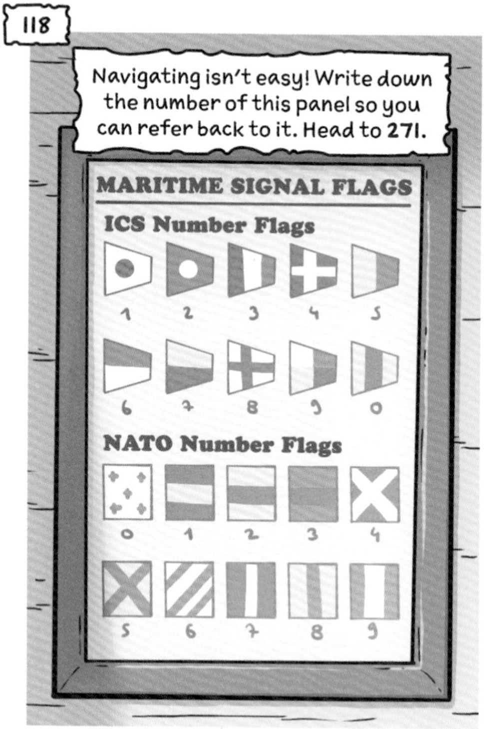
118
Navigating isn't easy! Write down the number of this panel so you can refer back to it. Head to 271.
MARITIME SIGNAL FLAGS
ICS Number Flags
1 2 3 4 5
6 7 8 9 0
NATO Number Flags
0 1 2 3 4
5 6 7 8 9

119

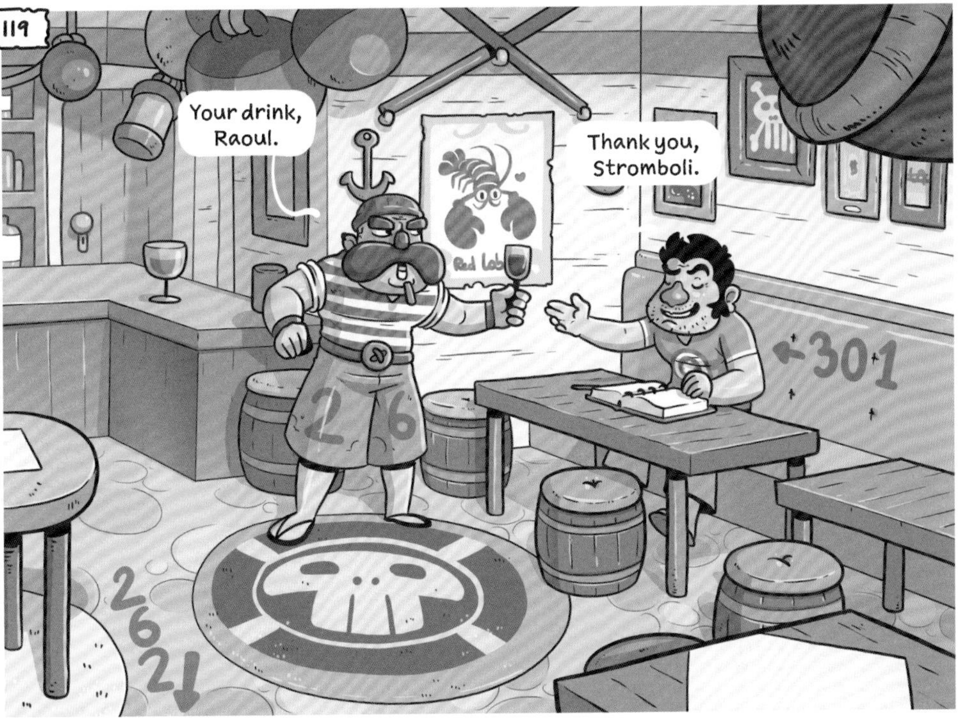

Your drink,
Raoul.
Thank you,
Stromboli.
26
301
262

120

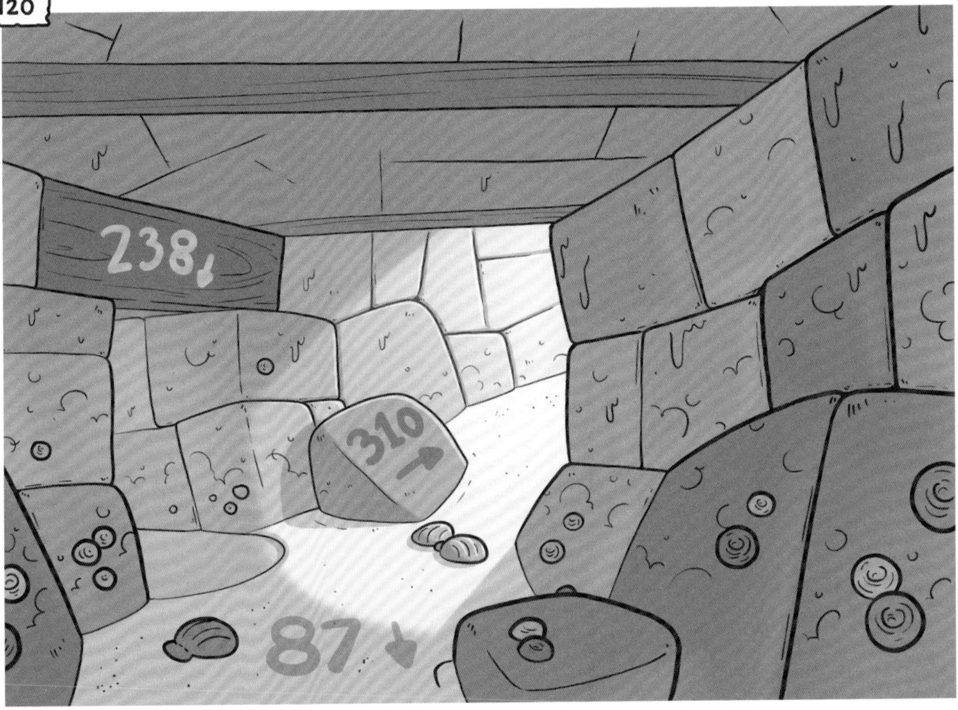

238
310
87

121

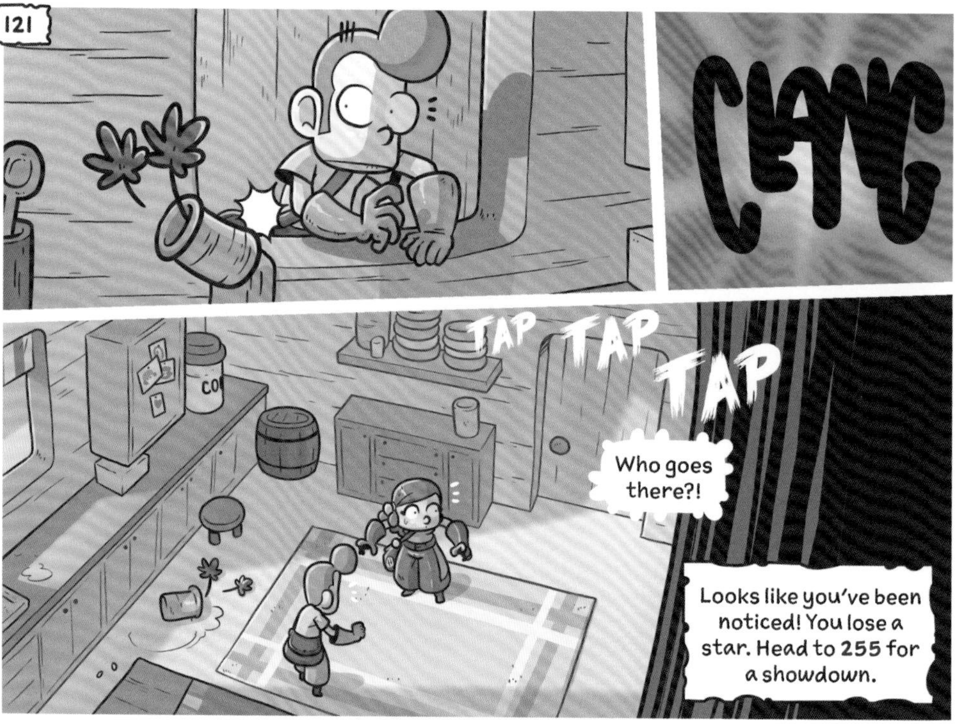
CLANG
TAP TAP TAP
Who goes there?!
Looks like you've been noticed! You lose a star. Head to 255 for a showdown.

122

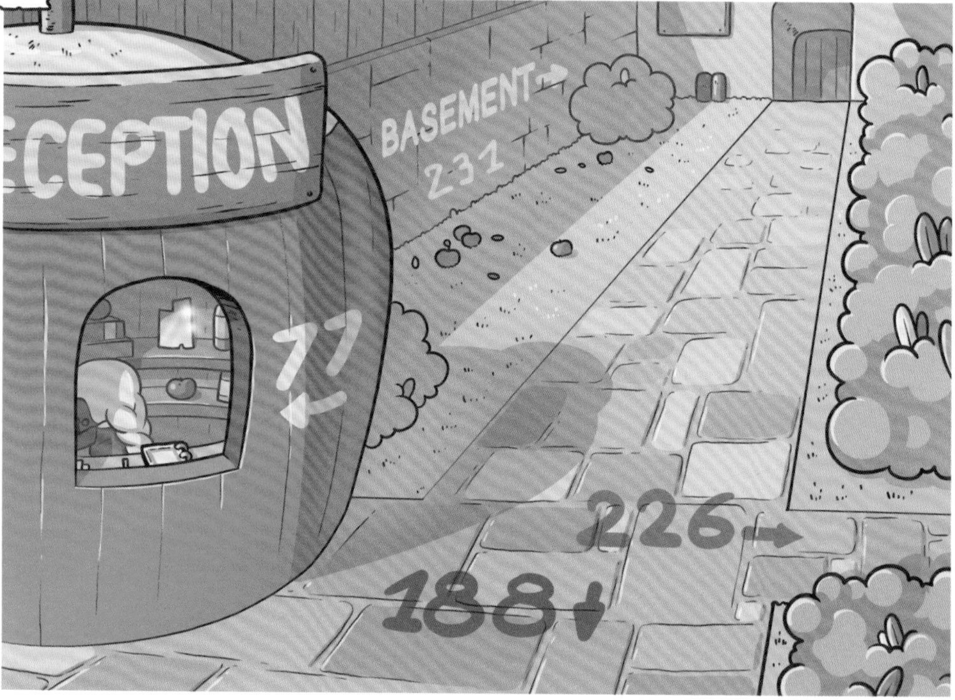
ECEPTION
BASEMENT→
231
226→
188↓

123

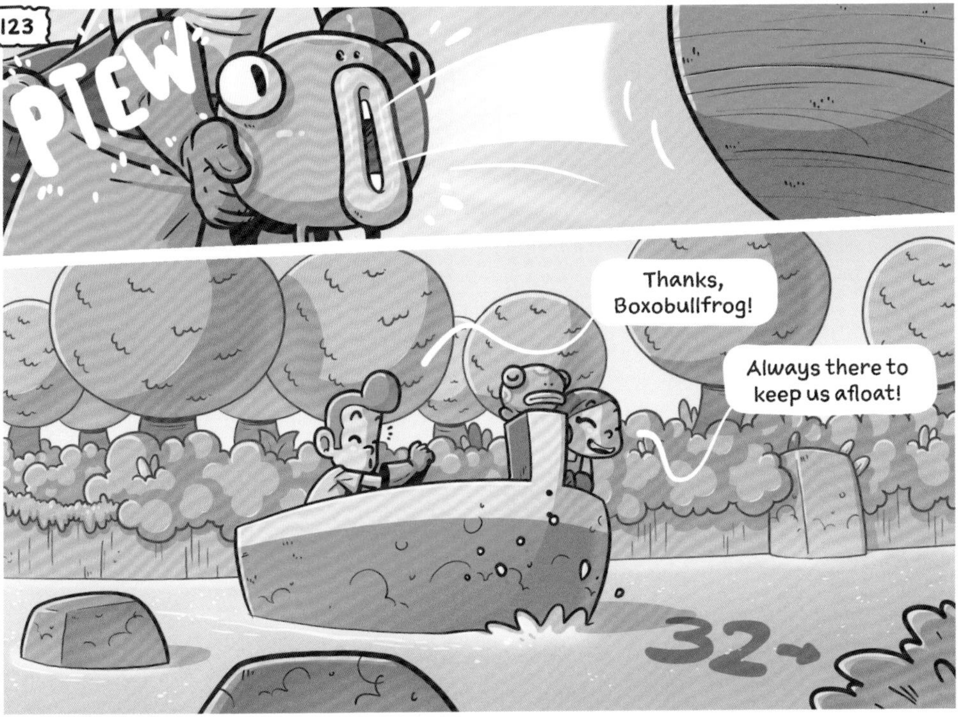
PTEW
Thanks, Boxobullfrog!
Always there to keep us afloat!
32→

124

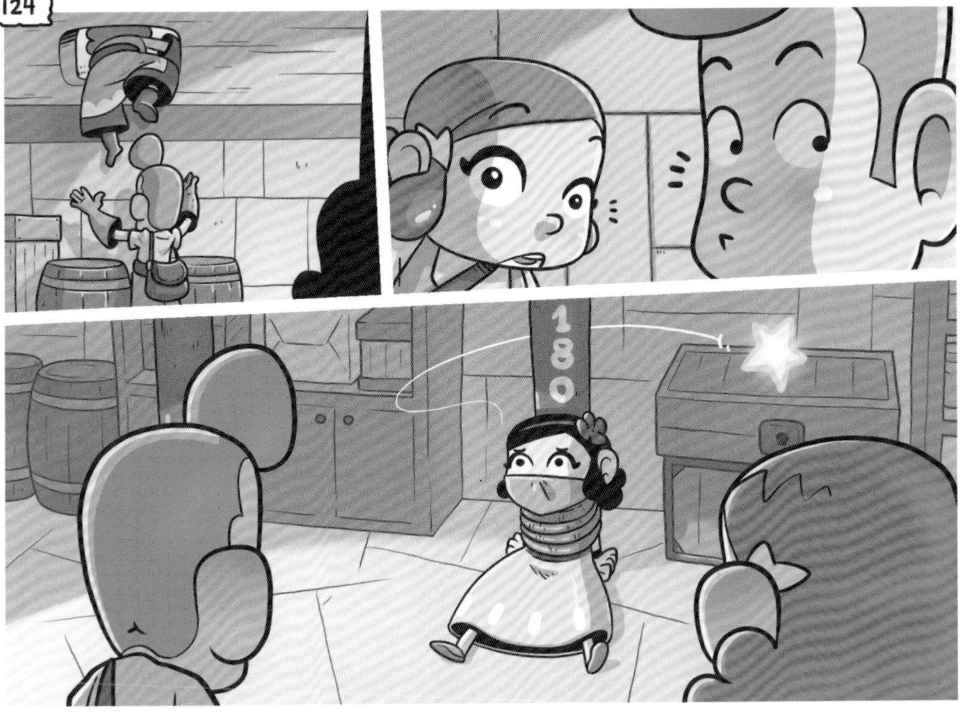
180

125

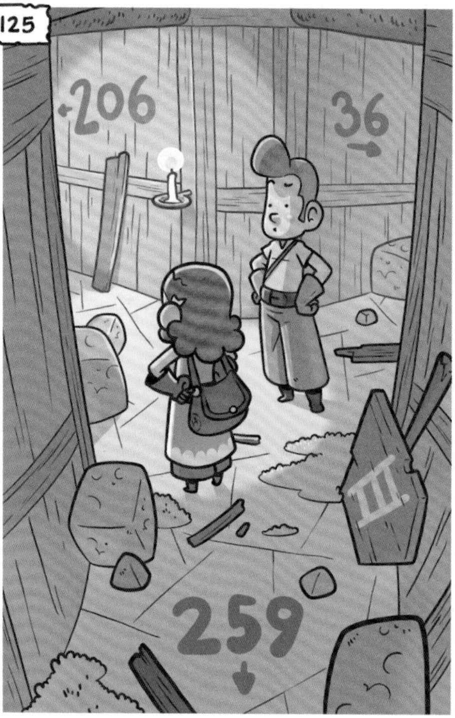
206
36
III
259

126

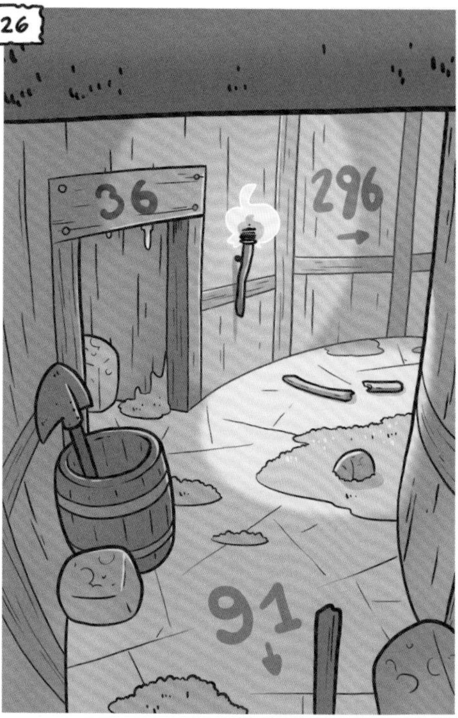
36
296
91

127

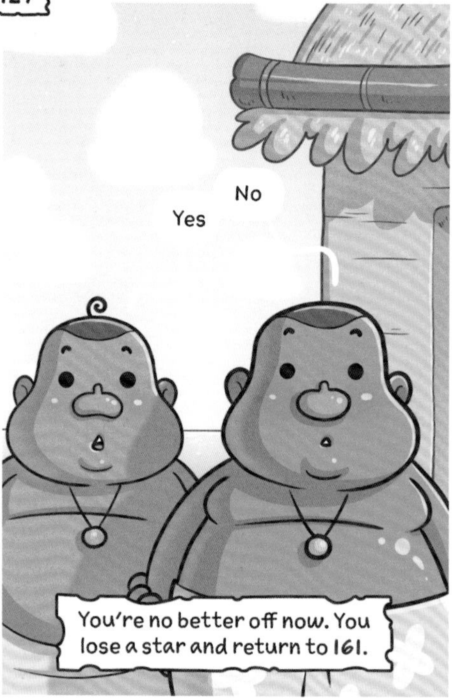
No
Yes
You're no better off now. You lose a star and return to 161.

128

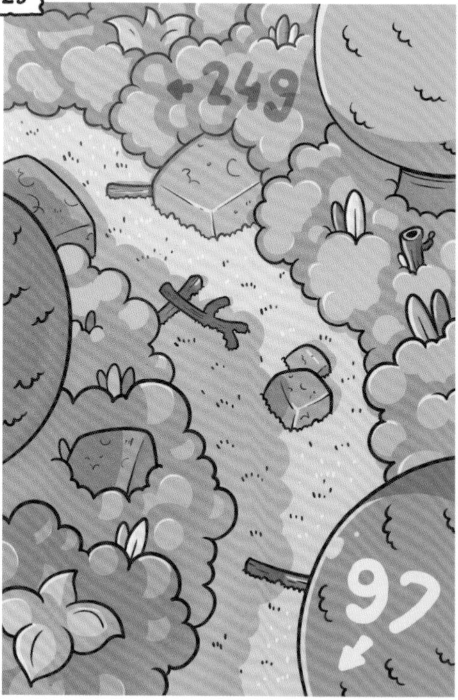
249
97

129

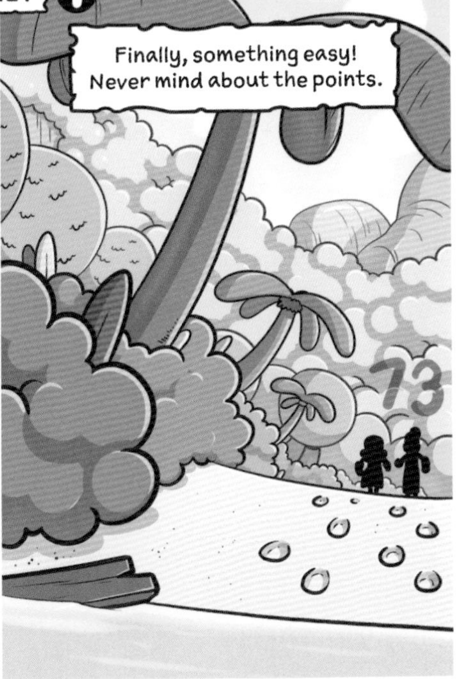
Finally, something easy!
Never mind about the points.
73

130

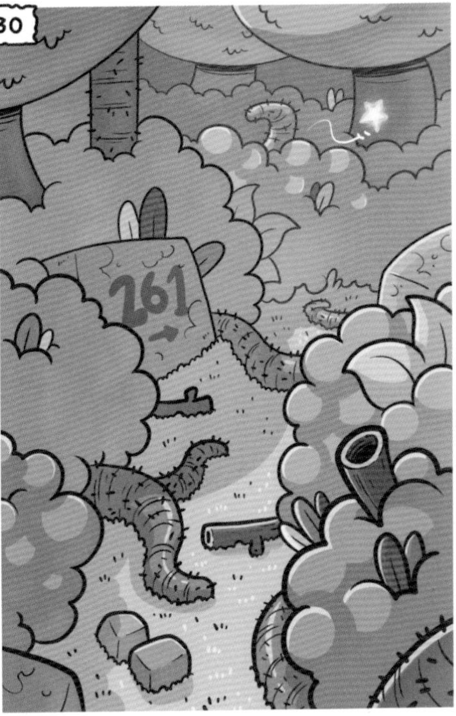
261

131

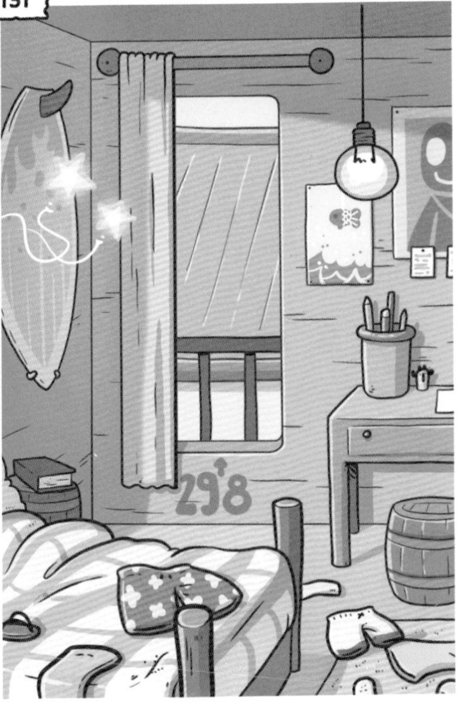
298

132

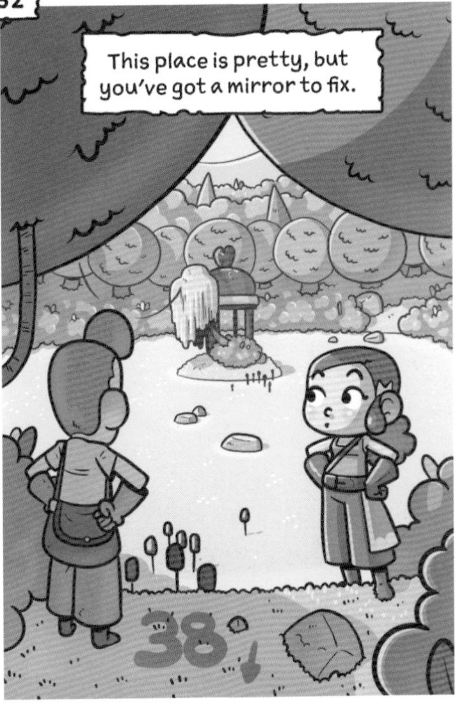
This place is pretty, but
you've got a mirror to fix.
38

133

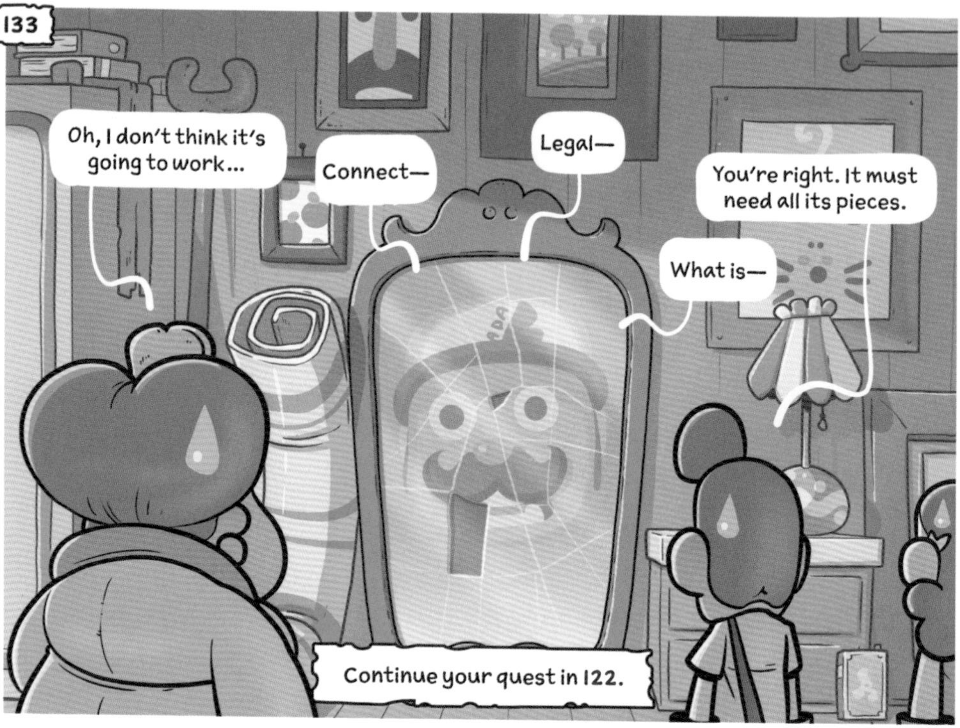
Oh, I don't think it's going to work...
Connect—
Legal—
You're right. It must need all its pieces.
What is—
Continue your quest in 122.

134

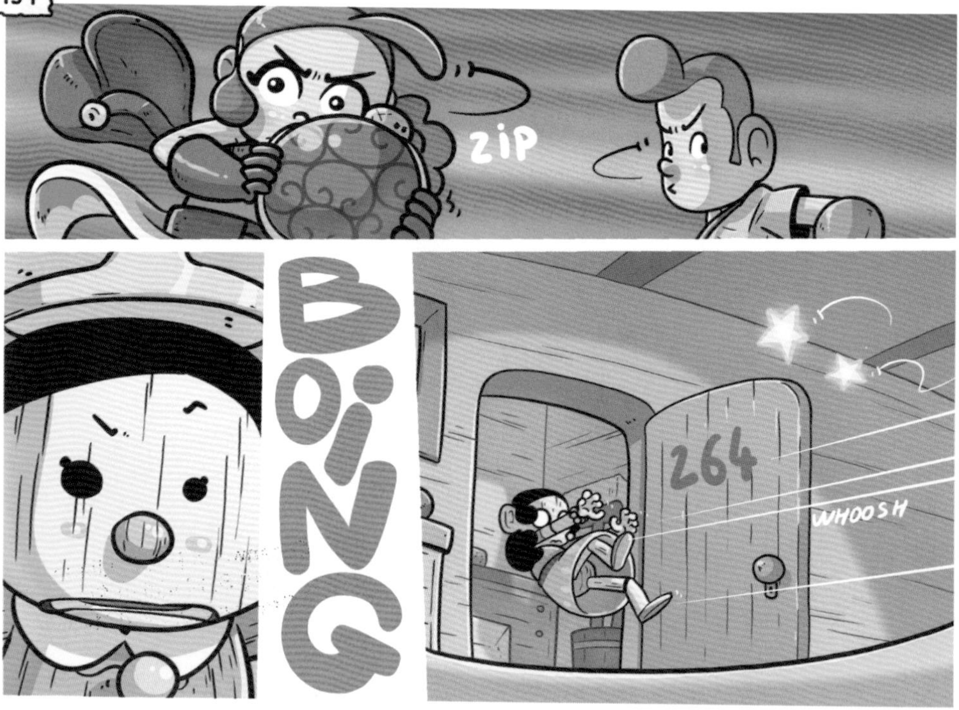
ZIP
BOING
264
WHOOSH

135

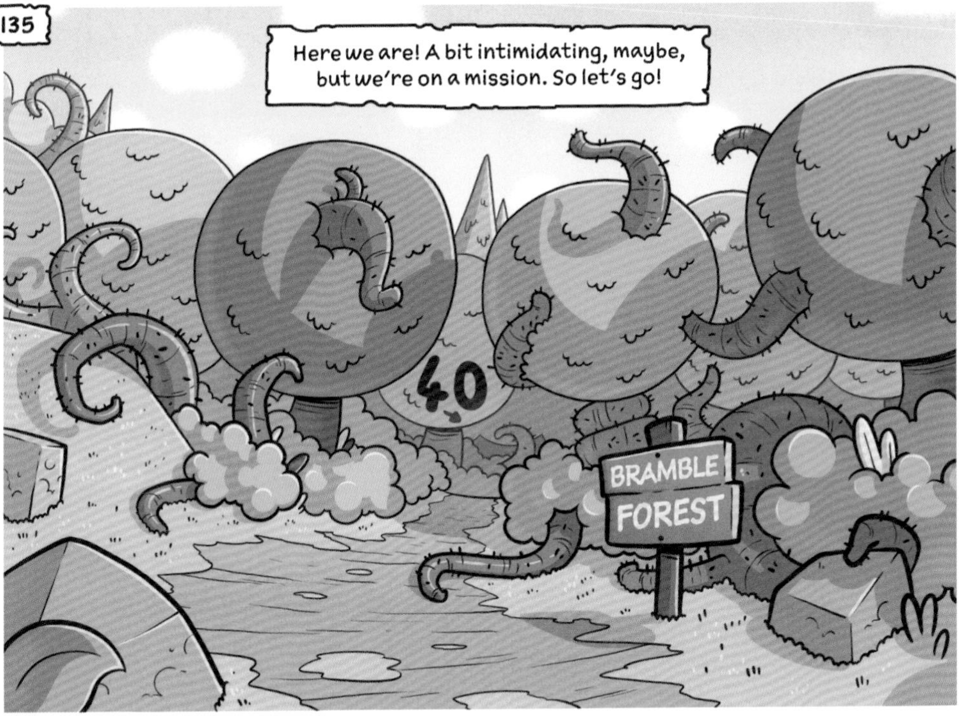
Here we are! A bit intimidating, maybe, but we're on a mission. So let's go!
40
BRAMBLE FOREST

136

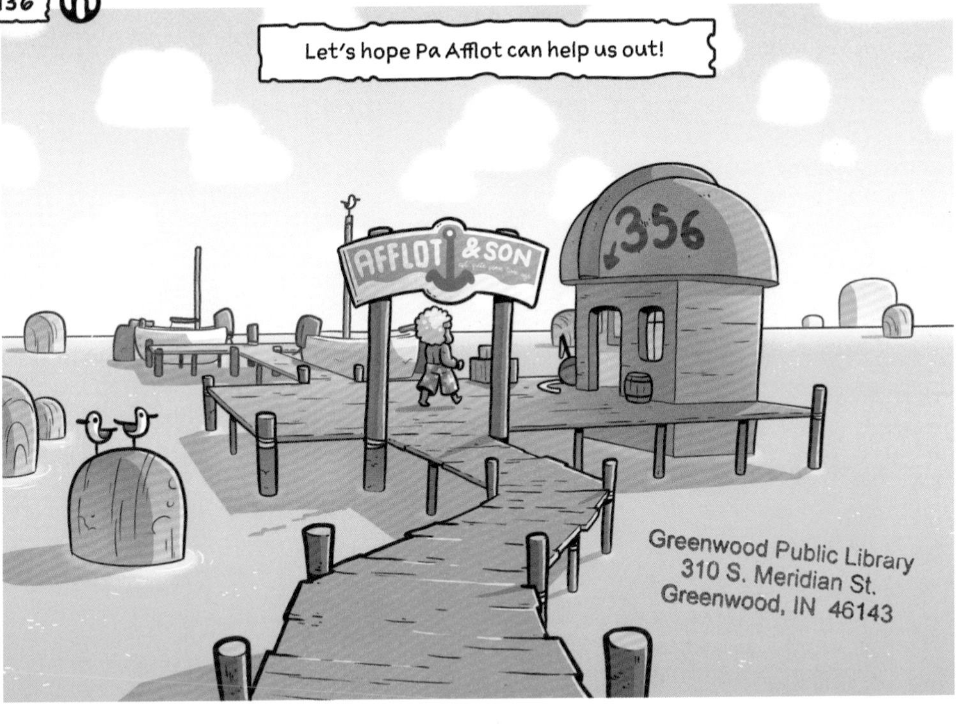
Let's hope Pa Afflot can help us out!
AFFLOT & SON
356

137

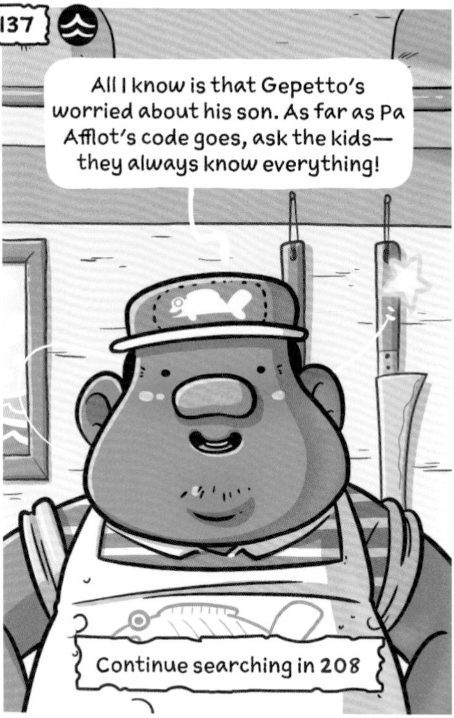
All I know is that Gepetto's worried about his son. As far as Pa Afflot's code goes, ask the kids—they always know everything!
Continue searching in 208

138

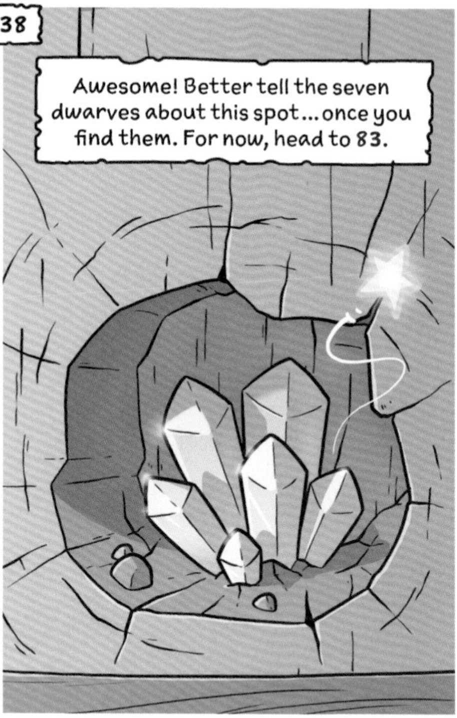
Awesome! Better tell the seven dwarves about this spot... once you find them. For now, head to 83.

139

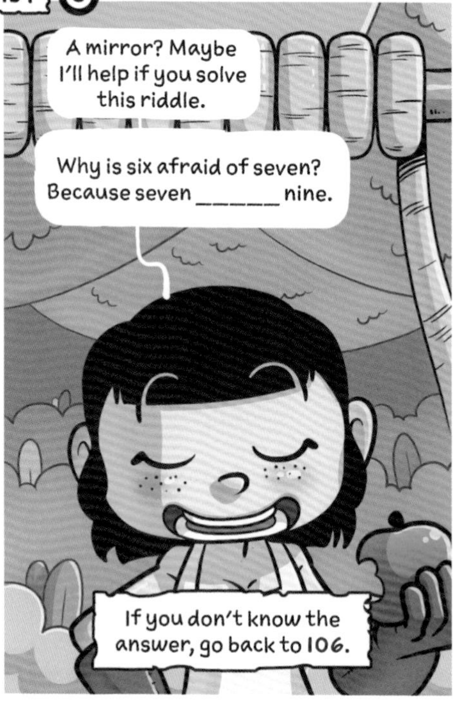
A mirror? Maybe I'll help if you solve this riddle.
Why is six afraid of seven? Because seven ______ nine.
If you don't know the answer, go back to 106.

140

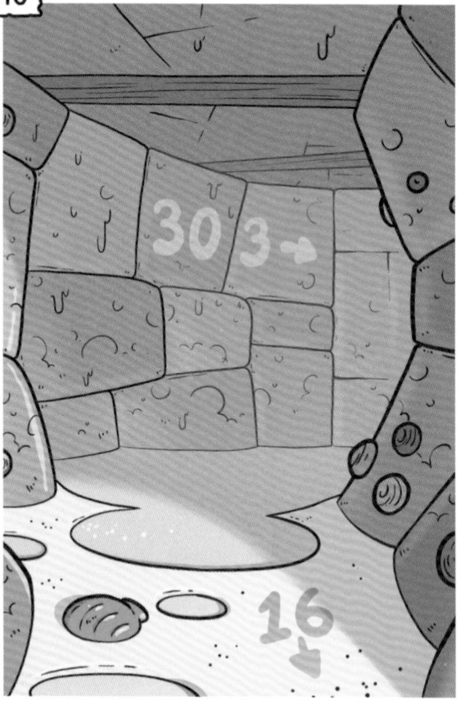
303
16

41

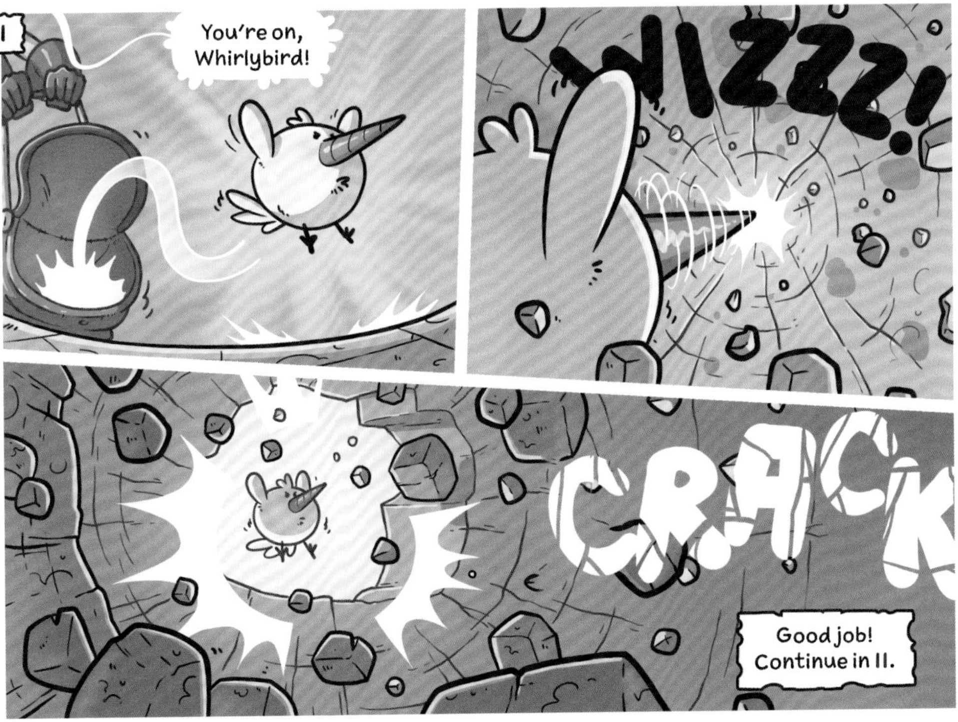
You're on, Whirlybird!
WIZZZ!
CRACK
Good job! Continue in 11.

42

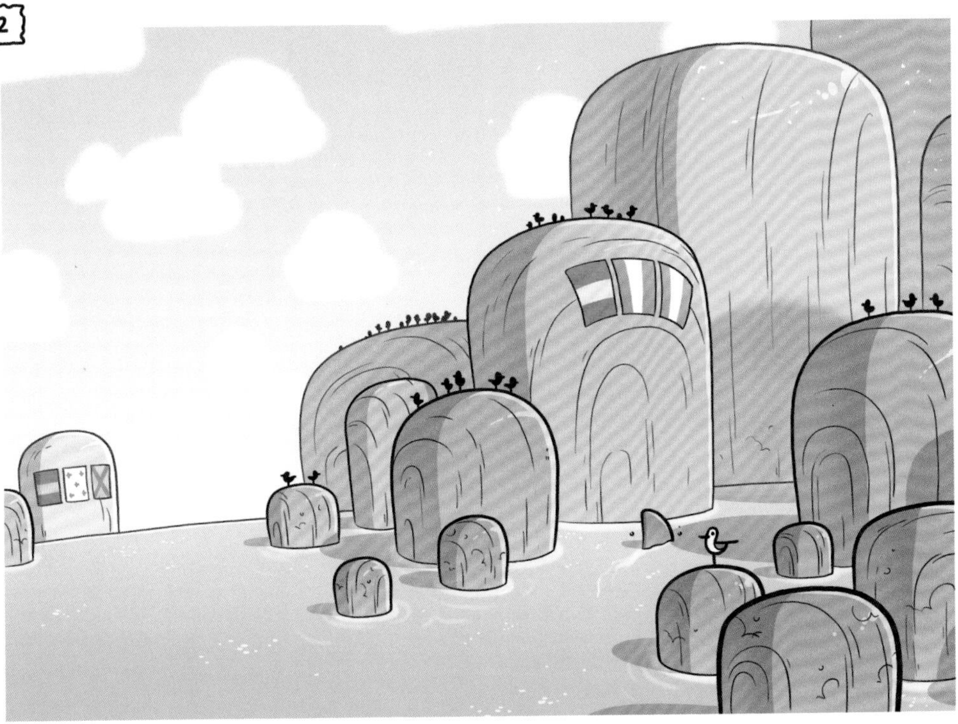

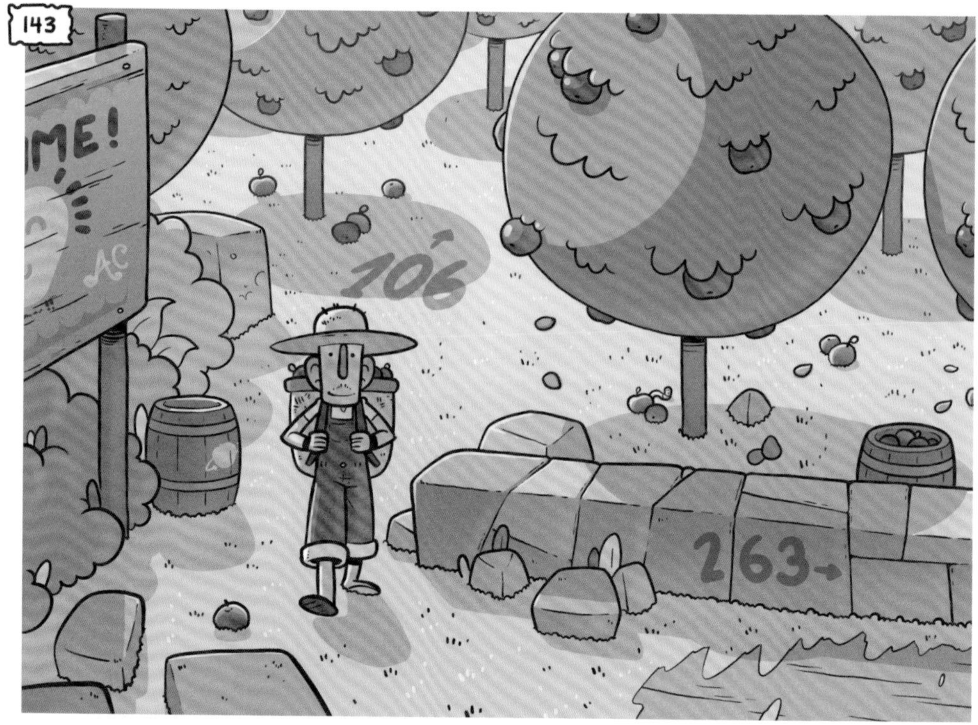
143
ME!
AC
106
263

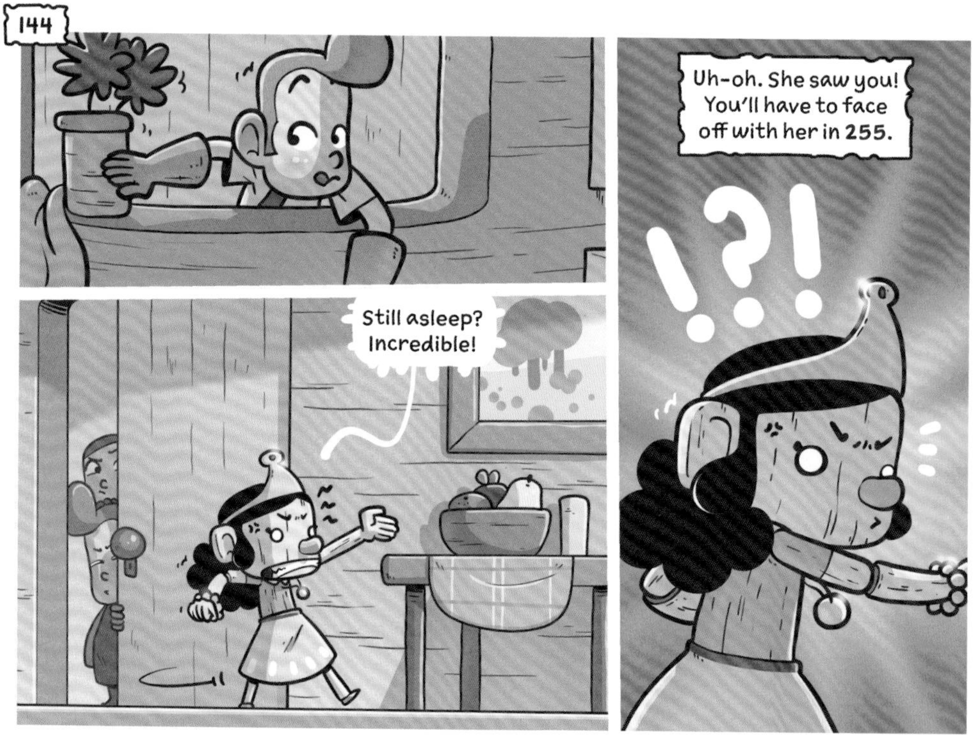
144
Still asleep? Incredible!
Uh-oh. She saw you! You'll have to face off with her in 255.
!?!

145

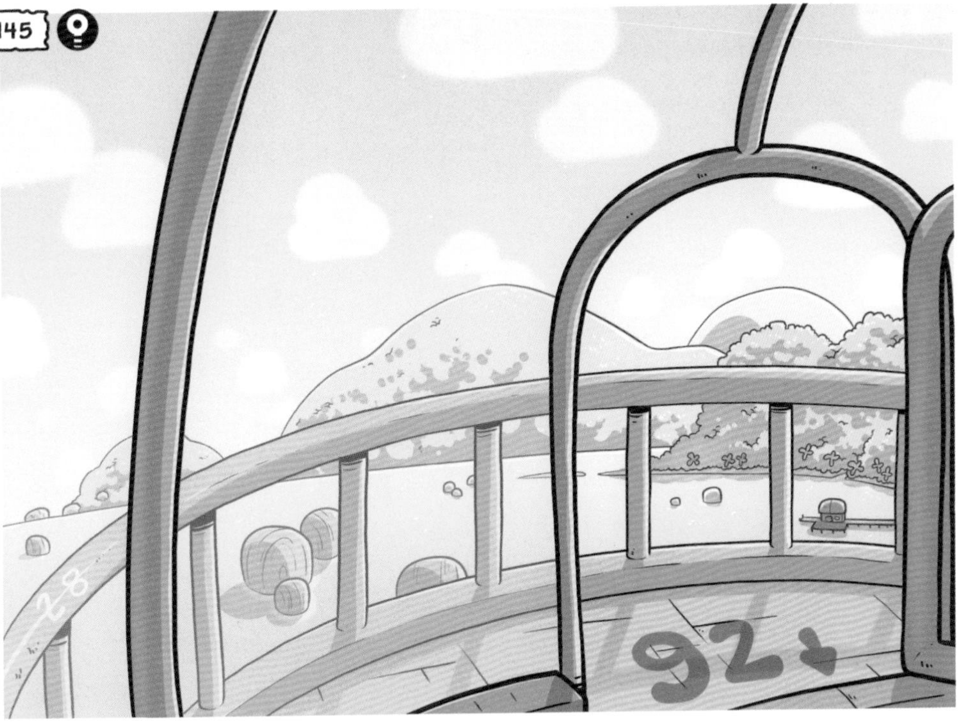
28
92

146

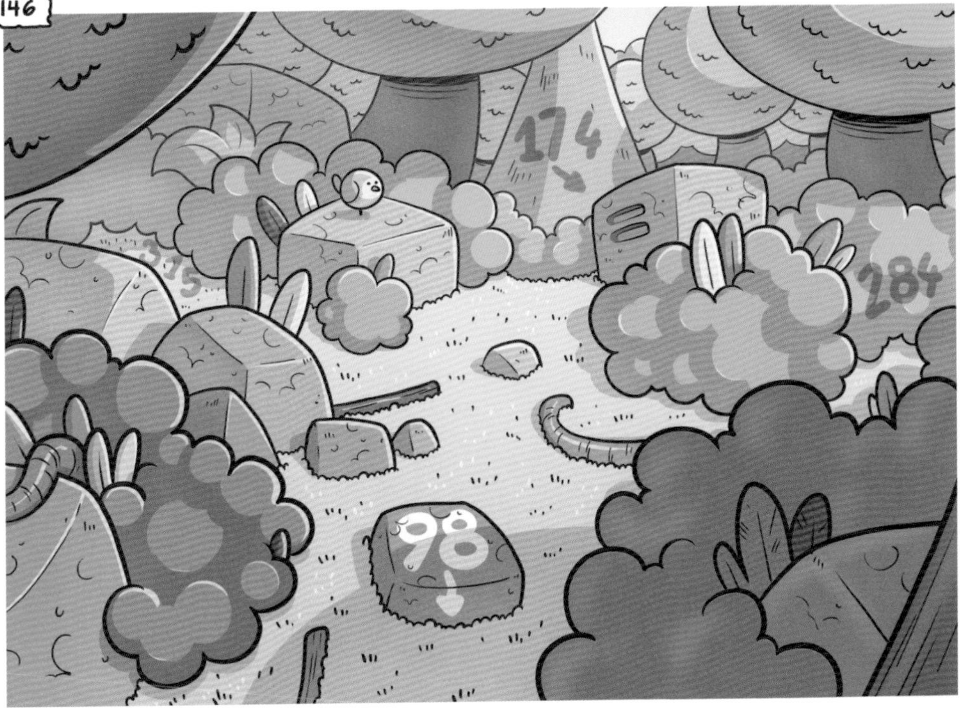
174
315
284
98

147
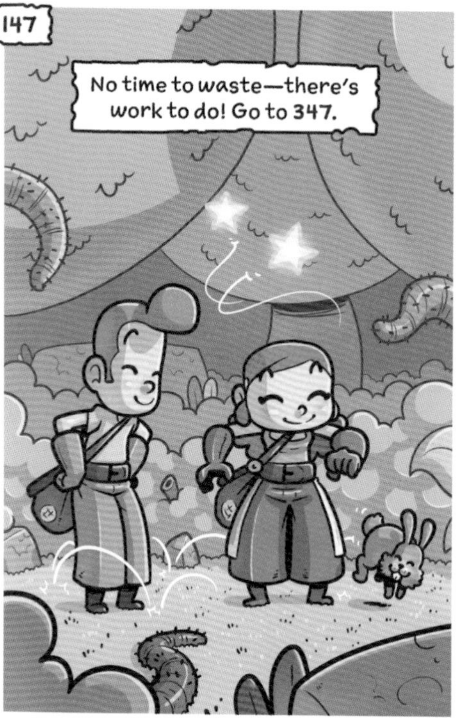
No time to waste—there's work to do! Go to 347.

148
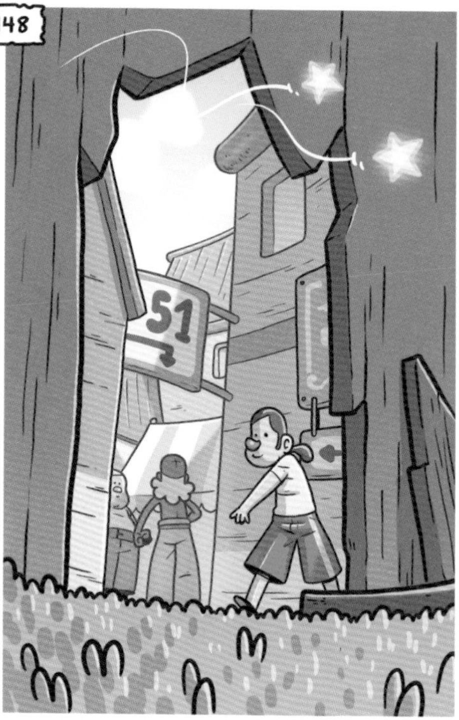
51

149
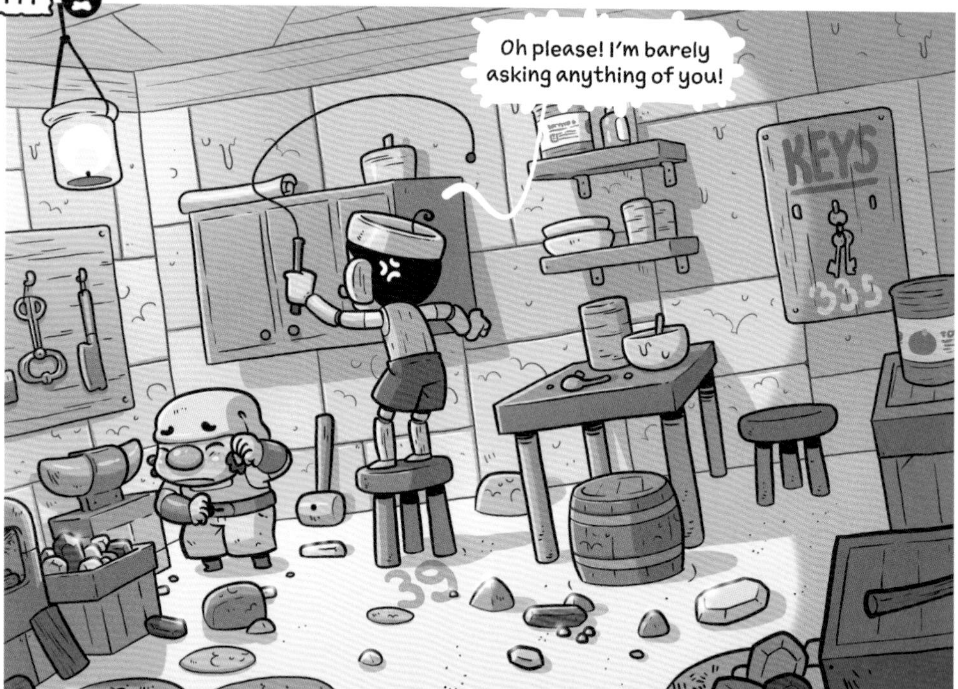
Oh please! I'm barely asking anything of you!
KEYS
335
39

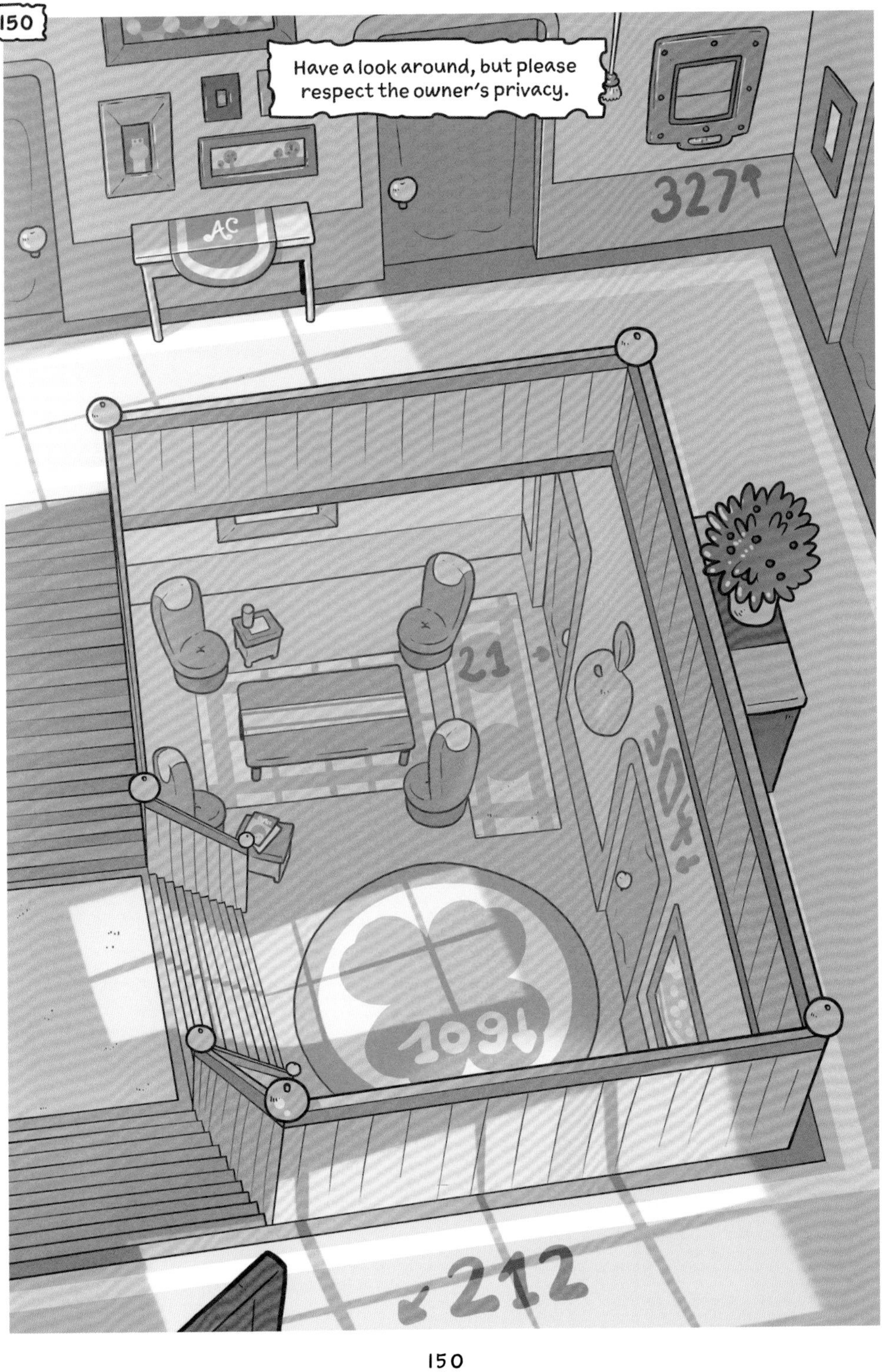
Have a look around, but please respect the owner's privacy.
AC
327
21
304
109
212

151

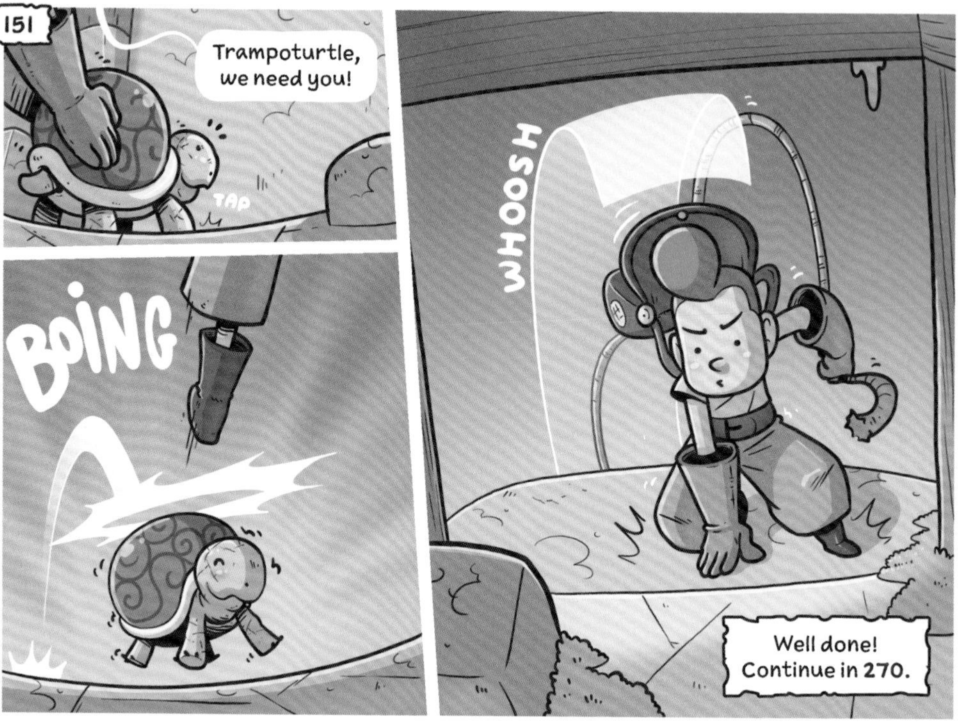
Trampoturtle, we need you!
TAP
BOING
WHOOSH
Well done! Continue in 270.

152

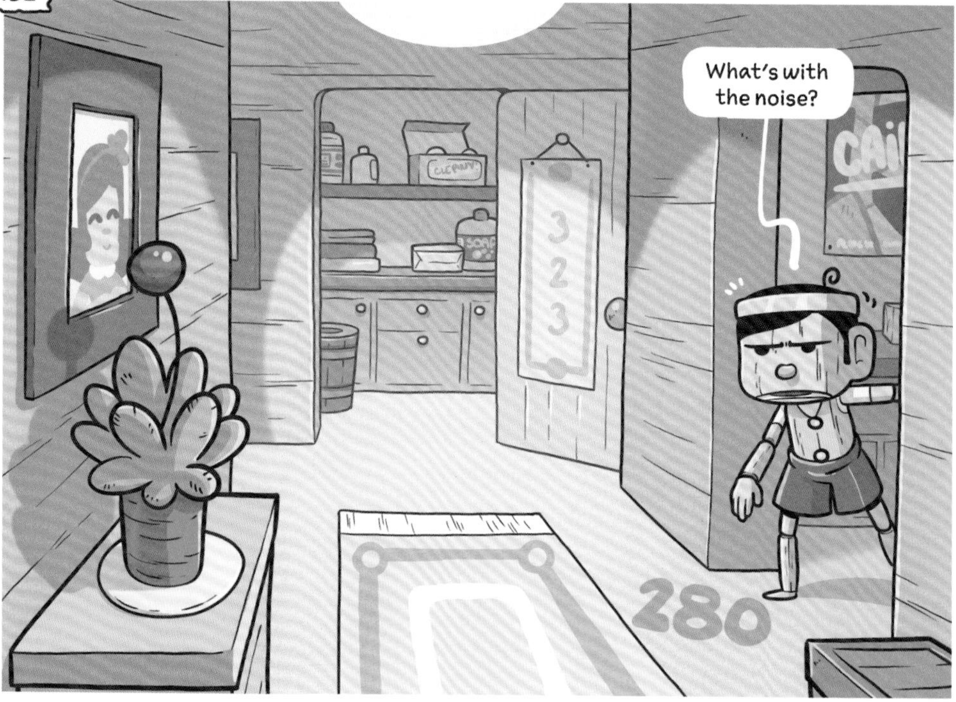
What's with the noise?
323
280

153

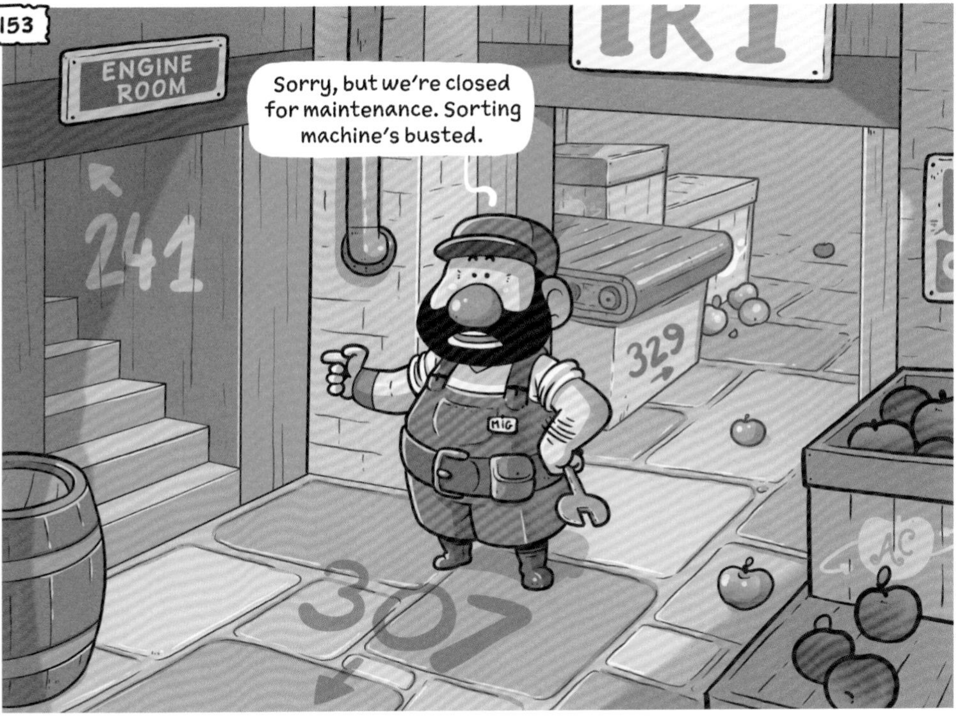
ENGINE ROOM
241
Sorry, but we're closed for maintenance. Sorting machine's busted.
MIG
329
307

154

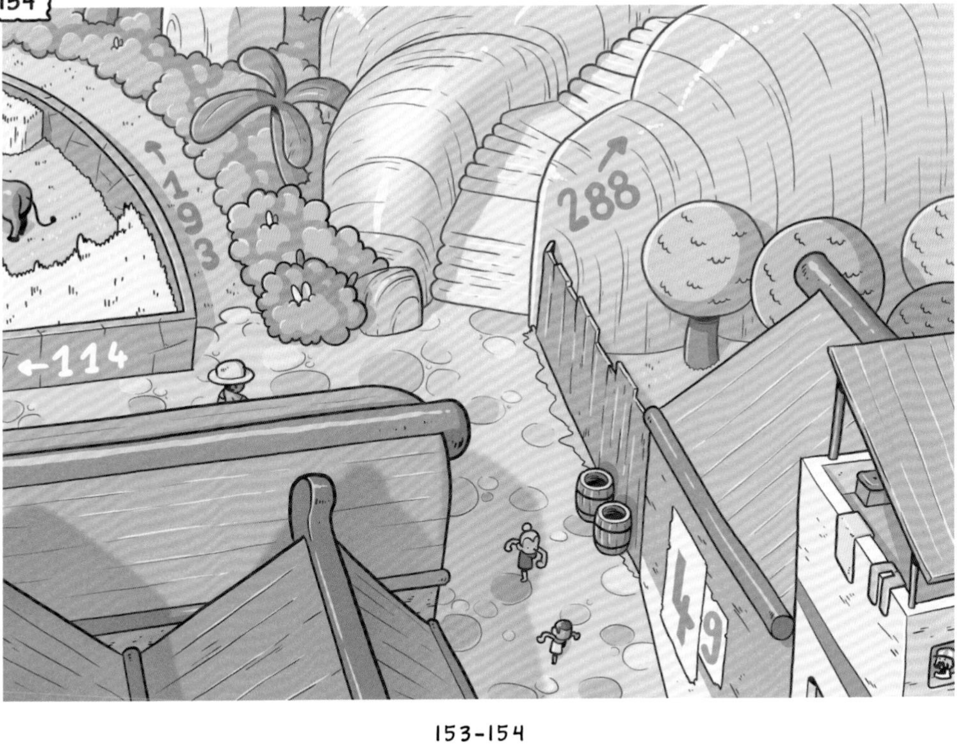
193
288
←114

155

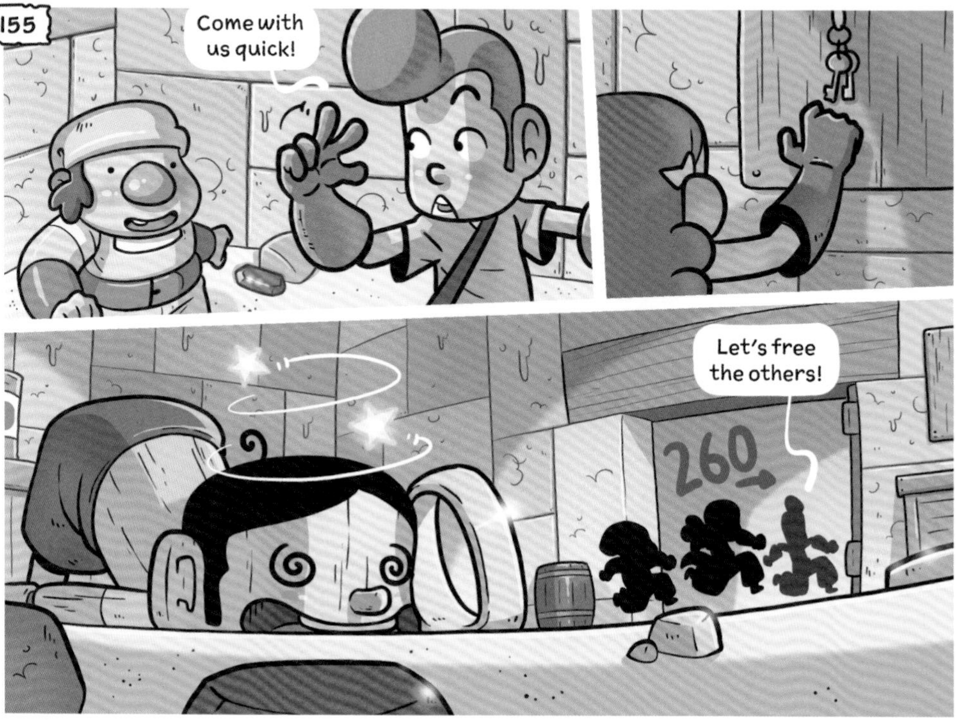
Come with us quick!
Let's free the others!
260

156

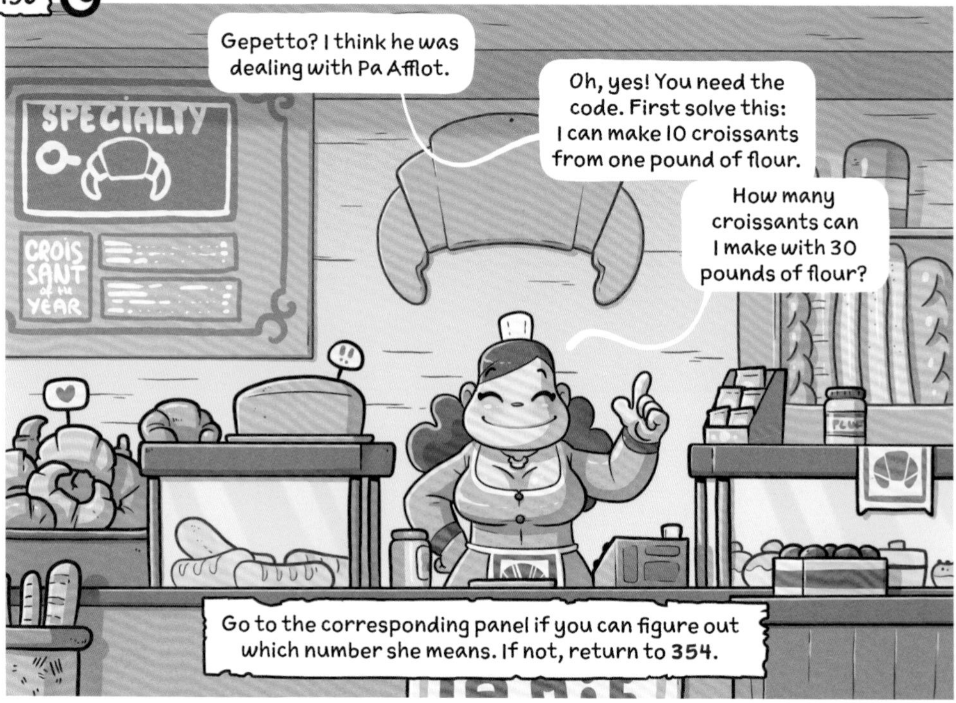
Gepetto? I think he was dealing with Pa Afflot.
Oh, yes! You need the code. First solve this: I can make 10 croissants from one pound of flour.
How many croissants can I make with 30 pounds of flour?
SPECIALTY
CROISSANT of the YEAR
Go to the corresponding panel if you can figure out which number she means. If not, return to 354.

157

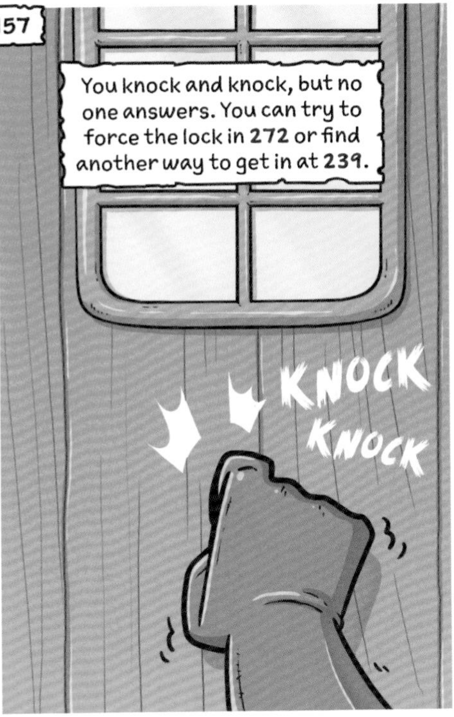
You knock and knock, but no one answers. You can try to force the lock in 272 or find another way to get in at 239.
KNOCK
KNOCK

158

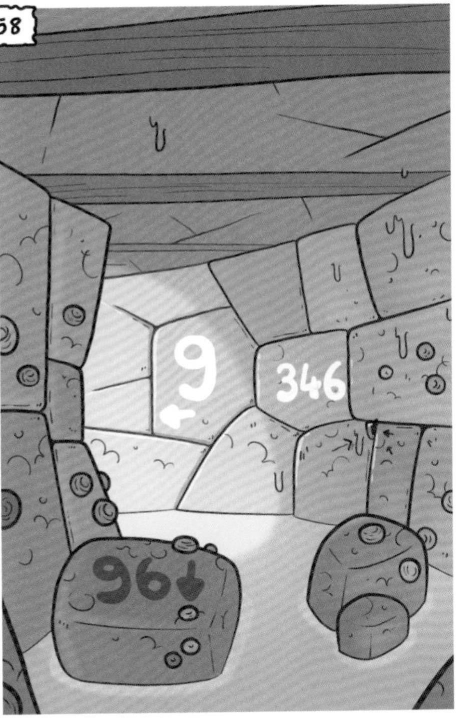
9
346
196

159

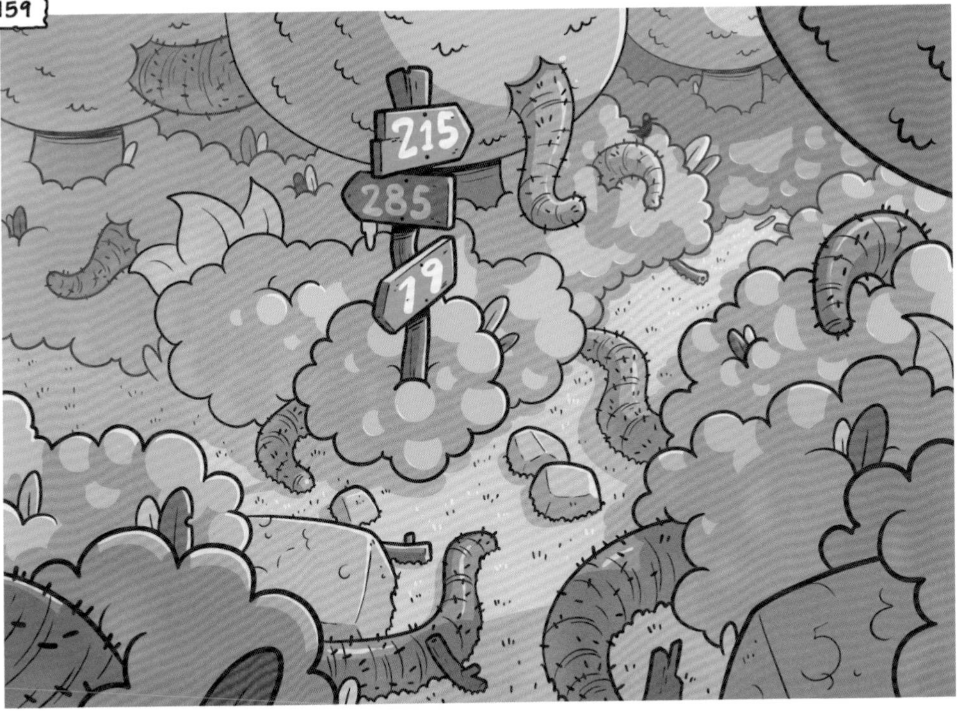
215
285
19

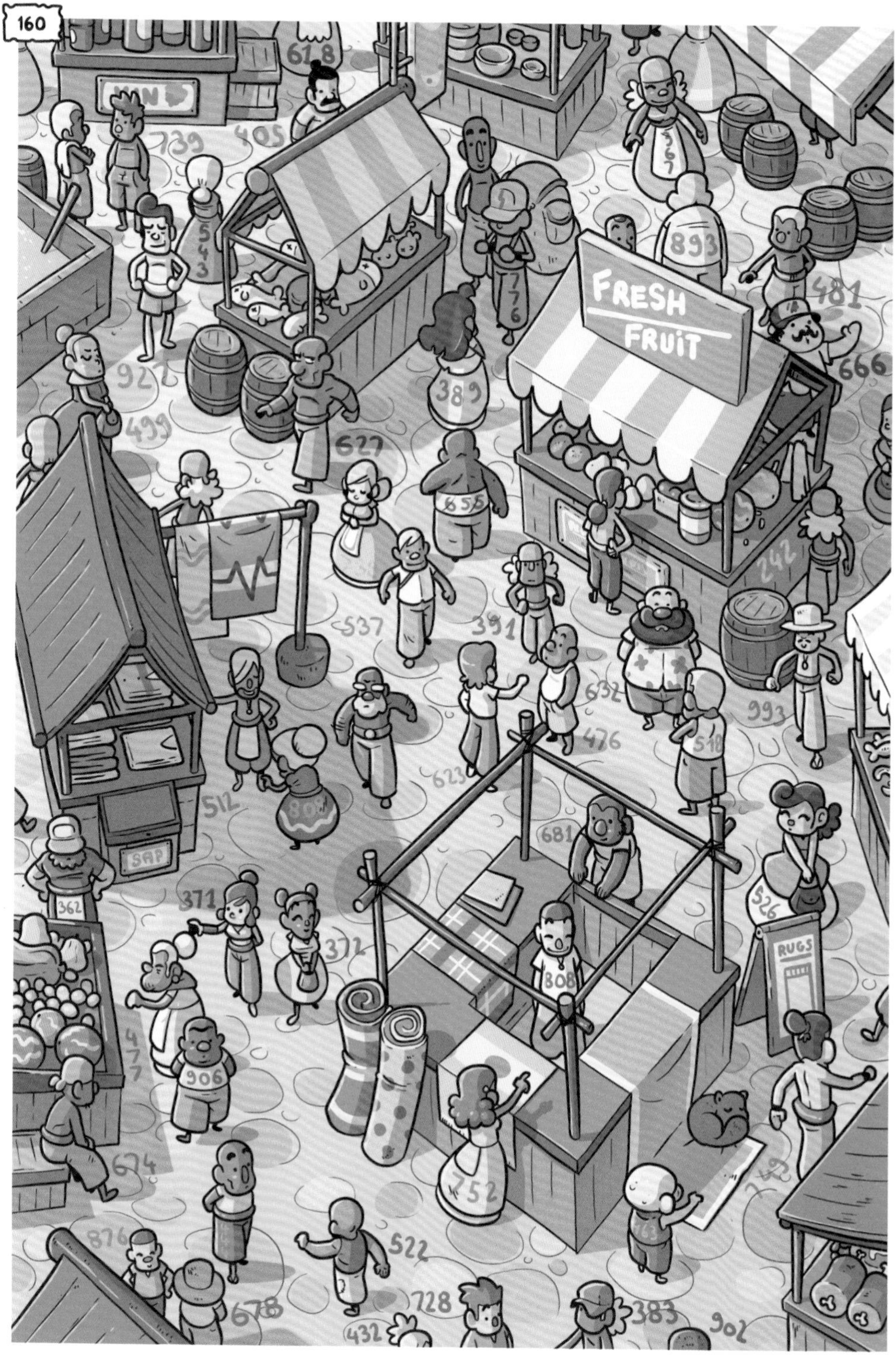
FRESH
FRUIT
RUGS
SAP
618
739
405
543
567
776
893
481
666
927
499
389
627
655
242
537
391
632
476
993
518
512
623
808
681
362
371
372
526
808
906
477
674
752
763
876
522
678
728
432
383
902

161

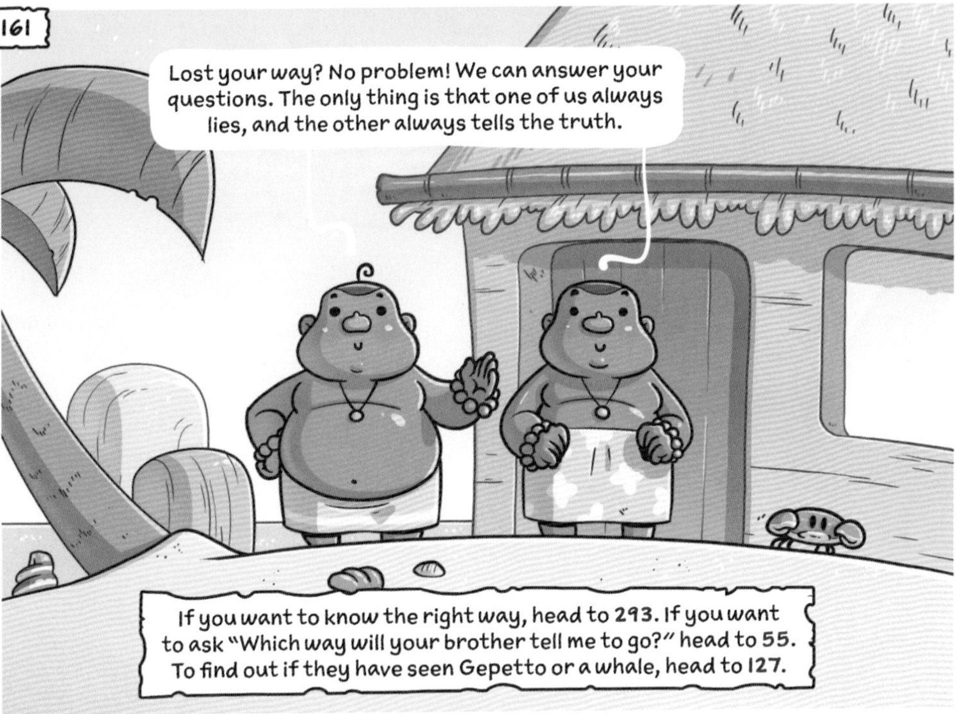
Lost your way? No problem! We can answer your questions. The only thing is that one of us always lies, and the other always tells the truth.
If you want to know the right way, head to 293. If you want to ask "Which way will your brother tell me to go?" head to 55. To find out if they have seen Gepetto or a whale, head to 127.

162

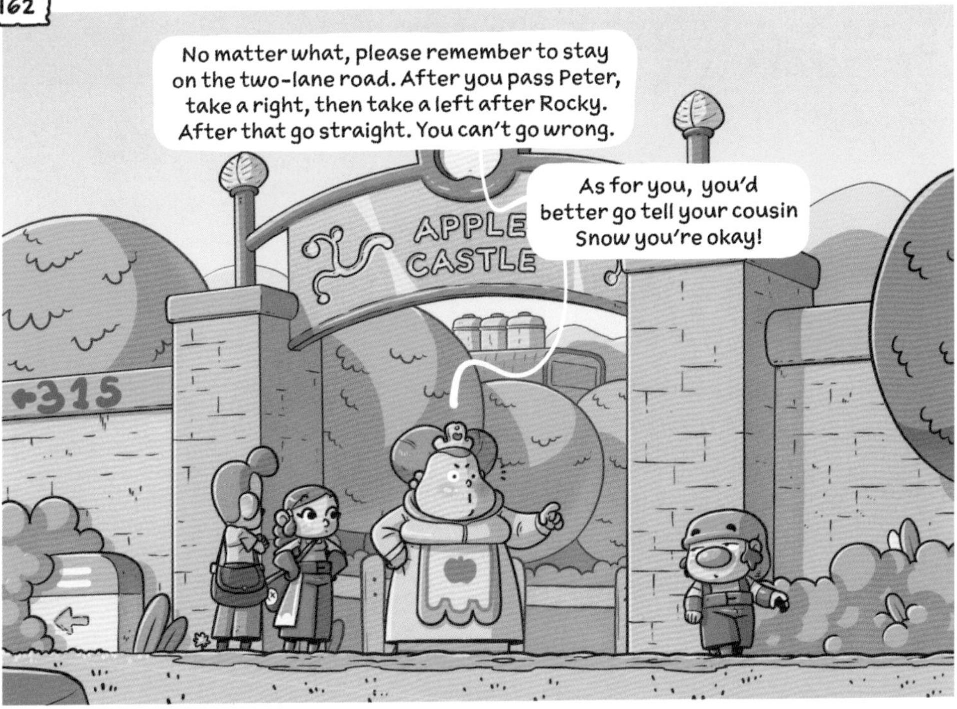
No matter what, please remember to stay on the two-lane road. After you pass Peter, take a right, then take a left after Rocky. After that go straight. You can't go wrong.
As for you, you'd better go tell your cousin Snow you're okay!
APPLE CASTLE
315

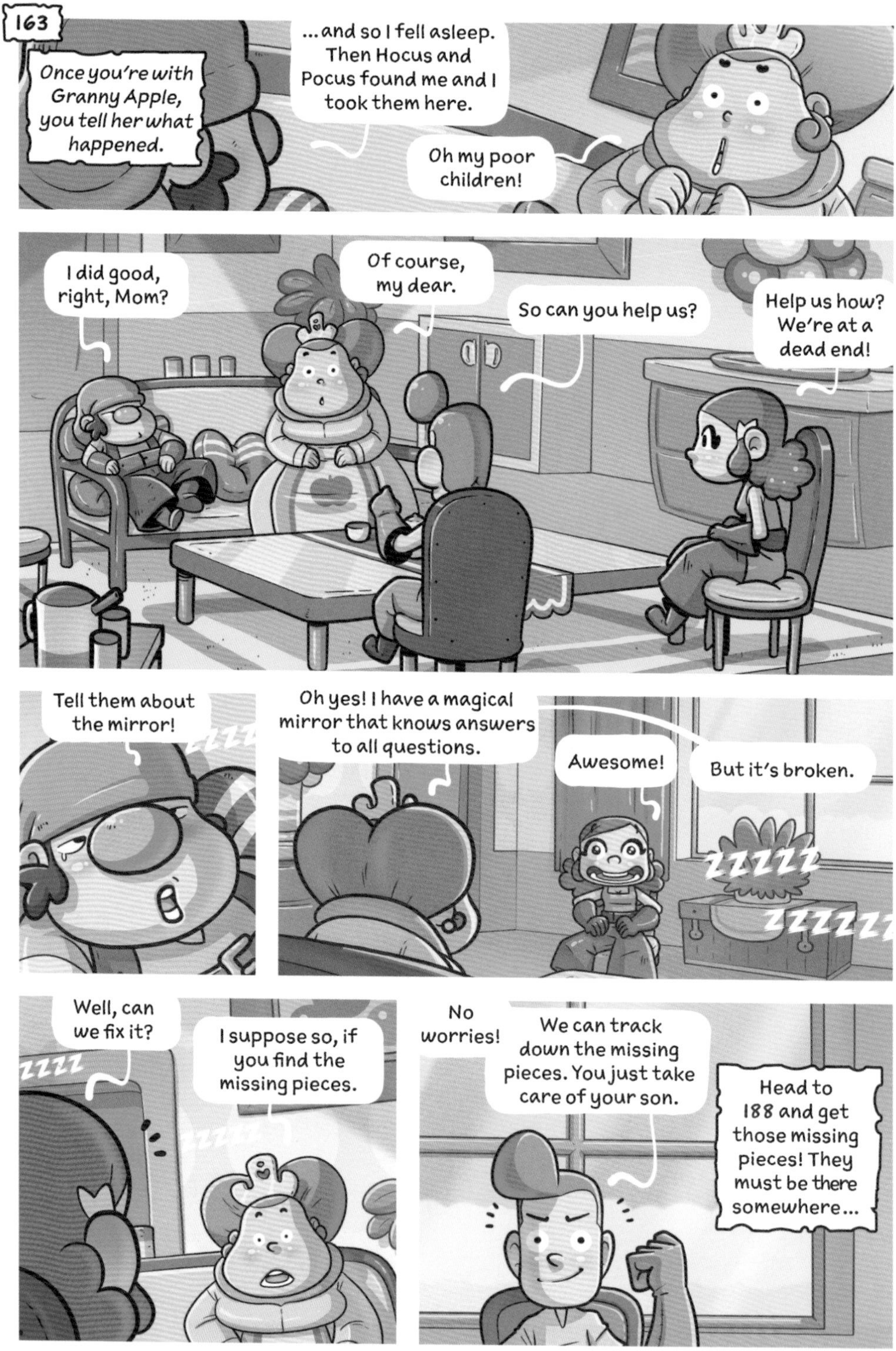
163
Once you're with Granny Apple, you tell her what happened.
...and so I fell asleep. Then Hocus and Pocus found me and I took them here.
Oh my poor children!
I did good, right, Mom?
Of course, my dear.
So can you help us?
Help us how? We're at a dead end!
Tell them about the mirror!
Oh yes! I have a magical mirror that knows answers to all questions.
Awesome!
But it's broken.
ZZZZZ
ZZZZZZ
Well, can we fix it?
I suppose so, if you find the missing pieces.
No worries!
We can track down the missing pieces. You just take care of your son.
Head to 188 and get those missing pieces! They must be there somewhere...

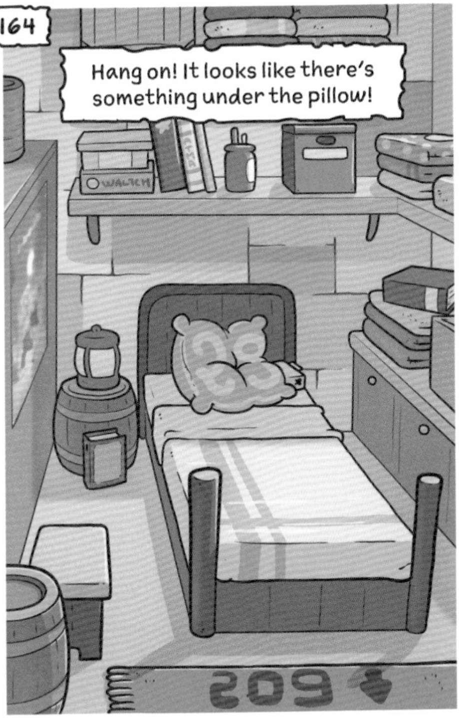
164
Hang on! It looks like there's something under the pillow!

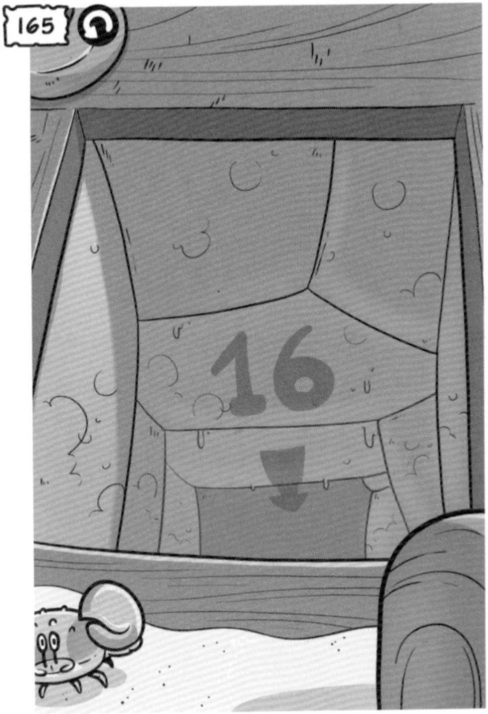
165
16

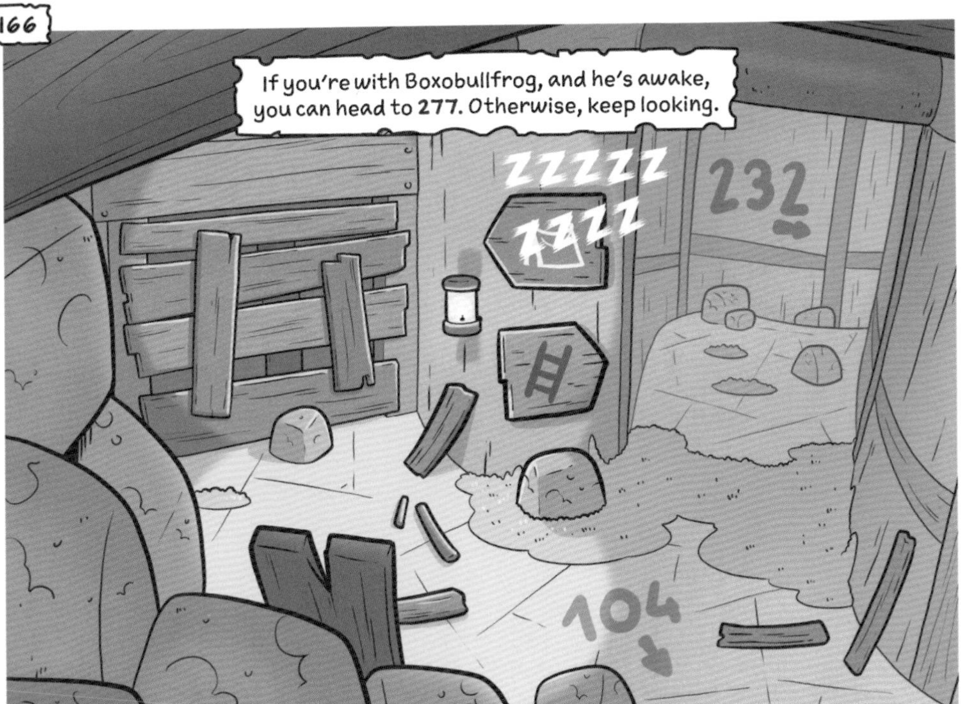
166
If you're with Boxobullfrog, and he's awake, you can head to 277. Otherwise, keep looking.
ZZZZZ
ZZZZ
232
104

167

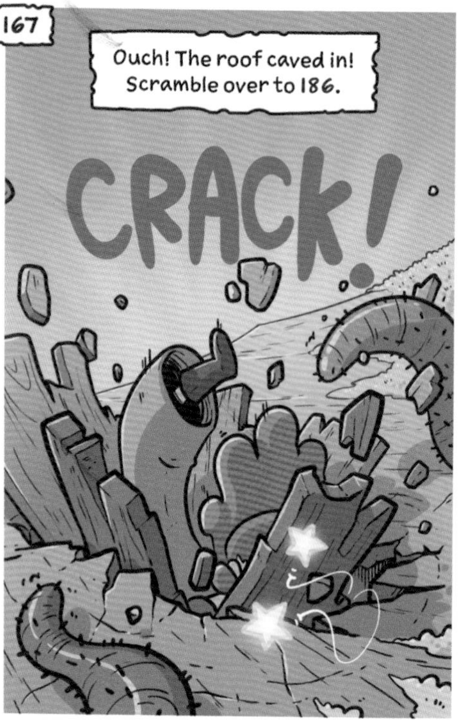

Ouch! The roof caved in! Scramble over to 186.
CRACK!

168

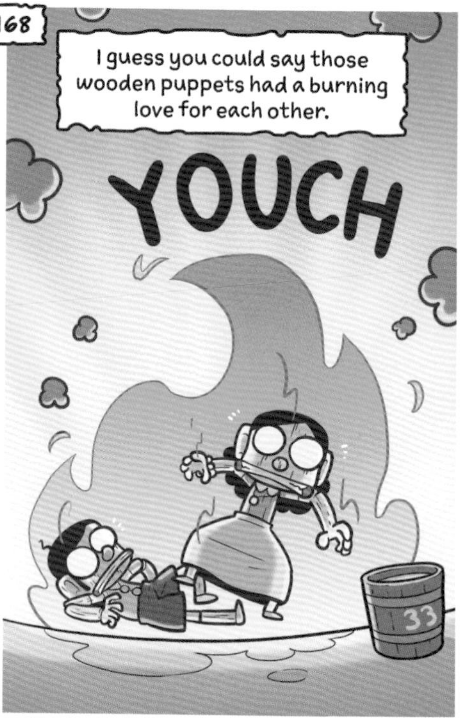

I guess you could say those wooden puppets had a burning love for each other.
YOUCH
33

169

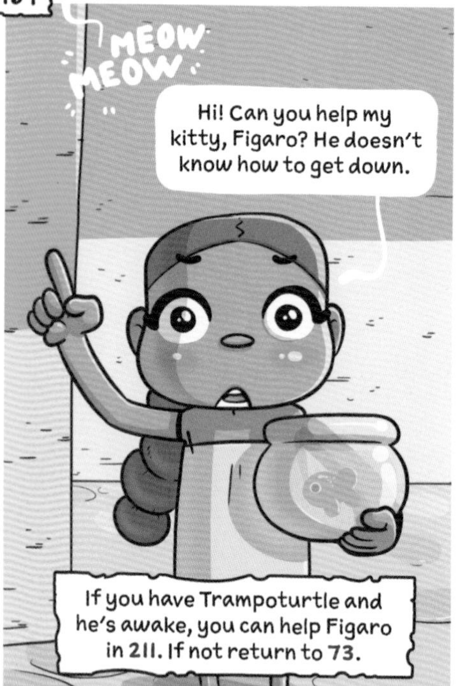

MEOW
MEOW
Hi! Can you help my kitty, Figaro? He doesn't know how to get down.
If you have Trampoturtle and he's awake, you can help Figaro in 211. If not return to 73.

170

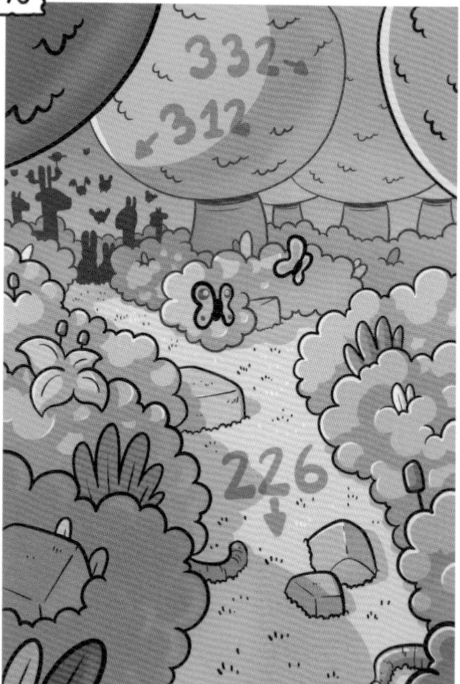

332
312
226

171

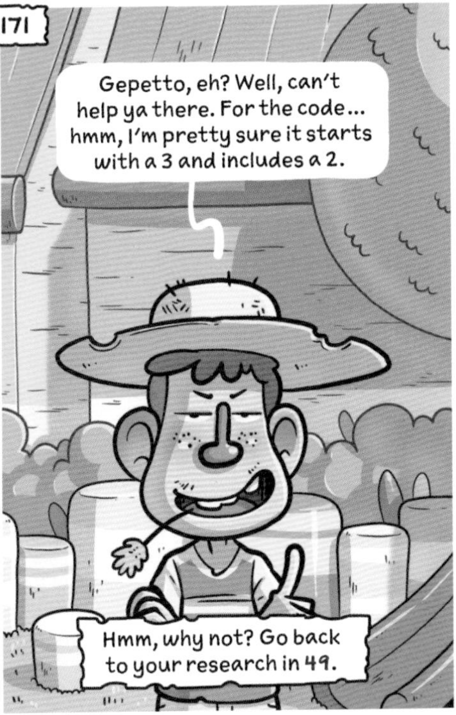

Gepetto, eh? Well, can't help ya there. For the code... hmm, I'm pretty sure it starts with a 3 and includes a 2.
Hmm, why not? Go back to your research in 49.

172

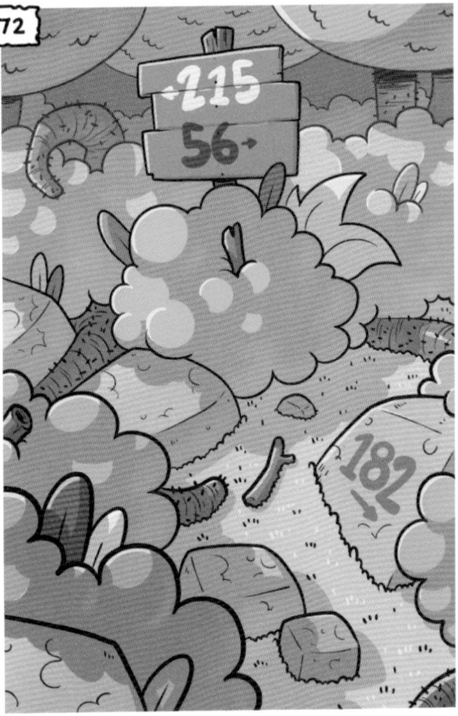

215
56
182

173

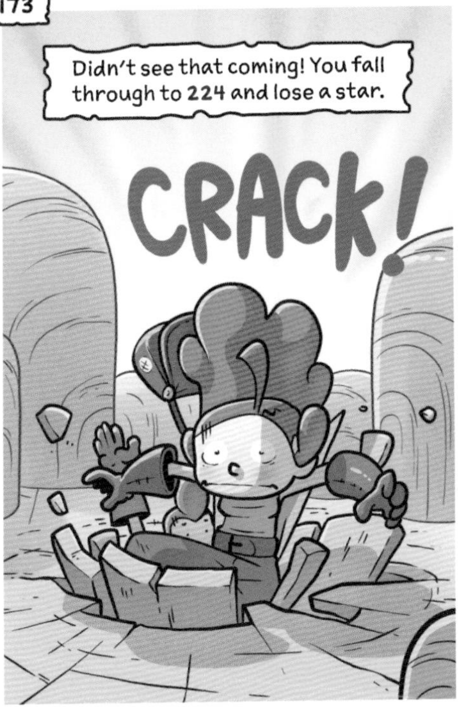

Didn't see that coming! You fall through to 224 and lose a star.
CRACK!

174

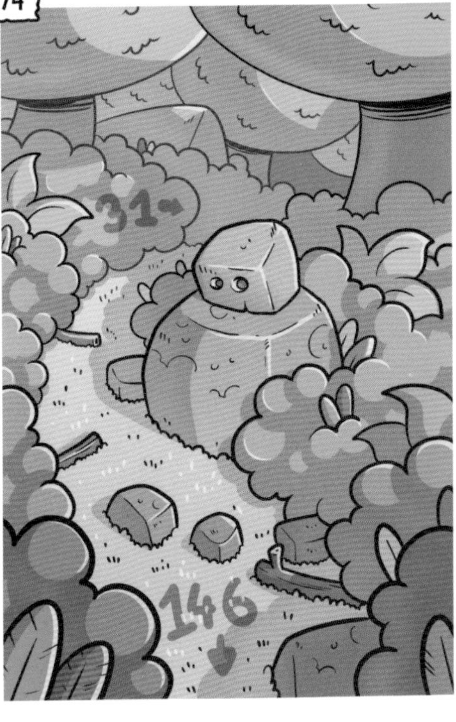

31
146

175

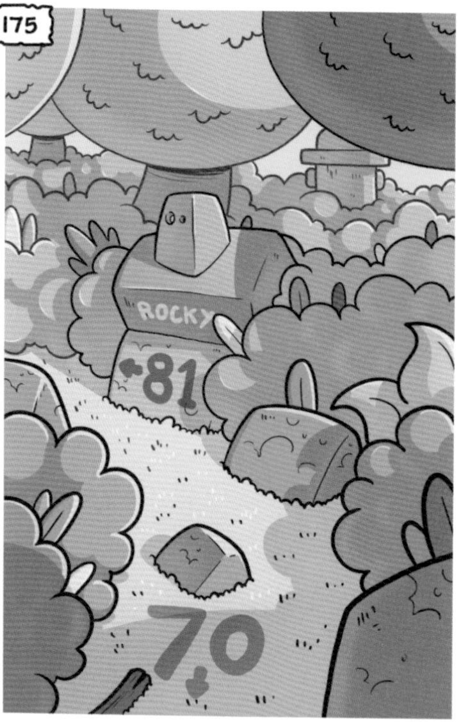
ROCKY
81
70

176

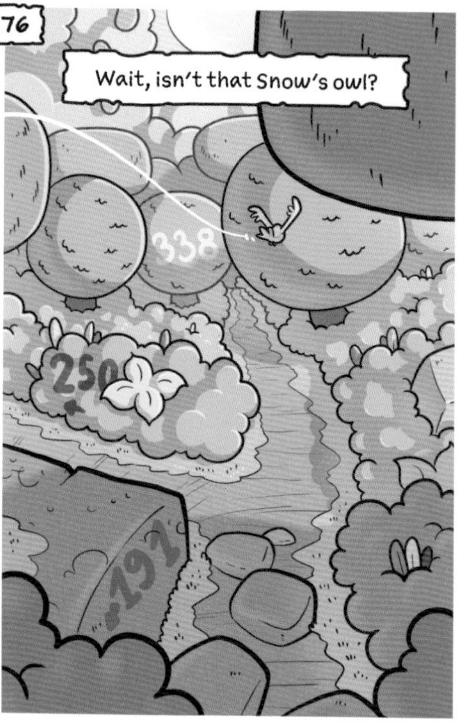
Wait, isn't that Snow's owl?
338
250
191

177

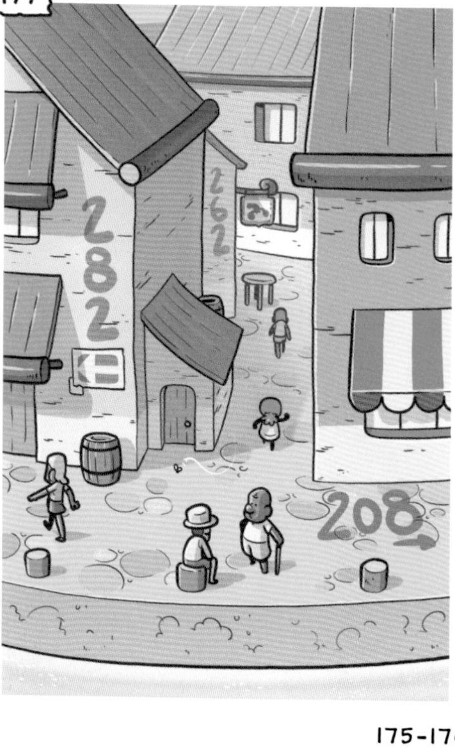
282
262
208

178

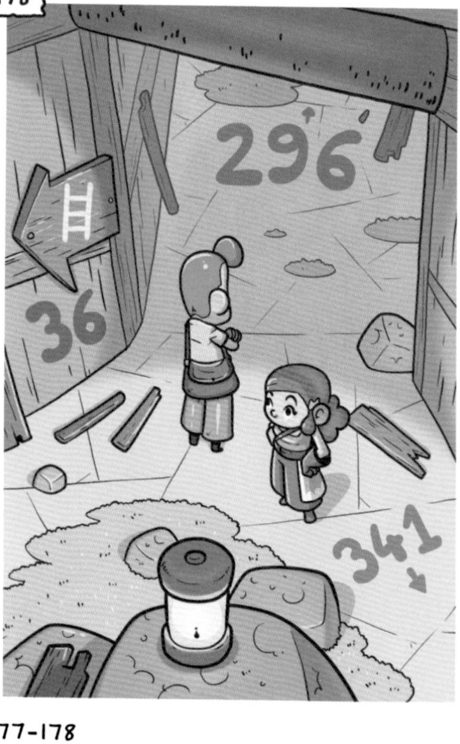
296
36
341

179

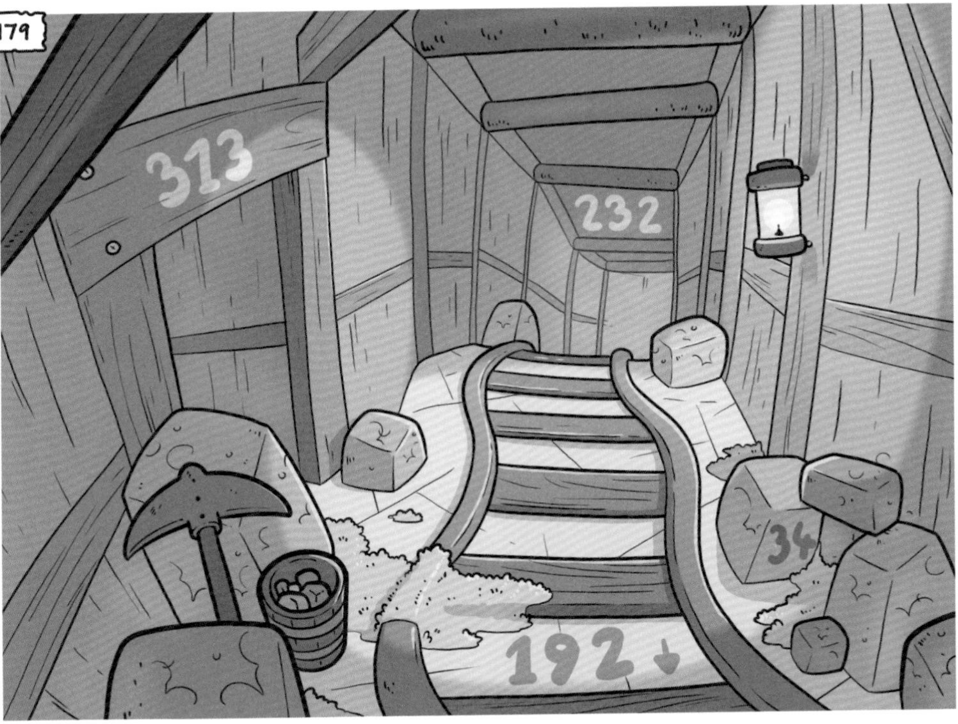
313
232
192
34

180

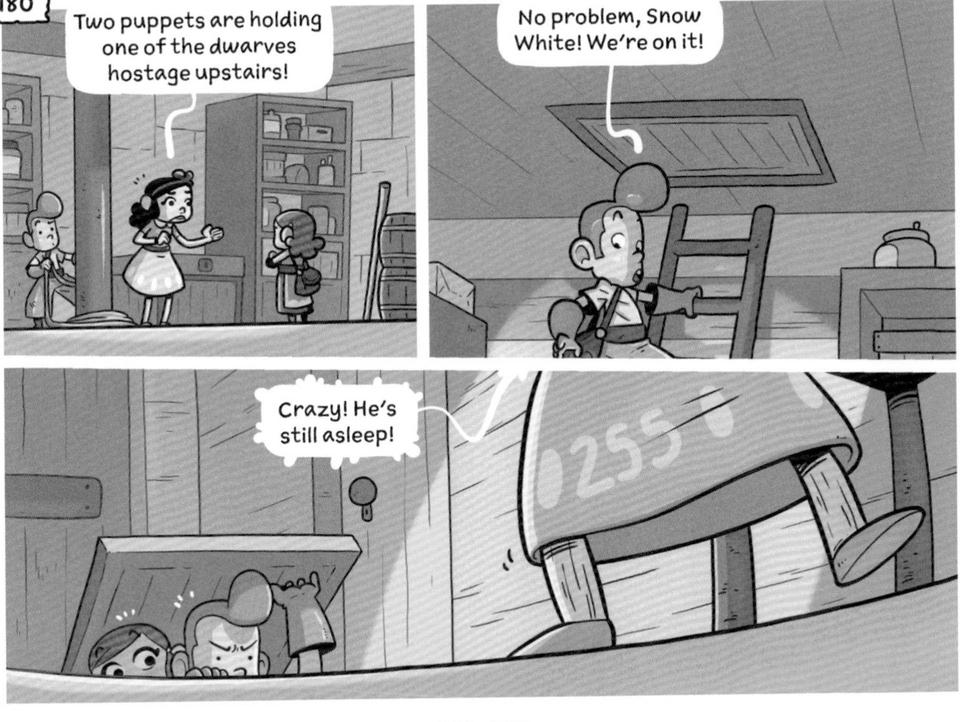
Two puppets are holding one of the dwarves hostage upstairs!
No problem, Snow White! We're on it!
Crazy! He's still asleep!

181

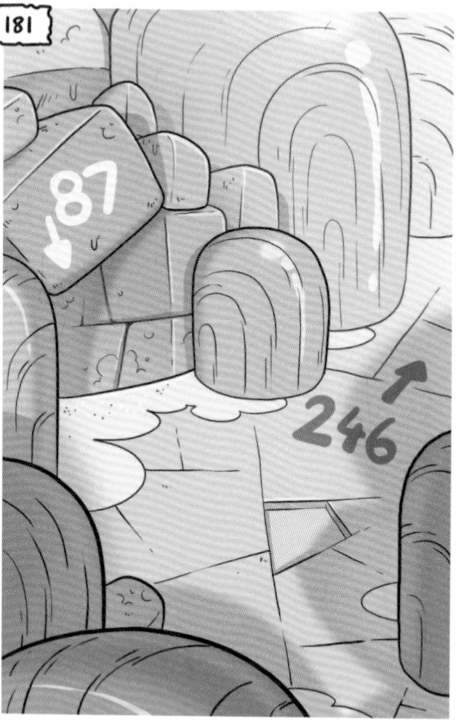
87
246

182

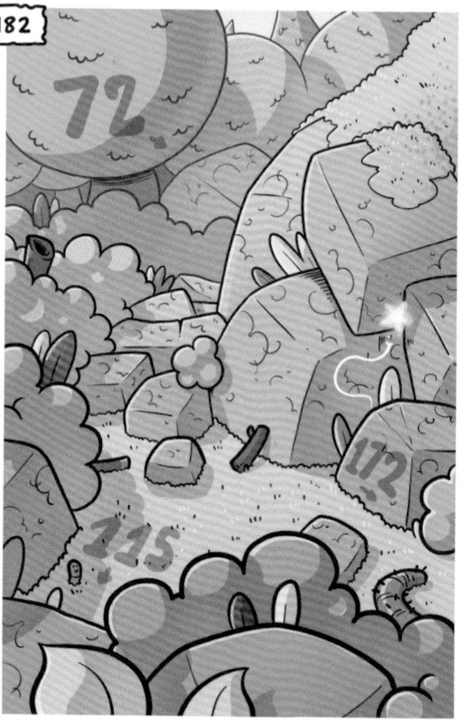
72
172
115

183

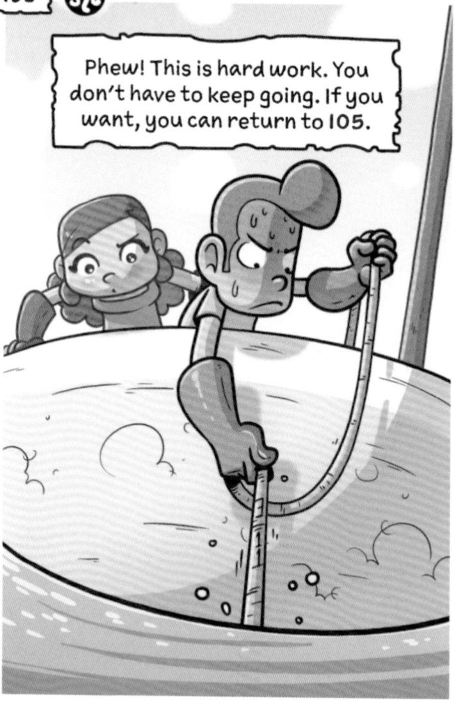
Phew! This is hard work. You don't have to keep going. If you want, you can return to 105.

184

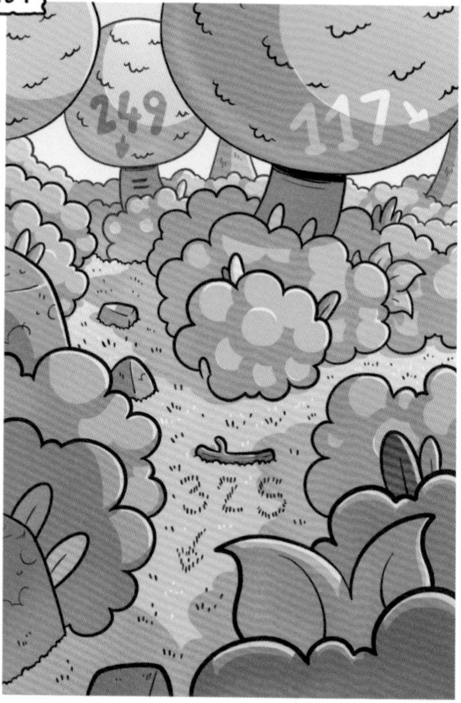
249
117
325

185

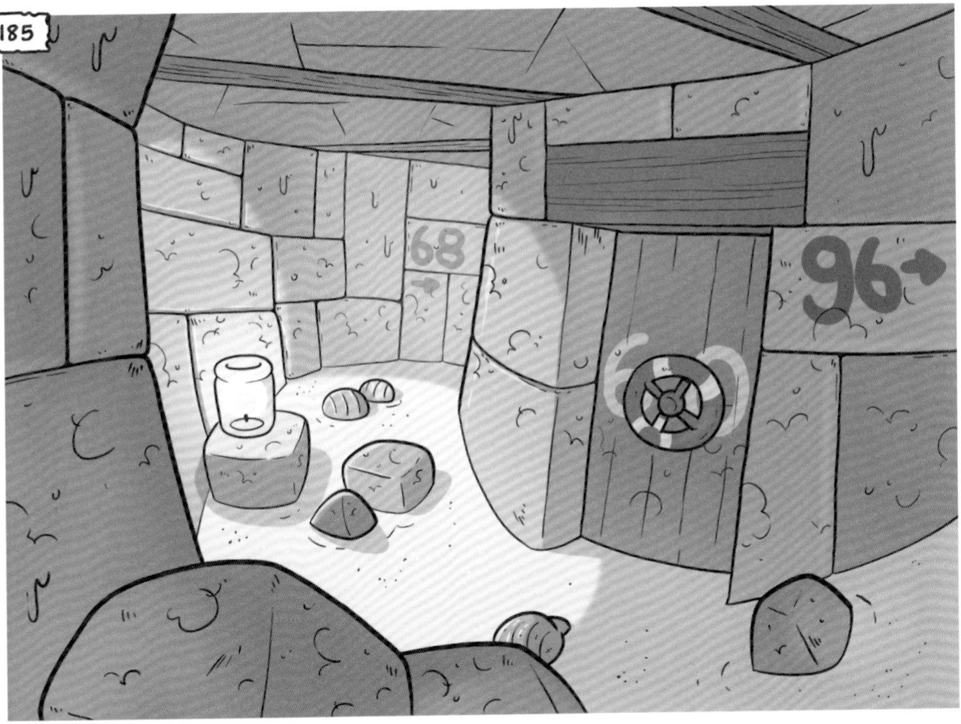
68
96

186

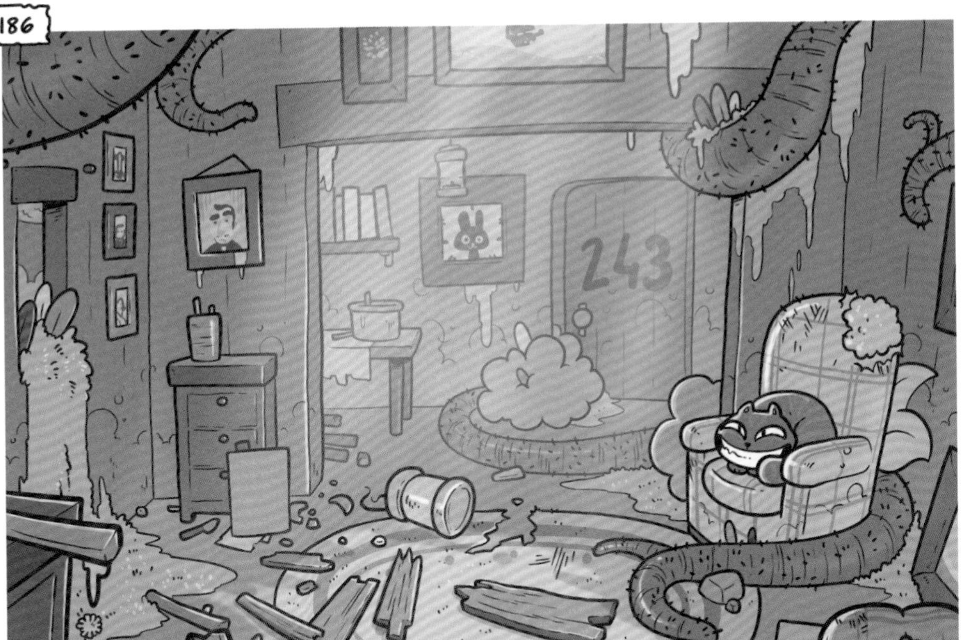
243

187

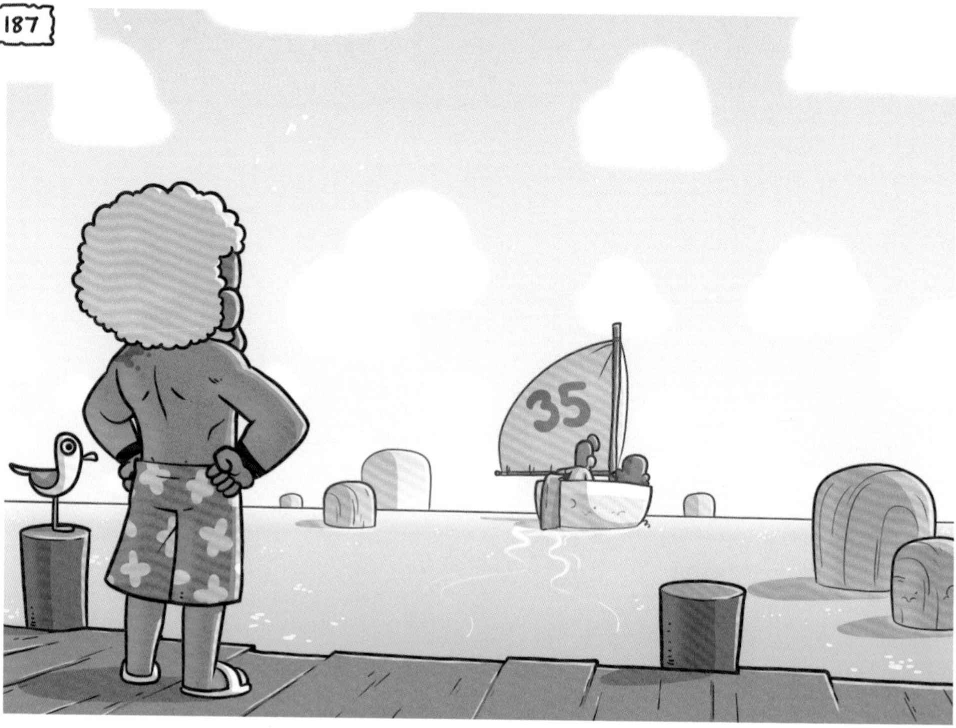
35

188

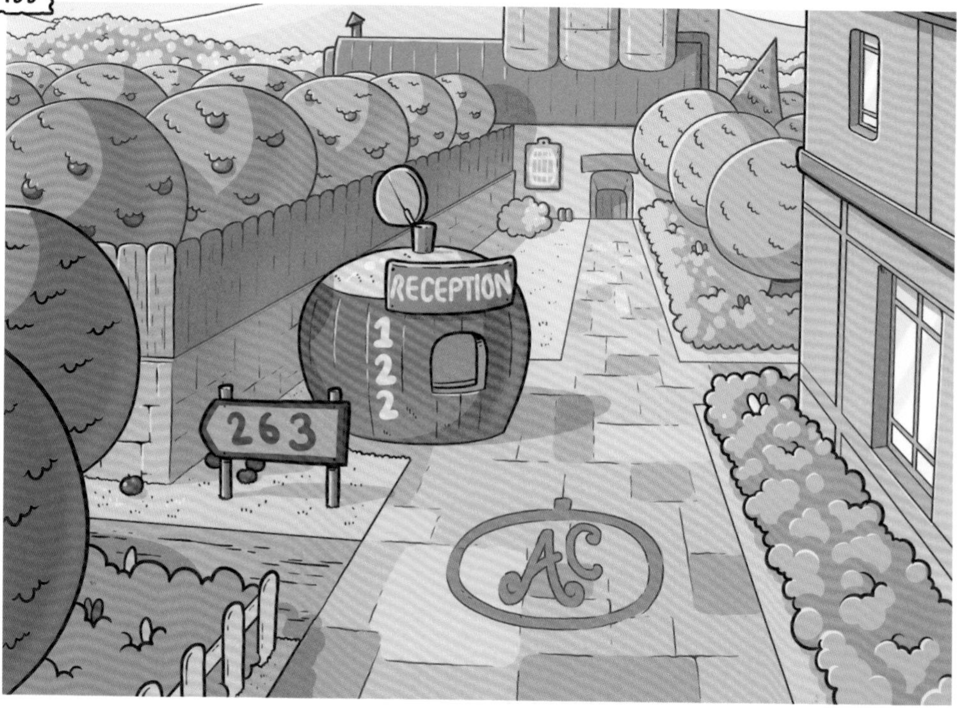
RECEPTION
122
263
AC

189

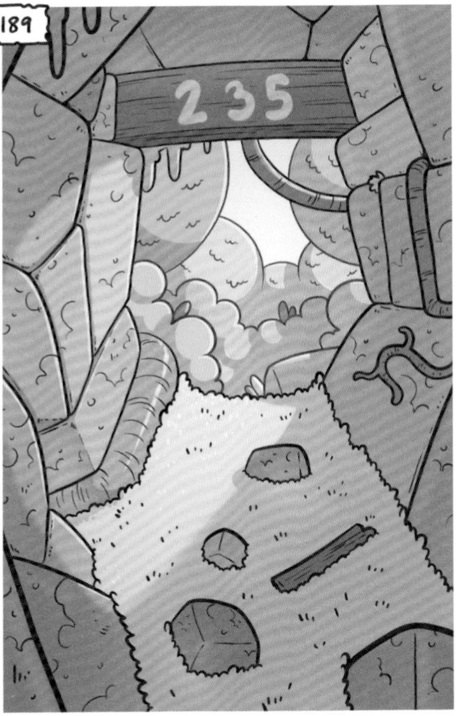
235

190

Yeah, the story of these puppets is weirdly similar to Jiminy and Snow White. Love makes you do crazy things, you know!

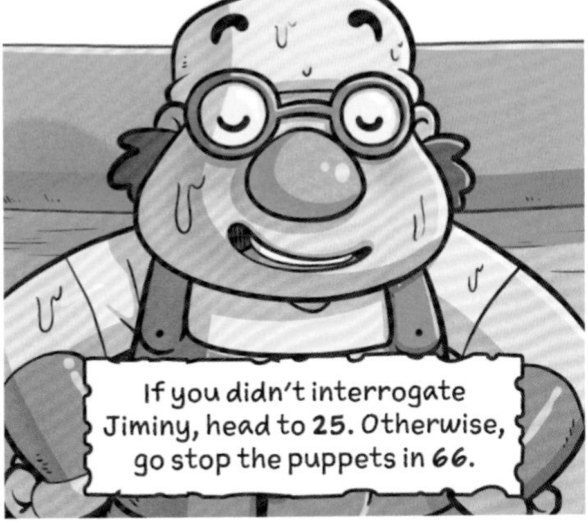
If you didn't interrogate Jiminy, head to **25**. Otherwise, go stop the puppets in **66**.

191

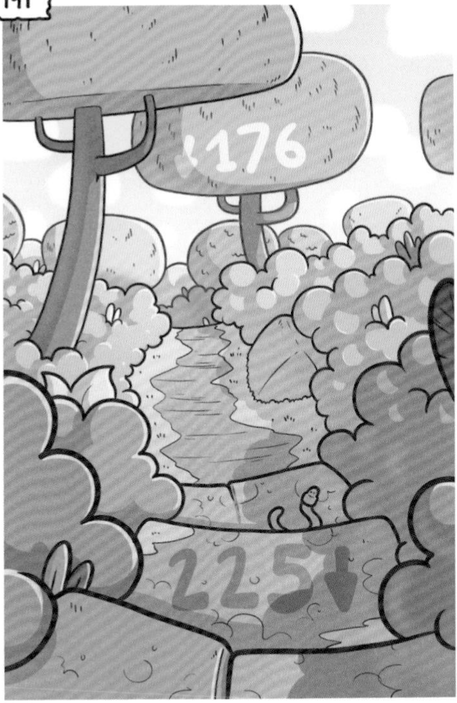
176
225

192

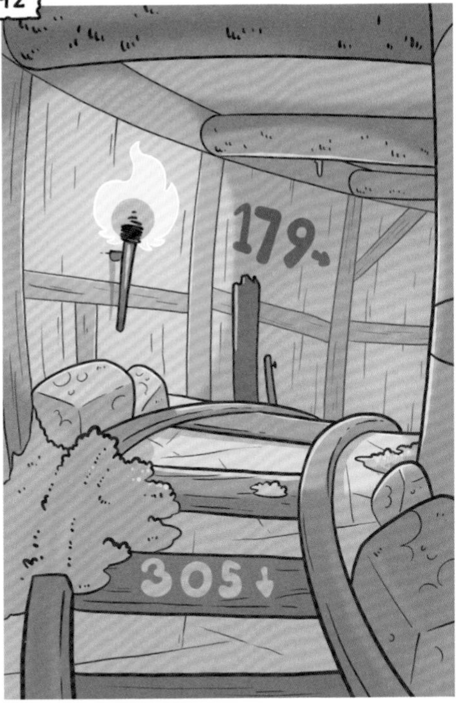
179
305

193

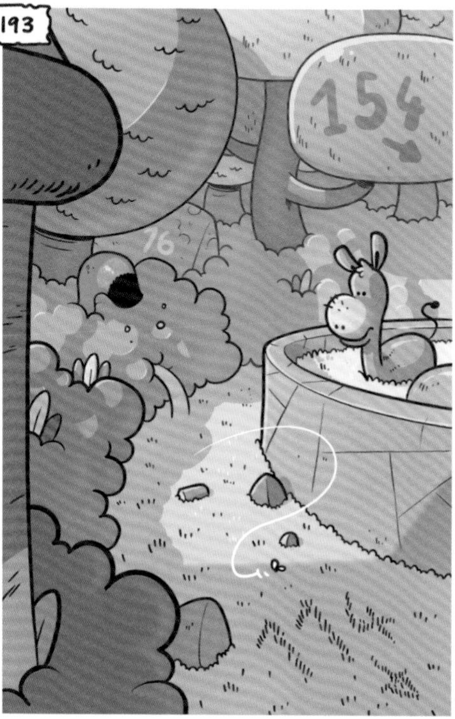
154
76

194

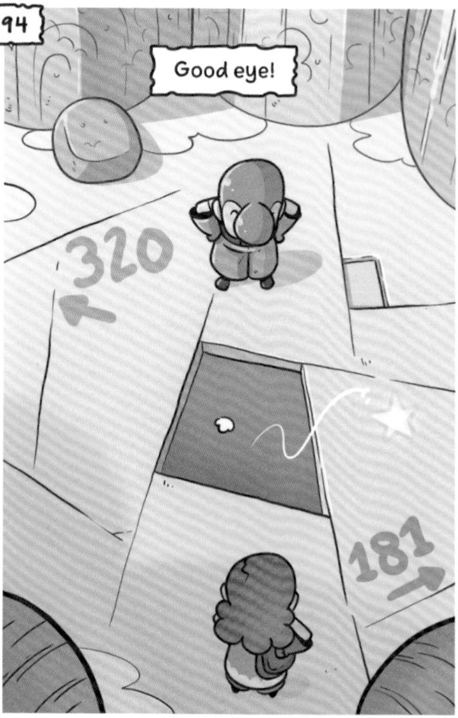
Good eye!
320
181

195

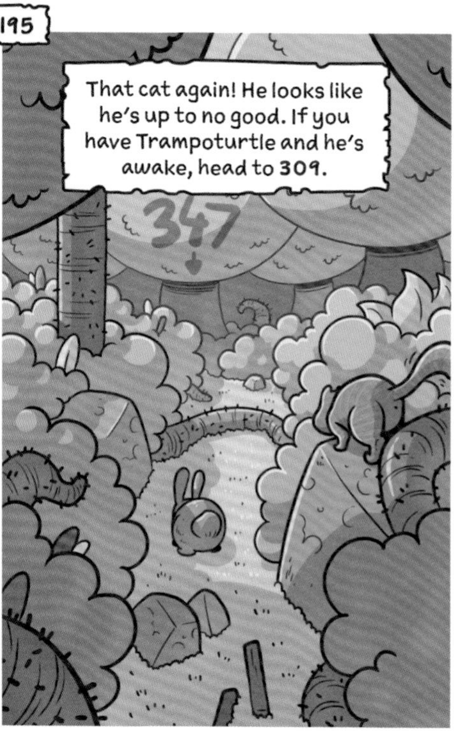
That cat again! He looks like he's up to no good. If you have Trampoturtle and he's awake, head to 309.
347

196

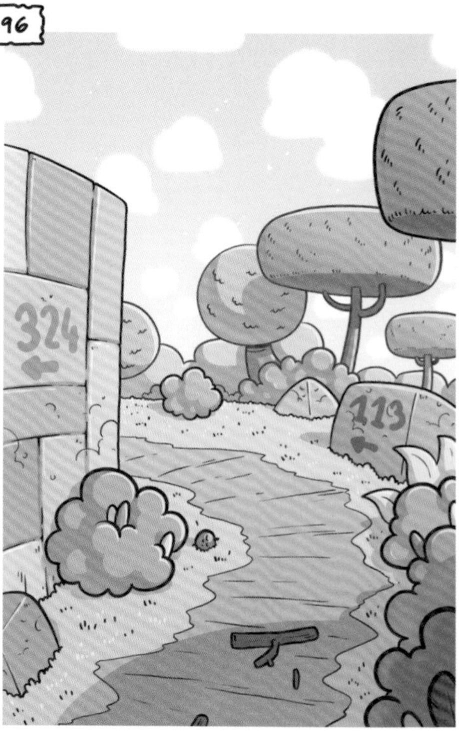
324
113

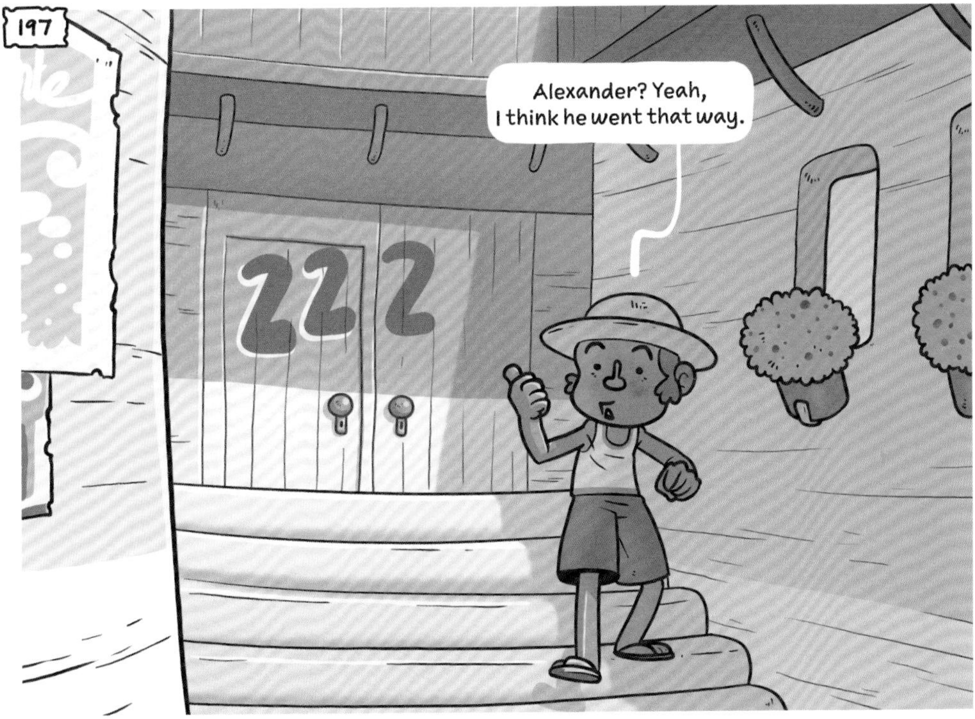
197
222
Alexander? Yeah, I think he went that way.

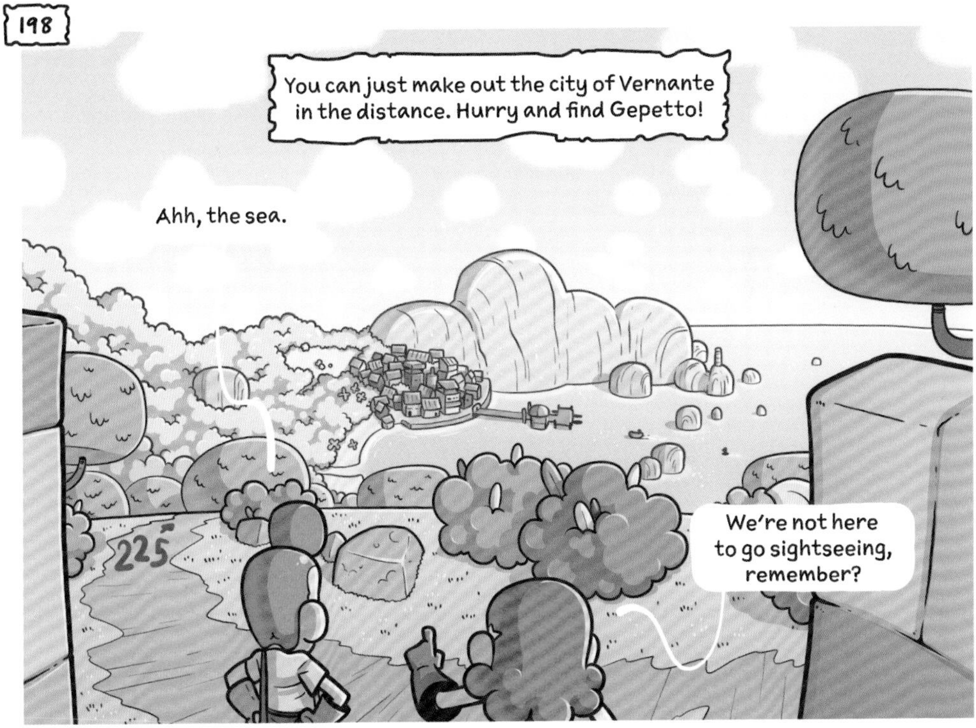
198
You can just make out the city of Vernante in the distance. Hurry and find Gepetto!
Ahh, the sea.
225
We're not here to go sightseeing, remember?

199

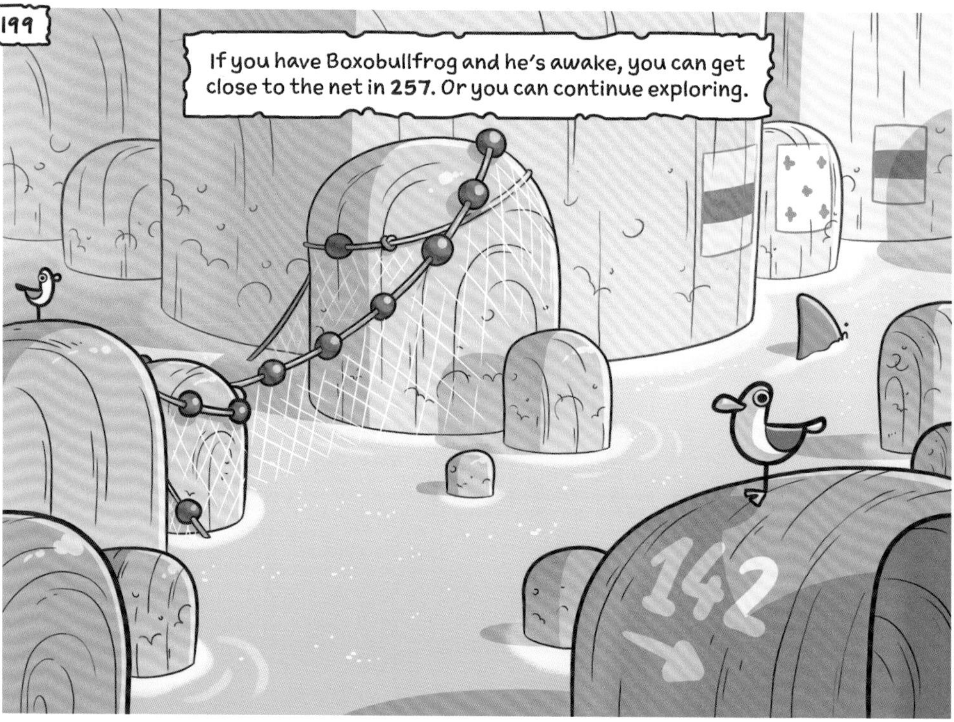
If you have Boxobullfrog and he's awake, you can get close to the net in **257**. Or you can continue exploring.
142

200

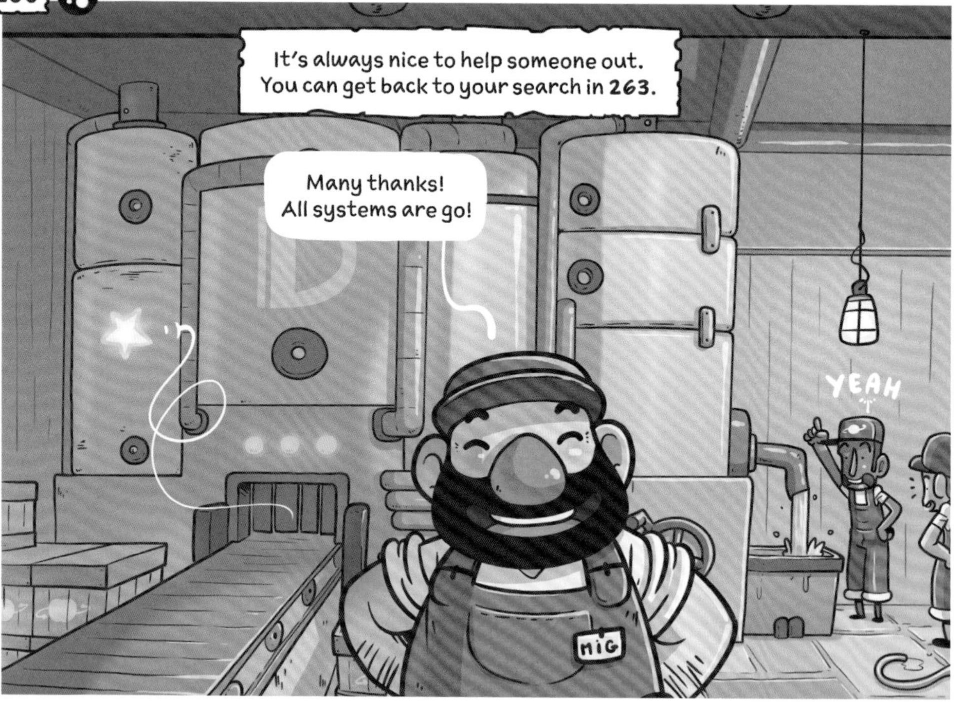
It's always nice to help someone out. You can get back to your search in **263**.
Many thanks! All systems are go!
YEAH
MIG

201

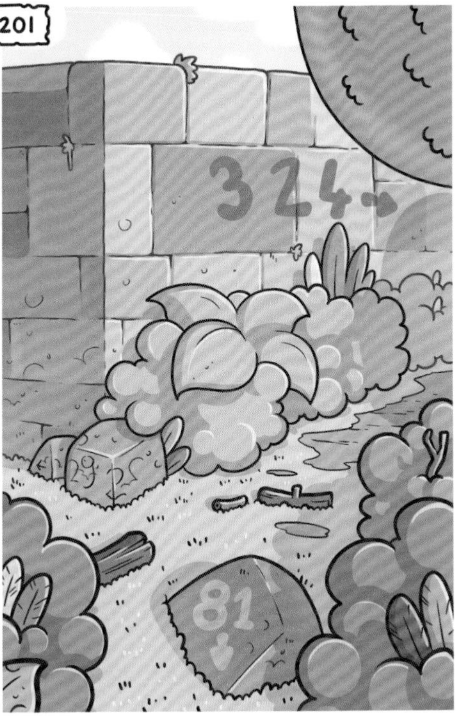
324
29
81

202

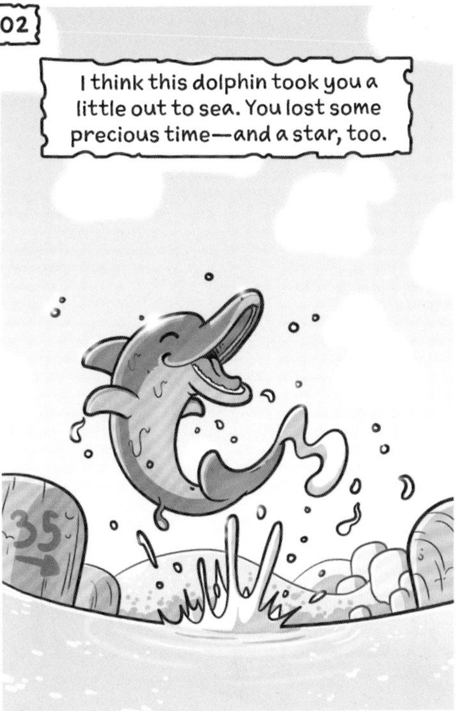
I think this dolphin took you a little out to sea. You lost some precious time—and a star, too.
35

203

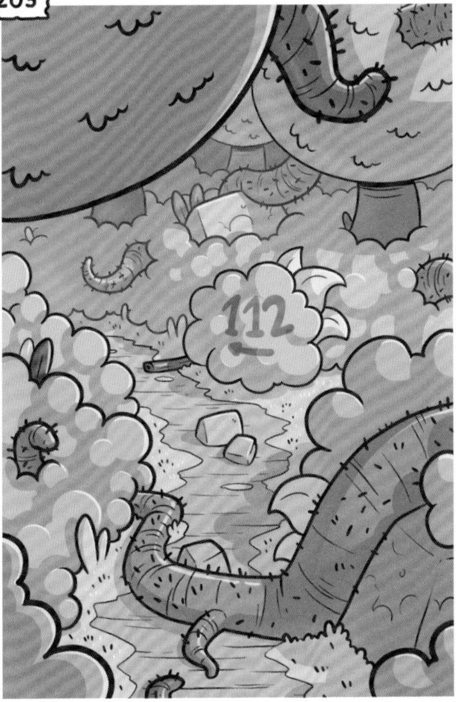
112

204

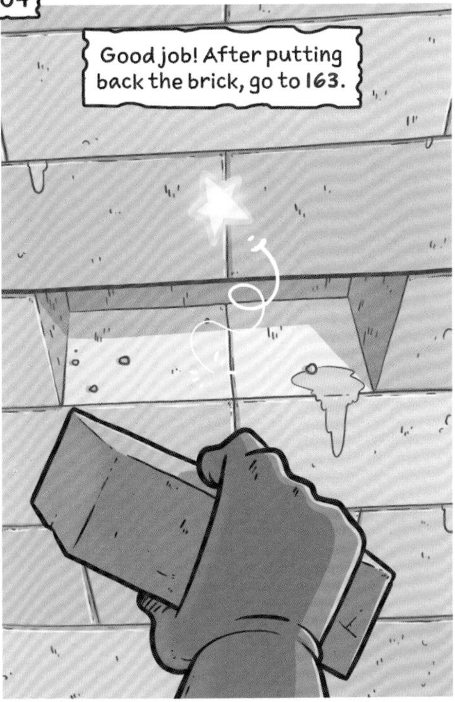
Good job! After putting back the brick, go to 163.

205

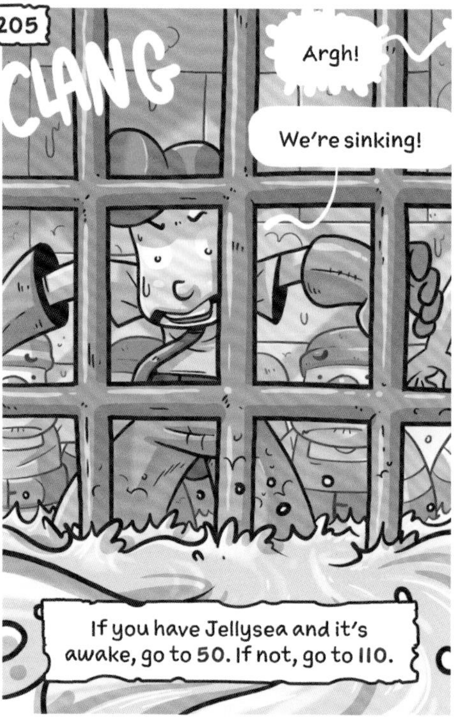
CLANG
Argh!
We're sinking!
If you have Jellysea and it's awake, go to 50. If not, go to 110.

206

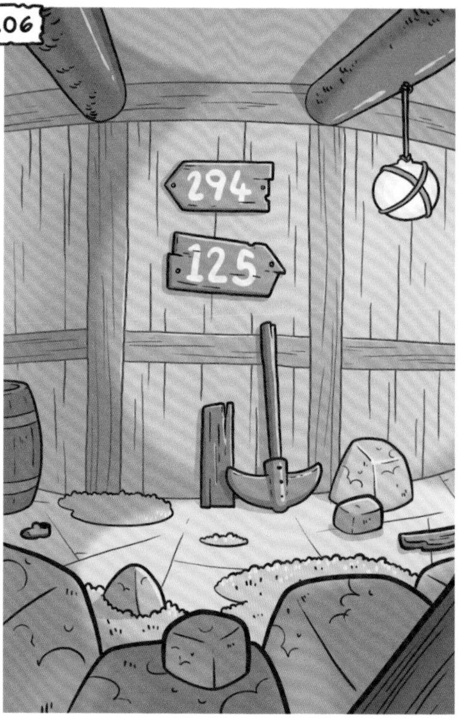
294
125

207

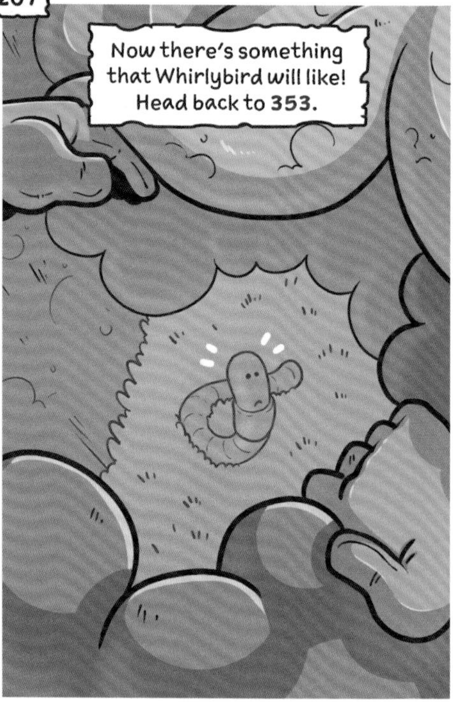
Now there's something that Whirlybird will like! Head back to 353.

208

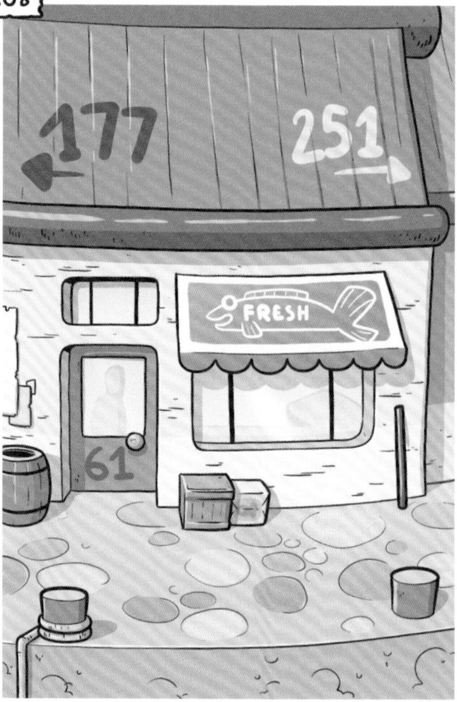
177
251
FRESH
61

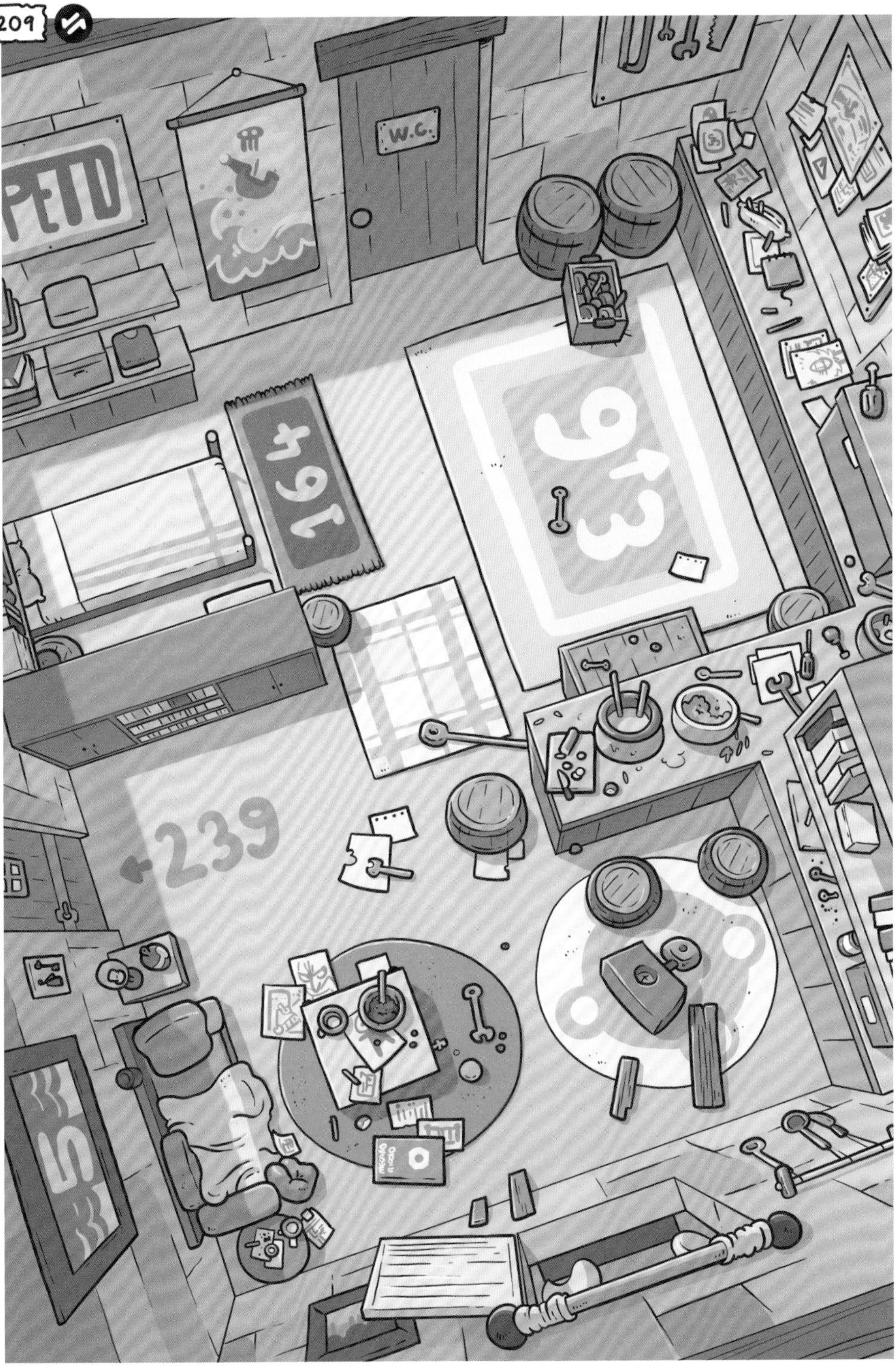
W.C.
9↑3
←239

210

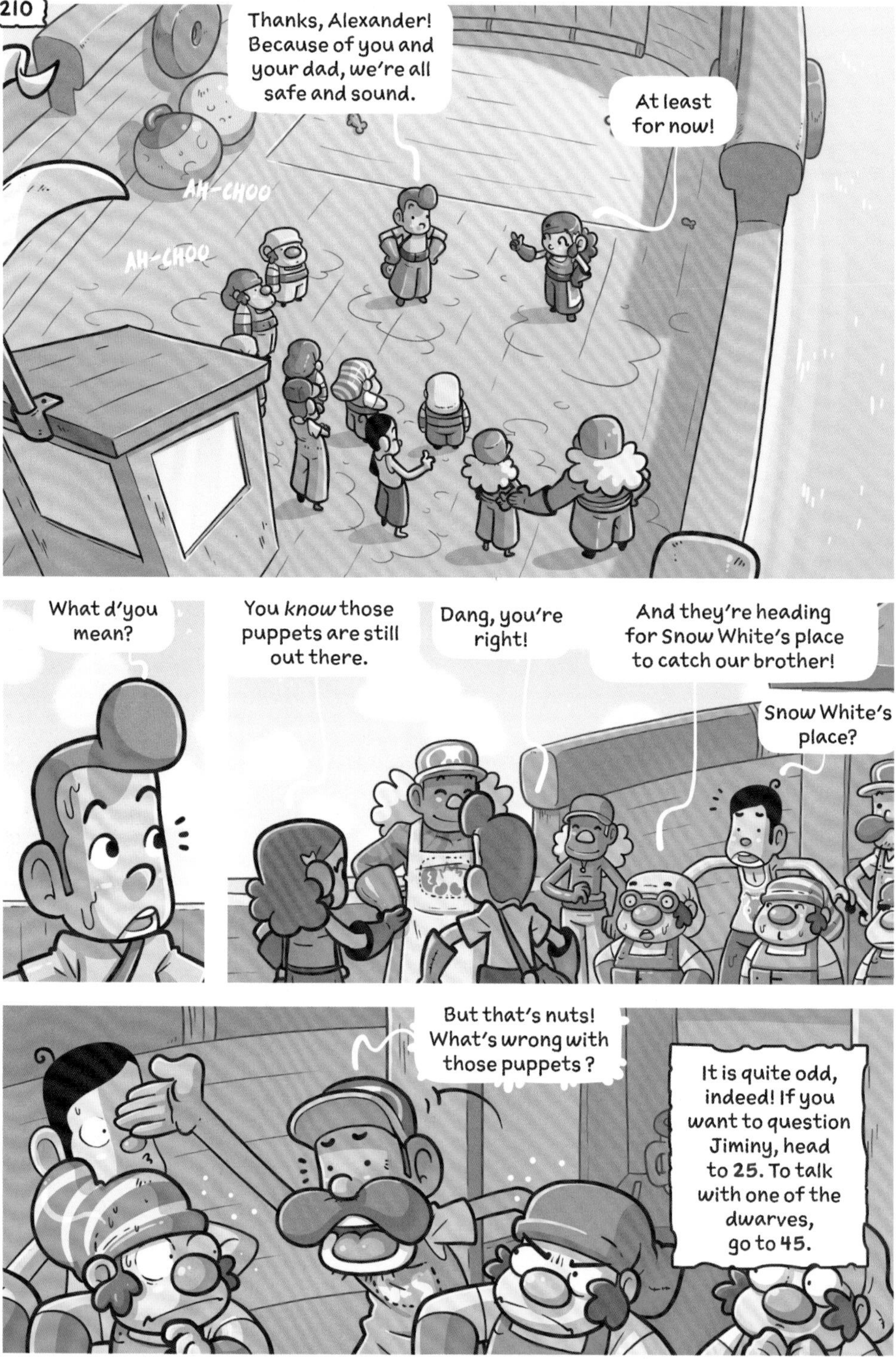

Thanks, Alexander! Because of you and your dad, we're all safe and sound.
At least for now!
AH-CHOO
AH-CHOO
What d'you mean?
You *know* those puppets are still out there.
Dang, you're right!
And they're heading for Snow White's place to catch our brother!
Snow White's place?
But that's nuts! What's wrong with those puppets?
It is quite odd, indeed! If you want to question Jiminy, head to 25. To talk with one of the dwarves, go to 45.

211

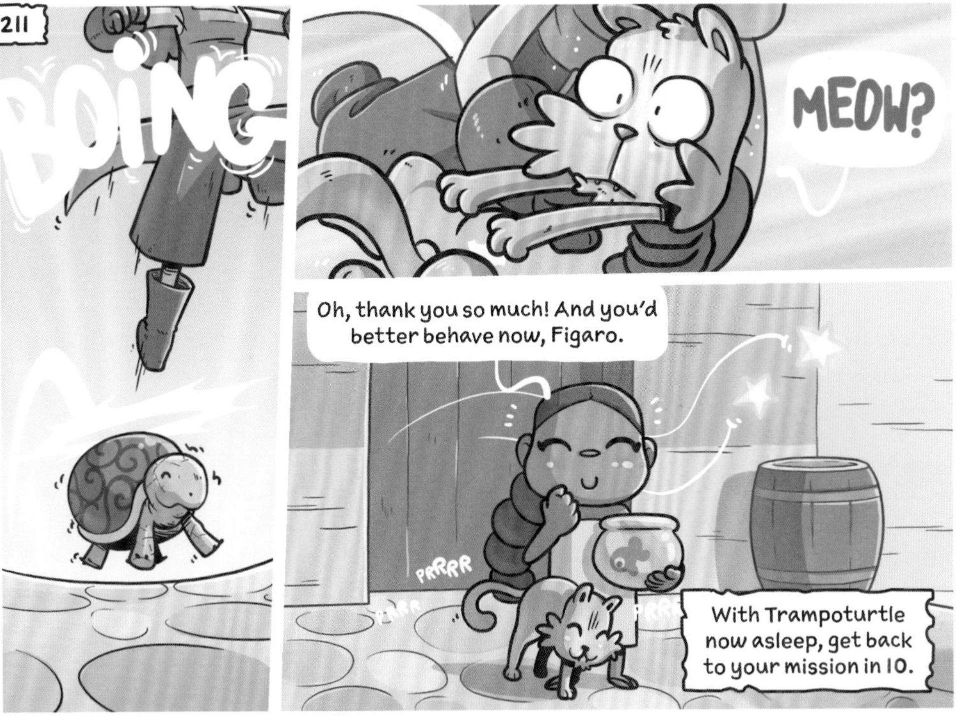
BOING
MEOW?
Oh, thank you so much! And you'd better behave now, Figaro.
PRRRR
PRRR
PRRR
With Trampoturtle now asleep, get back to your mission in 10.

212

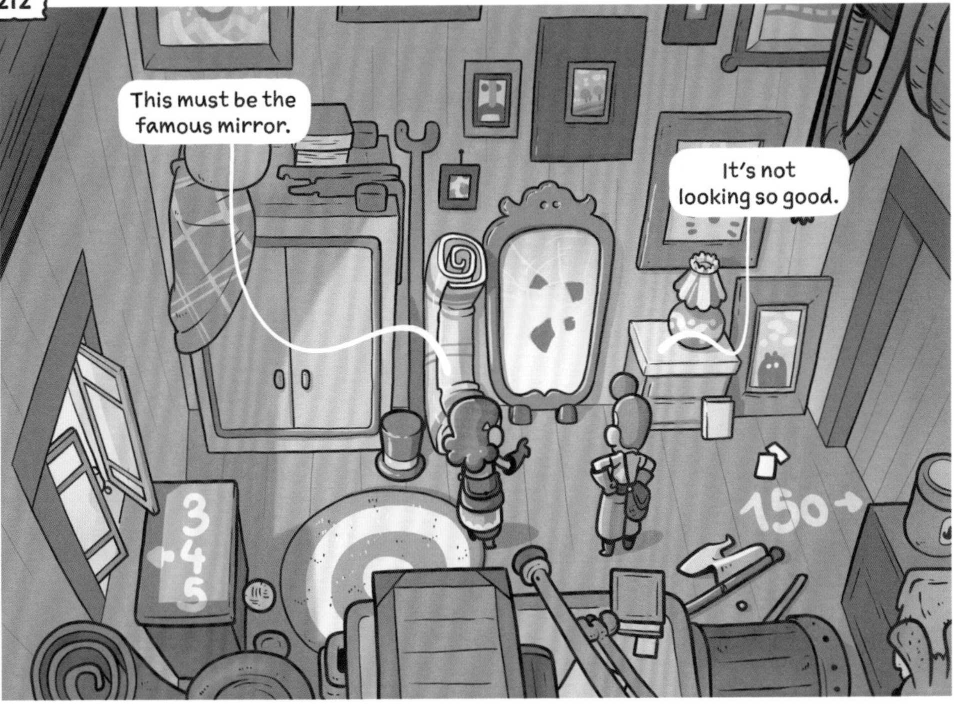
This must be the famous mirror.
It's not looking so good.
345
150→

213

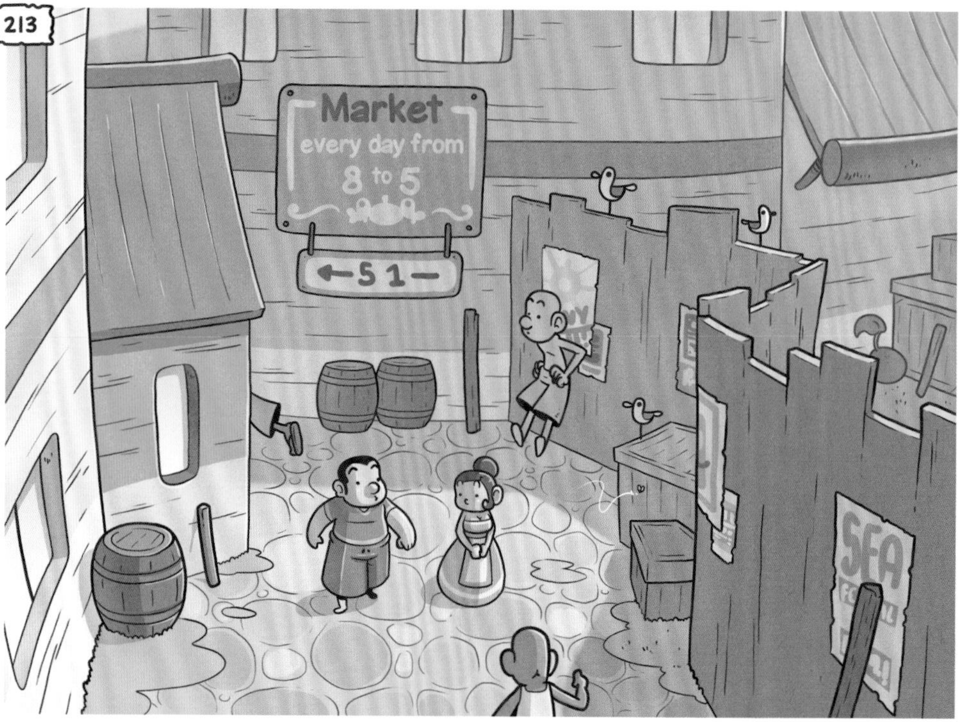
Market
every day from
8 to 5
← 51 –
SEA

214

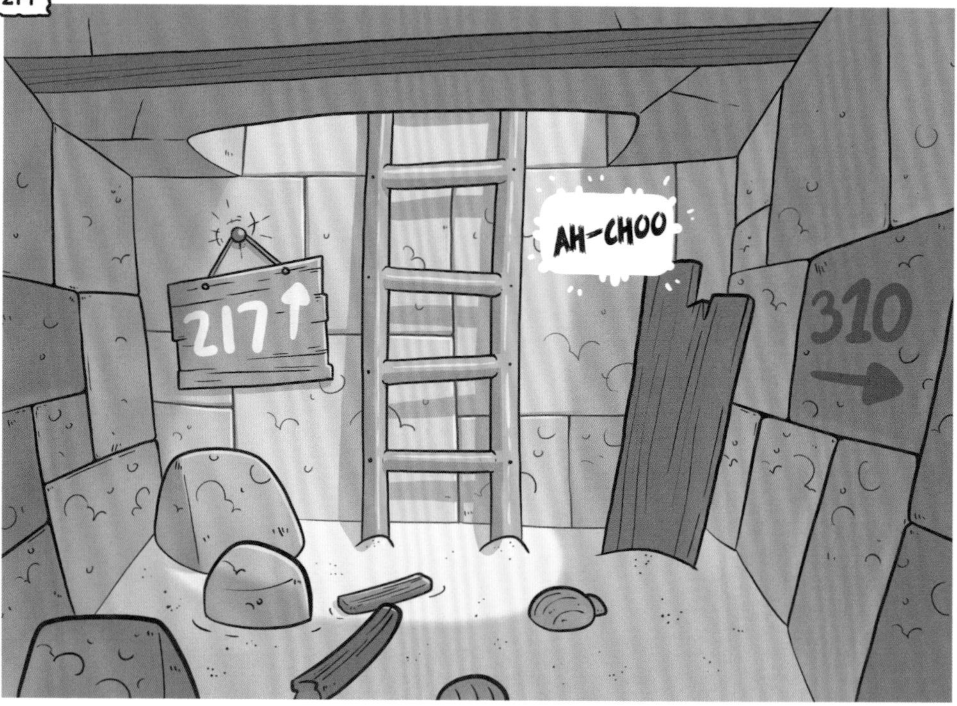
217 ↑
AH-CHOO
310 →

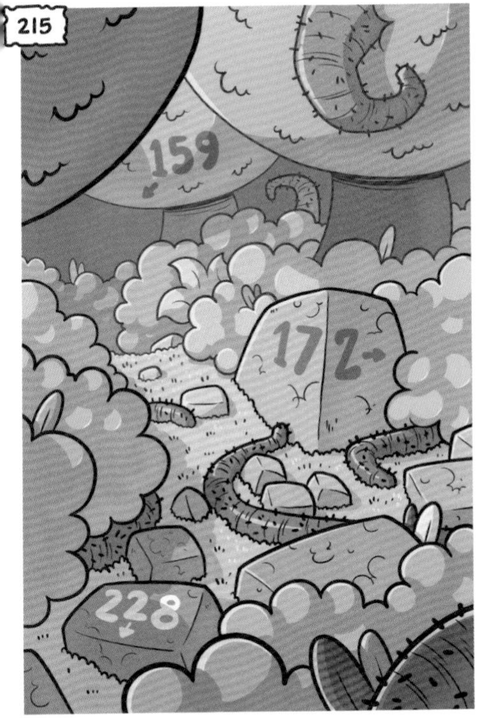
215
159
172
228

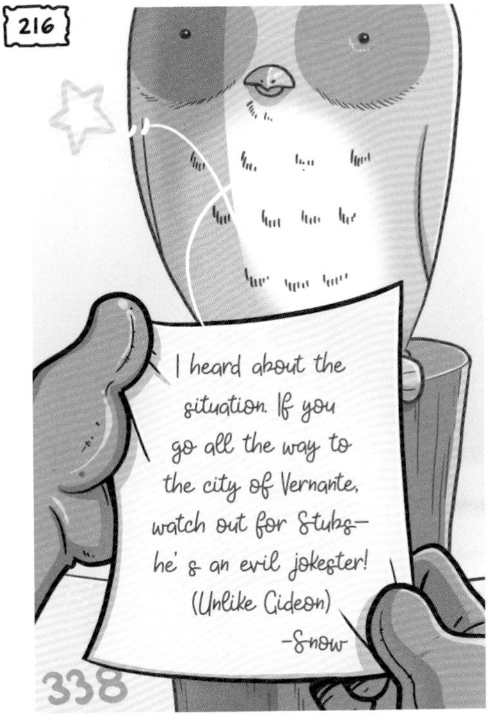
216
I heard about the situation. If you go all the way to the city of Vernante, watch out for Stubs—he's an evil jokester! (Unlike Gideon)
-Snow
338

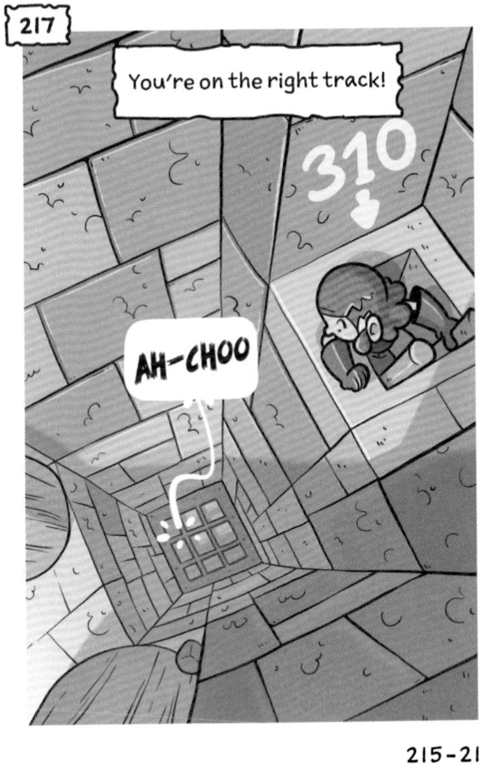
217
You're on the right track!
310
AH-CHOO

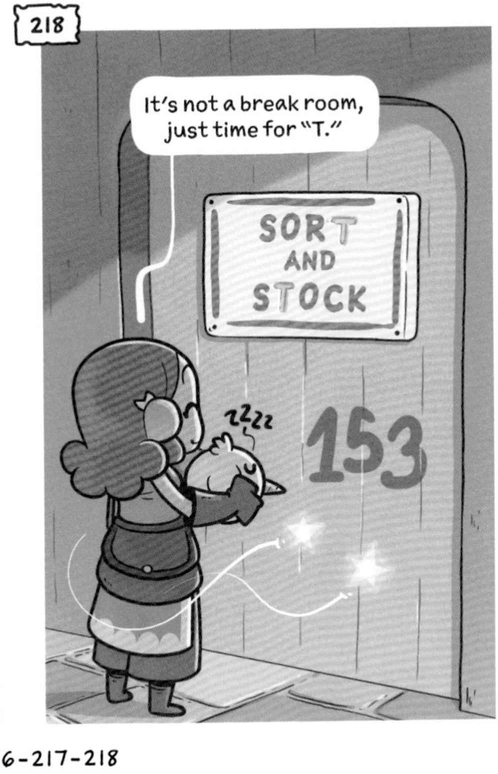
218
It's not a break room, just time for "T."
SORT AND STOCK
ZZZZ
153

219

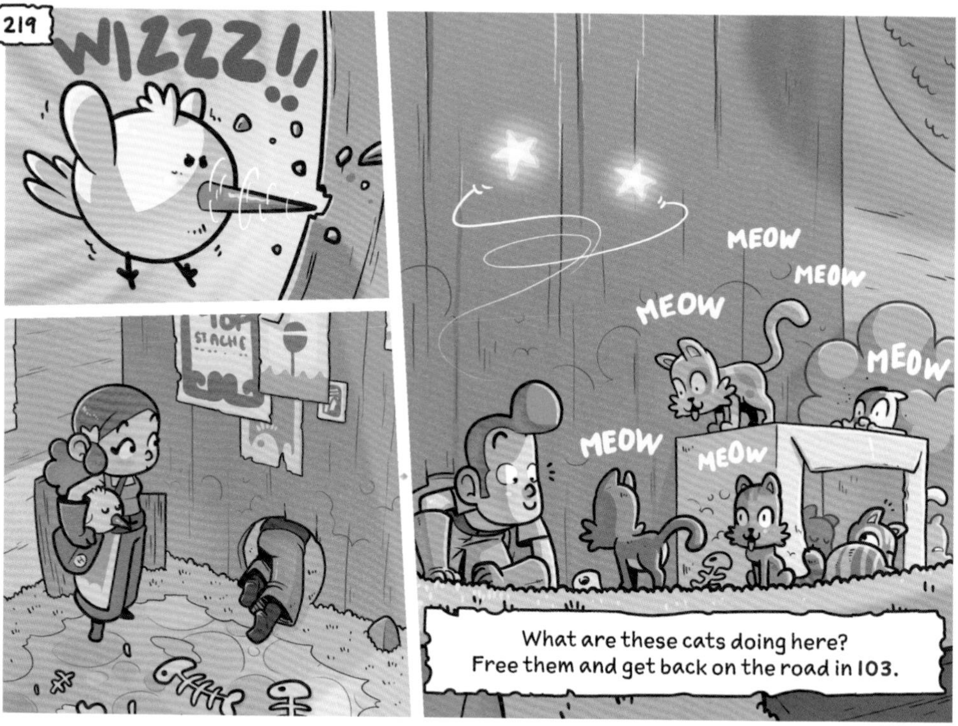
WIZZZ!
MEOW
MEOW
MEOW
MEOW
MEOW
MEOW
What are these cats doing here?
Free them and get back on the road in 103.

220

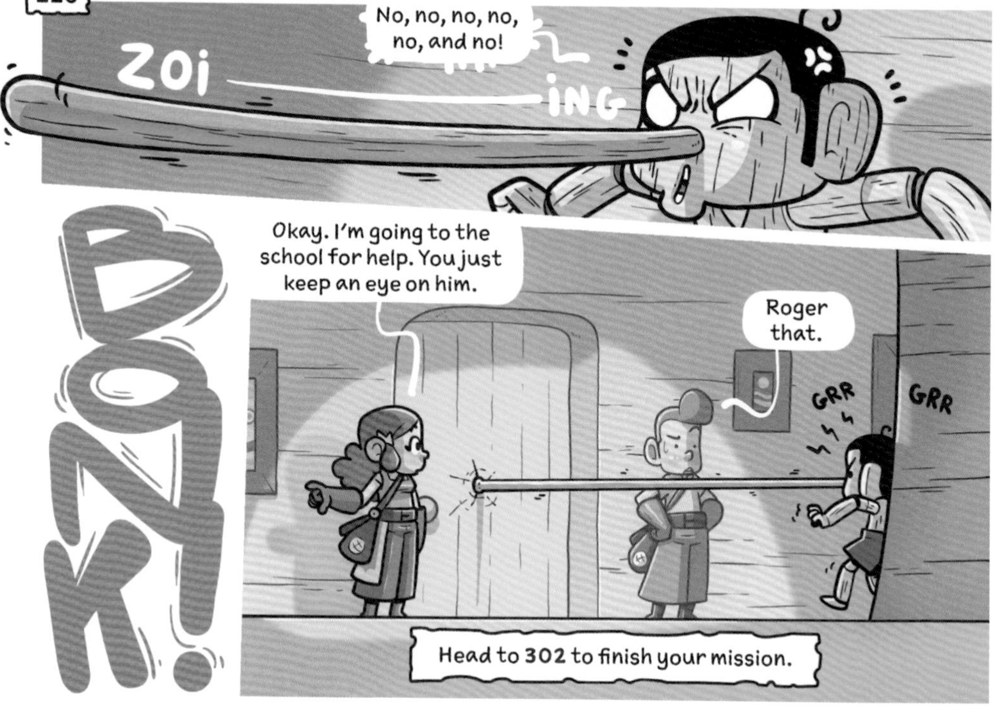
No, no, no, no,
no, and no!
ZOi—ING
KZOOB!
Okay. I'm going to the school for help. You just keep an eye on him.
Roger that.
GRR
GRR
Head to 302 to finish your mission.

221

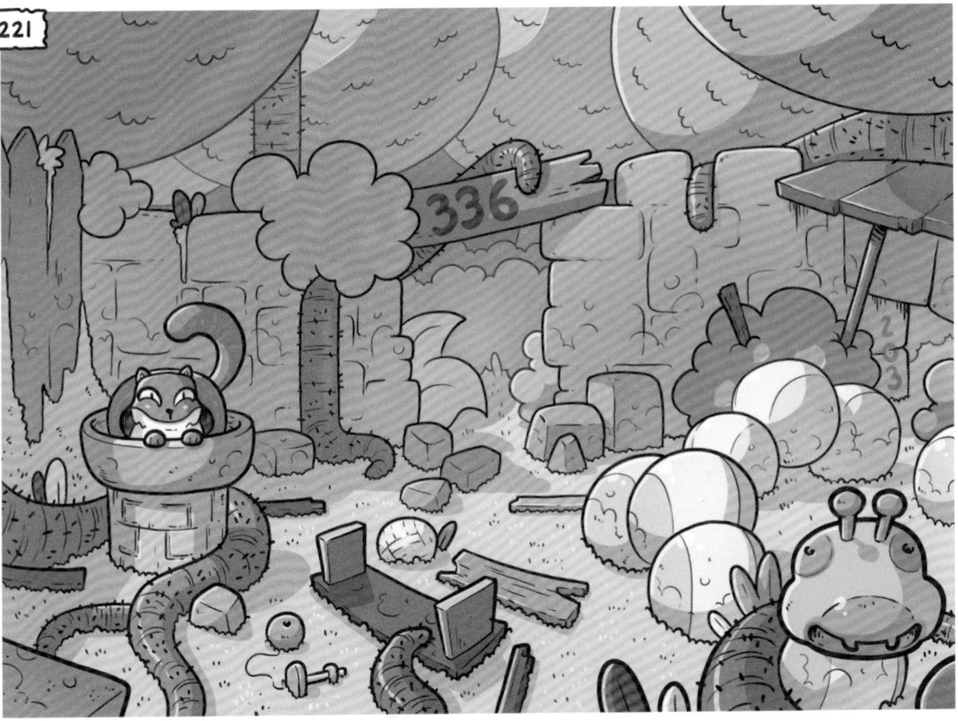
336

222

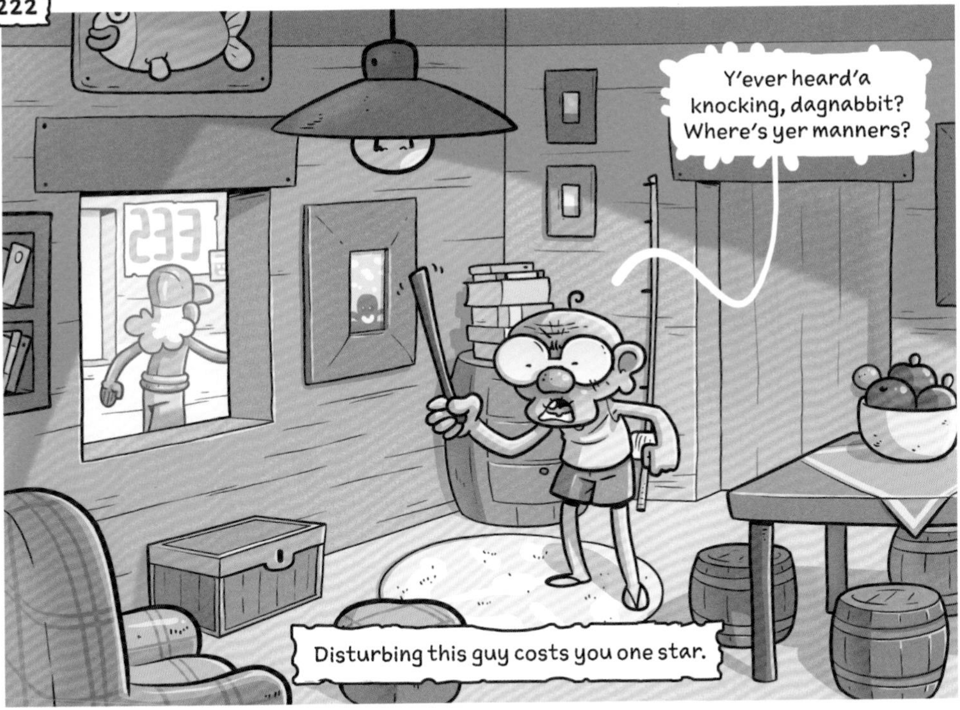
Y'ever heard'a knocking, dagnabbit? Where's yer manners?
Disturbing this guy costs you one star.

223

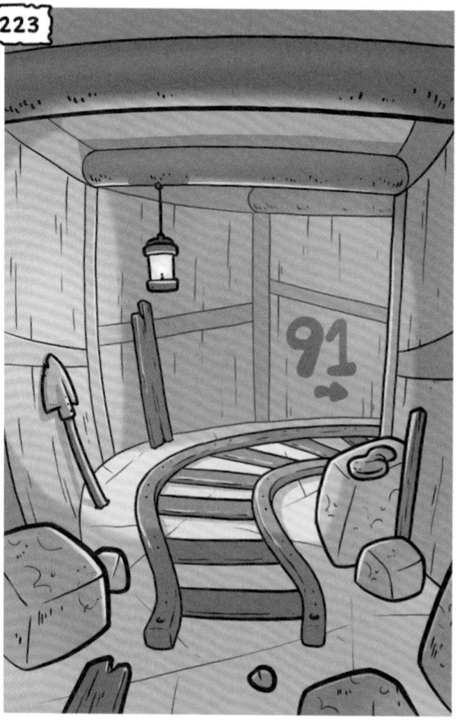
91

224

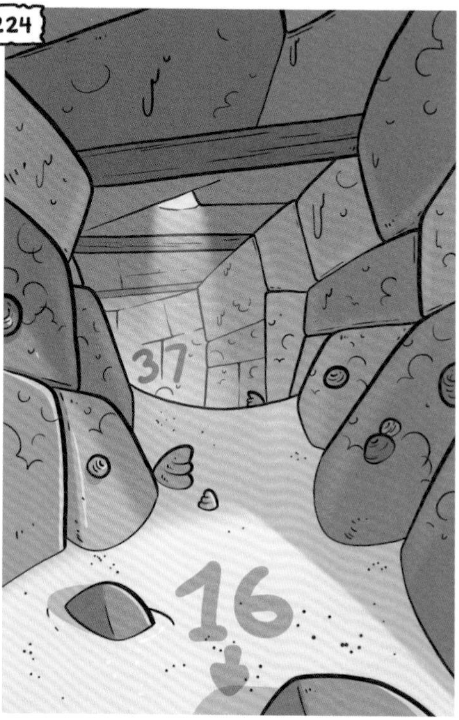
37
16

225

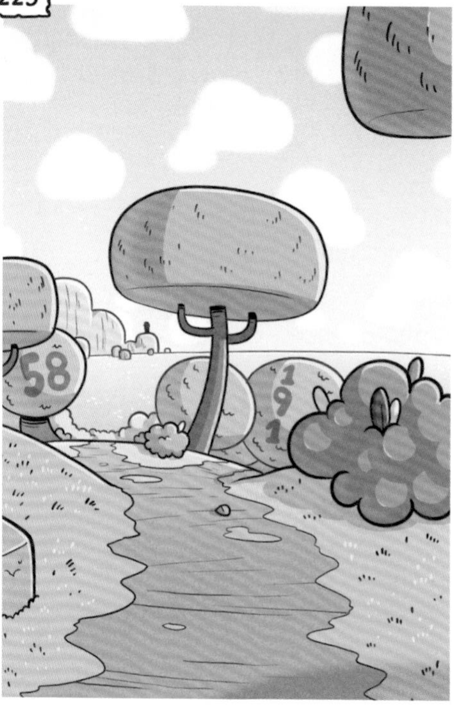
58
191

226

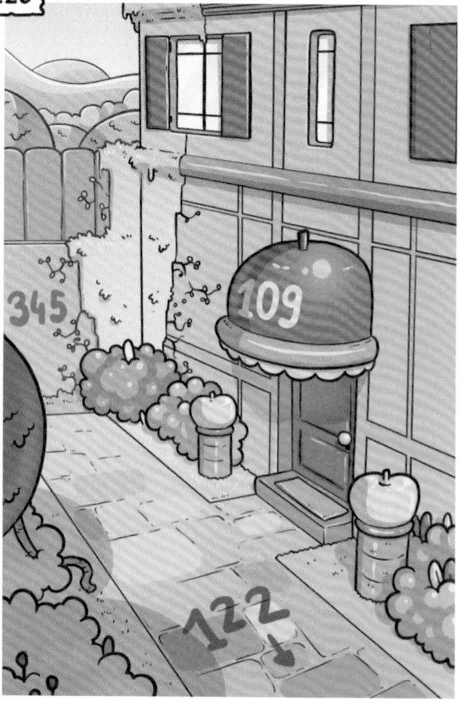
345
109
122

227

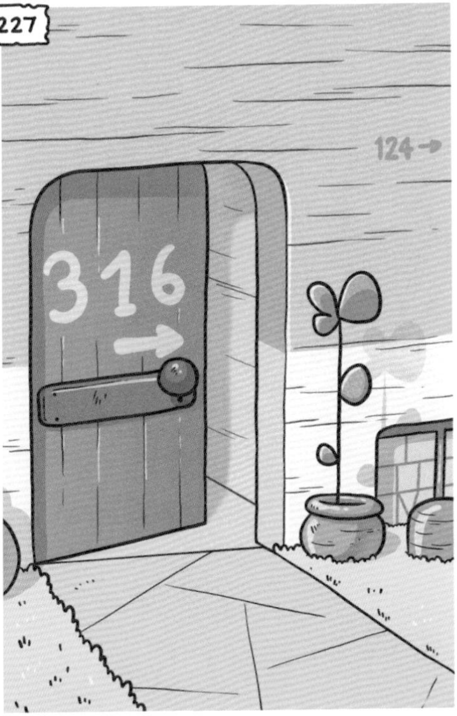
316
124

228

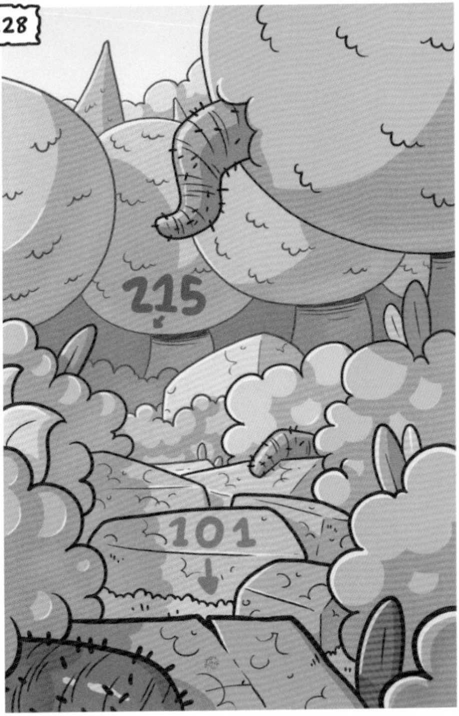
215
101

229

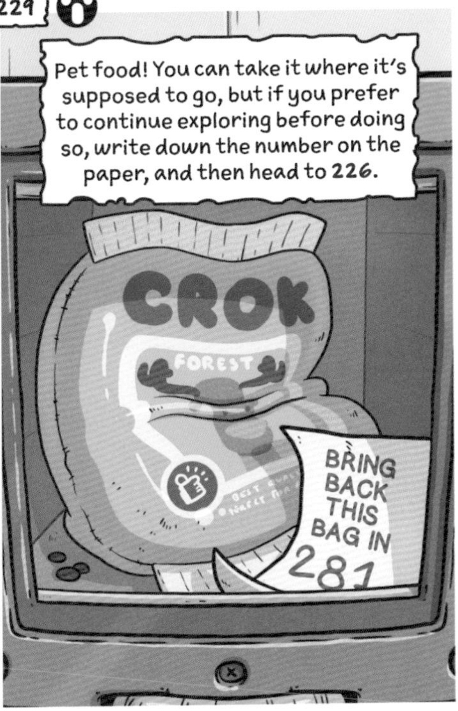
Pet food! You can take it where it's supposed to go, but if you prefer to continue exploring before doing so, write down the number on the paper, and then head to **226**.
CROK
FOREST
BRING BACK THIS BAG IN 281

230

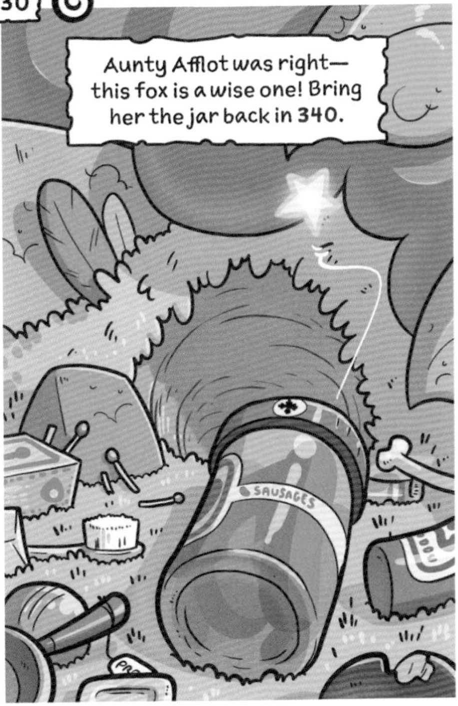
Aunty Afflot was right—this fox is a wise one! Bring her the jar back in **340**.
SAUSAGES

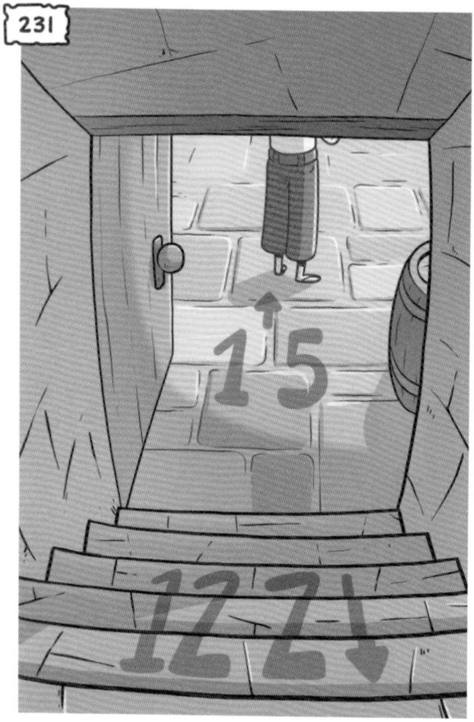
231
15
122

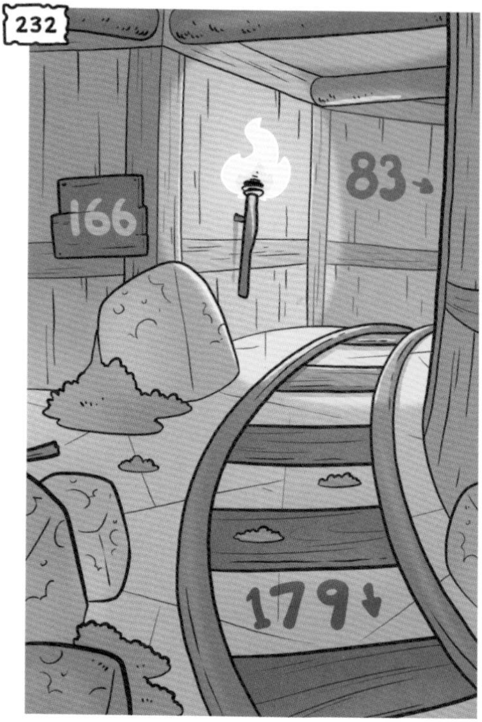
232
166
83
179

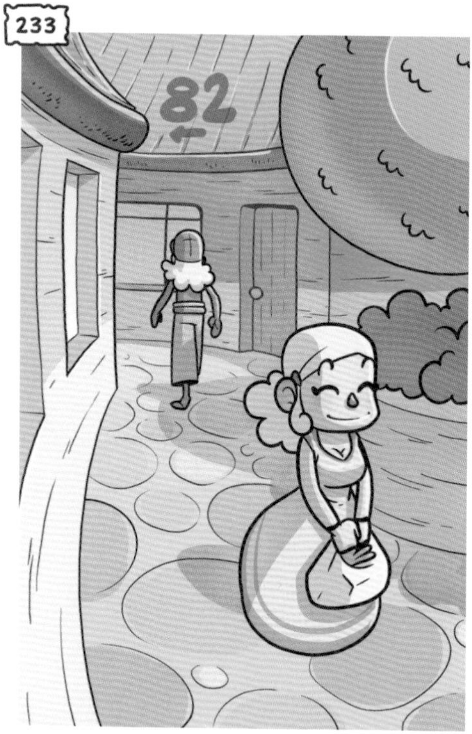
233
82

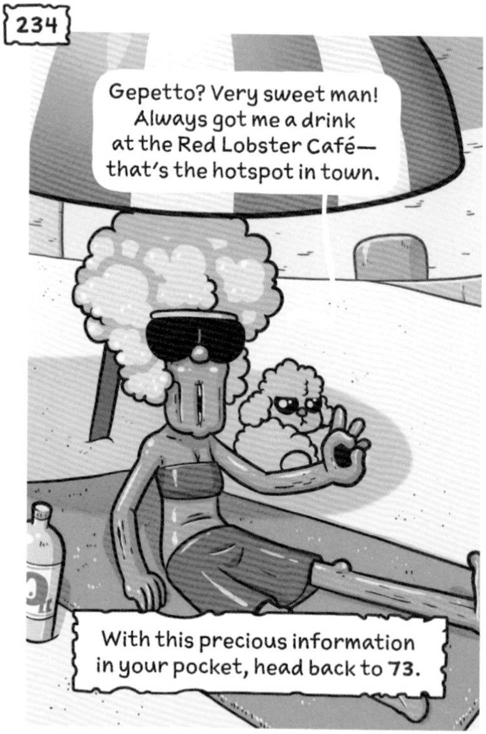
234
Gepetto? Very sweet man! Always got me a drink at the Red Lobster Café— that's the hotspot in town.
With this precious information in your pocket, head back to 73.

235

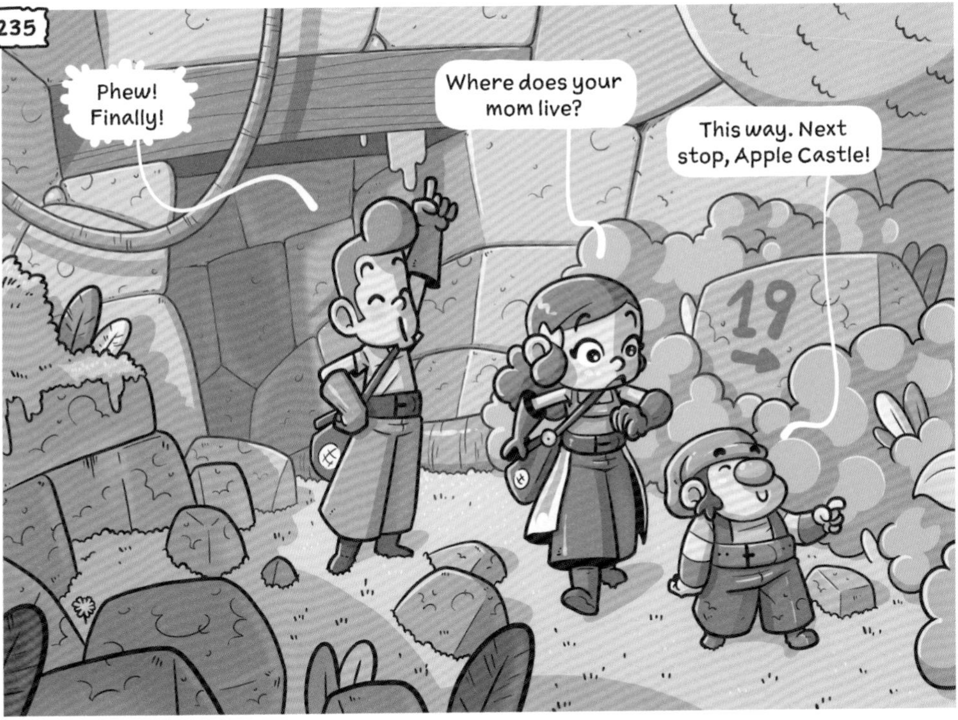

Phew! Finally!
Where does your mom live?
This way. Next stop, Apple Castle!
19

236

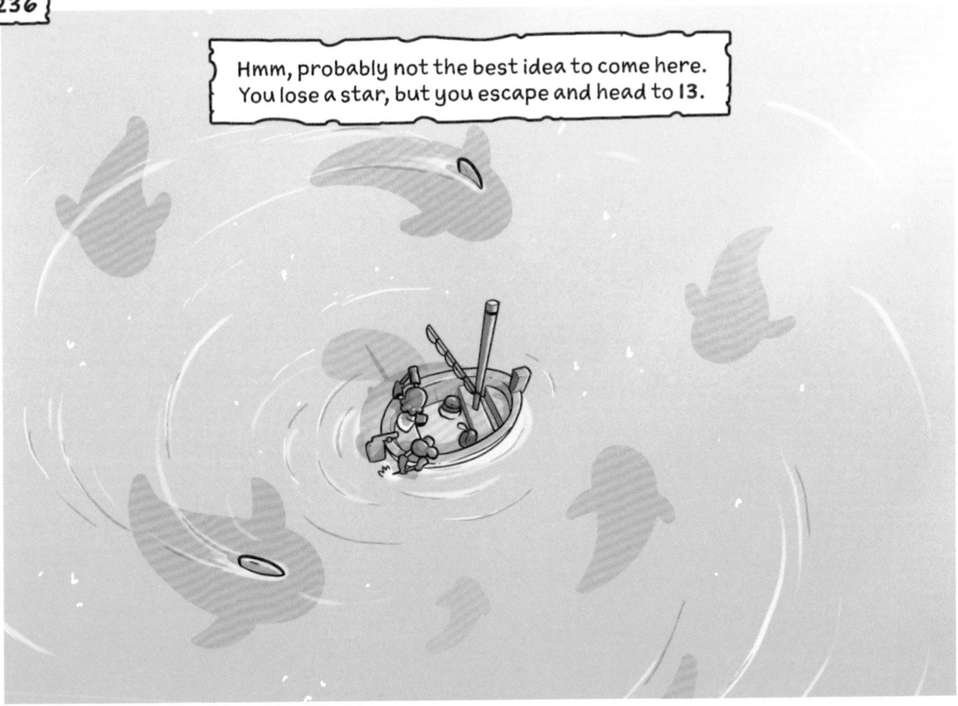

Hmm, probably not the best idea to come here. You lose a star, but you escape and head to 13.

237

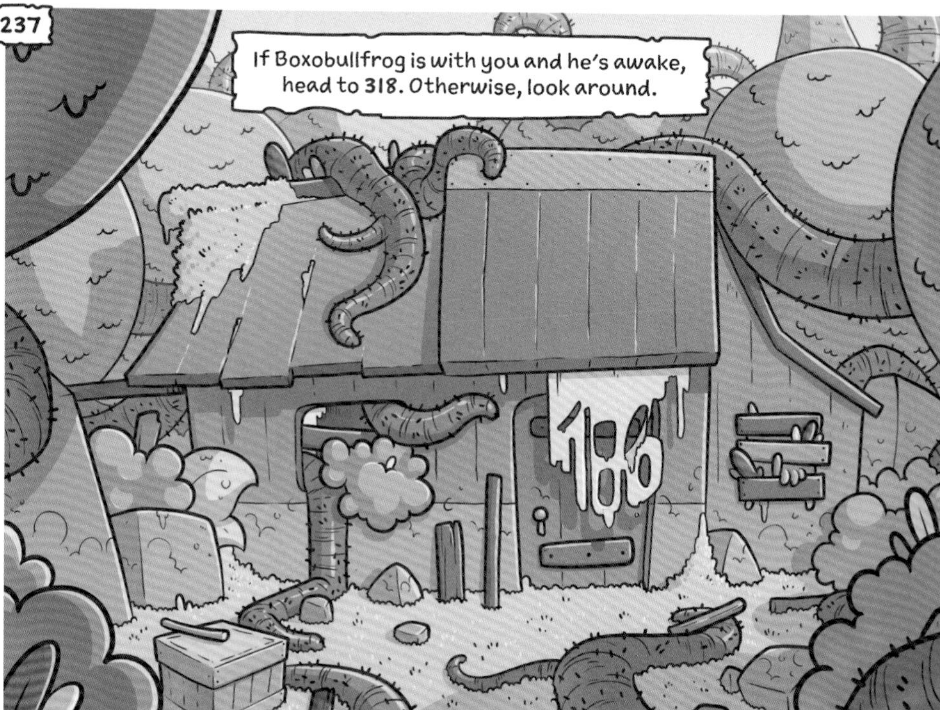
If Boxobullfrog is with you and he's awake, head to 318. Otherwise, look around.
180

238

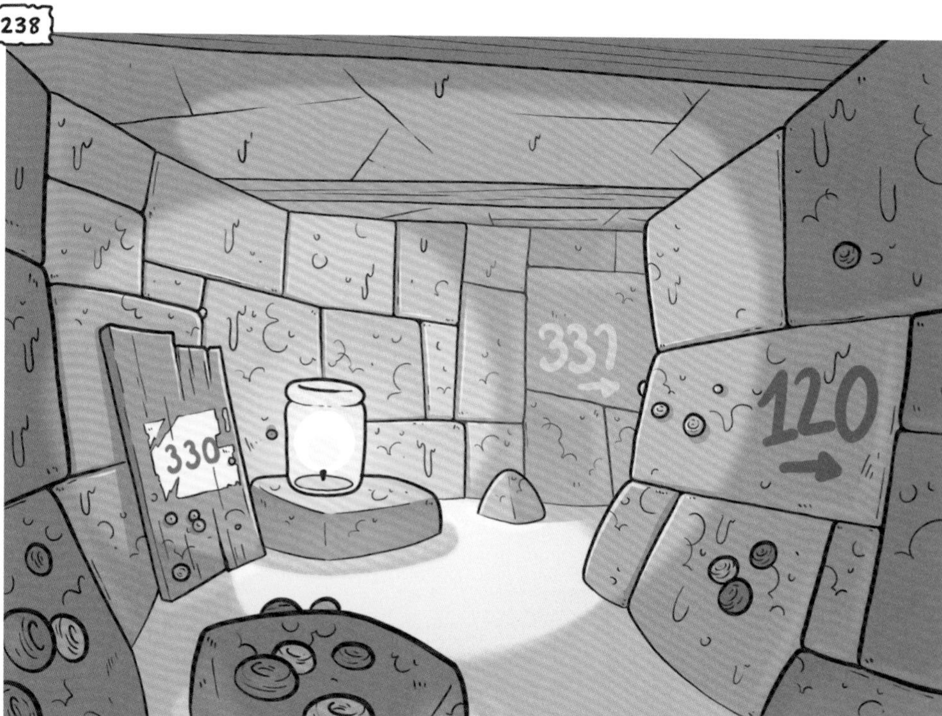
330
331
120

239

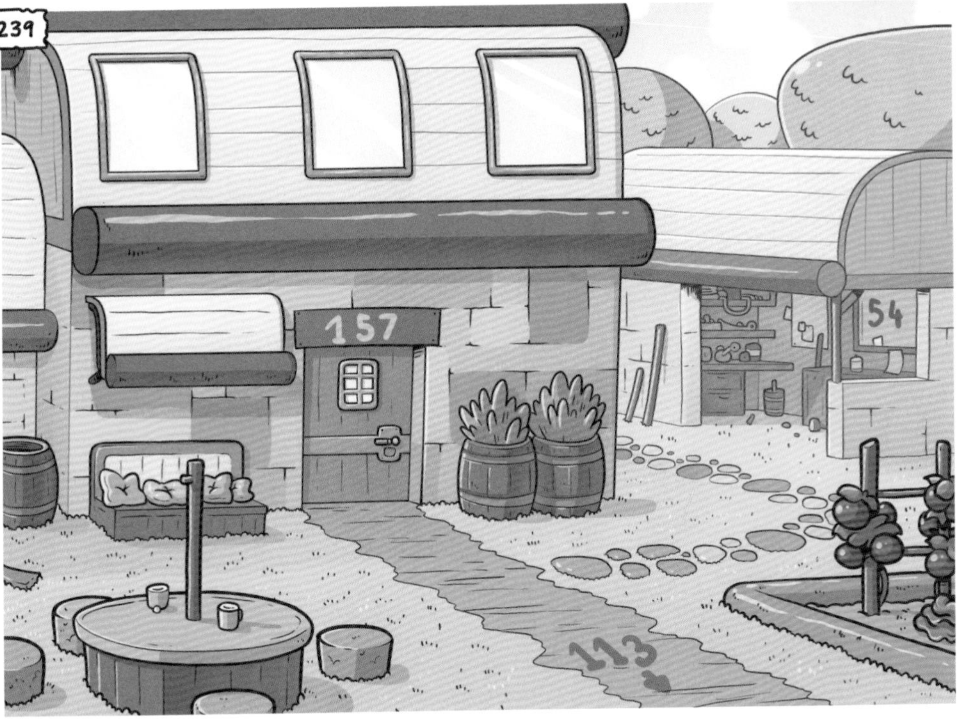
157
54
113

240

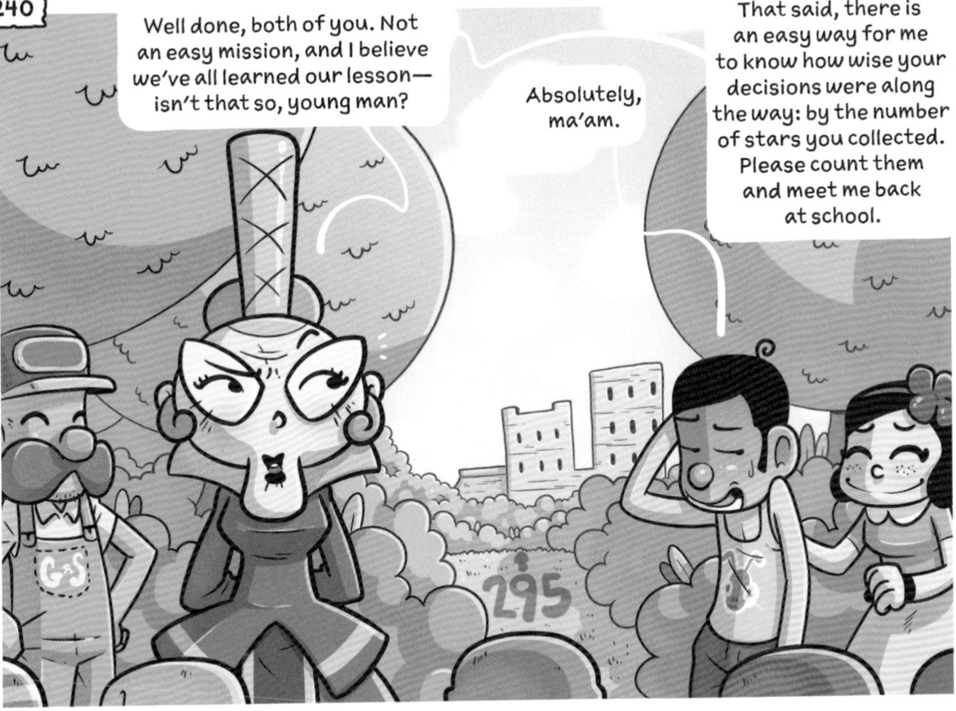
Well done, both of you. Not an easy mission, and I believe we've all learned our lesson—isn't that so, young man?
Absolutely, ma'am.
That said, there is an easy way for me to know how wise your decisions were along the way: by the number of stars you collected. Please count them and meet me back at school.
G&S
295

241

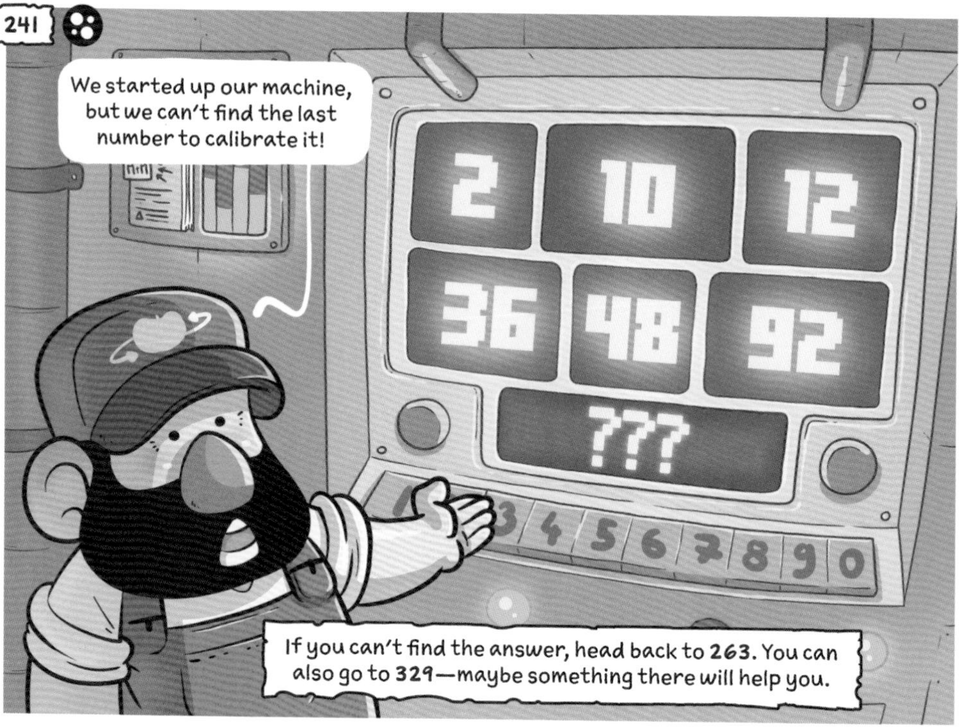
We started up our machine, but we can't find the last number to calibrate it!
2 10 12
36 48 92
???
3 4 5 6 7 8 9 0
If you can't find the answer, head back to 263. You can also go to 329—maybe something there will help you.

242

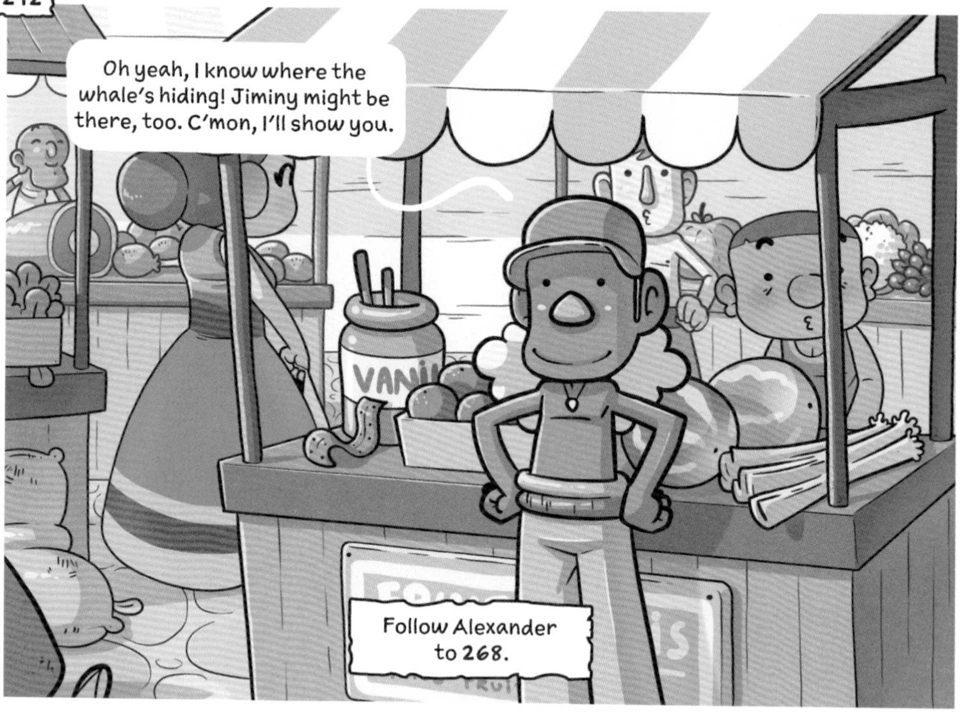
Oh yeah, I know where the whale's hiding! Jiminy might be there, too. C'mon, I'll show you.
VANI
Follow Alexander to 268.

243

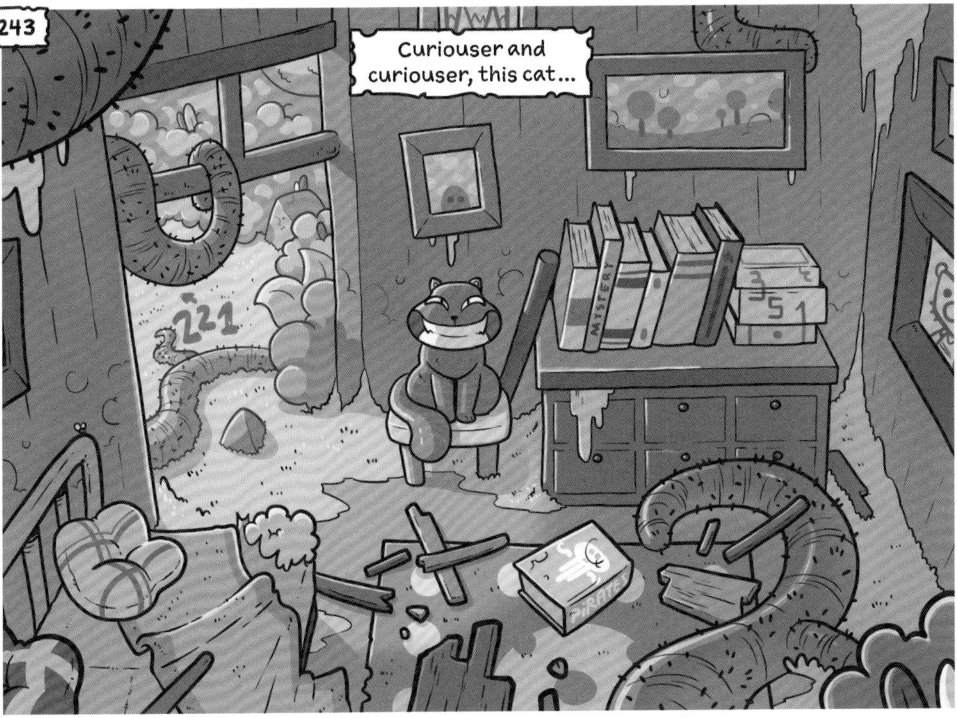
Curiouser and curiouser, this cat...
221
MYSTERY
PIRATES

244

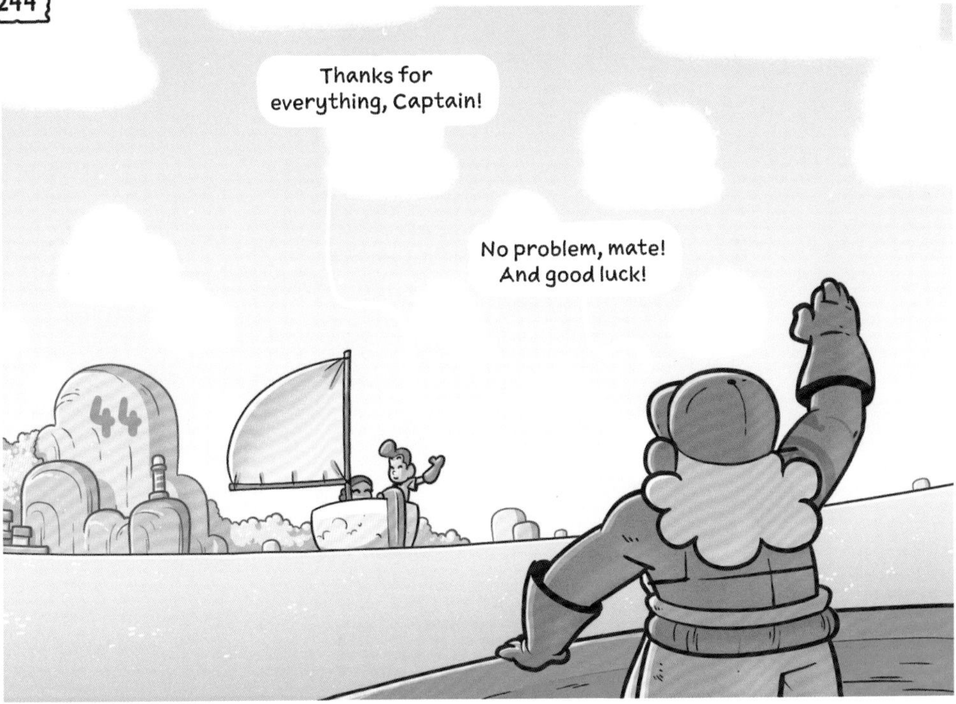
Thanks for everything, Captain!
No problem, mate! And good luck!
44

245

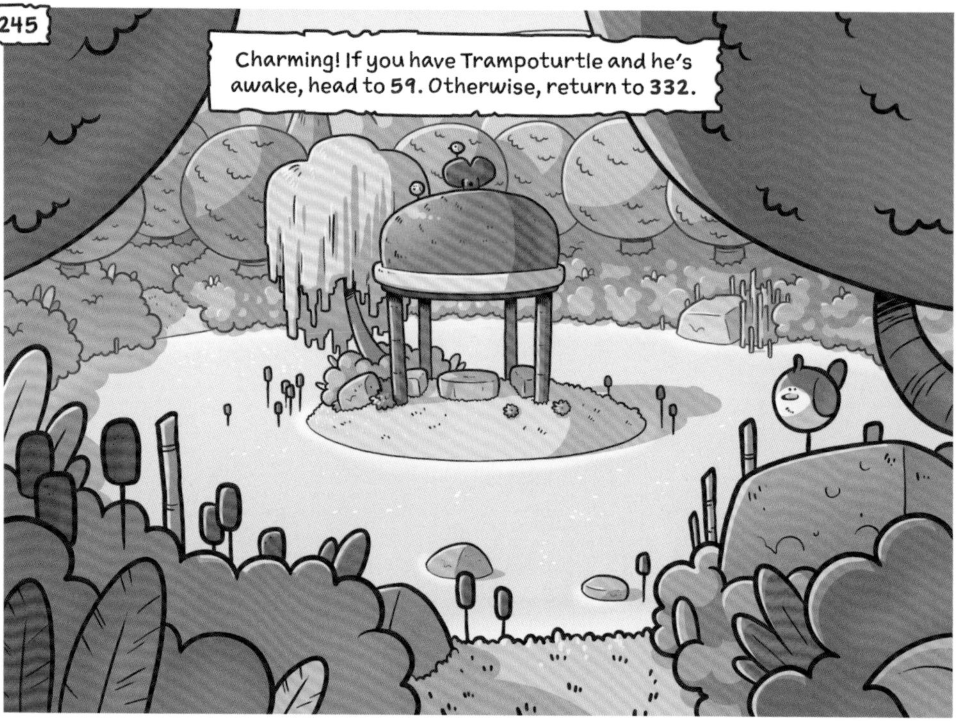
Charming! If you have Trampoturtle and he's awake, head to 59. Otherwise, return to 332.

246

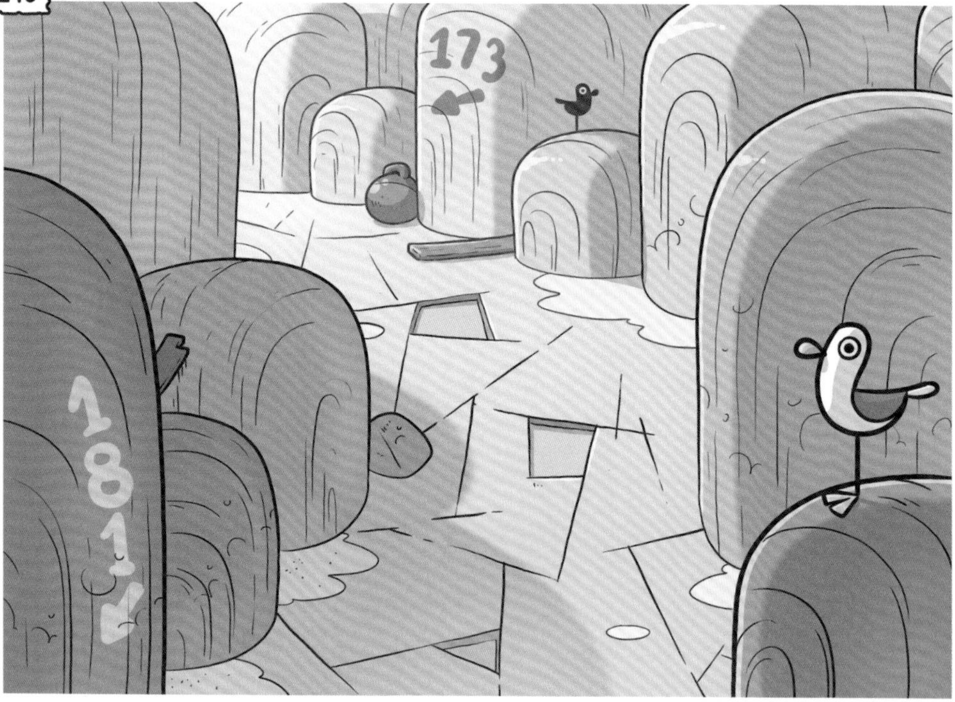
173
181

247

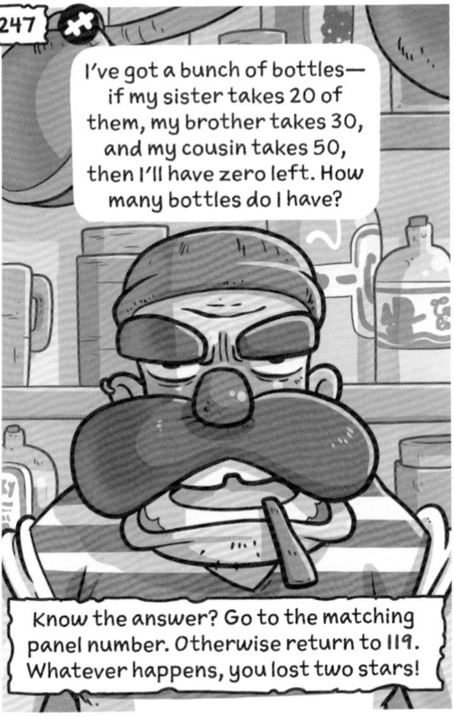

I've got a bunch of bottles—if my sister takes 20 of them, my brother takes 30, and my cousin takes 50, then I'll have zero left. How many bottles do I have?
Know the answer? Go to the matching panel number. Otherwise return to 119. Whatever happens, you lost two stars!

248

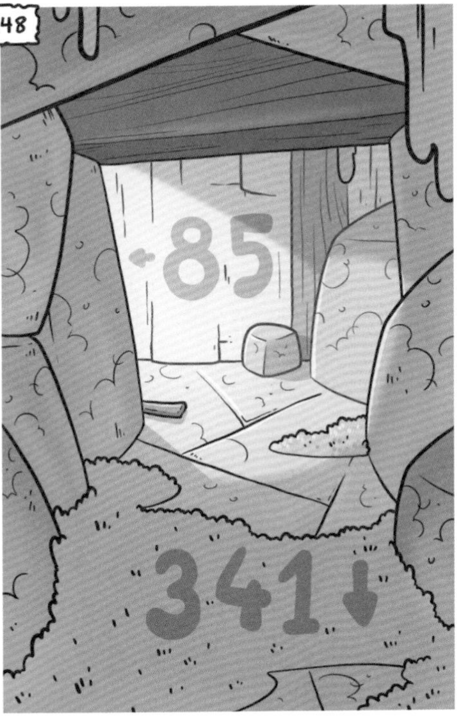

85
341

249

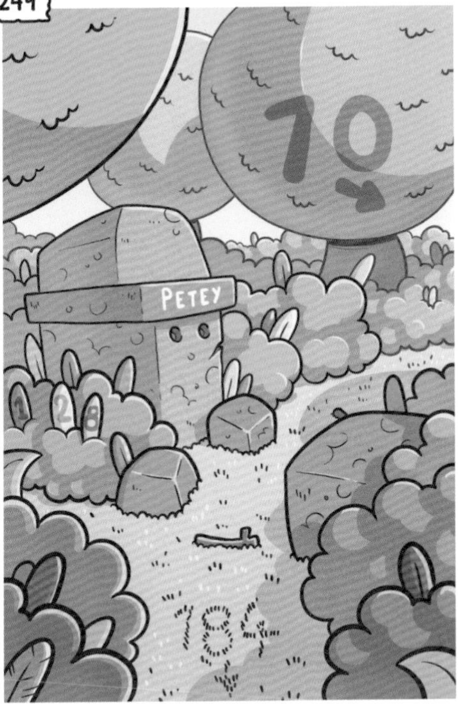

70
PETEY

250

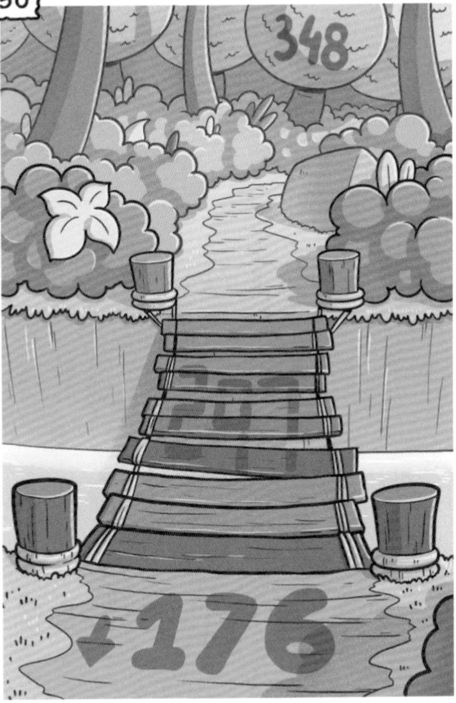

348
176

251

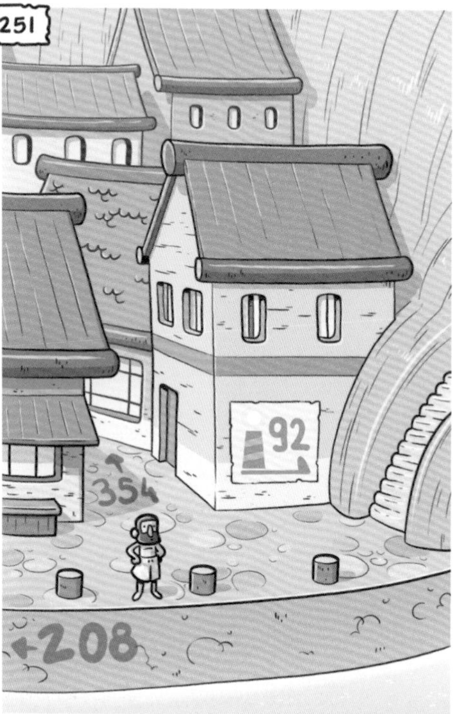
92
354
208

252

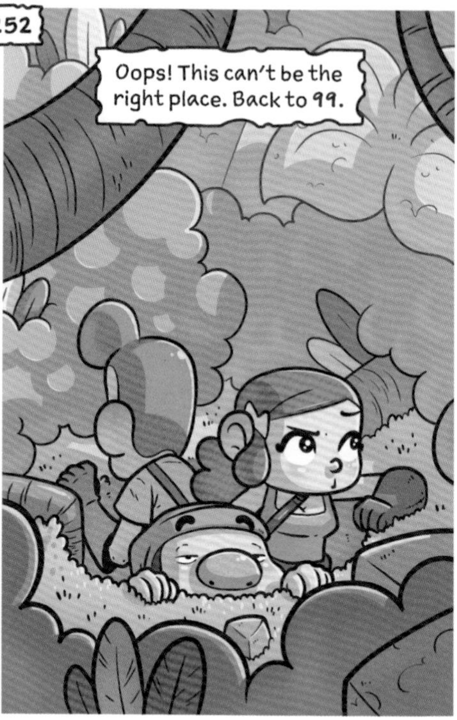
Oops! This can't be the right place. Back to 99.

253

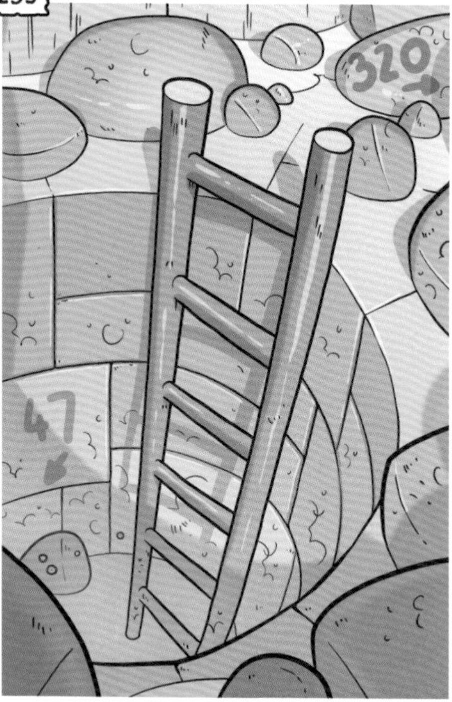
320
47

254

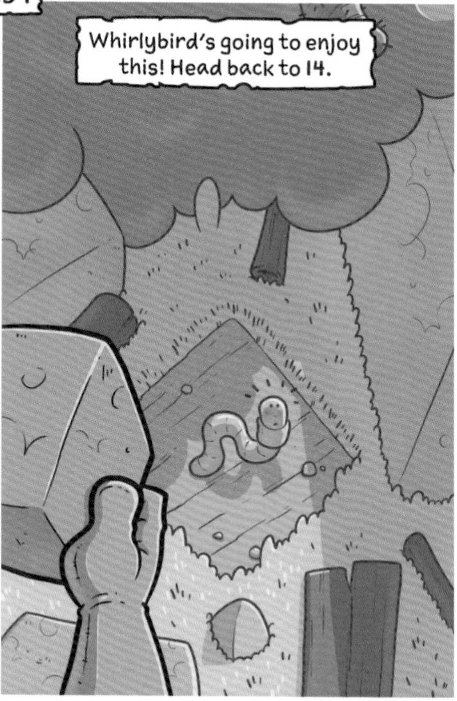
Whirlybird's going to enjoy this! Head back to 14.

255

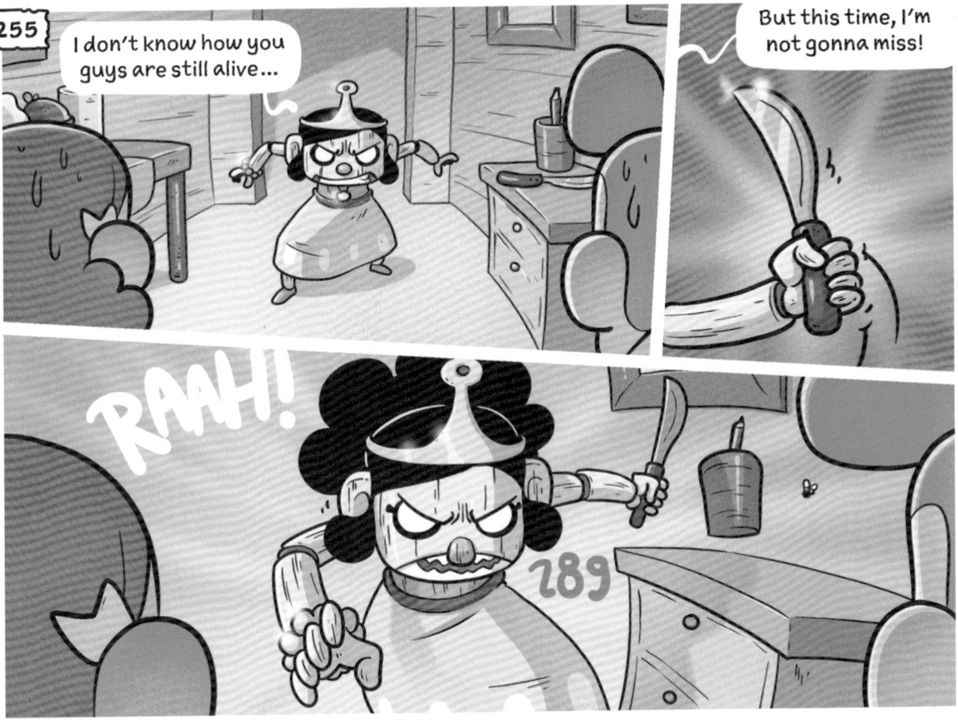
I don't know how you guys are still alive...
But this time, I'm not gonna miss!
RAAH!
289

256

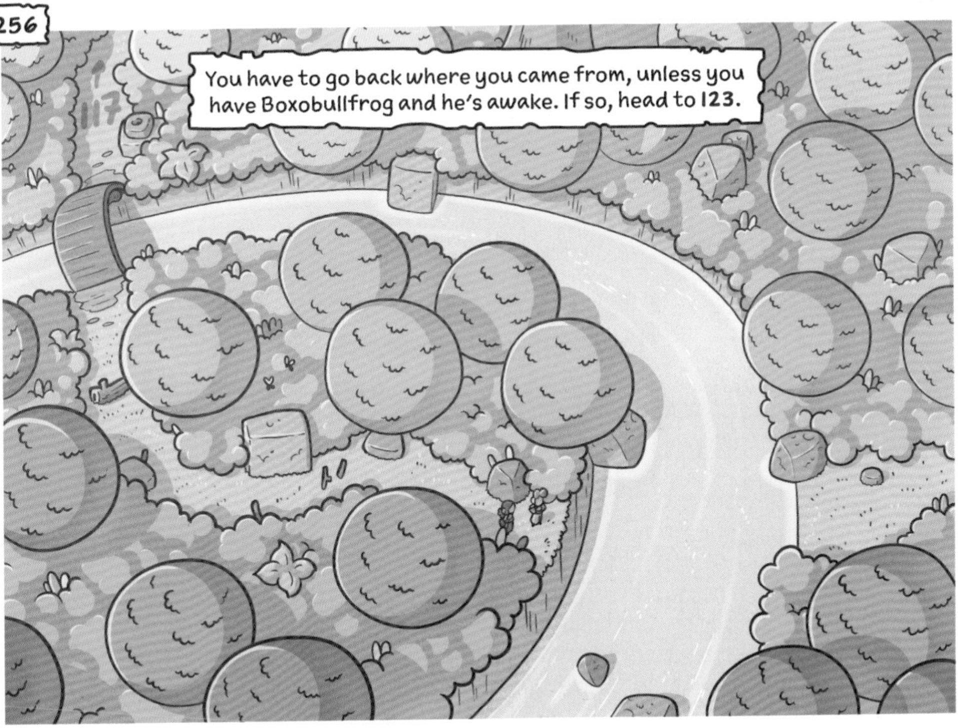
You have to go back where you came from, unless you have Boxobullfrog and he's awake. If so, head to 123.
117

257

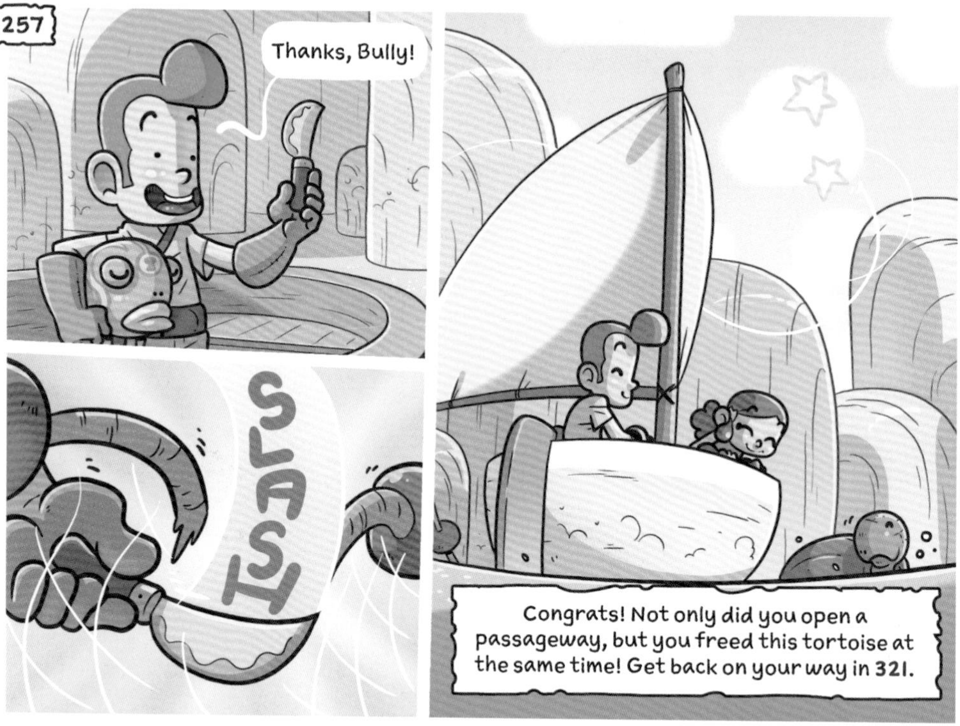
Thanks, Bully!
SLASH
Congrats! Not only did you open a passageway, but you freed this tortoise at the same time! Get back on your way in 321.

258

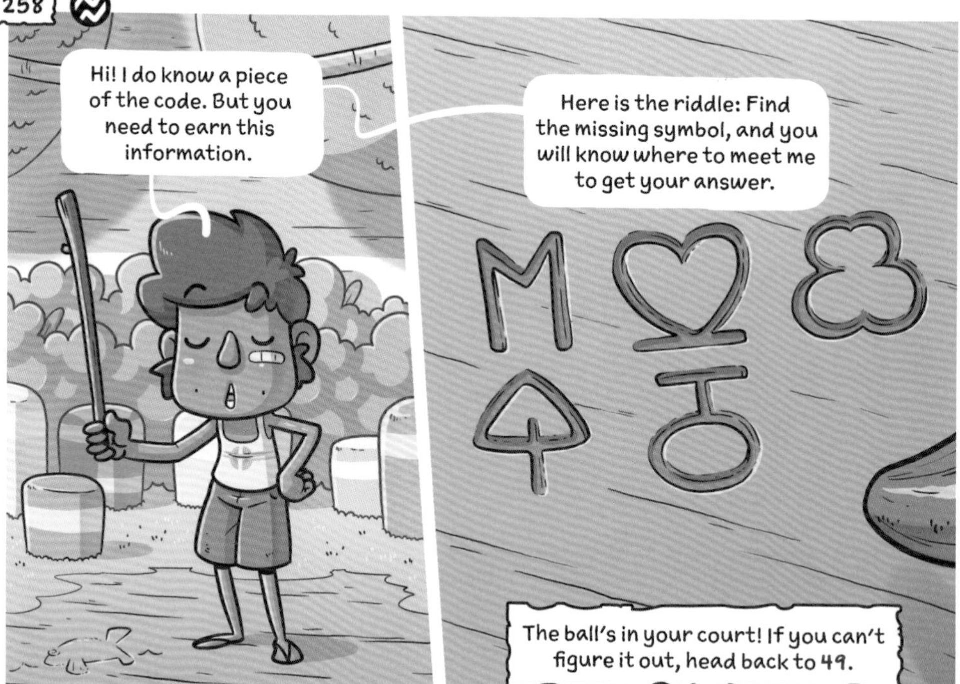
Hi! I do know a piece of the code. But you need to earn this information.
Here is the riddle: Find the missing symbol, and you will know where to meet me to get your answer.
The ball's in your court! If you can't figure it out, head back to 49.

259

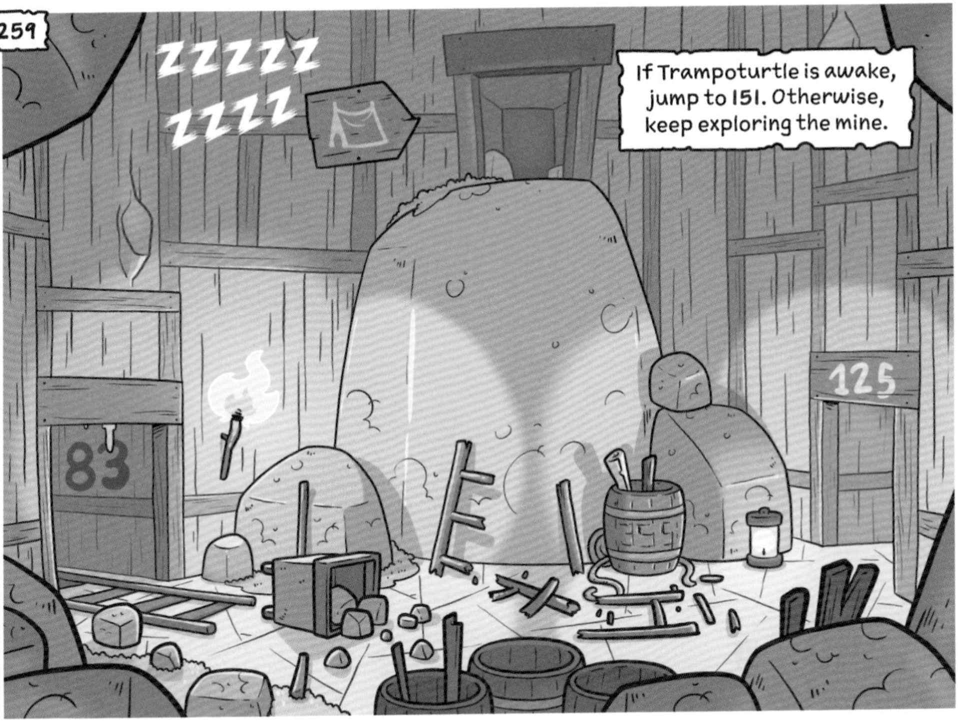
ZZZZZ
ZZZZ
If Trampoturtle is awake, jump to 151. Otherwise, keep exploring the mine.
83
125

260

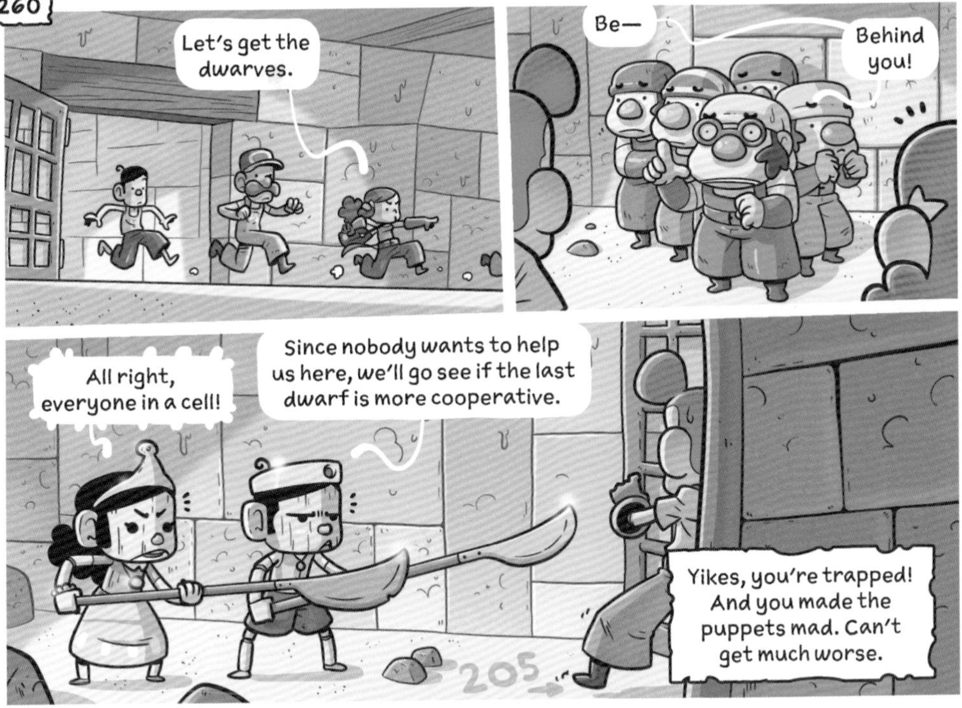
Let's get the dwarves.
Be—
Behind you!
All right, everyone in a cell!
Since nobody wants to help us here, we'll go see if the last dwarf is more cooperative.
Yikes, you're trapped! And you made the puppets mad. Can't get much worse.
205

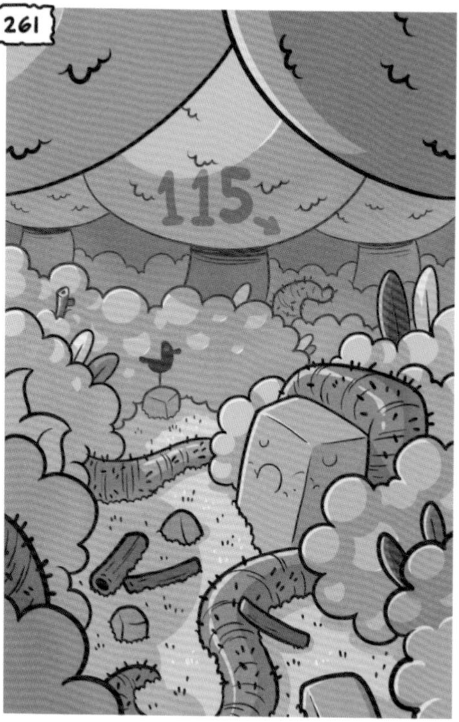
261
115

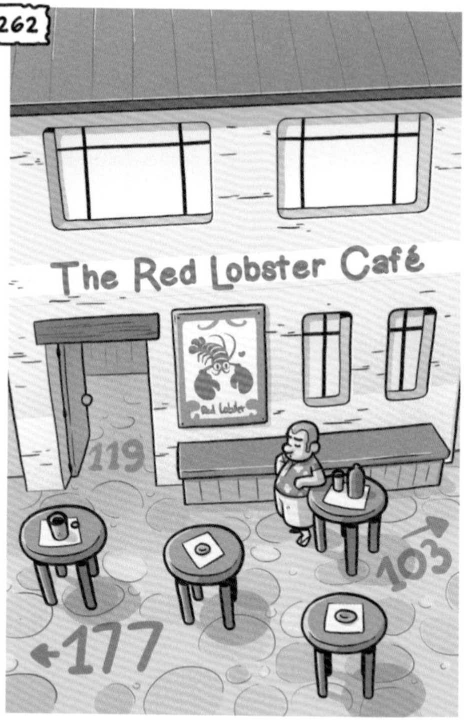
262
The Red Lobster Café
Red Lobster
119
103
177

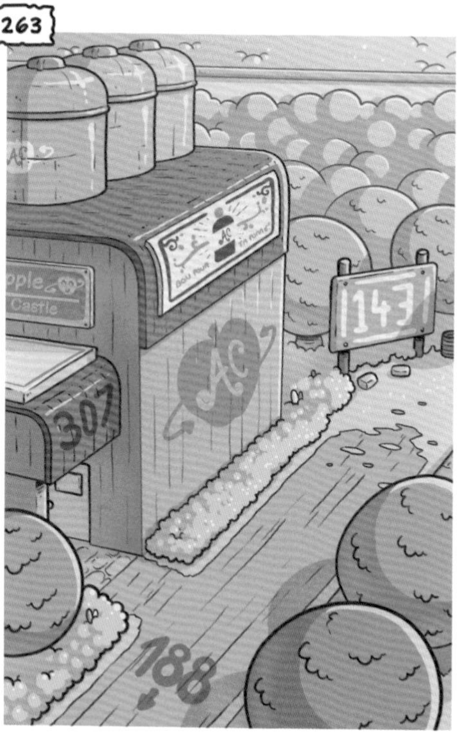
263
Castle
AC
143
307
188

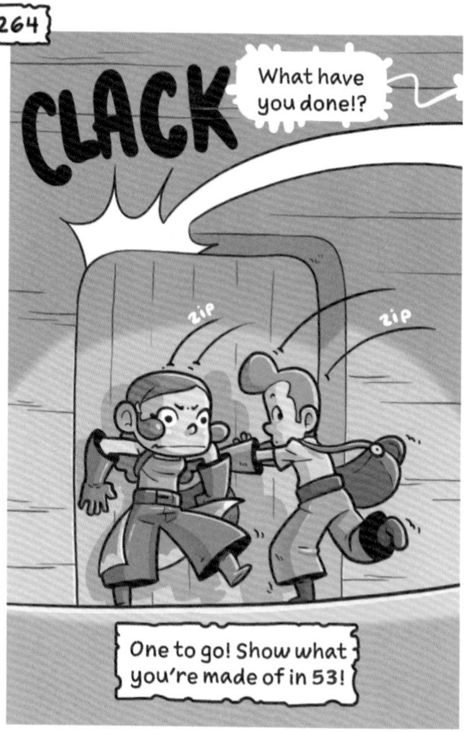
264
CLACK
What have you done!?
ZIP
ZIP
One to go! Show what you're made of in 53!

265

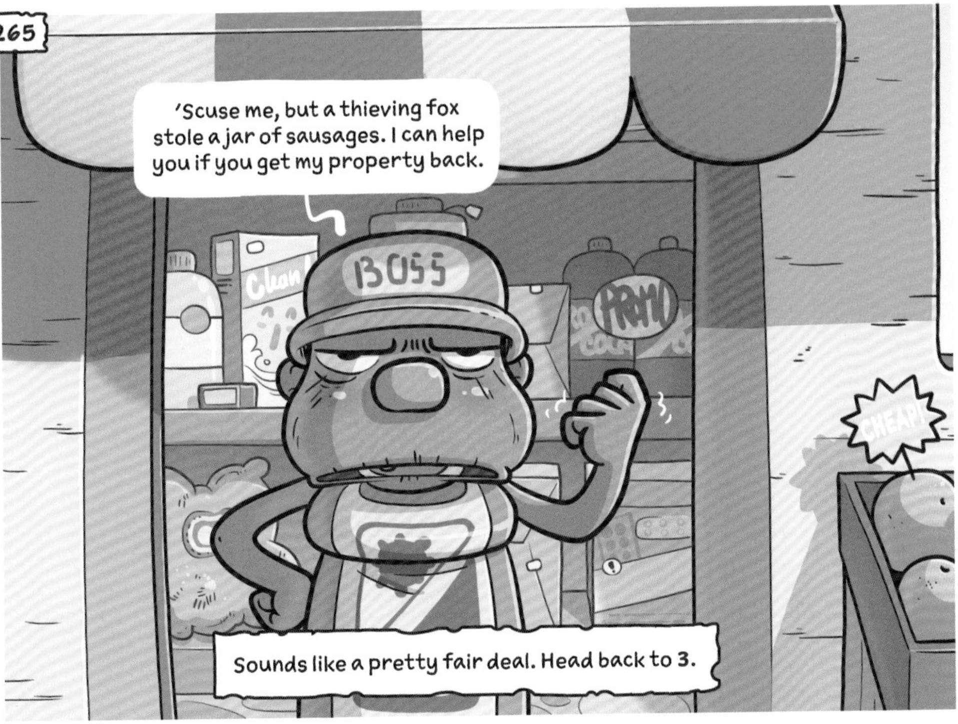
'Scuse me, but a thieving fox stole a jar of sausages. I can help you if you get my property back.
BOSS
CHEAP!
Sounds like a pretty fair deal. Head back to 3.

266

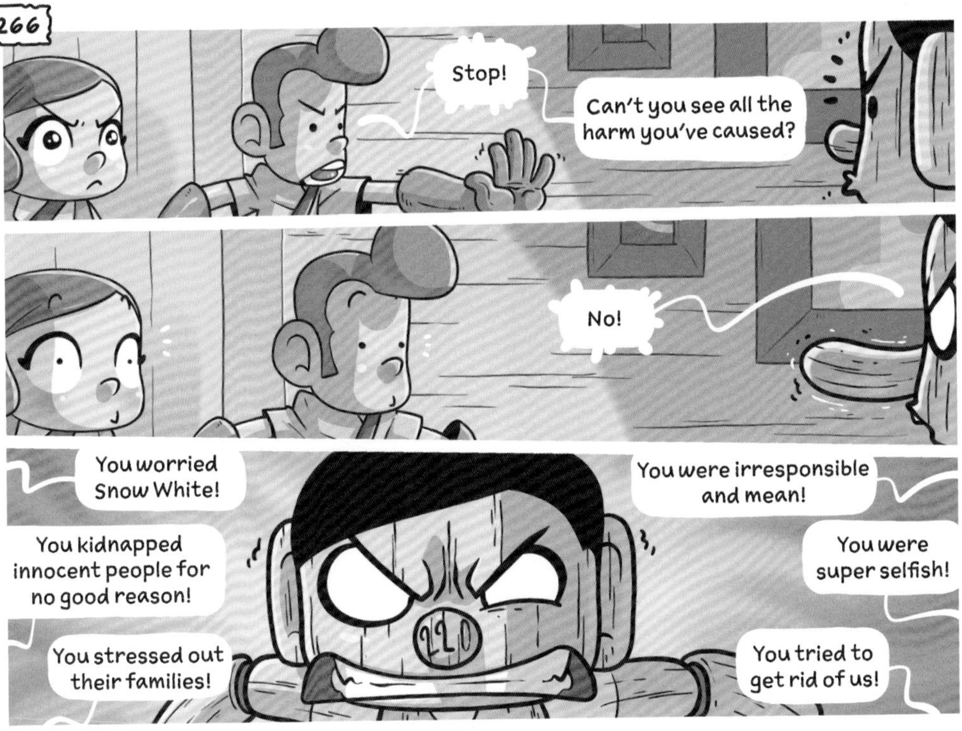
Stop!
Can't you see all the harm you've caused?
No!
You worried Snow White!
You kidnapped innocent people for no good reason!
You stressed out their families!
You were irresponsible and mean!
You were super selfish!
You tried to get rid of us!

267

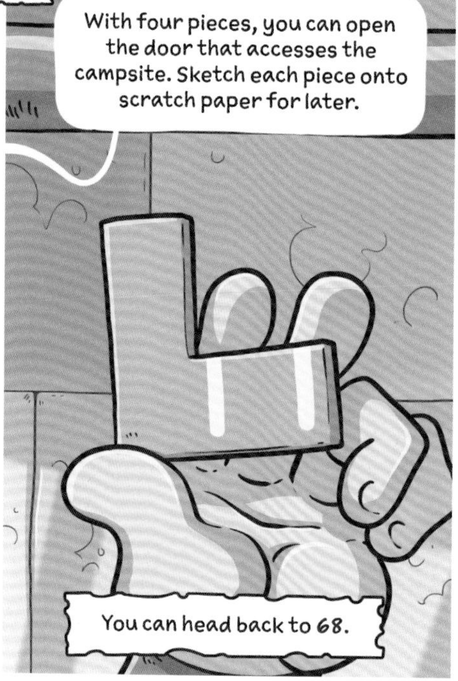
With four pieces, you can open the door that accesses the campsite. Sketch each piece onto scratch paper for later.
You can head back to 68.

268

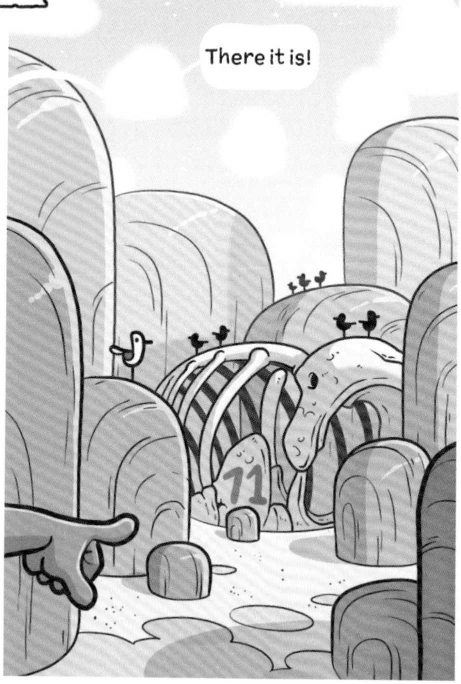
There it is!
71

269

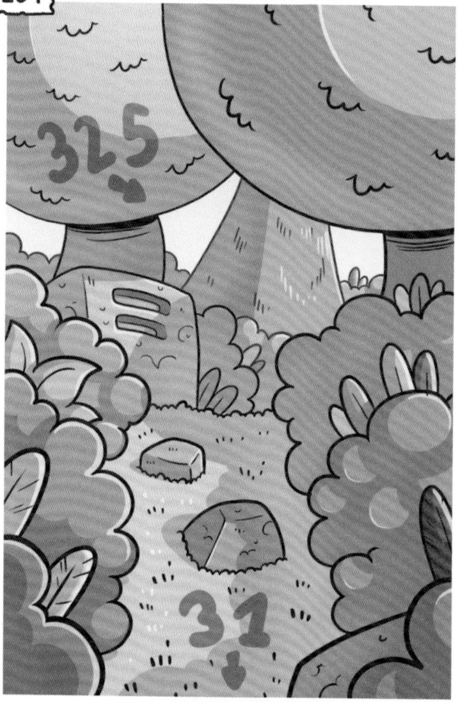
325
31

270

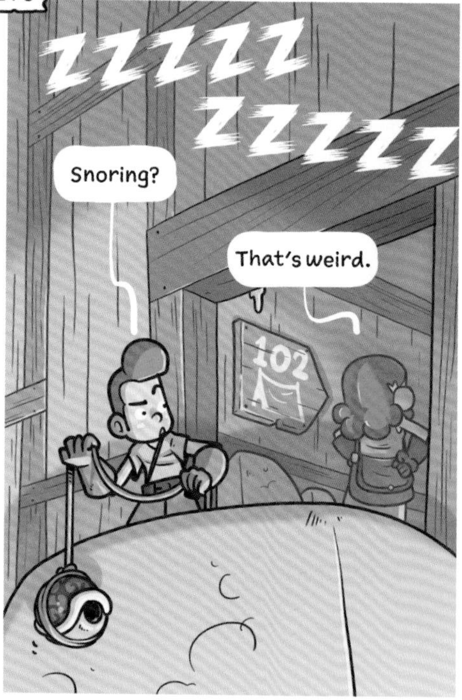
ZZZZZ
ZZZZZZ
Snoring?
That's weird.
102

271

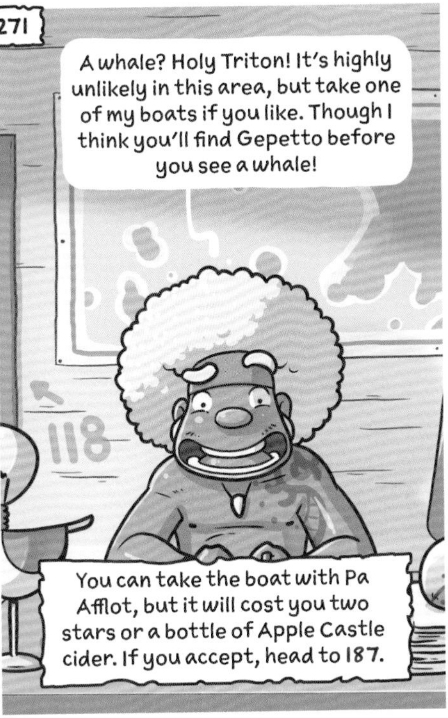
A whale? Holy Triton! It's highly unlikely in this area, but take one of my boats if you like. Though I think you'll find Gepetto before you see a whale!
118
You can take the boat with Pa Afflot, but it will cost you two stars or a bottle of Apple Castle cider. If you accept, head to 187.

272

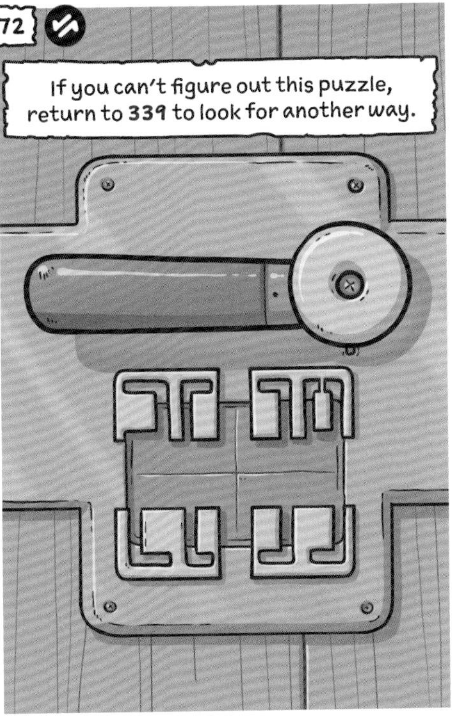
If you can't figure out this puzzle, return to **339** to look for another way.

273

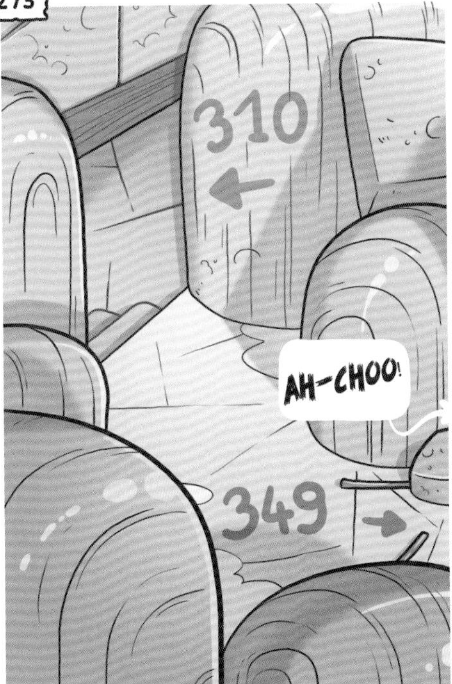
310
AH-CHOO!
349

274

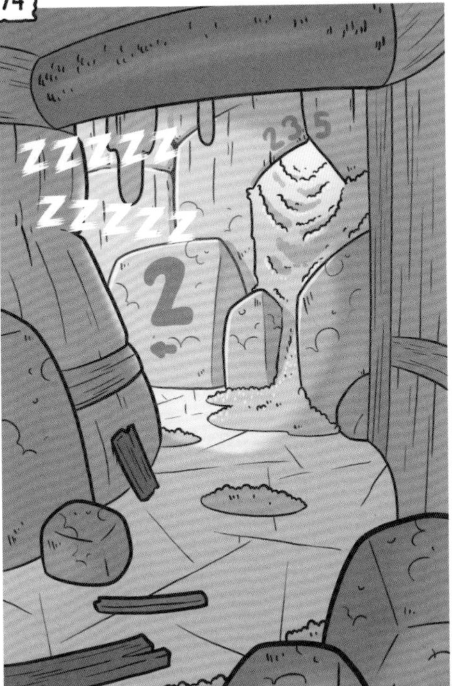
ZZZZZ
ZZZZZ
235
2

275

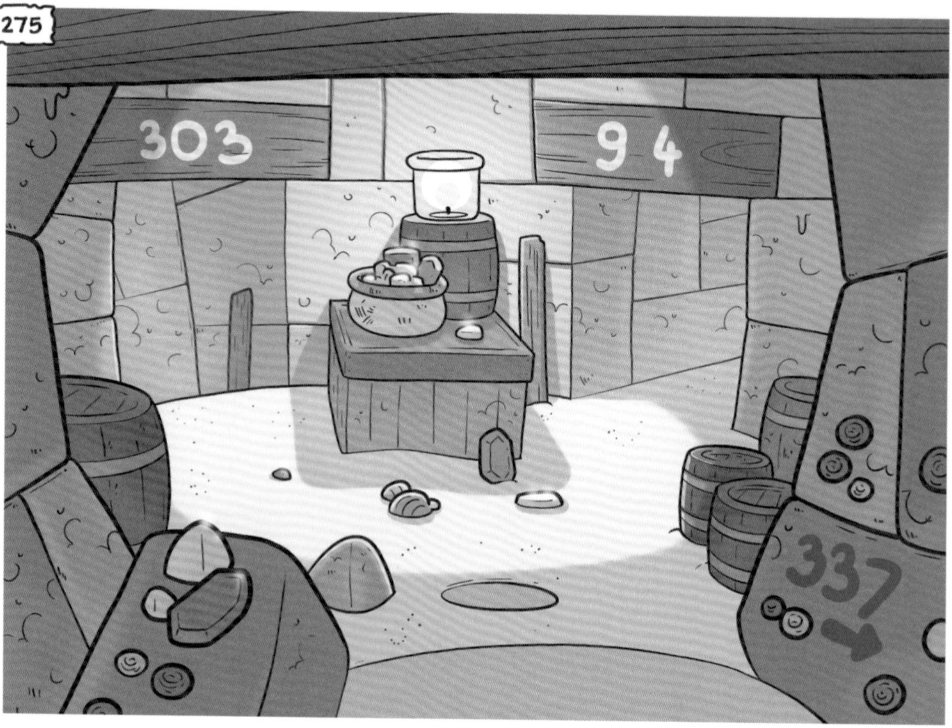
303
94
337

276

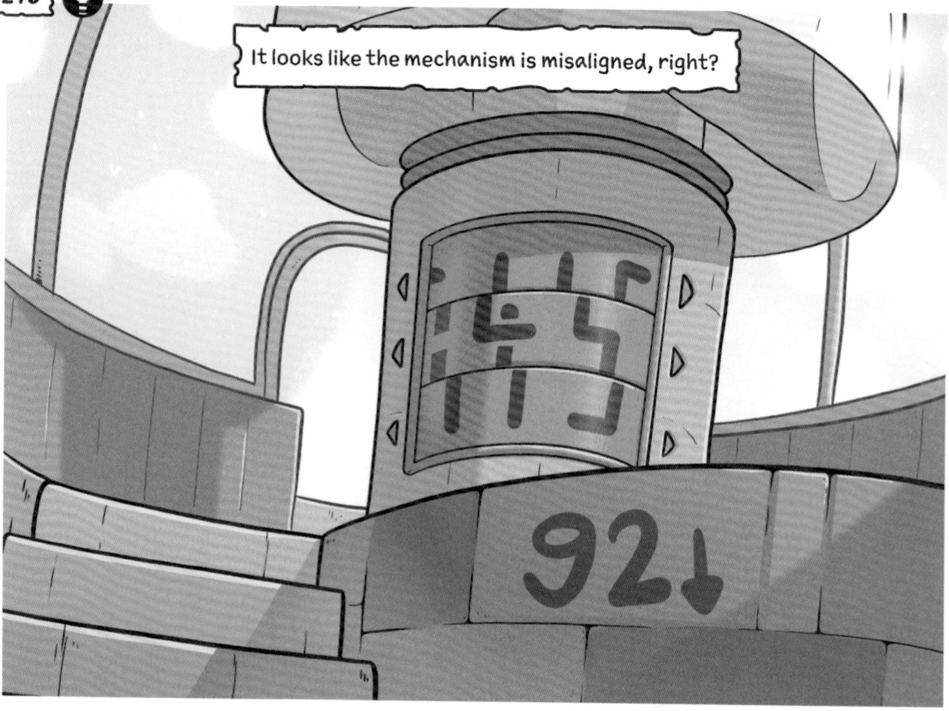
It looks like the mechanism is misaligned, right?
92

277

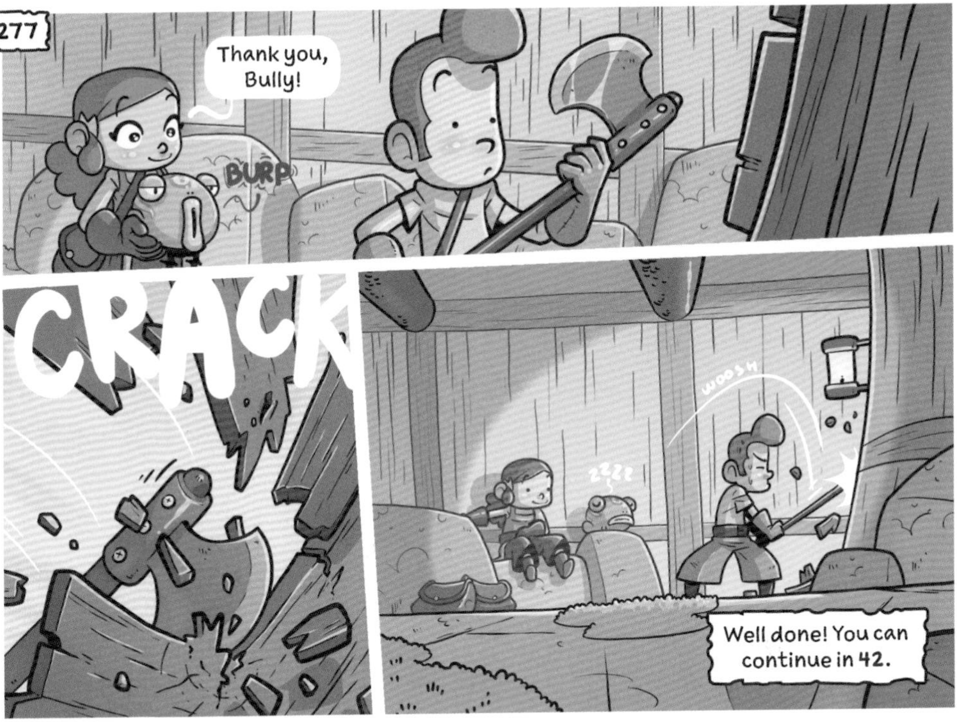
Thank you, Bully!
BURP
CRACK
WOOSH
ZZZZ
Well done! You can continue in 42.

278

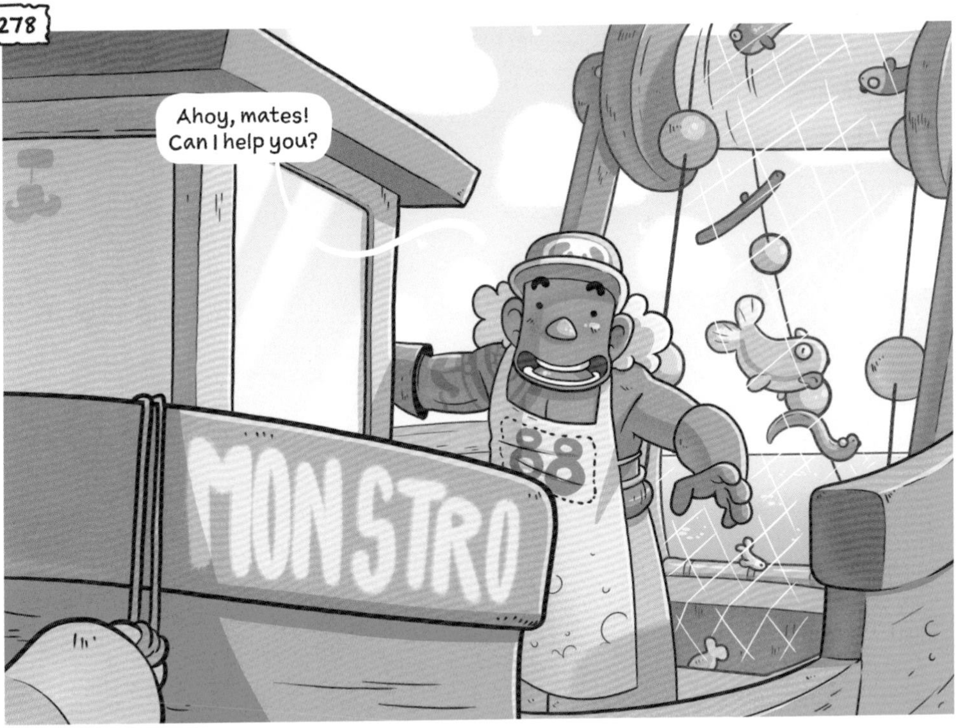
Ahoy, mates! Can I help you?
MONSTRO
88

279

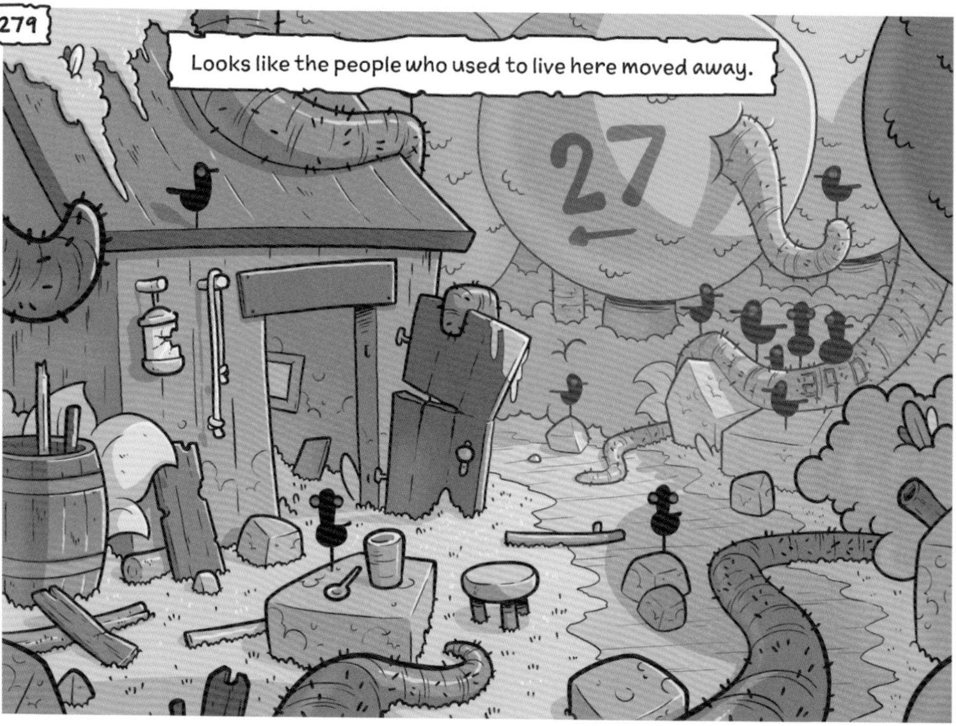

Looks like the people who used to live here moved away.
27

280

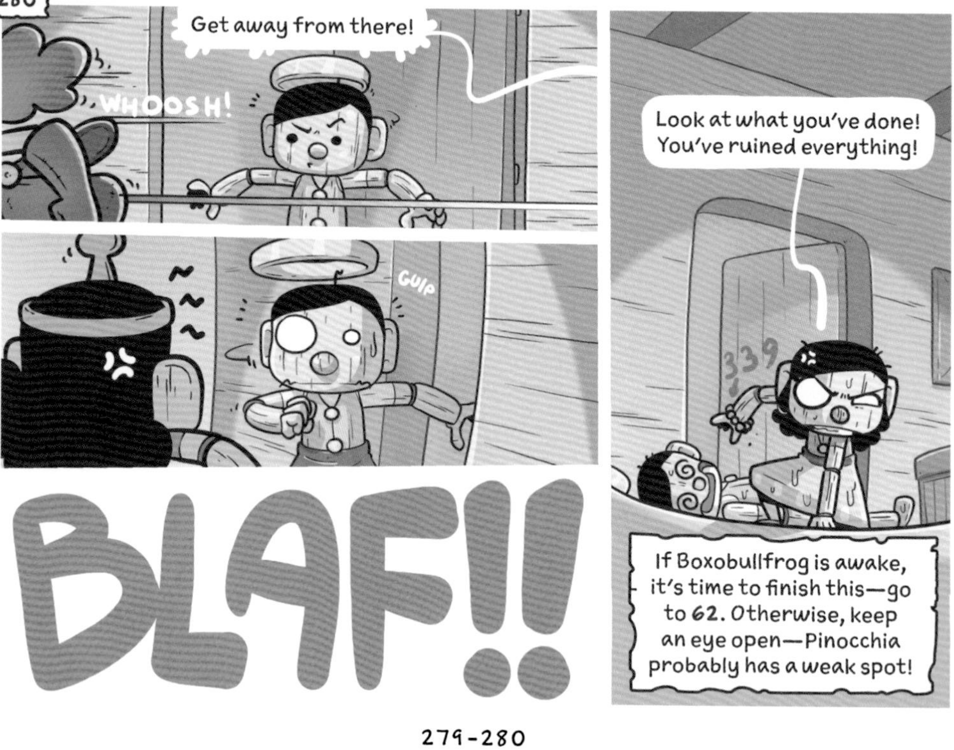

Get away from there!
WHOOSH!
GULP
BLAF!!
Look at what you've done! You've ruined everything!
339
If Boxobullfrog is awake, it's time to finish this—go to 62. Otherwise, keep an eye open—Pinocchia probably has a weak spot!

281

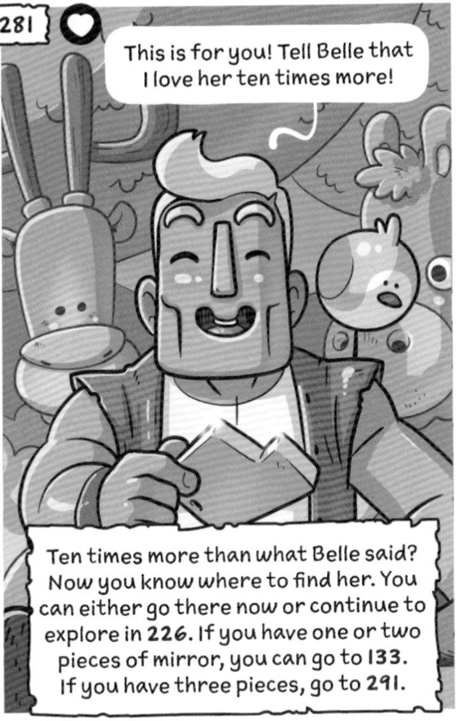
This is for you! Tell Belle that I love her ten times more!
Ten times more than what Belle said? Now you know where to find her. You can either go there now or continue to explore in **226**. If you have one or two pieces of mirror, you can go to **133**. If you have three pieces, go to **291**.

282

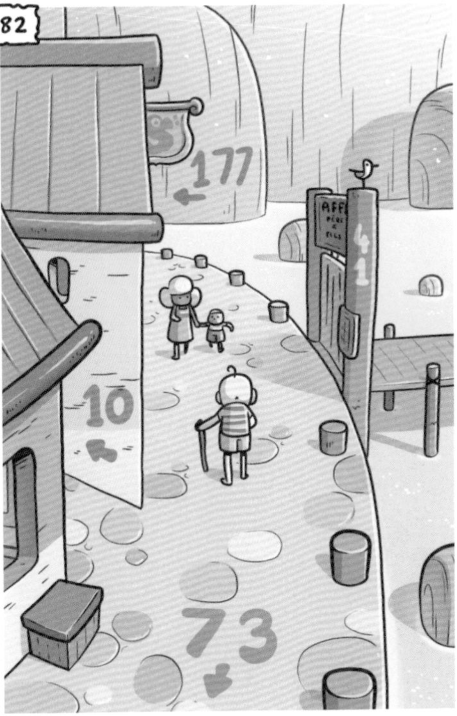
177
10
73

283

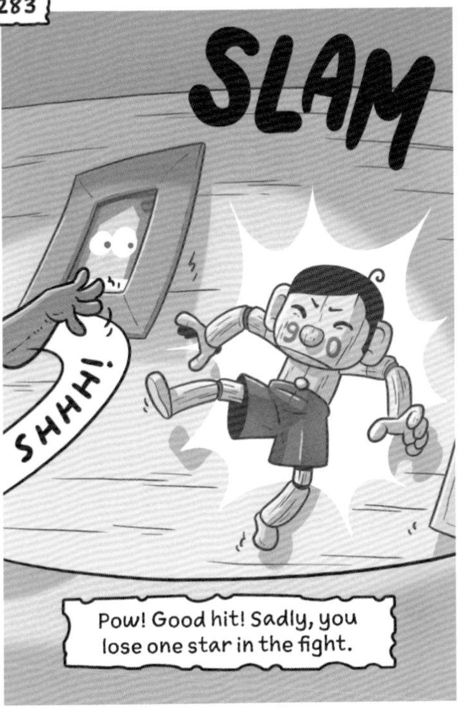
SLAM
SHHH!
Pow! Good hit! Sadly, you lose one star in the fight.

284

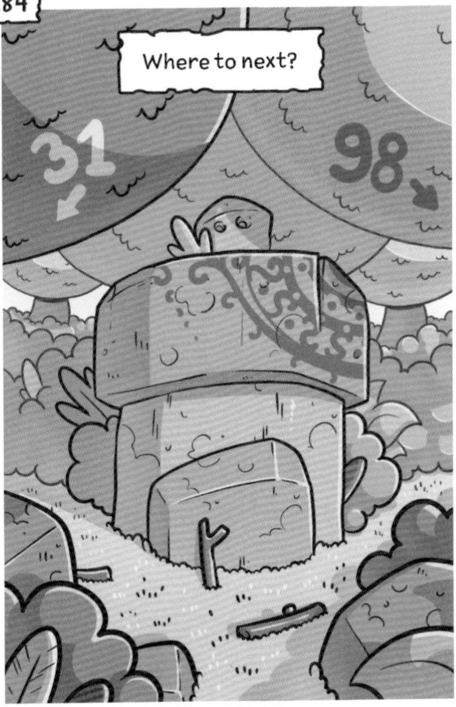
Where to next?
31
98

285

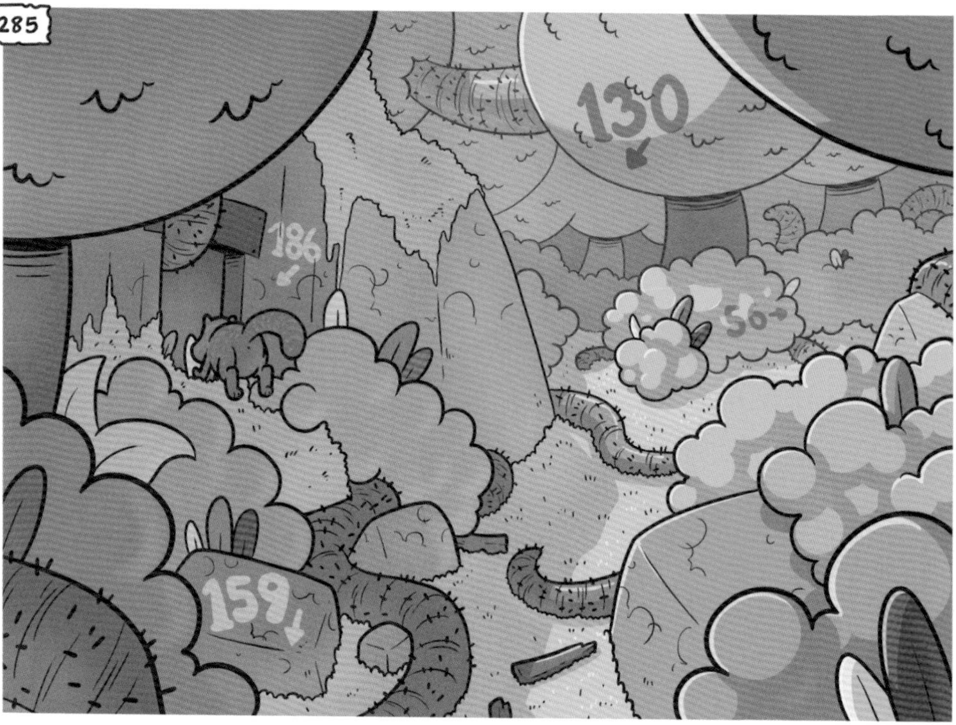
130
186
56
159

286

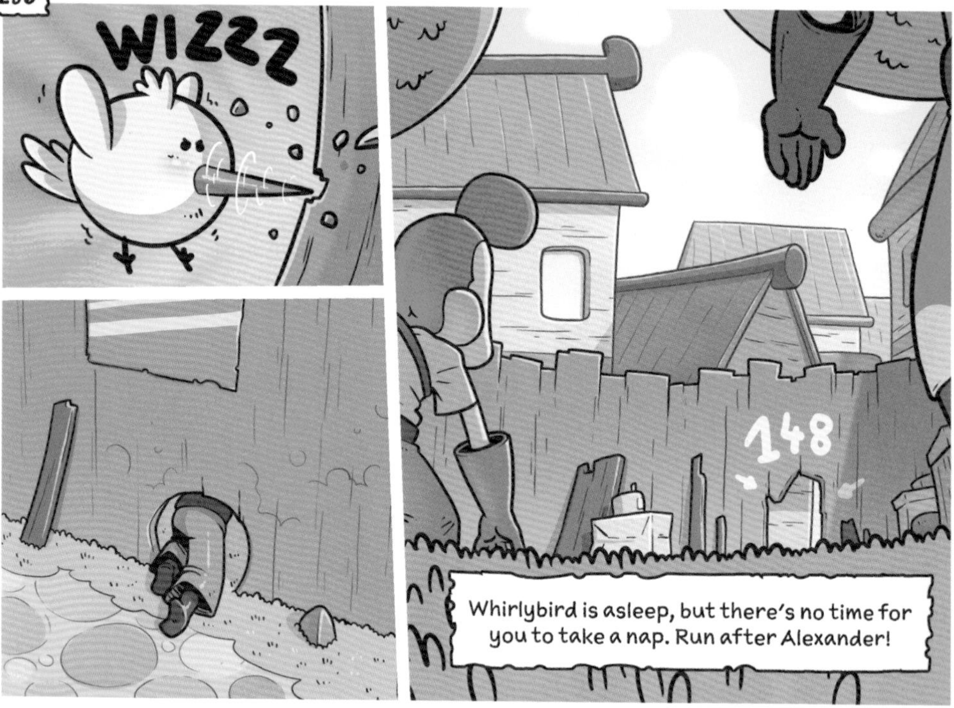
WIZZZ
148
Whirlybird is asleep, but there's no time for you to take a nap. Run after Alexander!

287

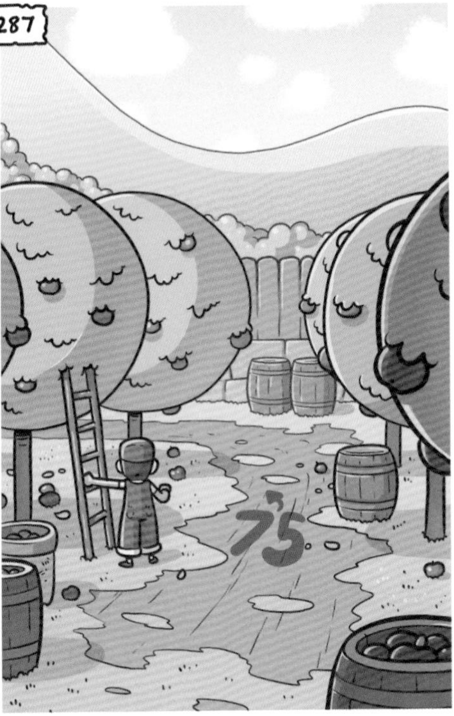
75

288

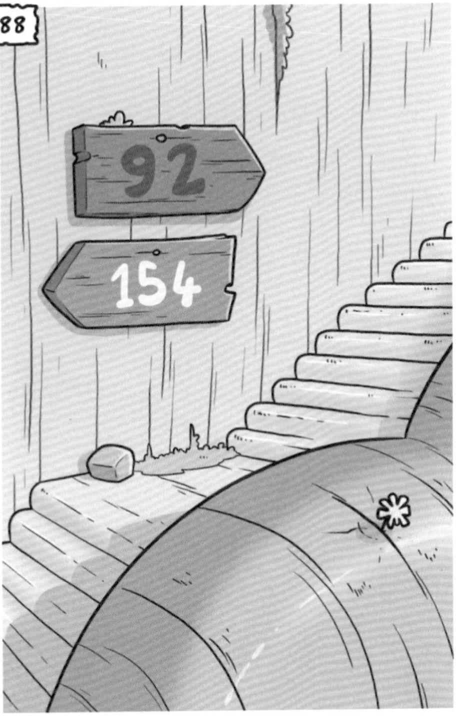
92
154

289

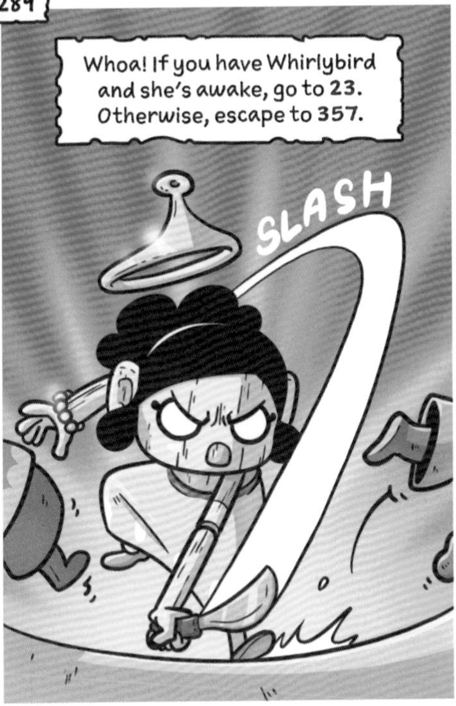
Whoa! If you have Whirlybird and she's awake, go to 23. Otherwise, escape to 357.
SLASH

290

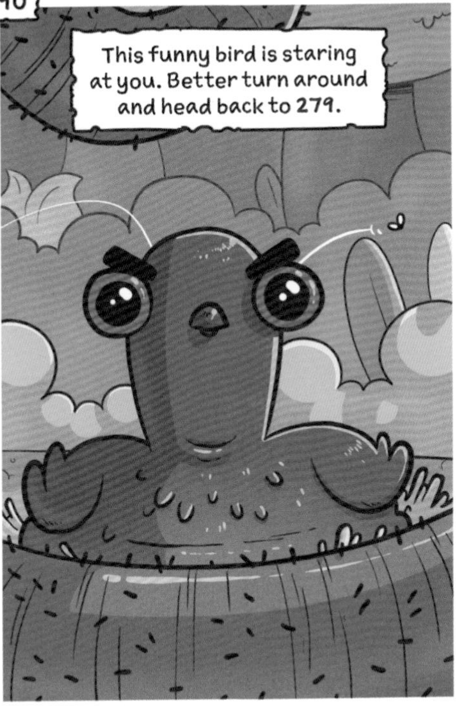
This funny bird is staring at you. Better turn around and head back to 279.

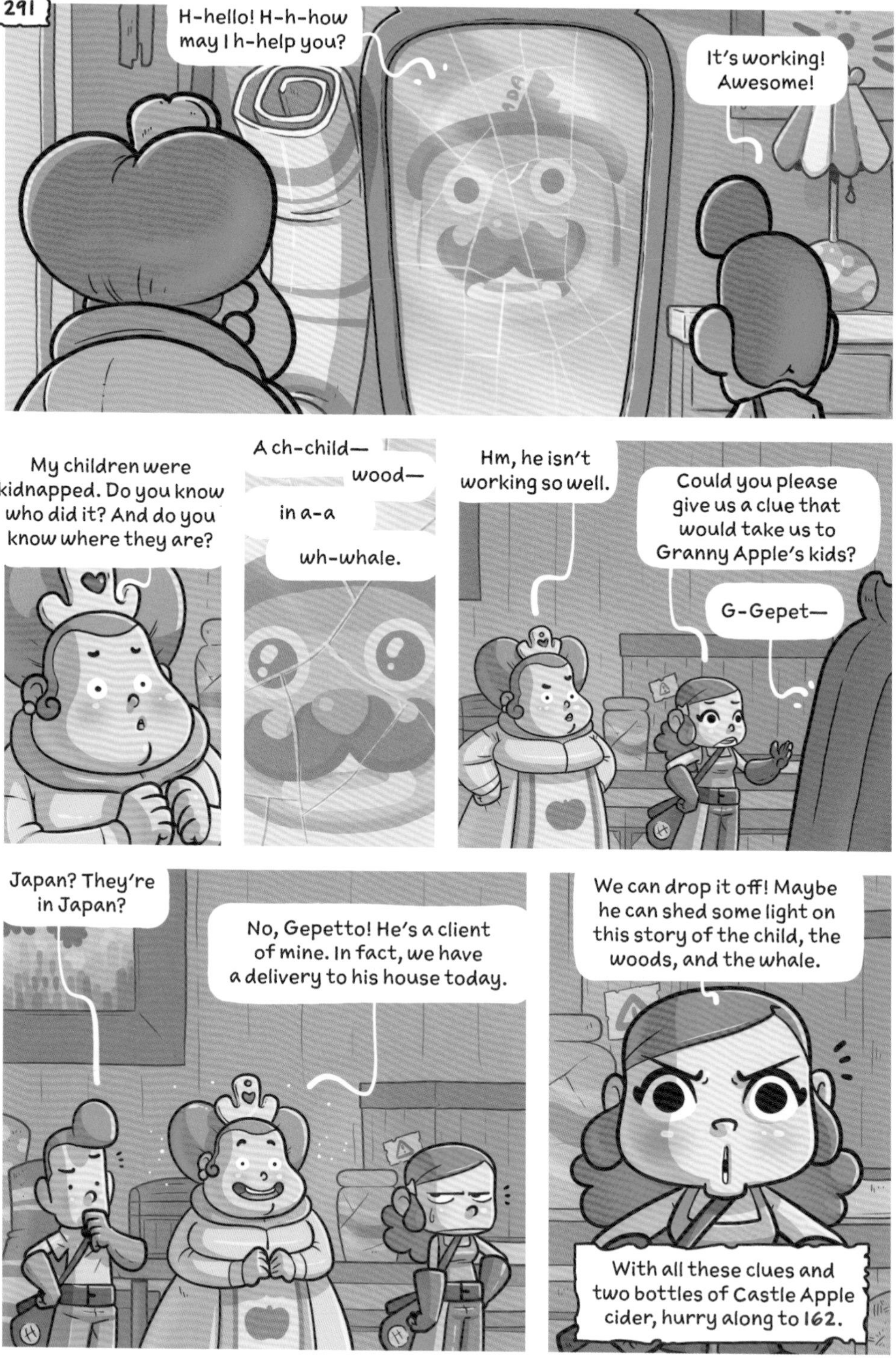
H-hello! H-h-how may I h-help you?
It's working! Awesome!
My children were kidnapped. Do you know who did it? And do you know where they are?
A ch-child—
wood—
in a-a
wh-whale.
Hm, he isn't working so well.
Could you please give us a clue that would take us to Granny Apple's kids?
G-Gepet—
Japan? They're in Japan?
No, Gepetto! He's a client of mine. In fact, we have a delivery to his house today.
We can drop it off! Maybe he can shed some light on this story of the child, the woods, and the whale.
With all these clues and two bottles of Castle Apple cider, hurry along to 162.

292

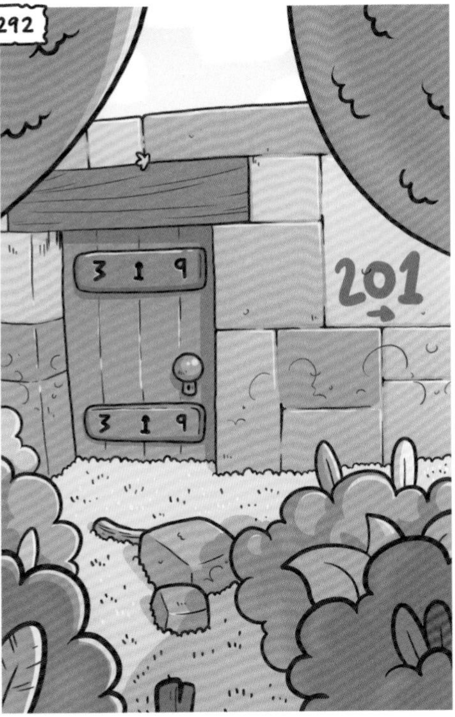
3 1 9
201
3 1 9

293

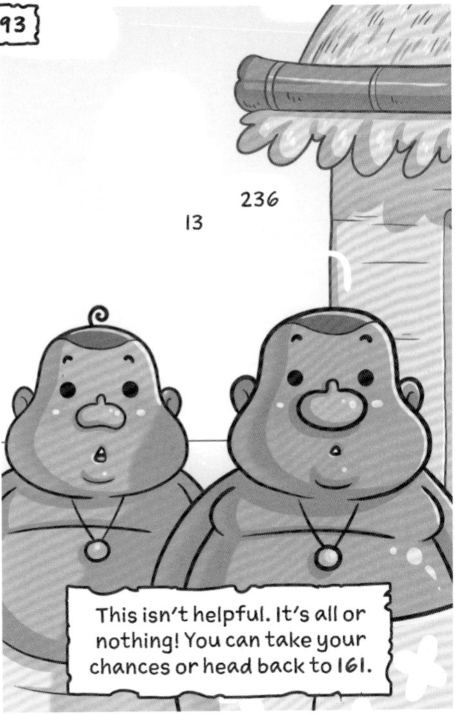
236
13
This isn't helpful. It's all or nothing! You can take your chances or head back to 161.

294

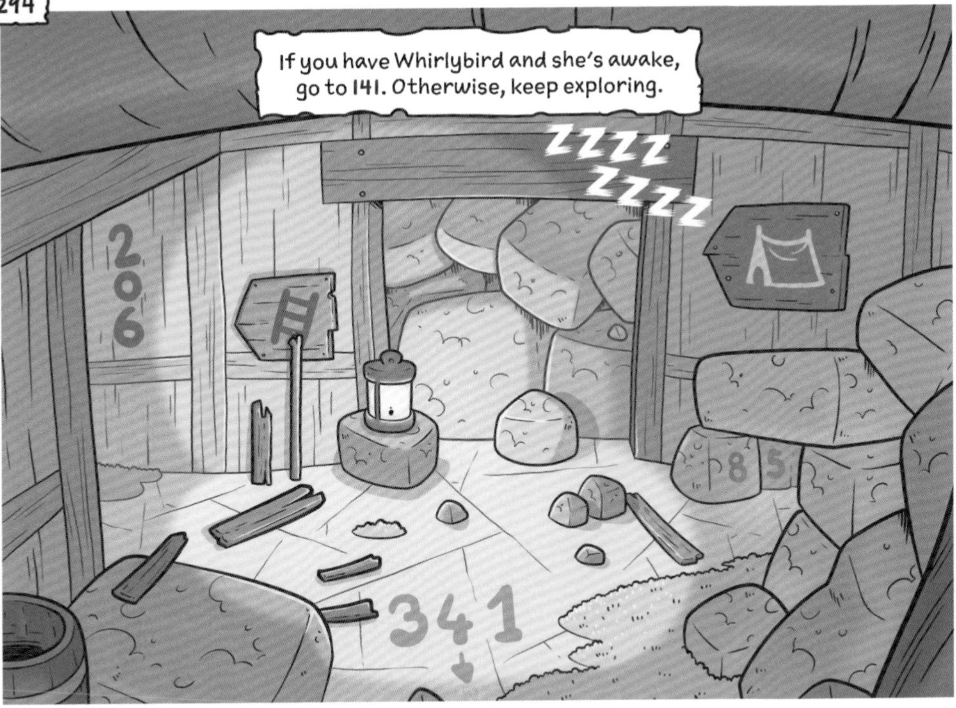
If you have Whirlybird and she's awake, go to 141. Otherwise, keep exploring.
ZZZZ
ZZZZ
206
85
341

295

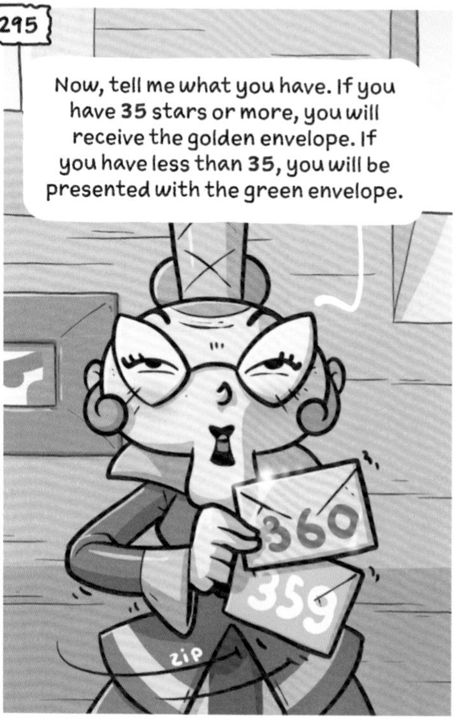
Now, tell me what you have. If you have **35** stars or more, you will receive the golden envelope. If you have less than **35**, you will be presented with the green envelope.
360
359
zip

296

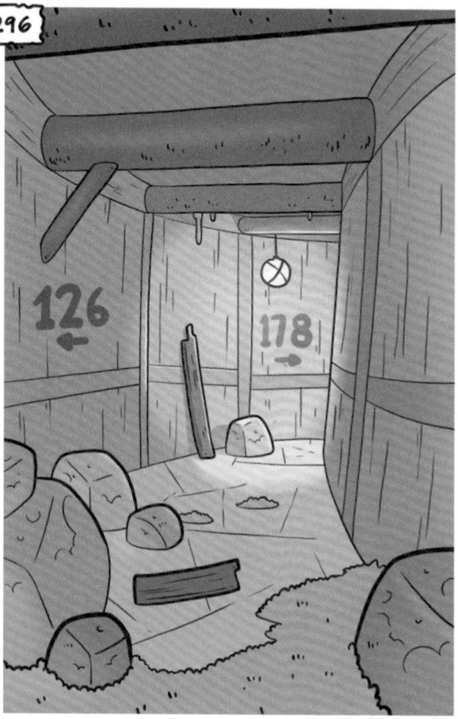
126
178

297

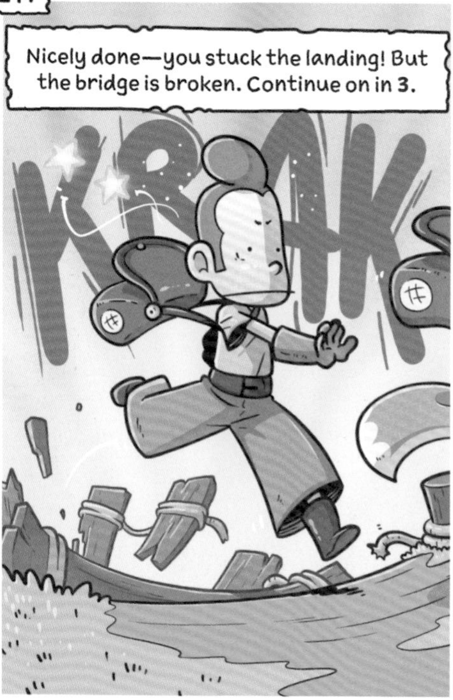
Nicely done—you stuck the landing! But the bridge is broken. Continue on in **3**.
KRAK

298

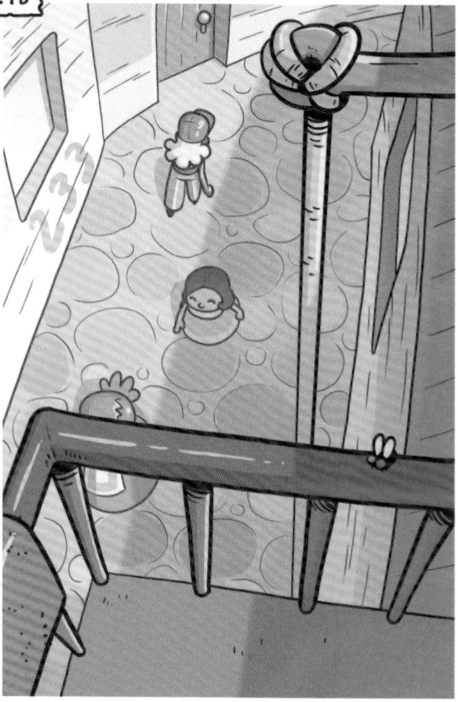

299

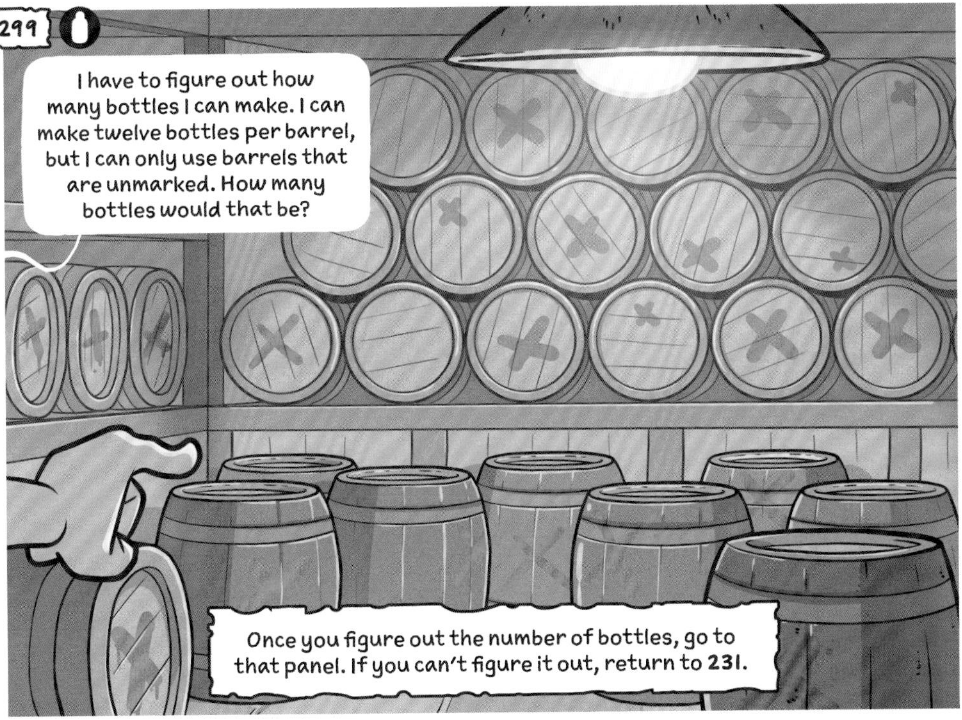
I have to figure out how many bottles I can make. I can make twelve bottles per barrel, but I can only use barrels that are unmarked. How many bottles would that be?
Once you figure out the number of bottles, go to that panel. If you can't figure it out, return to 231.

300

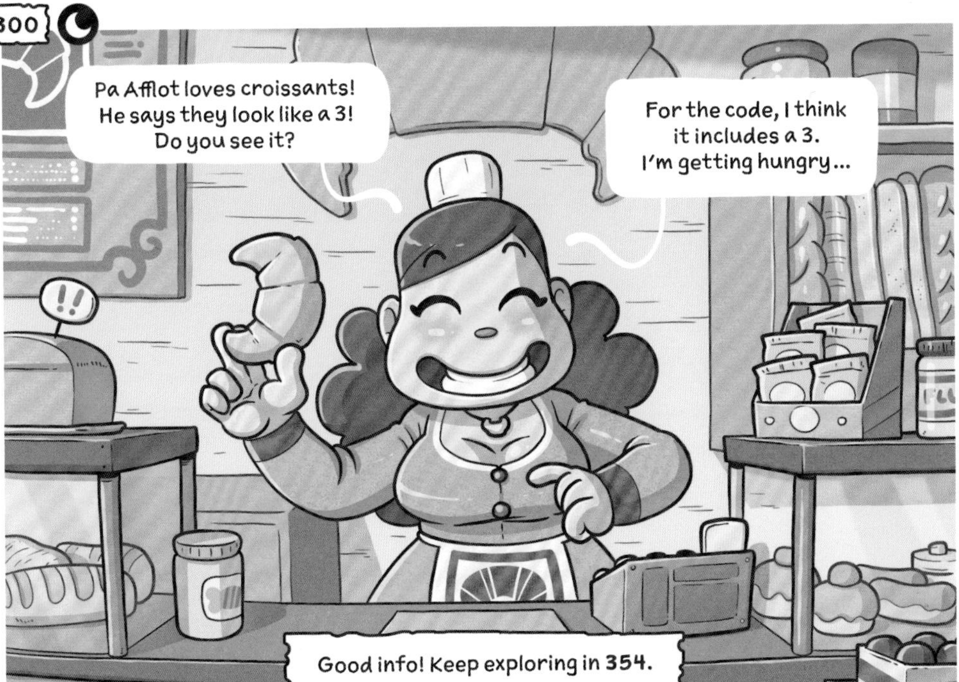
Pa Afflot loves croissants! He says they look like a 3! Do you see it?
For the code, I think it includes a 3. I'm getting hungry...
Good info! Keep exploring in 354.

301

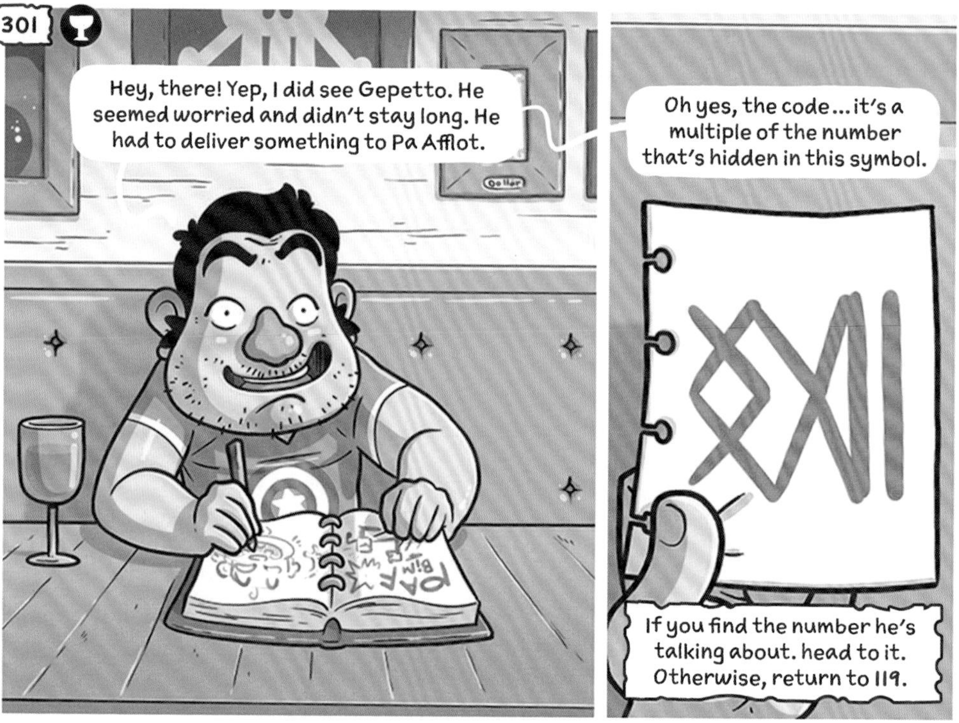
Hey, there! Yep, I did see Gepetto. He seemed worried and didn't stay long. He had to deliver something to Pa Afflot.
Oh yes, the code... it's a multiple of the number that's hidden in this symbol.
If you find the number he's talking about. head to it. Otherwise, return to 119.

302

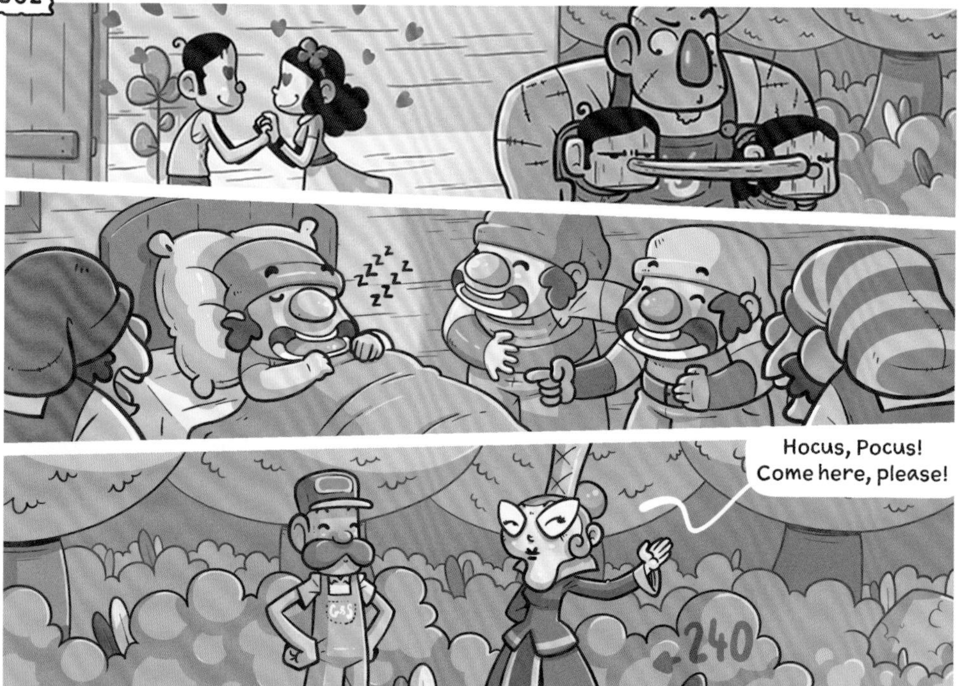
Hocus, Pocus! Come here, please!
240

303

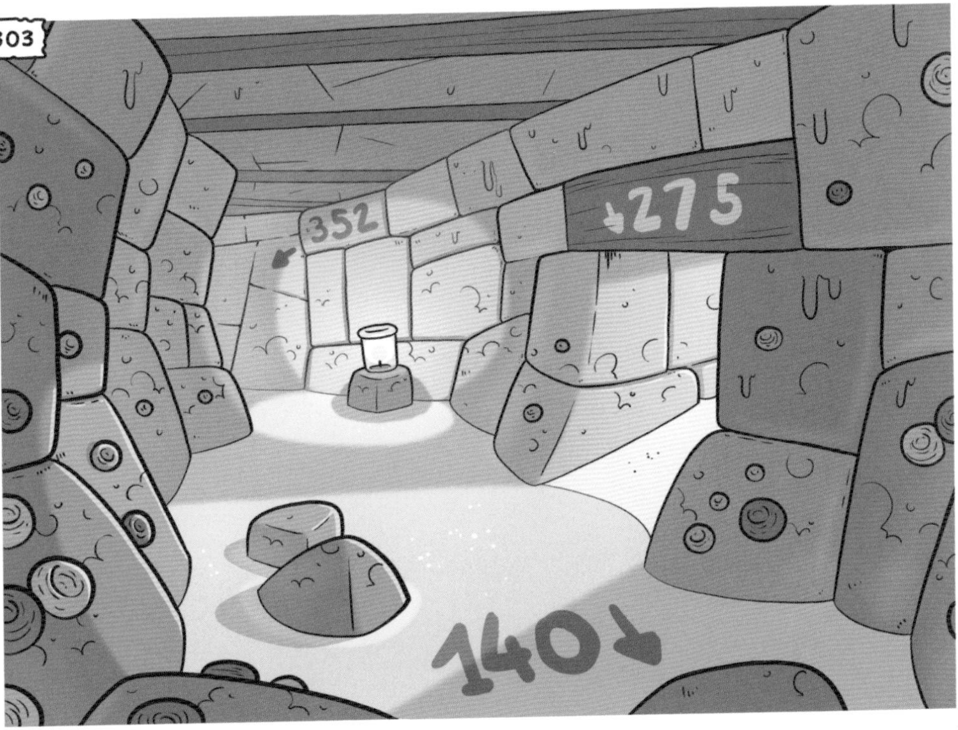
352
275
140

304

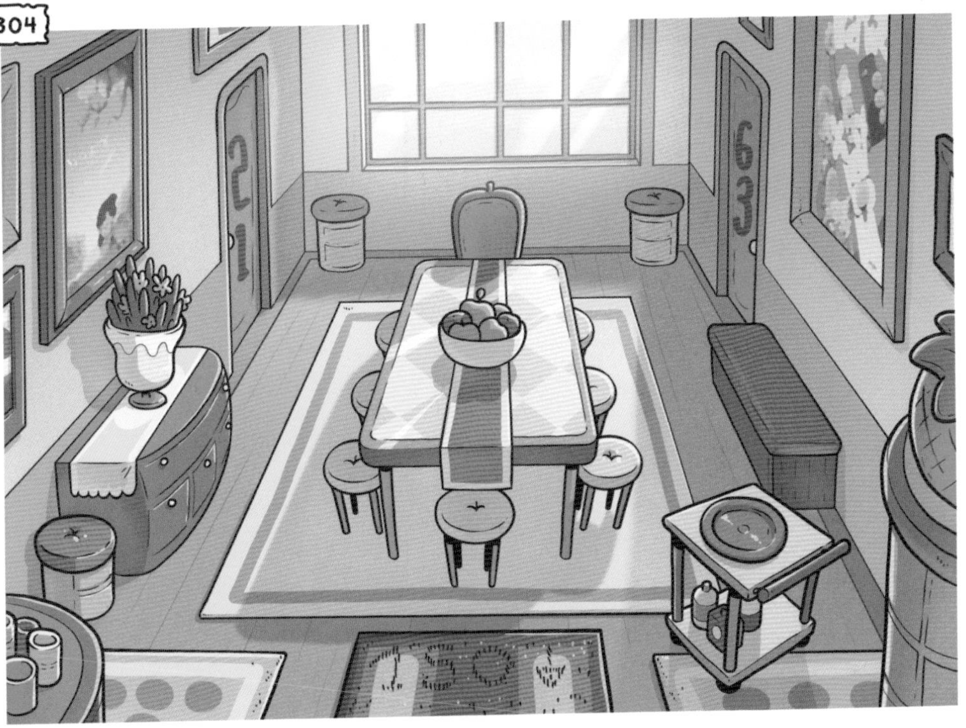
21
63

305

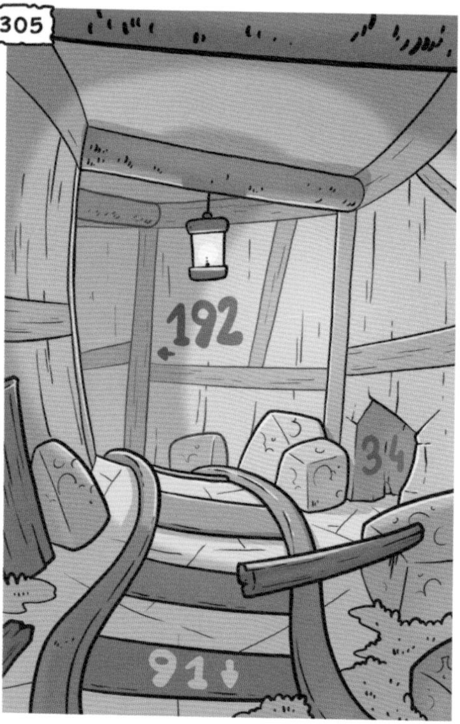
192
34
91

306

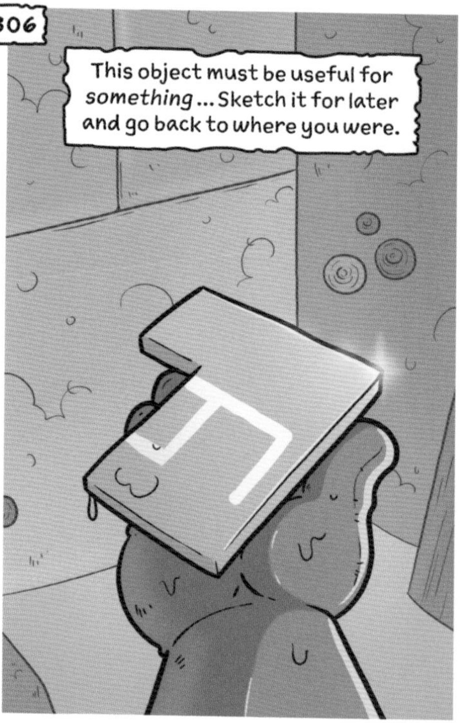
This object must be useful for *something* ... Sketch it for later and go back to where you were.

307

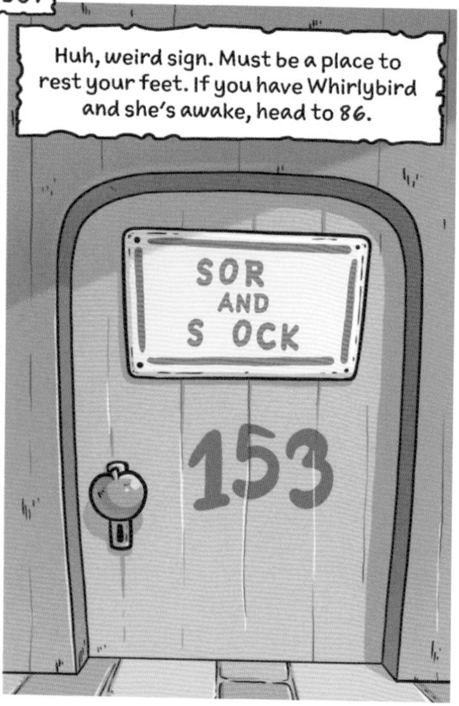
Huh, weird sign. Must be a place to rest your feet. If you have Whirlybird and she's awake, head to 86.
SOR AND S OCK
153

308

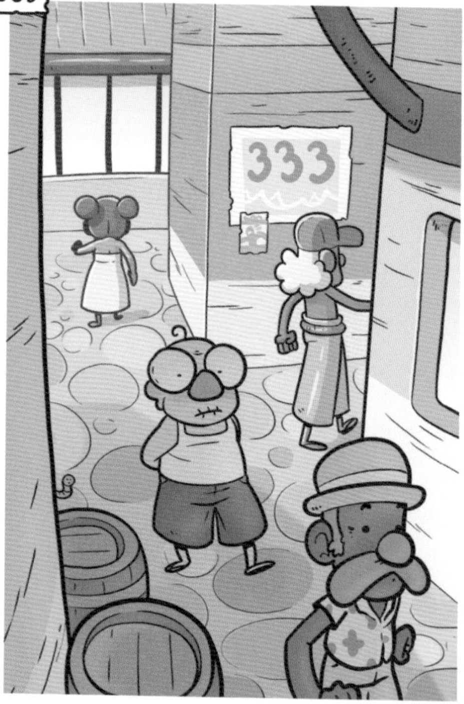
333

309

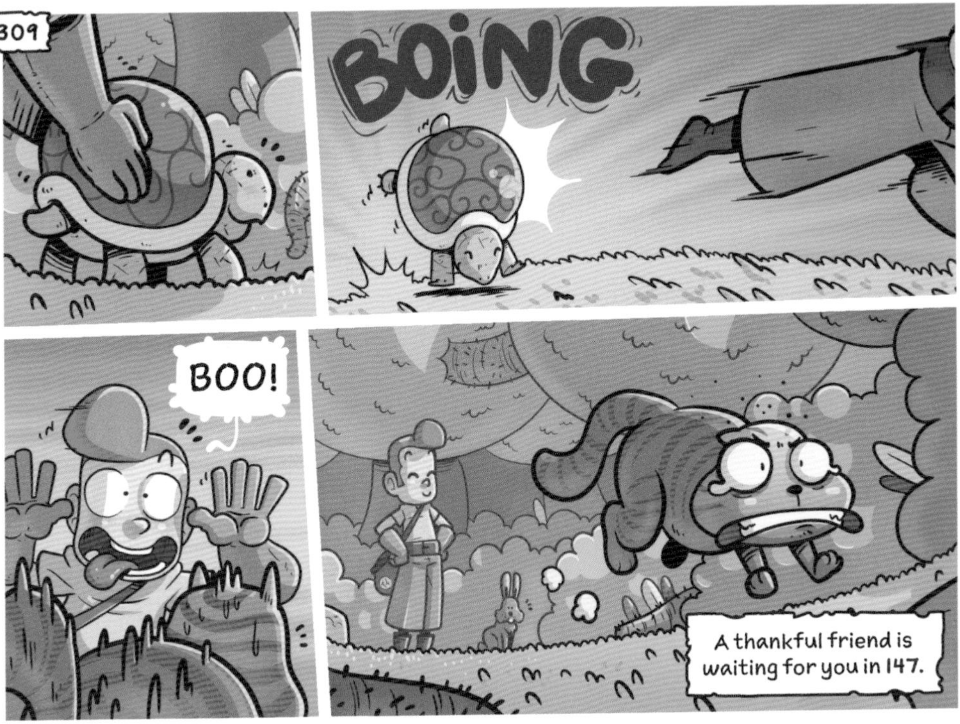
BOING
BOO!
A thankful friend is waiting for you in 147.

310

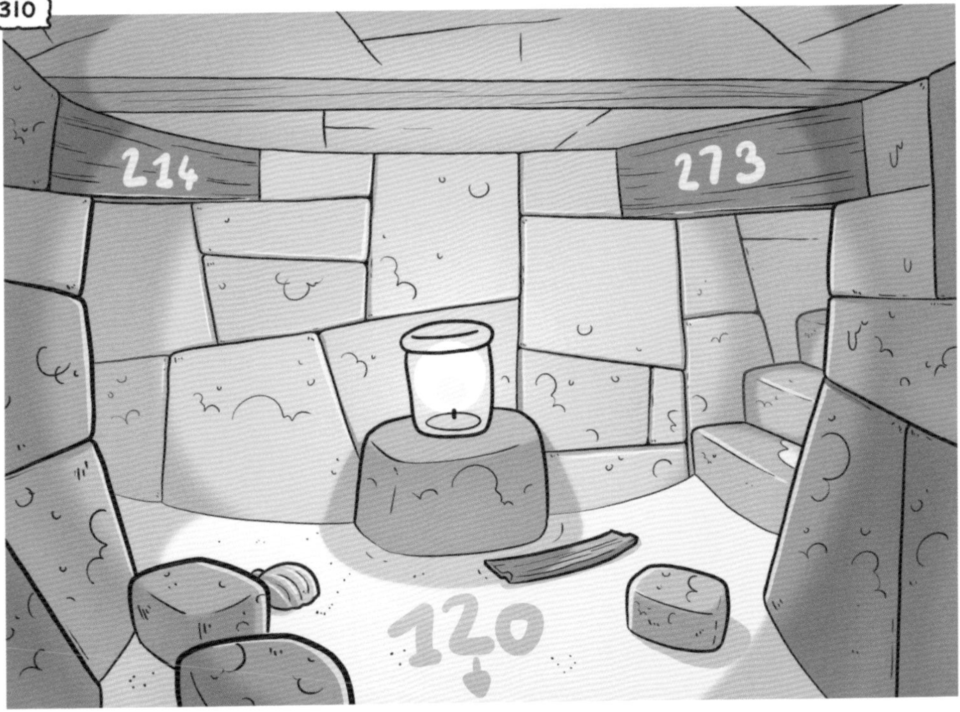
214
273
120

311

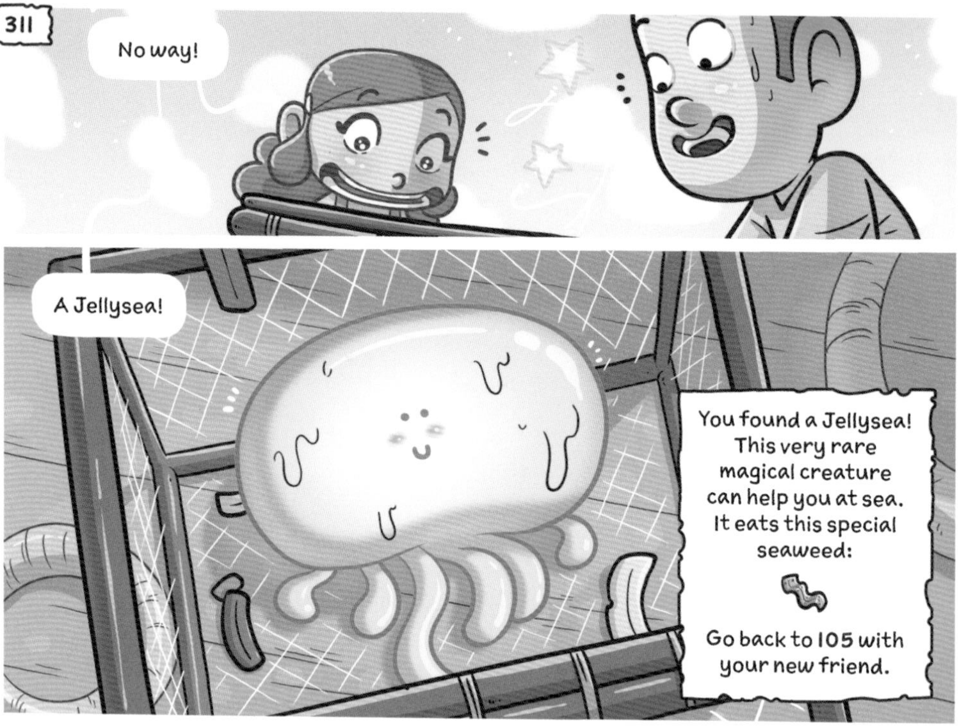
No way!
A Jellysea!
You found a Jellysea! This very rare magical creature can help you at sea. It eats this special seaweed:
Go back to 105 with your new friend.

312

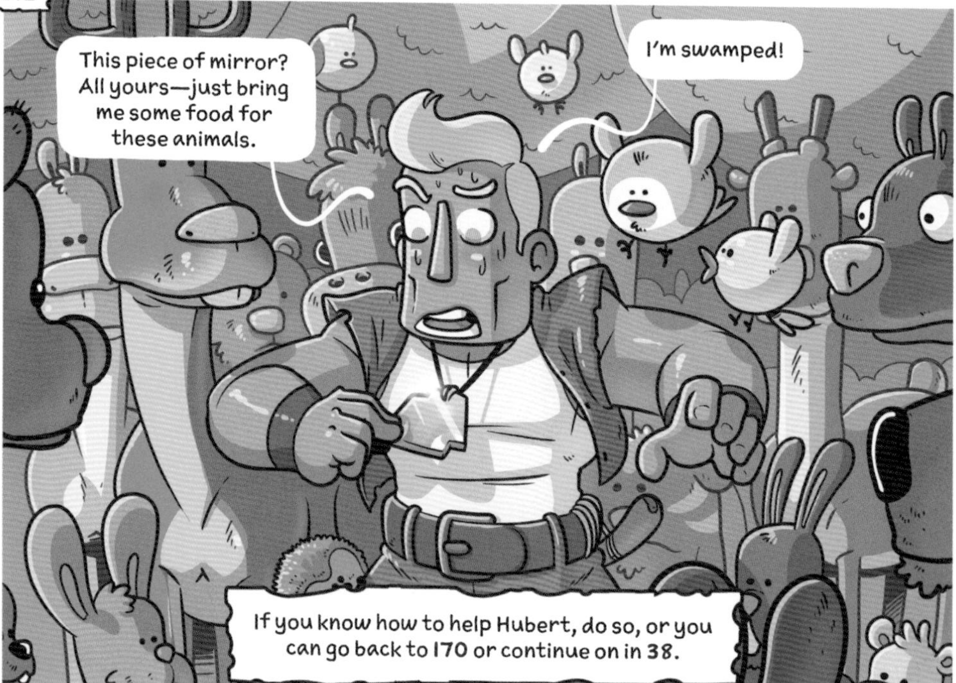
This piece of mirror? All yours—just bring me some food for these animals.
I'm swamped!
If you know how to help Hubert, do so, or you can go back to 170 or continue on in 38.

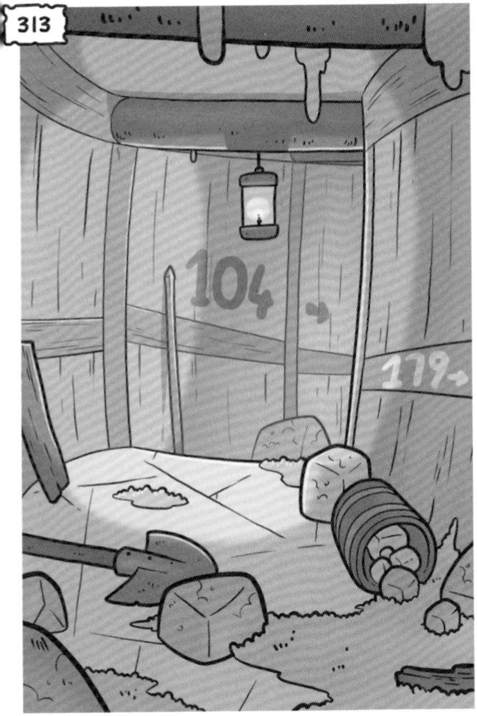
313
104
179→

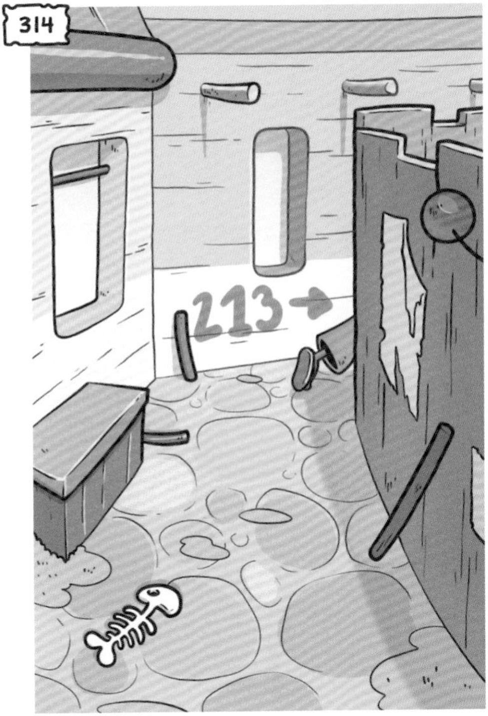
314
213→

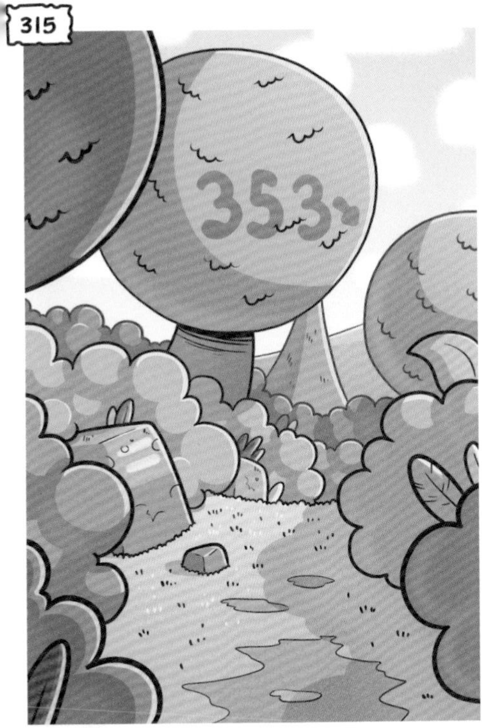
315
353→

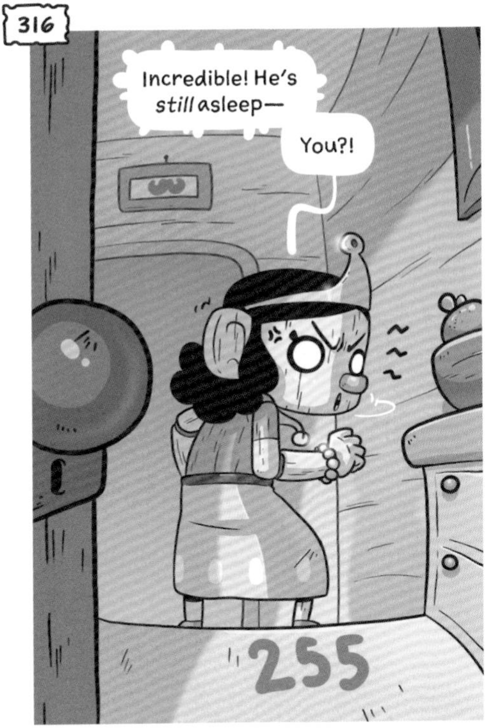
316
Incredible! He's *still* asleep—
You?!
255

317

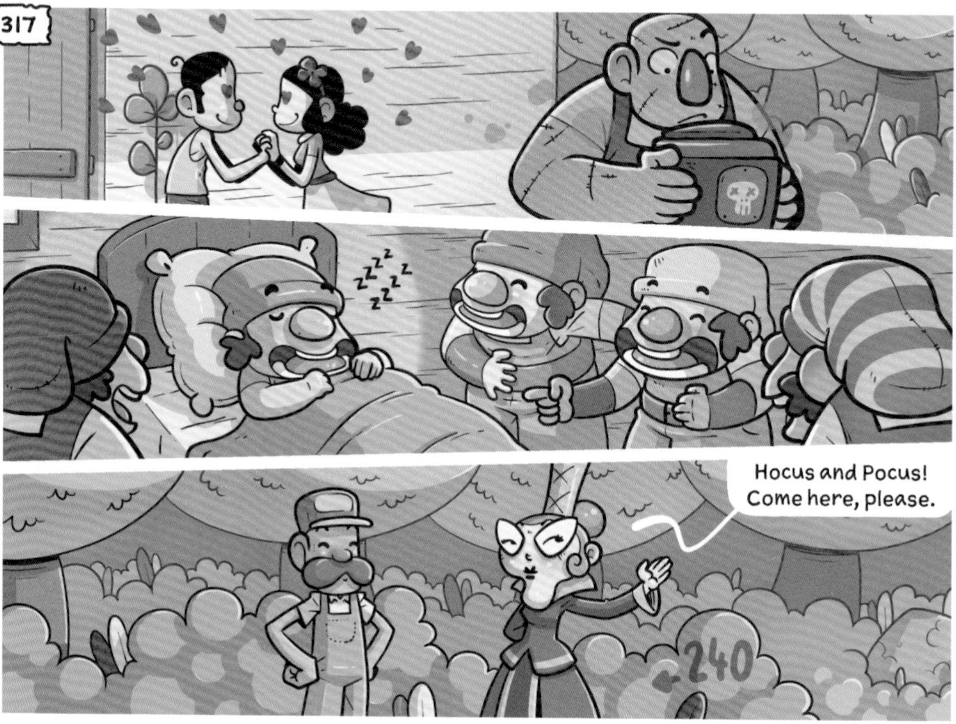
Hocus and Pocus!
Come here, please.
240

318

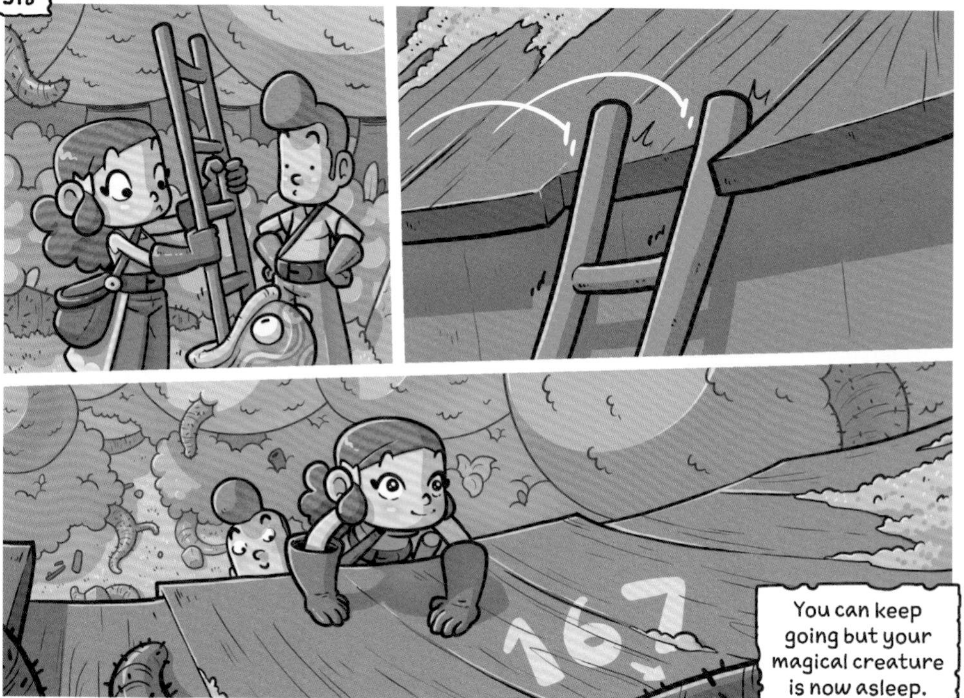
167
You can keep going but your magical creature is now asleep.

319

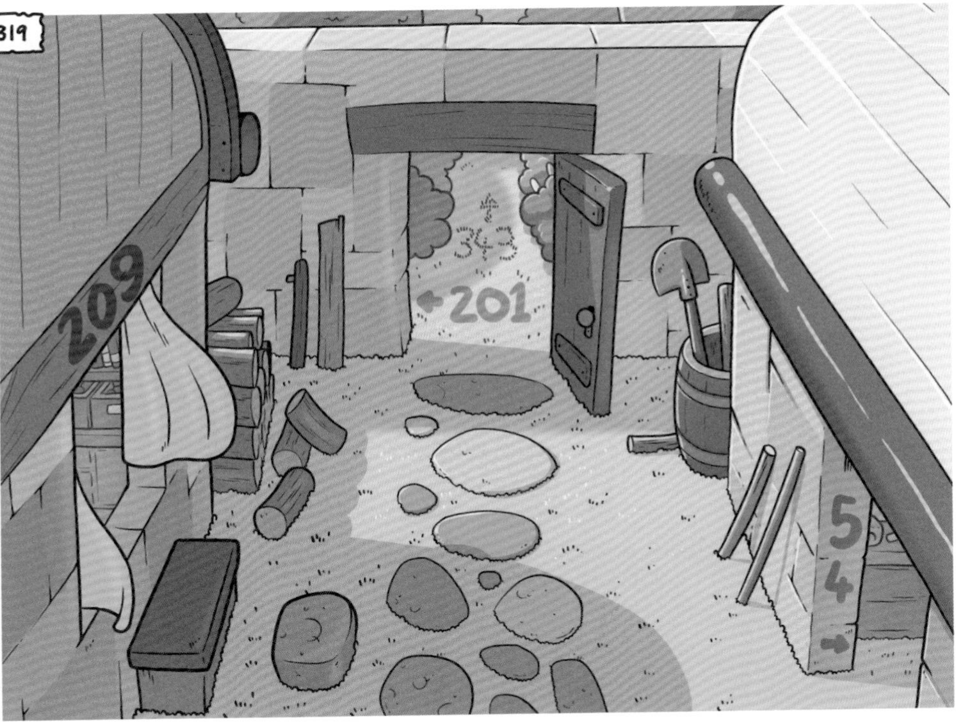
209
343
201
5
4

320

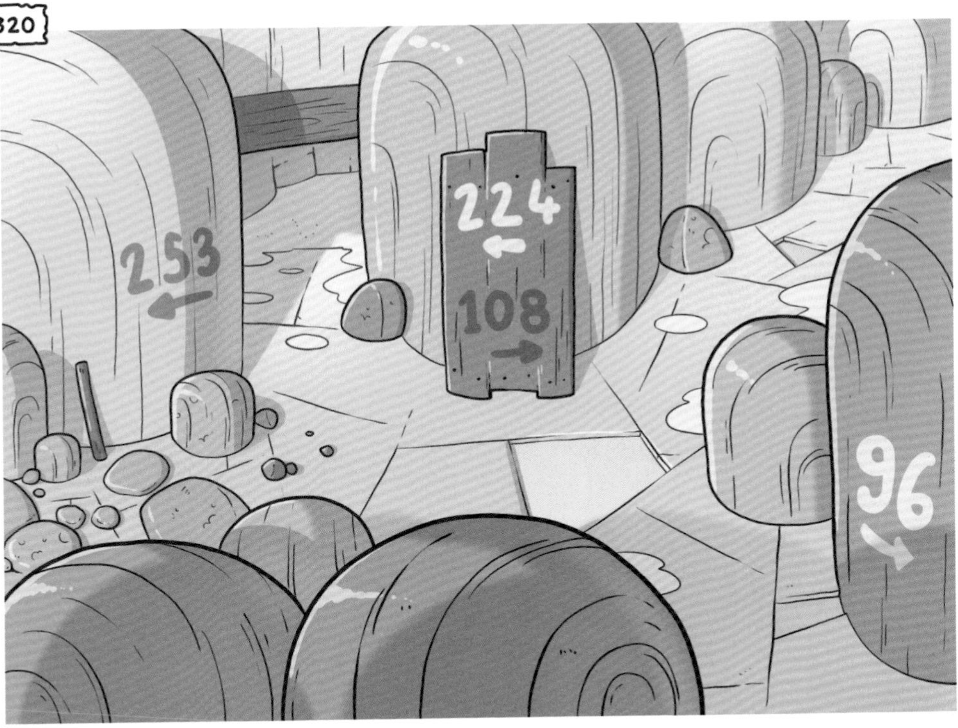
253
224
108
96

321

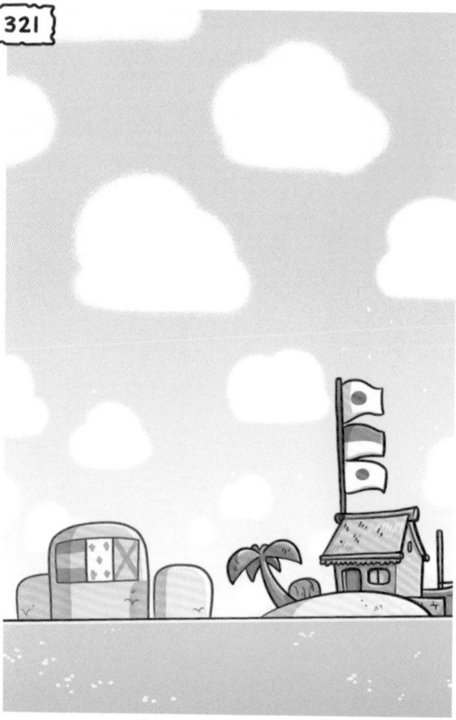

322

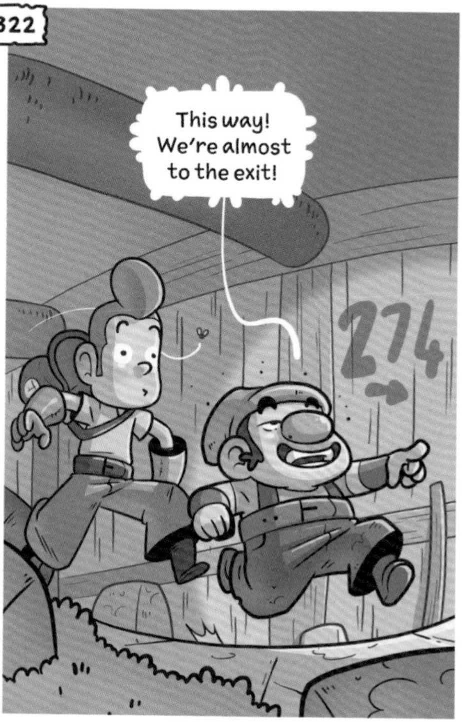
This way! We're almost to the exit!
274

323

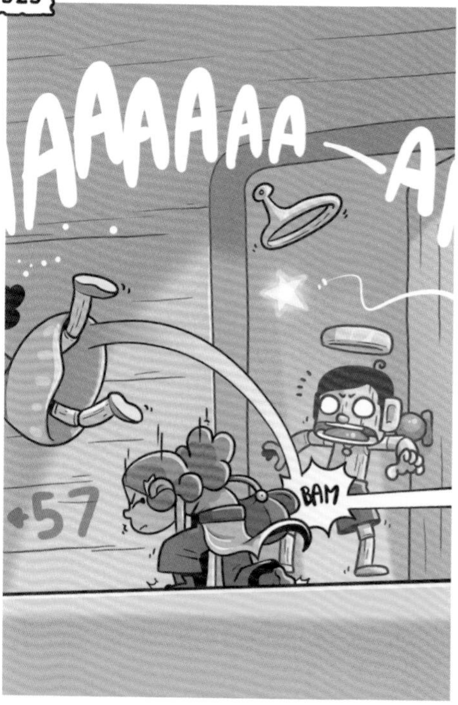
AAAAAAA—A
BAM
57

324

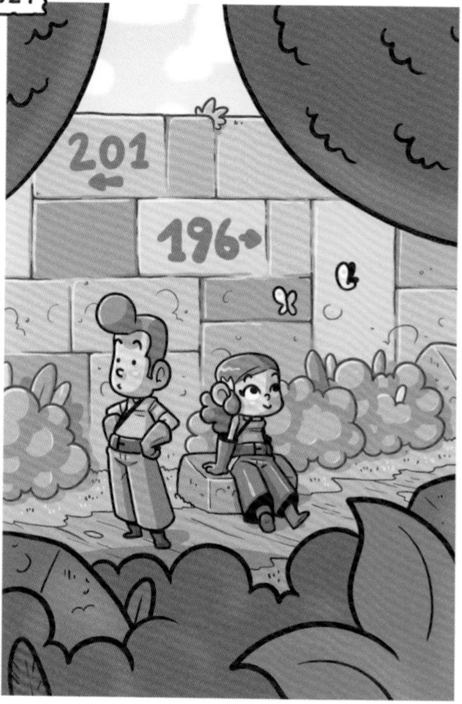
201
196

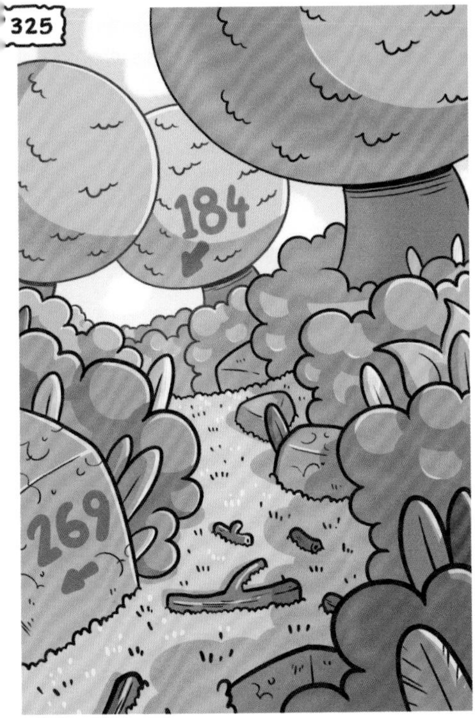
325
184
269

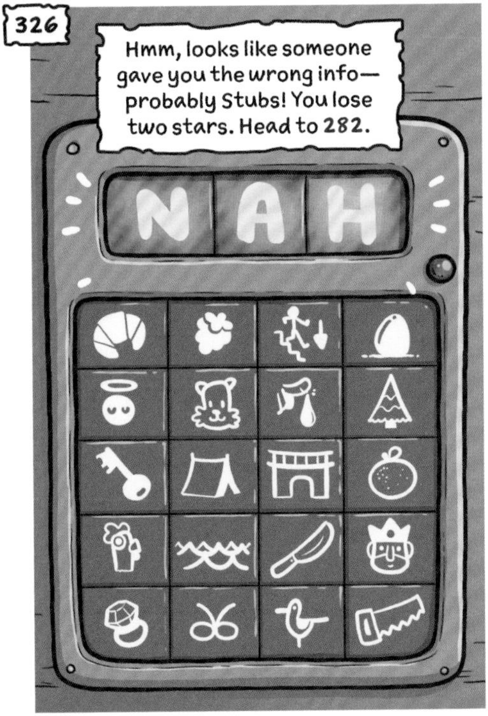
326
Hmm, looks like someone gave you the wrong info—probably Stubs! You lose two stars. Head to 282.
NAH

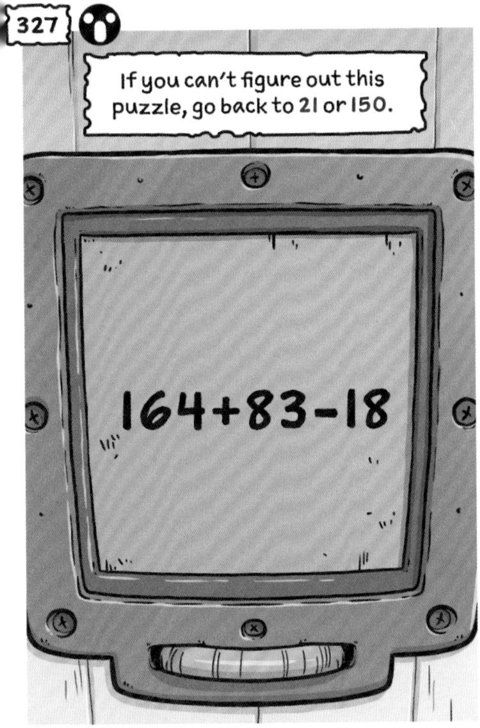
327
If you can't figure out this puzzle, go back to 21 or 150.
164+83-18

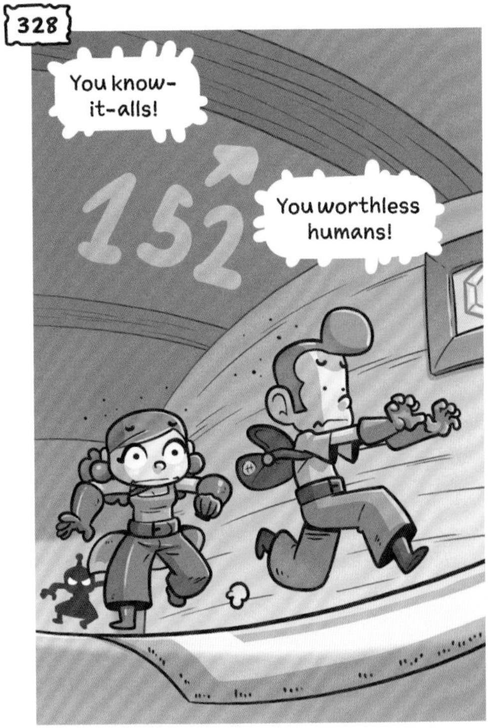
328
You know-it-alls!
152
You worthless humans!

329

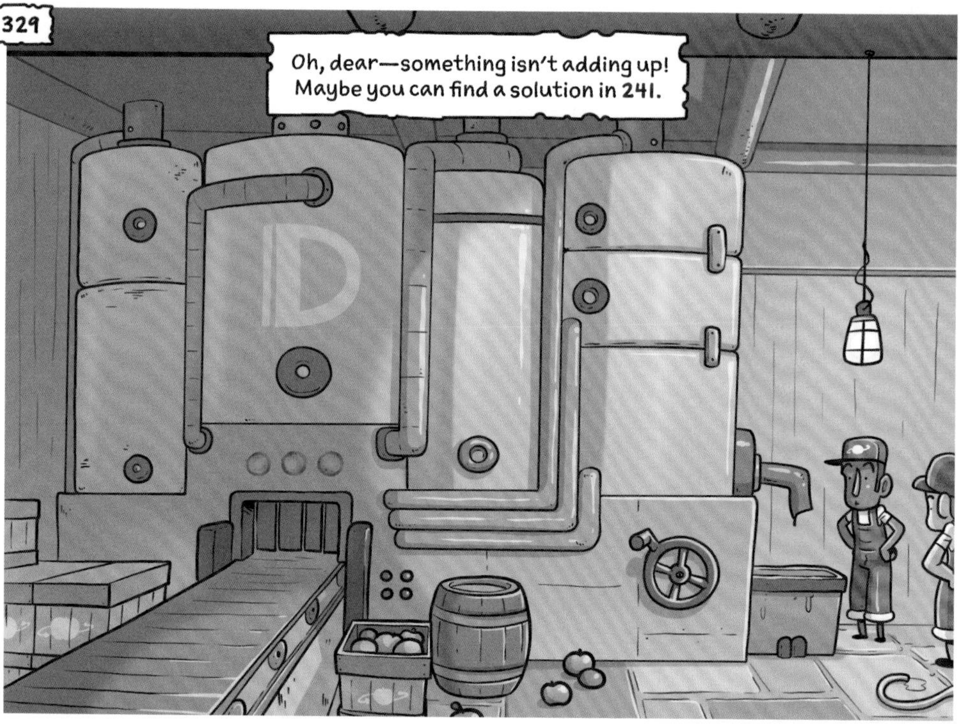
Oh, dear—something isn't adding up!
Maybe you can find a solution in 241.
D

330

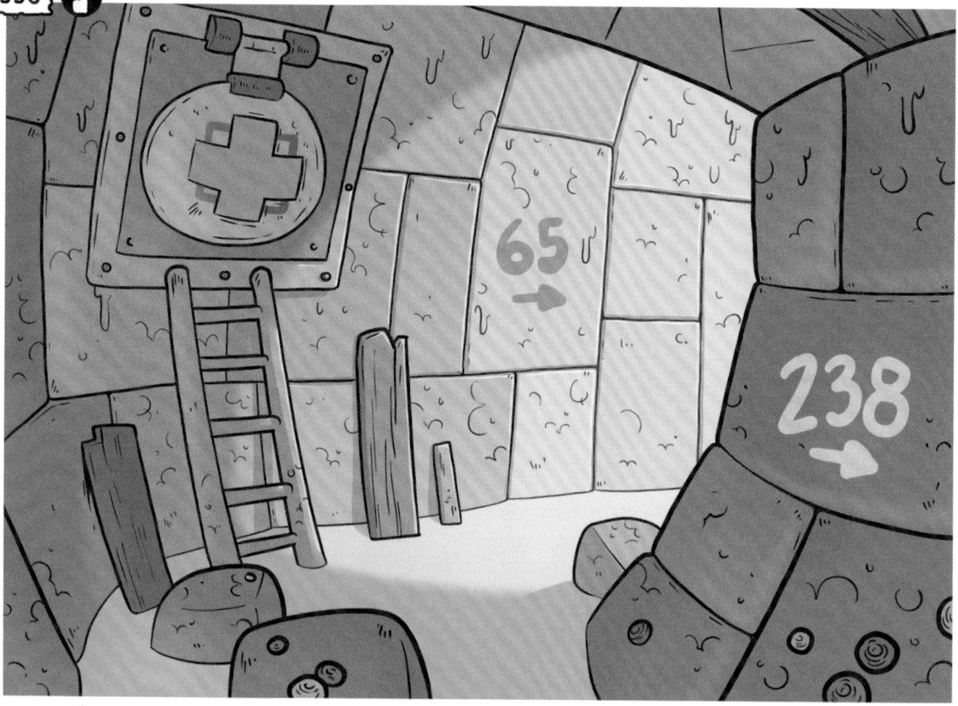
65
238

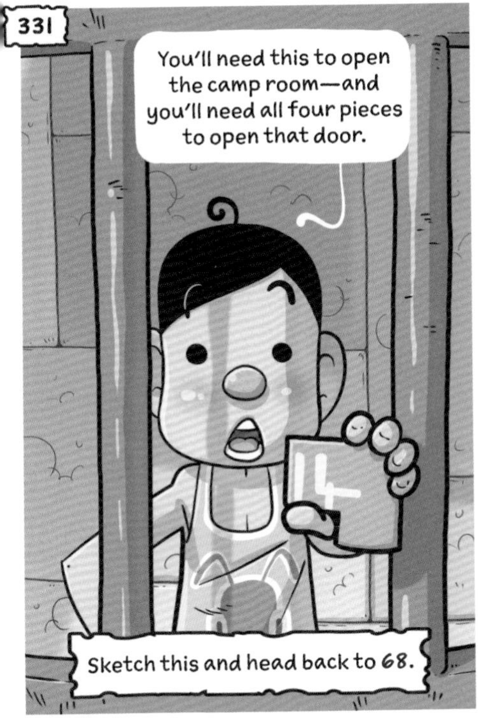
331
You'll need this to open the camp room—and you'll need all four pieces to open that door.
4
Sketch this and head back to 68.

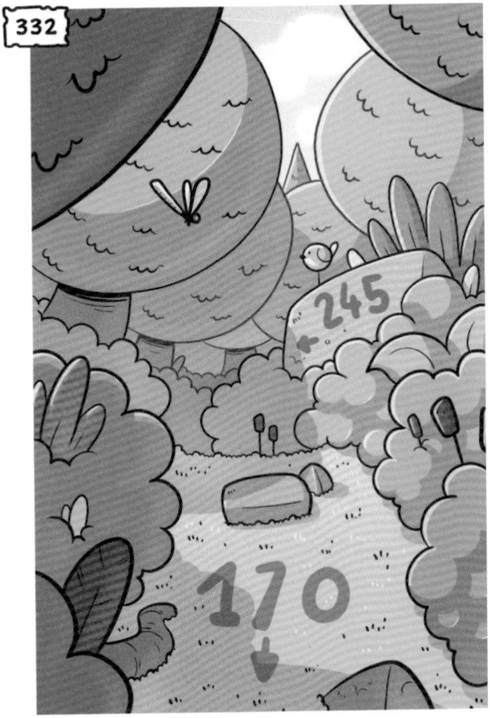
332
245
170

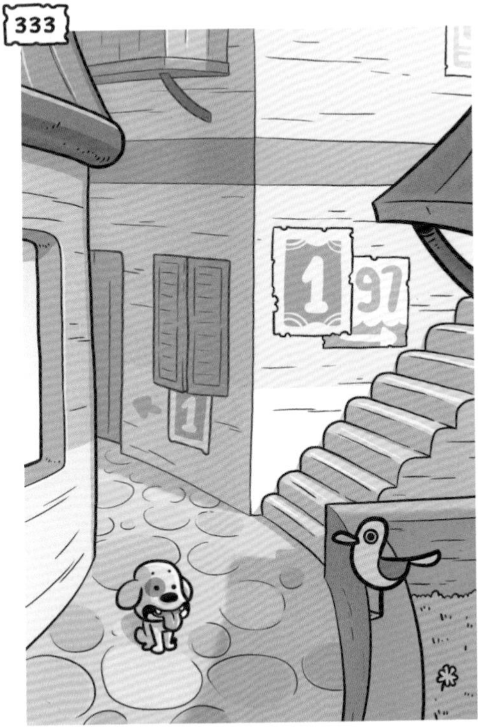
333
1
97
1

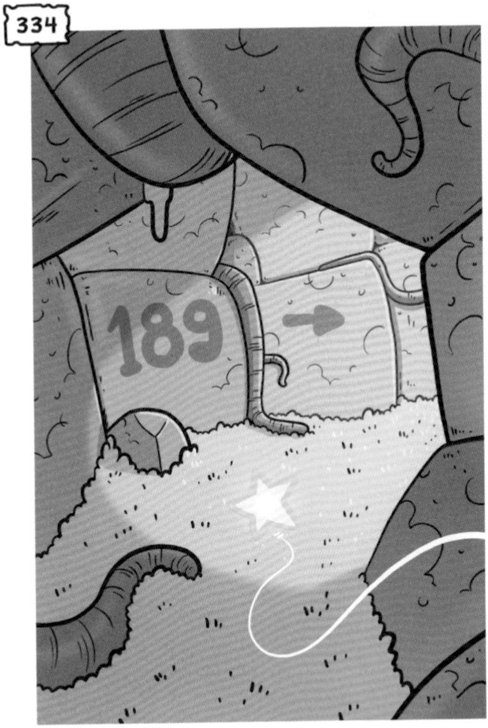
334
189

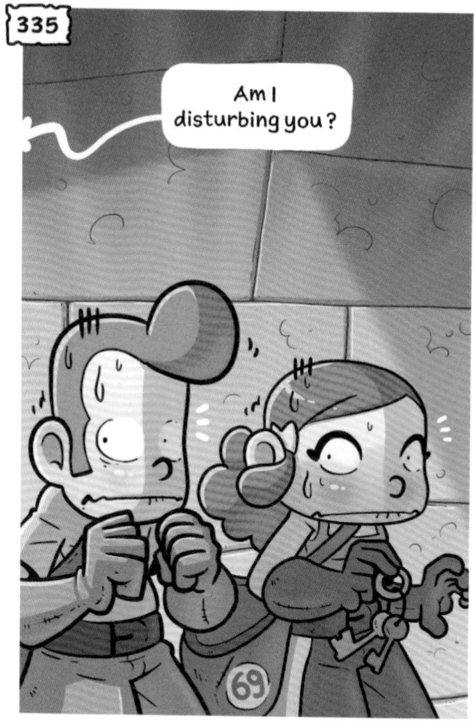
335
Am I disturbing you ?
69

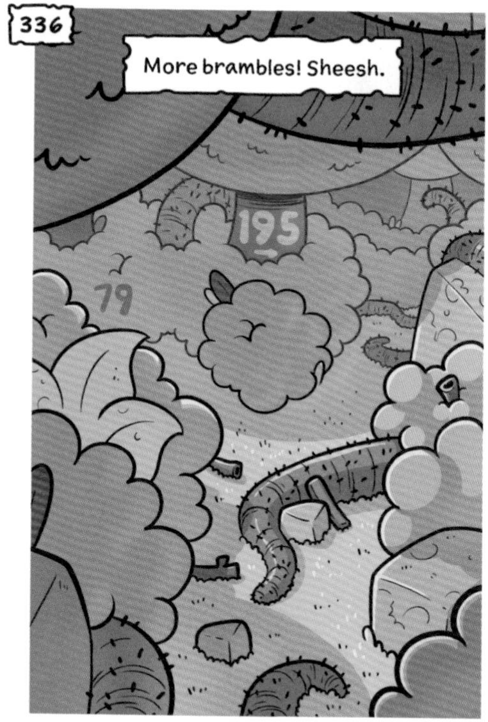
336
More brambles! Sheesh.
195
79

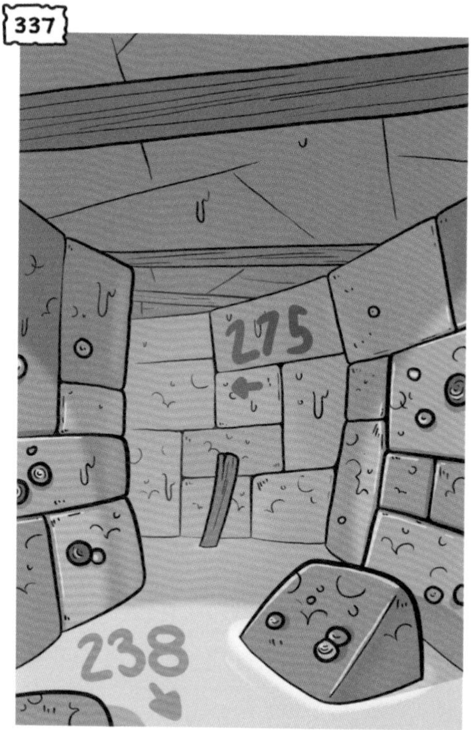
337
275
238

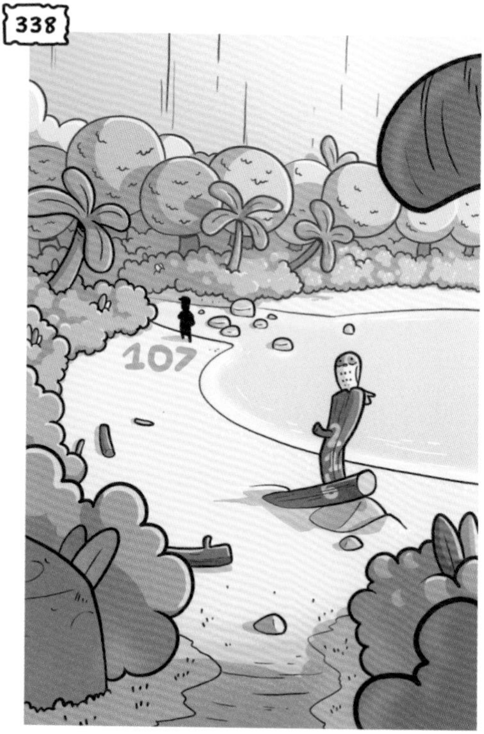
338
107

339

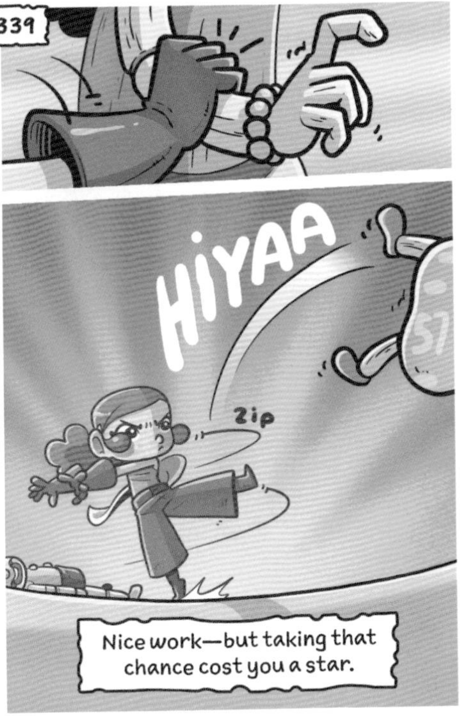
HIYAA
zip
Nice work—but taking that chance cost you a star.

340

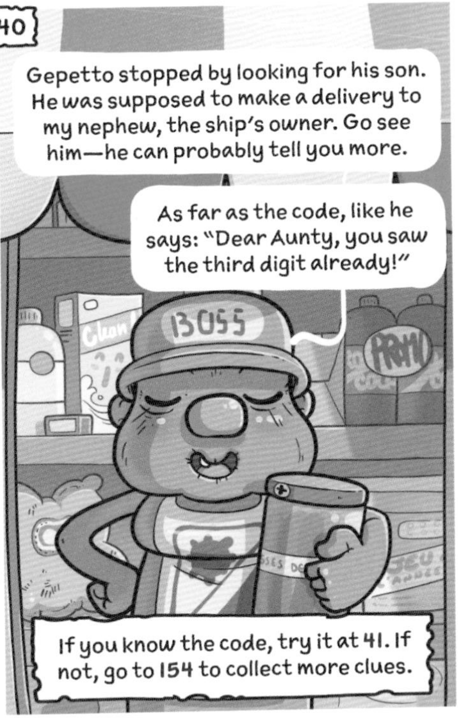
Gepetto stopped by looking for his son. He was supposed to make a delivery to my nephew, the ship's owner. Go see him—he can probably tell you more.
As far as the code, like he says: "Dear Aunty, you saw the third digit already!"
BOSS
If you know the code, try it at 41. If not, go to 154 to collect more clues.

341

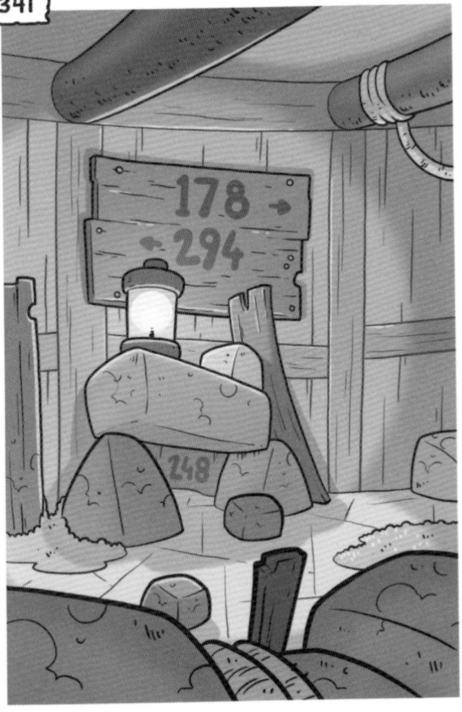
178 →
← 294
248

342

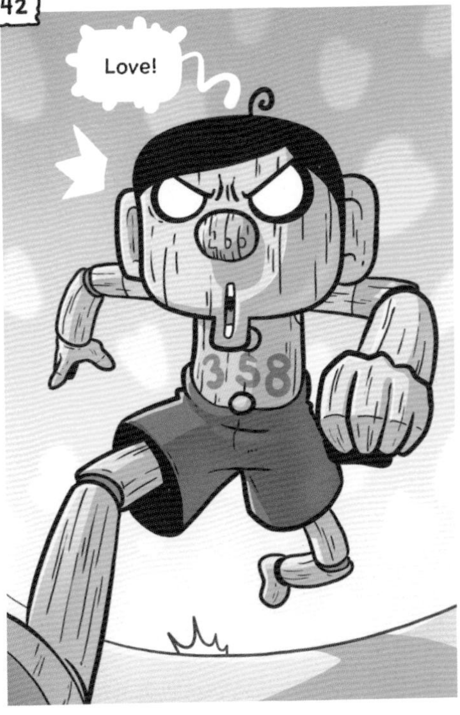
Love!
358

343

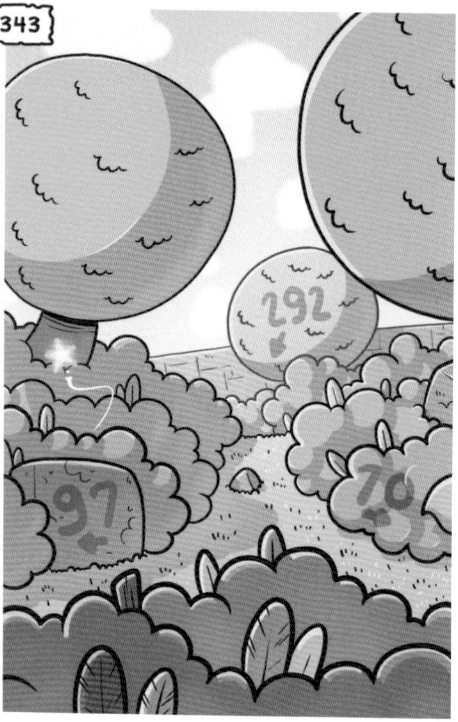
292
97
70

344

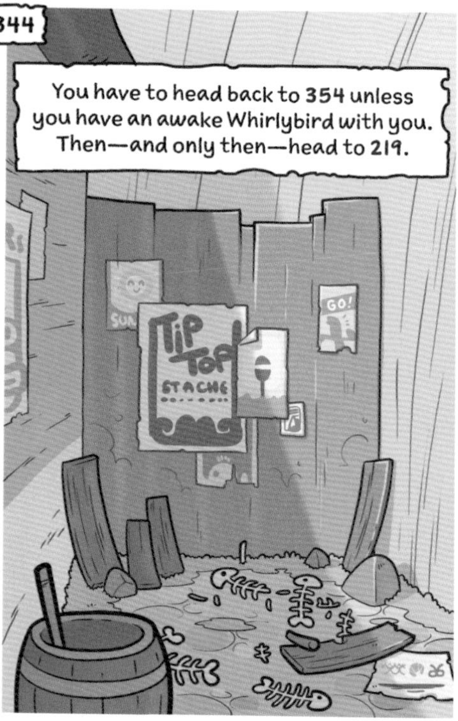
You have to head back to 354 unless you have an awake Whirlybird with you. Then—and only then—head to 219.
Tip Top
STACHE
GO!

345

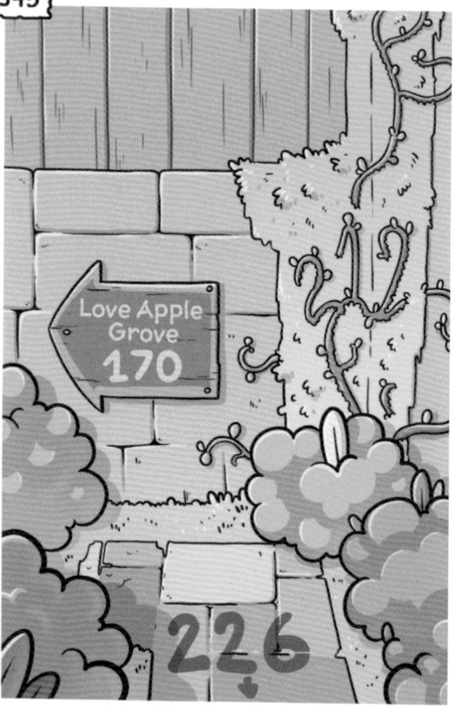
Love Apple
Grove
170
226

346

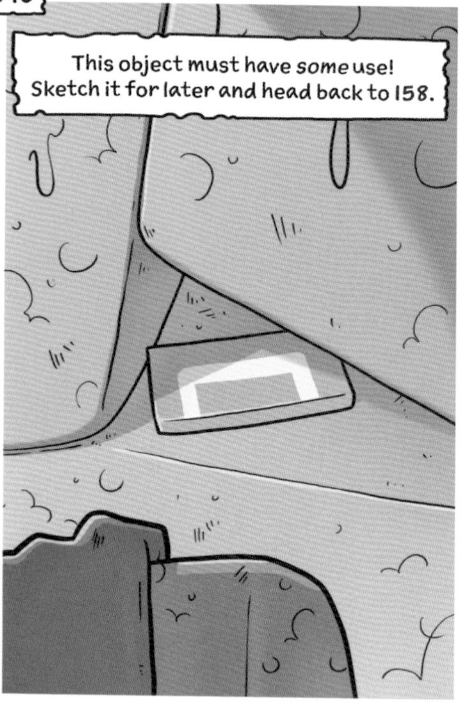
This object must have *some* use! Sketch it for later and head back to 158.

347

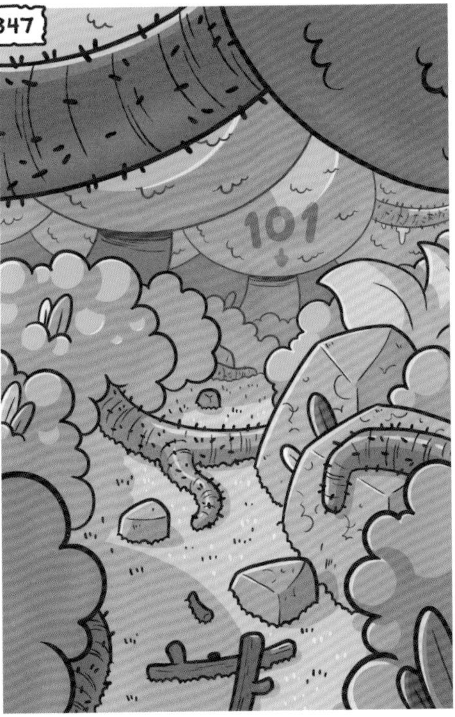

101

348

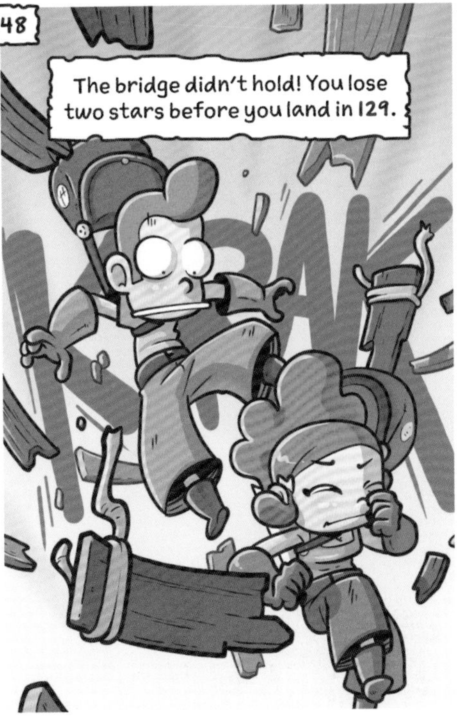

The bridge didn't hold! You lose two stars before you land in 129.

349

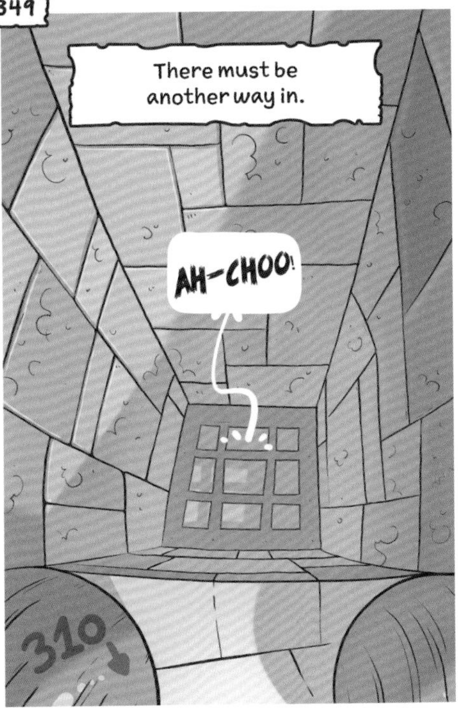

There must be another way in.
AH-CHOO!
310

350

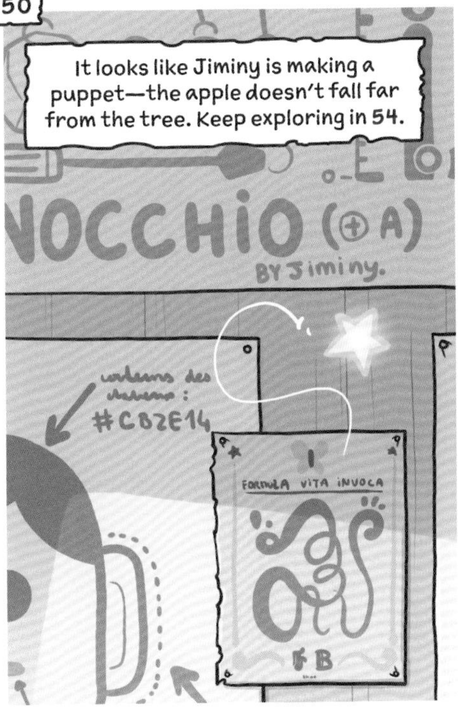

It looks like Jiminy is making a puppet—the apple doesn't fall far from the tree. Keep exploring in 54.
NOCCHIO (+A)
BY Jiminy.
#CBZE14
FORMULA VITA INVOCA
FB

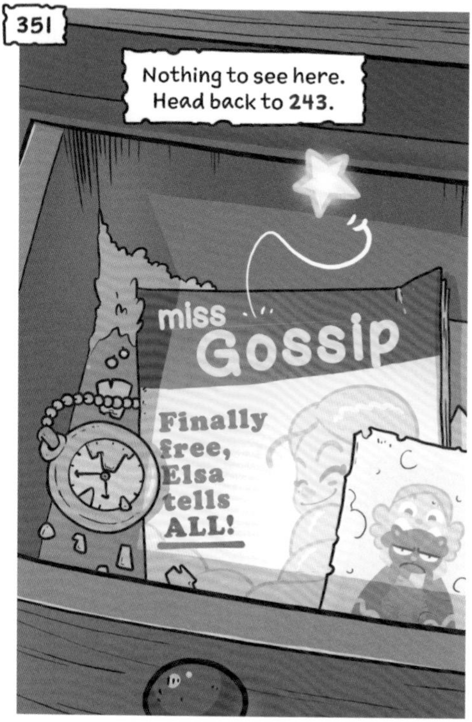
351
Nothing to see here.
Head back to 243.
miss Gossip
Finally free, Elsa tells ALL!

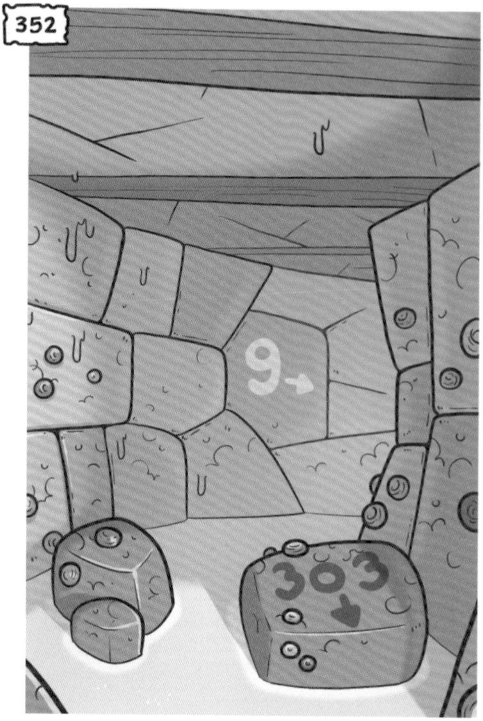
352
9
303

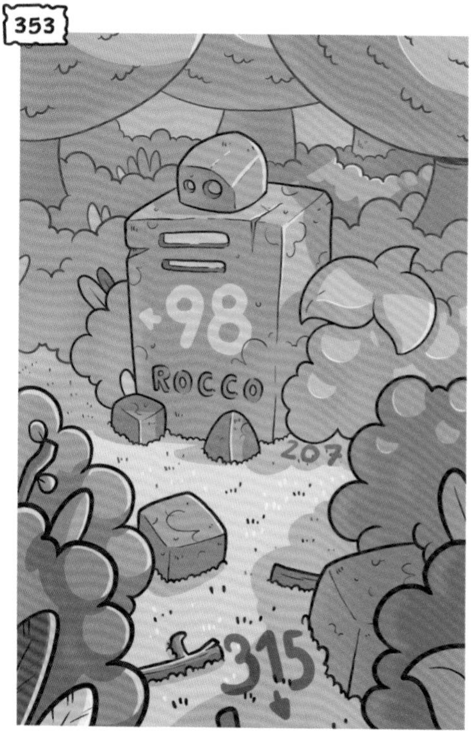
353
98
ROCCO
207
315

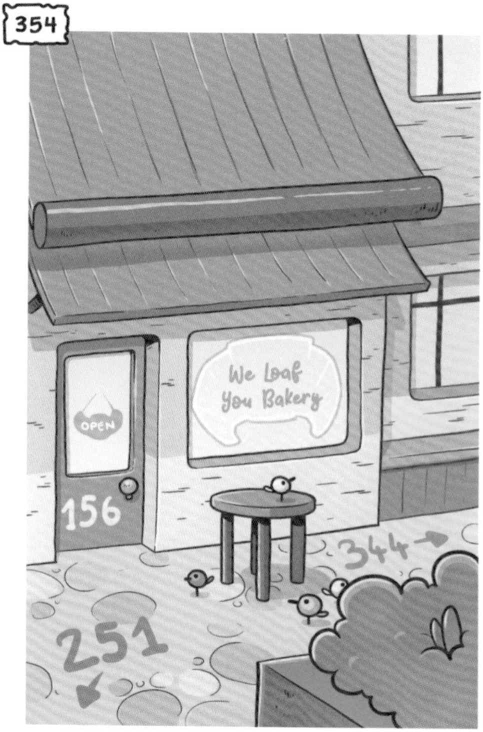
354
We Loaf You Bakery
OPEN
156
344
251

355

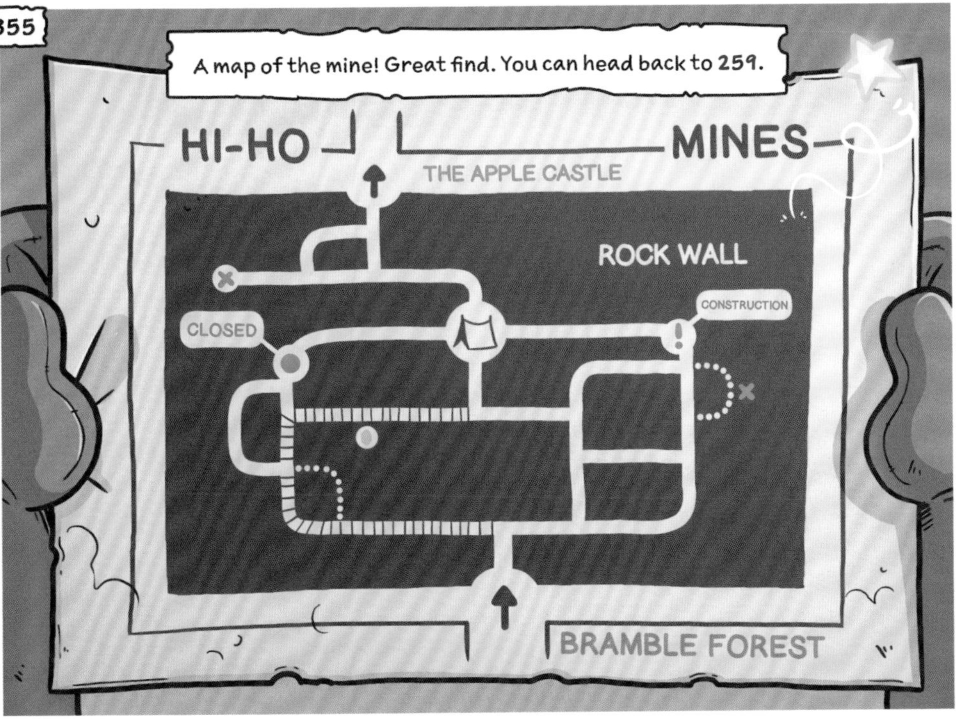
A map of the mine! Great find. You can head back to 259.
HI-HO MINES
THE APPLE CASTLE
ROCK WALL
CONSTRUCTION
CLOSED
BRAMBLE FOREST

356

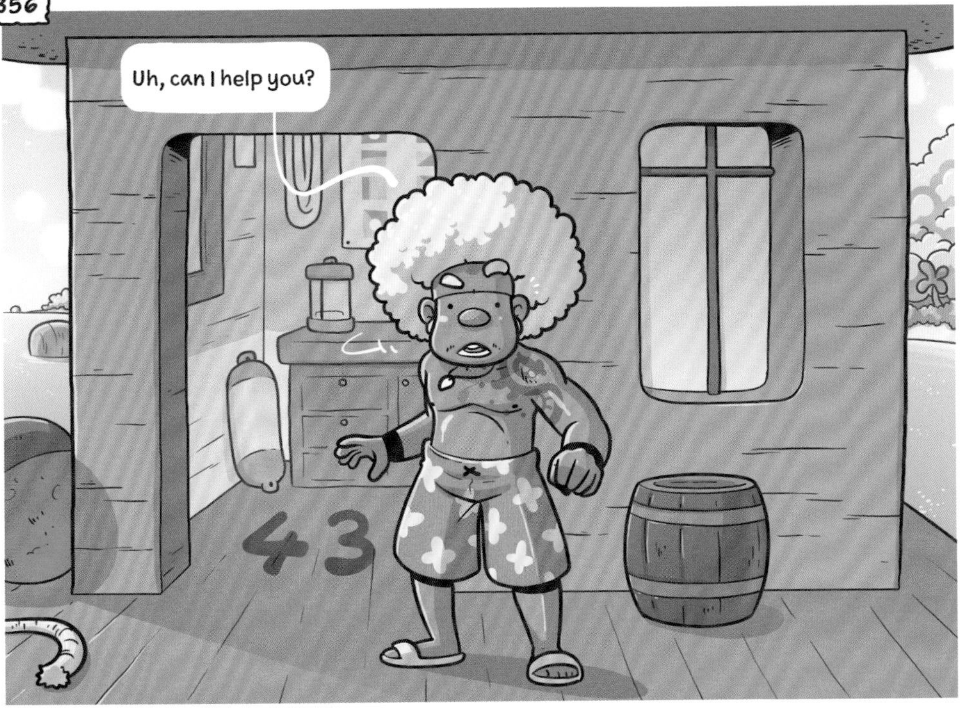
Uh, can I help you?
43

357

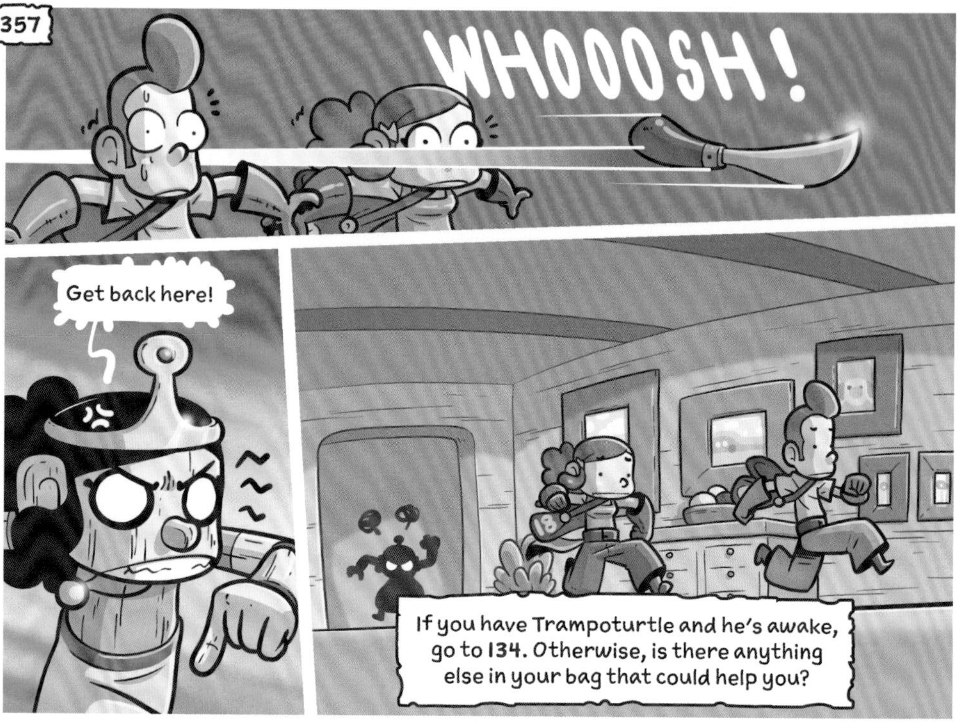
WHOOOSH!
Get back here!
If you have Trampoturtle and he's awake, go to 134. Otherwise, is there anything else in your bag that could help you?

358

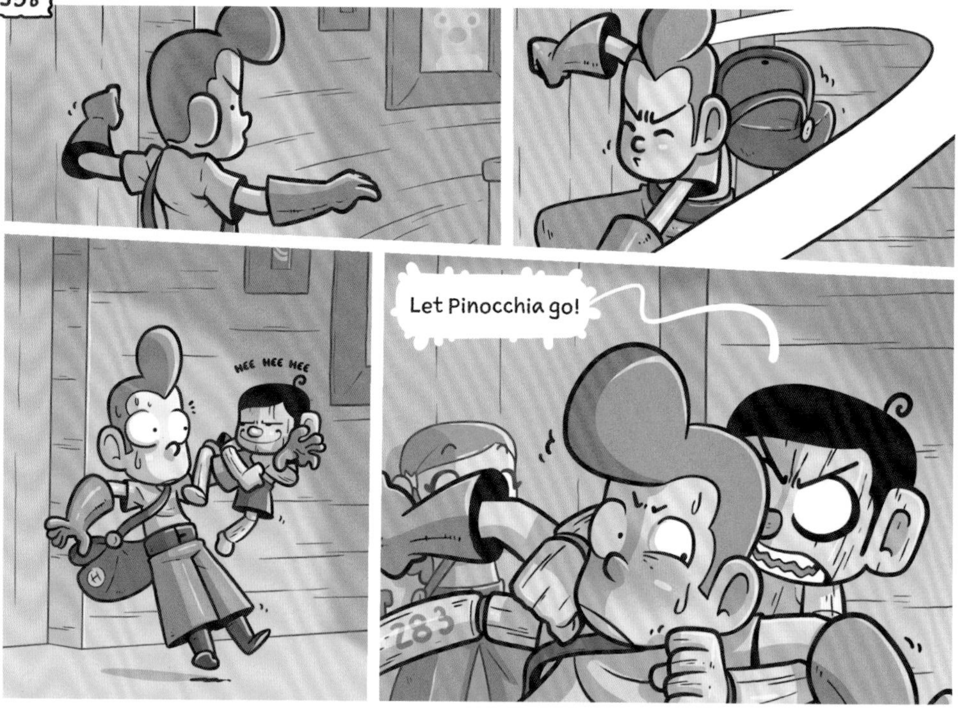
HEE HEE HEE
Let Pinocchia go!

359

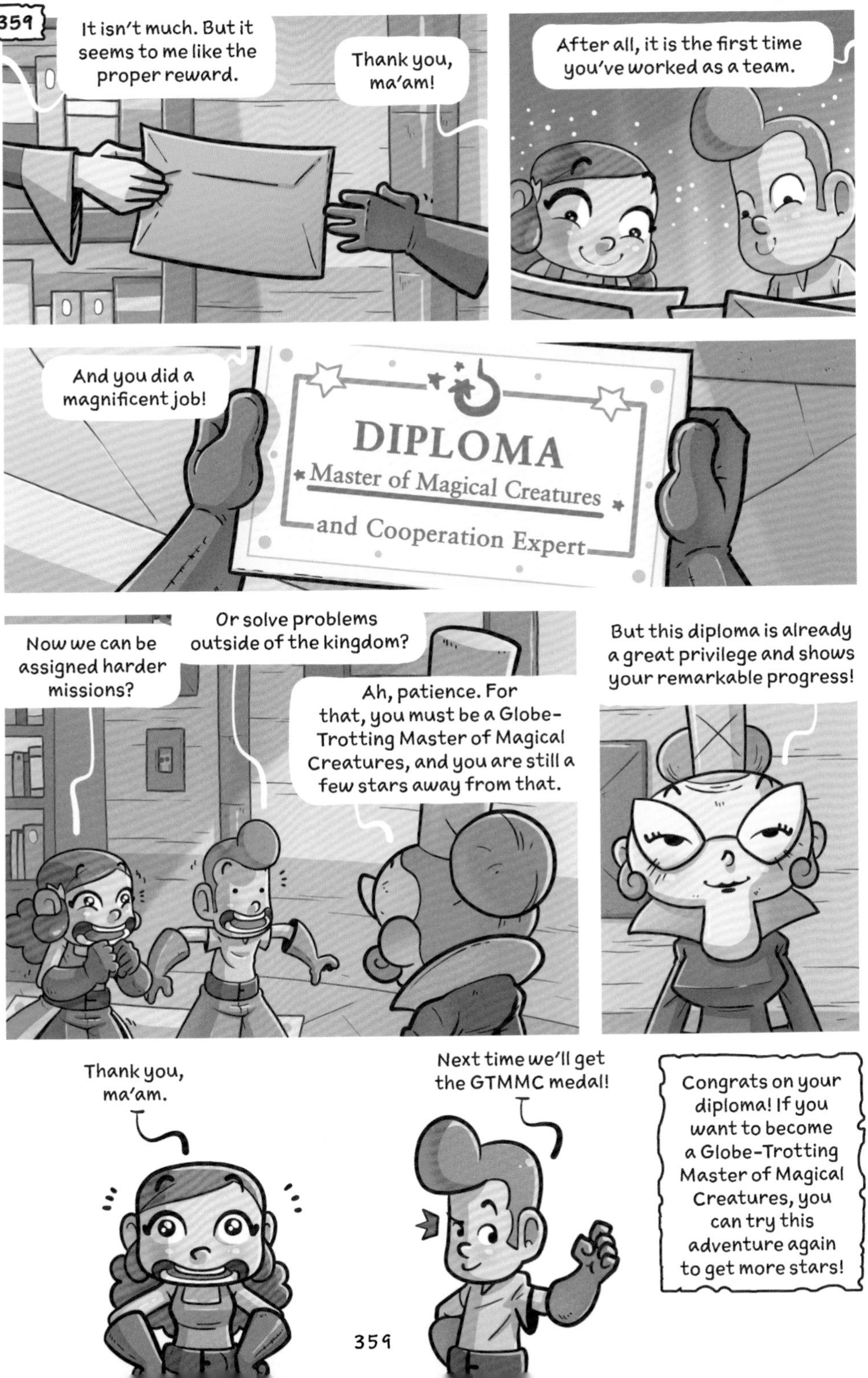

It isn't much. But it seems to me like the proper reward.
Thank you, ma'am!
After all, it is the first time you've worked as a team.
And you did a magnificent job!
DIPLOMA
Master of Magical Creatures
and Cooperation Expert
Now we can be assigned harder missions?
Or solve problems outside of the kingdom?
Ah, patience. For that, you must be a Globe-Trotting Master of Magical Creatures, and you are still a few stars away from that.
But this diploma is already a great privilege and shows your remarkable progress!
Thank you, ma'am.
Next time we'll get the GTMMC medal!
Congrats on your diploma! If you want to become a Globe-Trotting Master of Magical Creatures, you can try this adventure again to get more stars!

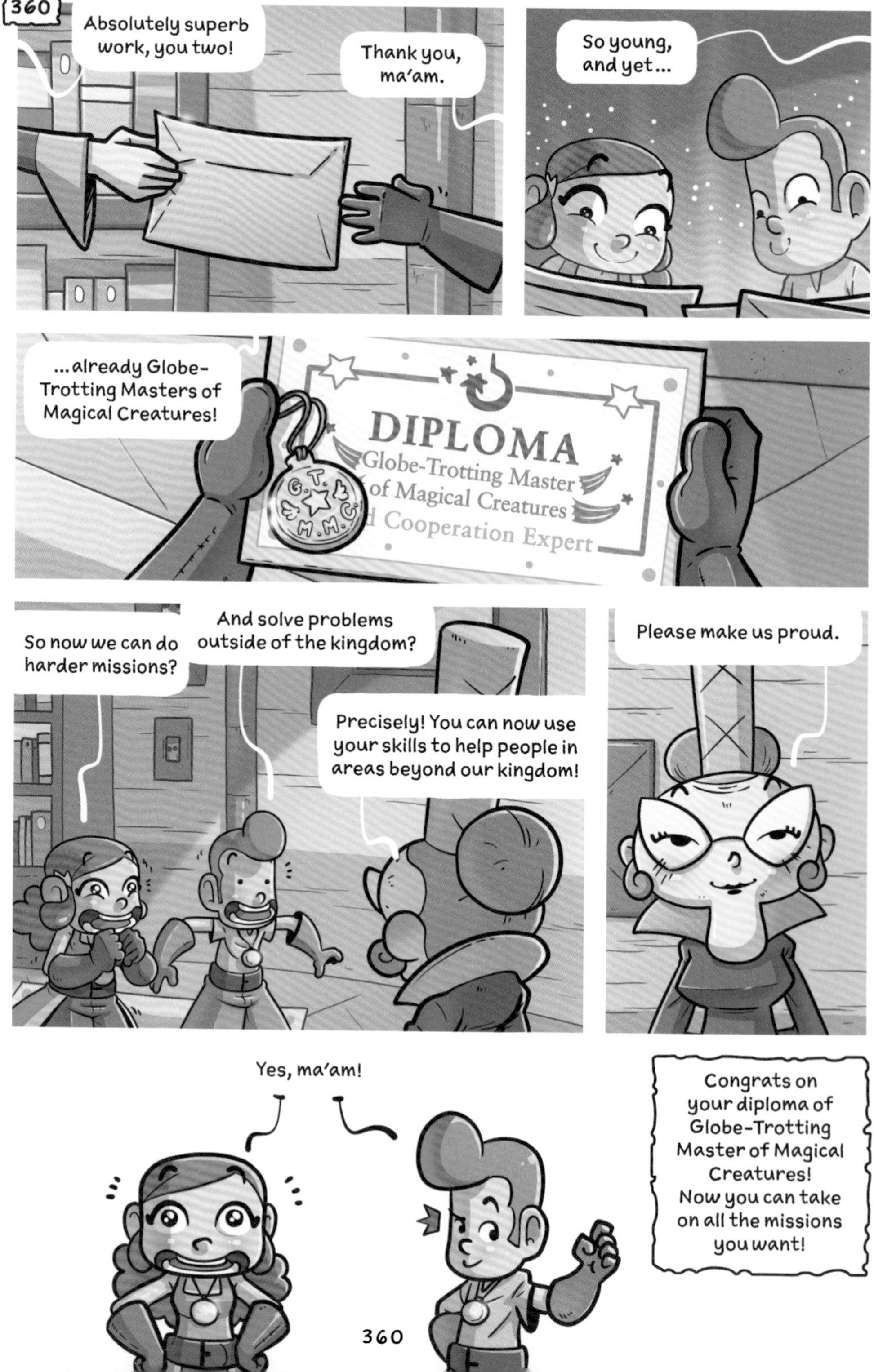
Absolutely superb work, you two!
Thank you, ma'am.
So young, and yet...
...already Globe-Trotting Masters of Magical Creatures!
DIPLOMA
Globe-Trotting Master of Magical Creatures
d Cooperation Expert
G.T. M.M.C.
So now we can do harder missions?
And solve problems outside of the kingdom?
Precisely! You can now use your skills to help people in areas beyond our kingdom!
Please make us proud.
Yes, ma'am!
Congrats on your diploma of Globe-Trotting Master of Magical Creatures! Now you can take on all the missions you want!

NOTES

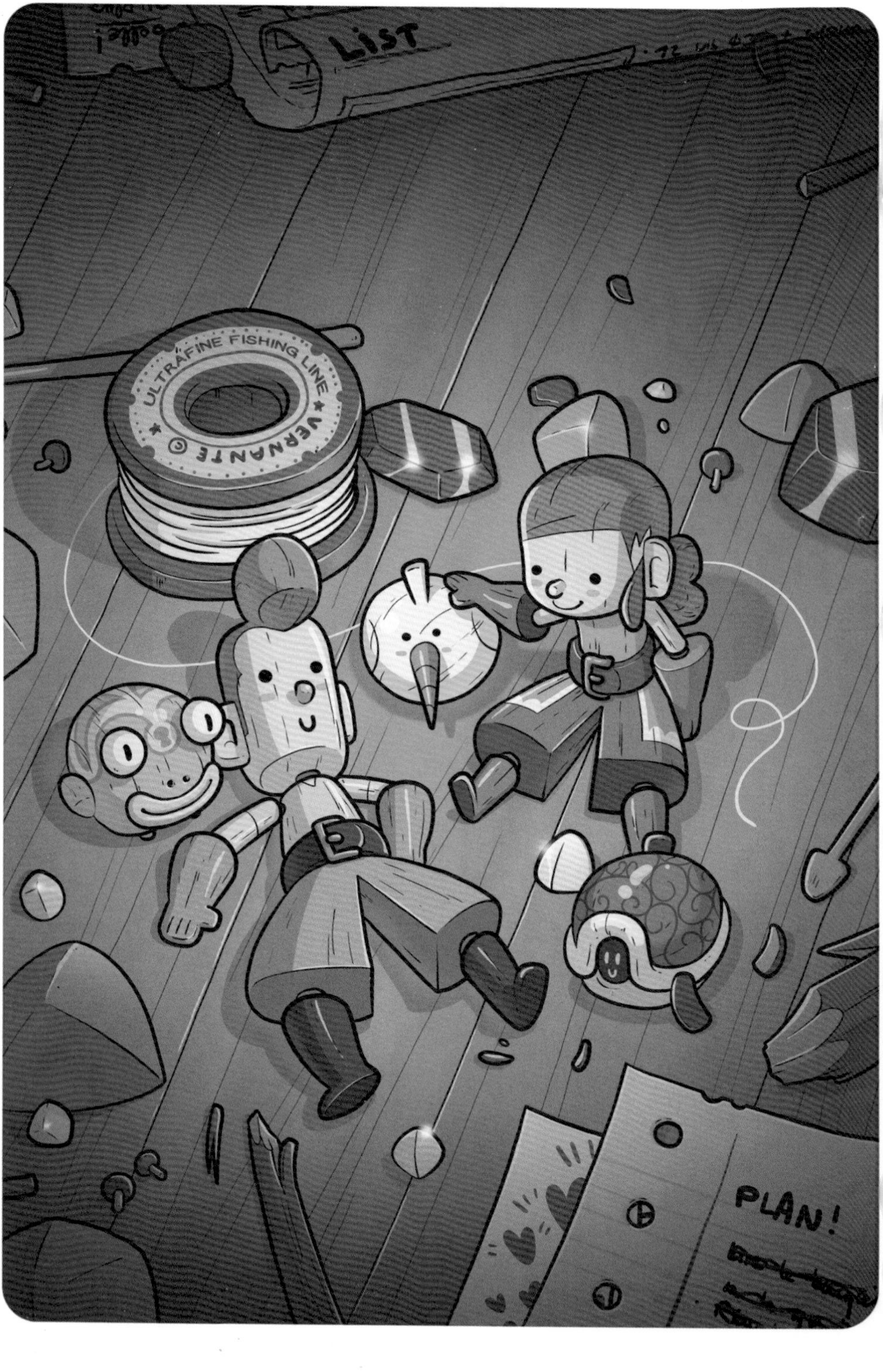
LIST
ULTRAFINE FISHING LINE
VERNANTE ©
PLAN!